Shaz is originally from England, but spends a lot of the year in Scotland. She has recently started her own floristry business and her own cut flower garden. She lives with her mother, father and two siblings. She hopes to publish more books in the future.

I dedicate this book to the great love of my life. I hope that wherever you are, you finally get to read this. I hope this reaches you into the skies above.

This is for my mother, who always told me my worth, my value, my ambitions were always stronger than anyone's opinion. That I can do anything if I set my mind to it. She taught me that being myself was as powerful as any weapon. And without her, I wouldn't be half the woman I am today.

She is the ink, the pen that helped me write this story.

This is for my father. The man that taught me how to smile, to play in the mud with pride. The man that taught me that there is no shame in failing as long as we get up and try again.

This is for my sister. My reflection in the mirror, the better version of myself. This is for the girl that inspired every great thing in this book, who inspires some of the greatest moments of my life. She is a gift to me from God.

This is for my brother. This is for the boy who showed me there is still kindness in humanity. For every time he showed love as if it was a habit.

You too are a gift from God.

Shaz M Willcocks

UNFORGIVABLE

AUSTIN MACAULEY PUBLISHERS™

LONDON • CAMBRIDGE • NEW YORK • SHARJAH

A CIP catalogue record for this title is available from the British Library.

ISBN 9781528929653 (Paperback)
ISBN 9781528965958 (ePub e-book)

www.austinmacauley.com

First Published (2019)
Austin Macauley Publishers Ltd
25 Canada Square
Canary Wharf
London
E14 5LQ

I would like to thank my family for all their love and support while writing this book, without them I would not be where I am today. But if it wasn't for my high school English teacher and her impeccable ability to whip even the most useless students into shape; I would not have made it this far. She was God in the classroom.

I would like to thank my incredible team at Austin Macauley. Their hard work and passion for our book touched my heart, and they made my dream a reality.

"The course of true love never did run smooth."

– William Shakespeare, A Midsummer Night's Dream, Act 1,
Scene 1

Prologue

The night was quiet. The stars up above her shined on like a never-ending sea of glitter and black ink.

There she stood, facing the night alone. Watching as the world carried on while her heart broke for her fallen lover.

She could hear his screams, his wails of defeat as he battered the Earth below her. She could feel the vibrations from his bruised fists hitting the newly formed dirt.

But she did not answer him.

And she did not let him return.

Instead she closed her eyes, took a deep breath and turned away.

The stars whispered as she passed them, hushing each other in awe as she entered her temple.

The temple was new; it was fresh with newly born prays for her reign. The statues' eyes focused on her as she too passed them. She could feel their stares, their sorrow for her. But she paid them no mind.

The guards opened the doors for her, their shining armour catching her eye as she walked into the huge white room before her. Then silently, as if they were scared to make a noise in case she snapped, they closed the doors behind her.

She was alone. Utterly alone.

Her reflection stared back up at her from the marble floor, a perfectly shaped face of horror and beauty. Unnoticeable tears streaked her face, but she paid them no mind.

On she walked, towards that great marble chair. That throne that has brought her so much pain. Its perfect purity boiling the rage within her, yet she did not let it show. The walls around her shifted within themselves; she could hear the pieces of rock sliding against each other, grating on her ears. She could feel each living creature's love and pain as if it was her own.

There she stood, her heart breaking, her mighty heart.

She let herself feel it for a moment; for a single second she allowed it all into her chest to swallow her whole. The pain engulfed her, all the memories of him, all the hurt and love she had for him consumed her.

And it nearly brought her to her knees. Nearly…

She hardly opened her heart to anyone. Sometimes to no one. But when she does, when she *did,* there was never quite a love like it again. And never quite a tragedy when she locked it away for the last time.

"May I come in?" a young male asked from the shadows.

The sun began to rise outside the stained glass windows; the light shone onto the throne giving it its own halo.

Without looking away from the light, she answered. "You have already."

"Yes, yes, I'm sorry to intrude."

The male was hunched over, his arms deformed from punishments of the past, for his betrayals of mankind. His hair was grey, his eyes black. He was scorched with distaste.

"Get on with it!" she snapped, her voice tired.

He was hesitant to go on. "Is… is it done?"

"It is done," she answered defeated, no longer wanting to talk. "Now get out."

He scurried away like a rat, his feet scuffing the floor as he went. Her body hummed with rage, quite rage that demanded to be released. But just like before, so many times before, she crushed it down. Just like the perfect creature they all thought she was. The perfect creature she *had* to be.

"Are you ok?"

She turned to find her friend there, his face as broken as hers, as he too had just loved and lost. He stood taller than her, his hands clasped behind his armoured back. His amour shone as much as his violet eyes did, stark against his pale skin.

"I don't think I'll ever be ok again," she admitted to only him.

He said nothing, but touched her shoulder in comfort.

"What should I do with the infant?" he asked. The child, the infant; the only way she could think about the baby was think of it as a foetus, a monster. "Should I bring him to you?"

"No." She knew she could never care for the child, not now. Not when it looked so much like its father. "Send it to him, let him care for the monster he created. And if he doesn't want it, cast it out too."

And without another word she turned away yet again, letting his hand fall away like a leaf in autumn. She could hear the cries of her child. Her new born. The baby she gave birth to just hours ago. But she couldn't go to him. Her heart cried out to him, it wanted to love and hold him. But she couldn't. The stars up above wouldn't allow it. So she ignored his beautiful cries, cries that were pouring out for her.

For his mother to go to him.

But she couldn't.

She only got to hold him once. She remembered his soft skin brushing hers, his soft dark hair. He settled down completely as soon as he was placed into her arms. He was so small. So delicate.

Her first baby.

Her baby boy.

Her beautiful baby boy with his father's eyes. Those beautiful, stark, entrancing eyes that mirrored the world.

Those perfectly crystal blue eyes…

Chapter 1

"When I discover who I am, I'll be free."
                    – Ralph Ellison, 'Invisible Man'

Lucinda

For most of my life, I've been curious about everything. I've questioned everything. I never spoke out unless I was asking a question to something that hadn't been answered before. But as I grew older, I realised that maybe, just maybe, I shouldn't have been asking all these questions. But I didn't expect them to lead me down such a dark and twisted path that even the Devil himself wouldn't dare set foot upon. But after everything I've finally found the one answer to all my questions.

What is the point in it all? I asked myself.

Love. Love is the point of it all.

The darkness. A suffocating, irrational complication that kills the world's light. I awoke with a throat-curdling scream to the void of my bedroom. Nearly every night it was the same terrifying dream. Demons and twisted creatures begging for a release that I could not seem to give. They did nothing but terrorise and confuse me more and more every day, and if they didn't stop, I believed that I would wake up one morning and my mind would've snapped during the night. Sometimes I think it already has…

A few hours passed before I even thought about getting up. I knew I had to get ready for work, but my body just didn't have it in me anymore.

Yet I did it.

I followed the same routine as I usually did: shower, dress, and do my hair. I stood before my full-length mirror, drying my golden-brown hair before putting it up into a ponytail. My hair had grown past my bottom years ago, but I never wore it down. I was pretty, but I wasn't beautiful. I never saw anything special when I looked at my reflection; all I saw were big brown eyes and pale skin. Eyes that have been bitterly empty for so long. Too long.

I turned away and went to check if my mum was sober enough to take me to work. I crept downstairs and stepped over cans of beers and whiskey bottles, the air stung with the scent of alcohol. People always told me that the loss would dull over time, that everything would heal itself. I think in my own way I did heal; or I shut myself away from it instead. But my mother never did.

I found her passed out on the sofa. I nudged her leg to bring her round, but she was too hung over to notice. So I left her alone and took the keys to the car so I could drive myself to work. I never really blamed her for being the way she was. I wasn't such a great daughter either if I was being honest with myself. I accepted that many years ago, and that my life wasn't going to get better than what it was now, I wasn't going to get the chance to change my life, or travel to my heart's content. Maybe I even wanted the kind of adventure that makes a person lose their mind. Maybe…

I climbed into our old Mini copper and started the engine. The rumble of the car reminding me of the horrid day I had ahead of me.

I drove out of the driveway.

But before I bothered to focus on the road, I reached the local pub that I'd been working at for the past year. I sat for a few moments and gazed at the cracked walls and washed out paint, at the old Oak trees that hung over it like a shadow. I realised that this was the best I would ever have for my life. This was it for me.

I shook the thought off and grabbed my bag from the front seat and collected the rest of my scattered thoughts before engaging with the rest of the day, and as I entered the old back door to the pub, Jane burst through the hallway.

"There you are!"

She threw a smile at me, but I could only grimace in return to the very early morning, I could never understand how she was so happy when it was so early in the day. She walked with arms open for an embrace. I went stiff as she engulfed me. She was lucky because she was the only person that I could endure a hug from. Although I was relieved when she released me.

"How's it looking in there?" I dared to ask. She pulled a funny face and pushed me through the door. She passed me my freshly washed apron, notebook and pen.

"It's a battle field." She giggled while walking away into the office. I always liked Jane; she was one of the only people I could stand to be around. But she also seemed oblivious to the bad side of the world, as if she was a part of secret one that no one else could enter. She even looked too perfect to be from this world. Her hair was almost a fiery red; it was short but it suited her. It framed her highly structured cheeks with perfect definition. Her eyes were a bright green, like the deepest of murky seas. Daring you to look further, either to be washed clean or drowned in their depths. Her skin was perfect and creamy, like the best of vanilla ice cream. Every girl would be deadly jealous of her, but it wasn't her fault she was extremely yet unnaturally beautiful. She reminds you of the first time you ever felt alive.

Here we go.

I mentally groaned as I tied my apron around my waist and took a deep breath before approaching the first table with a fake smile.

It was hours later of taking orders and pouring drinks for sleazy old men and intolerable women before I could finally take a break. I pulled out my sandwich from my lunch box and sat behind the bar with a book. I savoured the dry ham and the butter, my stomach gurgling for more. I liked to tell myself that I read so many books to escape my own life, even if it's just for a little while; any escape would be fulfilling.

"Don't you dare come here!" Jane hissed from the back office; it was so vicious it snapped me out of my trance of reading. I tried to listen more closely as she continued to argue with someone. I assumed she was on the phone because I couldn't hear another voice arguing back.

"If you do this, it will be the biggest mistake you'll ever make," she tried to plead with them. I inched towards the back as quietly as I could and saw her stalking back and forth in the office. I'd never seen her so angry. I don't think I'd *ever* seen Jane angry. "You've done enough damage already! Leave it be. It's been so long, just leave her be!" She braced her hands against the front of her desk and leaned forward, her body stiff from aggravation.

I poked my head into the office.

She finally huffed with defeat. "I just don't want to see either of you hurt from this."

She wasn't making any sense, so I turned away to get back to work. *"Lucinda doesn't deserve this and neither do you."*

I froze. Then I heard a phone slam down onto a hard surface, probably shattering the screen. She walked out of the office and locked the door, and when she turned to face me, we both froze.

She appeared shocked and seemed to have forgotten that I was even in the building.

She blinked before speaking. "What are you doing?"

I was speechless for a few seconds before stammering to answer her.

"I–I was just–" I opened and closed my mouth like a gold fish, she raised her hand to interrupt me. I went silent as she placed the keys to the office into her pocket.

"I'm sorry for snapping Lucinda, but I'm guessing from how loud I was speaking you can understand that I'm quite stressed right now." She placed her hand on my shoulder. I tried to smile to the best to my ability, which wasn't much. She smiled bright just like she usually did, and walked passed me to grab her jacket.

"I'll be gone for the rest of the day, but I'm sure you can close up without me, right?" She glanced at me while putting her arms through her sleeves. I nodded and she winked while rushing out of the door, leaving me alone with the very few customers that were left.

How joyful.

It was midnight when I finally finished closing. I grabbed the keys and turned to lock the back door. It was quiet outside, only the moonlight for company in the centuries old pub garden.

But I felt eyes on me. They were clawing at my back, trying to get me to turn and face them. I just kept my head turned to the door. I fumbled with the keys trying to find the right one with my numb fingers. I felt someone behind me stroke my ponytail. Yet when I spun round to face whoever it was, nothing was there. I found the key and with a racing heart I locked up the door; then I rushed to my car and spun out the car park as fast I possibly could. My heart didn't stop pounding until I got into the front door of my house.

"Where the hell have you been?!" my mother shouted from the sofa in the living room. I walked past and tried to ignore her. But she got up and followed me to my bedroom door. I threw my bag onto the bed, waiting for her to argue with me again.

She swayed in the doorway. "I have been waiting all day for you to return the car. *My* car by the way."

She shouted while alcohol dripped from her chin. I rolled my eyes and placed the keys back onto the bed.

"It's nice to know that you worry about me instead of your shitty car Mum," I scoffed as she grabbed her keys and sat back onto the bed, a beer hanging from her fingers.

She smirked. "You're lucky you're back in time. This is my last beer," she mumbled as she took another sip. I rolled my eyes again and changed into my pyjamas.

"I have work again tomorrow Mum. I need sleep, so can you please leave," I demanded without looking at her. But I knew she was hurt by my words, yet she left without another word. I didn't fall asleep straight away. I kept replaying Jane's conversation that she had on the phone repeatedly in my head. Wondering what I had to do with it. But finally sleep drew me into its arms. Yet I didn't sleep well that night; the wind made the tree outside rack its branches against my bedroom window. The cold sank into my bones and froze the workings of my body.

When I finally woke up after drifting through wake and sleep, the sunlight streaked into the room through the curtains.

Another day…

I groaned in annoyance as I pulled myself out of bed and got dressed, I took my time as I didn't want to see my mother so quickly this morning. But I had to face her sooner or later. I passed my full-length mirror and stopped. I stepped closer, and noticed that my skin had more of a glow to it today, and my eyes… they didn't look so tired. They shone for the first time in a long time. I smiled. When I got down stairs she was waiting with keys in hand. I looked her up and down and saw that she was dressed today. Her hair was brushed and sat on her shoulders with a shimmer, but she still looked quite pale.

I approached with caution. "What are you doing?"

She smiled shyly, jingled the keys and opened the door.

"I thought I could take you to work today," she said with a little caution of her own. I studied her as I passed through the door, but let it go as she got into the front seat of the car.

"Thanks," I mumbled as the car started. We drove in silence; the air was awkward and thick with tension.

But the day was warm outside the car; the birds were out and the sun was shining. When we finally reached the pub, I jumped from the car and she didn't say a thing. I didn't say goodbye. I left the car in the dust of my shoes.

I opened the back door and could already tell it was busy…

Lord give me strength.

I placed my bag away and made my way around the bar for my pen and note book and found Jane talking loudly in the back. I didn't want to know what she was talking about this time; I didn't want to know if she was talking about me again. Instead I took orders and smiled as usual. Some time passed before I noticed that I could feel eyes on me again, those crawling eyes, as if I was a target of some kind. But no one was looking at me when I looked around. So I tried to shrug it off and get back to work.

Jane squealed from her office, "Lucinda?"

I followed the sound to find her looking through some papers on her desk. When she looked up I couldn't help but giggle at her appearance.

"What?"

She laughed with me even though she was the joke. I pointed to her crazy red hair that was sticking up in every direction. She looked like a red porcupine, and when she looked into the mirror she tried to smooth it down while only making it funnier. Finally she pulled it up into a short ponytail and sat back down into her old leather chair behind her desk.

"I just wanted to make sure that you're alright." She clasped both of her hands onto the table before her and looked at me, almost studying me.

"Yeah I guess, why?" I asked. She didn't say anything until she stood up and placed a book that was laying on her desk on the shelf behind her.

"I snapped at you yesterday and I didn't mean to. I just want you to know it wasn't anything you did," she said.

"I know, I'm fine though," I said again to reassure her.

"Ok, well I just wanted to make sure." She turned and looked at me as if she was waiting to study my next expression.

"Yep…" I rocked back and forth on my heels and she smiled yet again.

"Ok then, well you go on without me. I'll be back out in a second."

She sat back down at her desk, so I left without another word. When I reached the bar, I placed my pen and book down to take my hair out of its ponytail, losing myself in the relief of having it down. But it was ruined as a group of immature men came tumbling through the door, obviously already drunk. They sat down at the table closet to the bar, whistling and shouting at me. I thought about just ignoring them, but I didn't want to get into trouble with my boss. So I grabbed my notebook and pen to take their order just so I could get away from them just as quick.

When I reached their table I smiled sarcastically.

"What can I get you?"

The ginger one on the left looked me up and down with a smirk, dirty humour gleaming in his eyes. He smacked my ass. I yelped and stepped back with a glare, thinking about pouring a beer over his largely sized head.

He oozed self-confidence. "I would definitely like that ass of yours on a plate if it's not too much trouble," he replied to my glare.

"No," I simply said.

His face fell once he realised his pickup line hadn't worked on me.

But it perked up just as quick. "Ok. I can just eat it now then."

He reached to pull me into his lap, but strong hands pulled me back. I didn't even turn around to see who had saved me.

But a smooth, strong voice answered him. "Sorry mate, but she's not on the menu." Whoever he was, his hold on my waist was soothing, yet I could feel the strength under his fingers. He held me close, making me stand right up against him. From what I could feel, he was lean but quite muscular. He was at least six foot as I could feel the bottom of his chin brush the top of my head. The ginger's face went hard like stone and he turned away and with a wave of his hand. We backed away. I turned to thank the stranger but couldn't find the words.

He was beautiful…

I was correct in guessing his size; he was very muscular but was also lean with it. His chest was broad but tucked into a narrow waist. I tore my eyes away to look up. His face was breath taking, all angles and smooth skin. A perfect canvas for an old Florence master to paint upon. He had high cheekbones, a strong jaw line that looked like it could cut metal and a straight nose that has obviously never been broken before. His hair shone like burning bronze as the sunshine streaked through the window; it was short around the sides and longer on top. But what captivated me most were his eyes. They were a striking crystal blue, like an exotic ocean concealed in his irises. They had a sad shape to them. From far away they might look stronger, sharper, but this close, with that kind of colour, they were devastatingly beautiful.

And they were looking straight at me.

I struggled to speak as he smiled down at me, perfect teeth revealed.

"I think the word you're looking for is thank you," he said chuckling slightly, and for the first time in a very long time I wanted to smile back. So I did.

18

"Thank you," I said still smiling. He still hadn't let my waist go. Instead his hand trailed down to hold my hip, making my skin shudder. As if tiny fairies were dancing across my fair skin. He seemed to be lost in thought as he gazed down at me, but he finally broke his siren's trance and pulled his arm away, clearing his throat; he smiled again.

"So, do you think I could get a beer?" He turned slightly, indicating to the bar. I snapped out of the trance and rushed behind the bar to get him a glass. He chuckled again as I poured him his drink.

Our fingers brushed as I passed him the glass. "What's your name?" he asked while sitting in one of the chairs in front of me. He was watching me, waiting for his answer. I shyly tucked my hair behind my ear.

"My name is Lucinda."

But as I tucked my hair away I realised it was still down, and as I went to pull it back into a pony tail, my hand was stopped by his.

"Why don't you leave it down? It suites you better that way."

He traced me with his eyes, and I didn't look away as I took my hands away from my hair.

I cleared my own throat. "I never really have it down anymore," I explained. He looked at me as if he didn't understand something he thought he once did.

"That's a shame," he said as if it really was a great shame. He continued to drink his beer as I continued to serve other customers. He watched me as if he was thinking about what to say next.

I came back to the bar.

"Can I have another beer please?" he asked. I lifted my eyebrow at his request but said nothing. "What?" he teased as I poured him another drink. I handed him the glass.

"I hope you're not driving," I said as he took another sip. But he just grinned as he set his glass back down. He leaned forward as if he wanted to tell me something in secret. So I leaned forward too.

"No, my little Lucinda. I'm not driving. But I'll be flying," he whispered. As if he was telling a great confession. I laughed at his words and leaned away from his sweet scent. The smell of his cologne; it smelled like old pianos and red roses, or was that just him? "No, I'm not driving. You don't have to worry about me."

He pulled out the money for the beers and I placed it into the till. I lifted my eyebrows playfully.

"Who said I cared about what happens to you?" I said arching an eyebrow. But he just leaned forward again, closer to me so I could smell his sweet scent again, and smiled that smile.

"Then why did you bother to ask me in the first place?" His tone was hush. He didn't look away, and neither did I. I didn't reply; in a way there wasn't anything left to say. But the moment was ruined by Jane.

"What are you both doing?" We both jumped back as she appeared next to us. I didn't even know how she got there; she was like a ninja. A red headed ninja. We cleared our throats in unison while she smirked at us both. Yet there was something she was hiding behind that grin, something wasn't quite right about it. It wasn't as wide as it normally was.

I shifted on my feet. "Hi Jane, what is it you need?" I tried to act natural while trying not to look at either of them. She couldn't stop grinning at both of us, and there was something unnerving about it.

"Peter." she turned to him. So that was his name, yet the way she said it, as if she was accusing him of something. "Can I see you out back please brother?" Wait. He was her brother?

Brilliant.

"If we have to," he said innocently.

He stood up and she playfully scolded him as he passed by the bar. But as a little bit of time passed I could hear them both speaking in whispers in the office, and I knew it was a heated conversation just based from their tones. As if both their voices were colliding like stones. Soon after I walked back to the bar from getting more glasses, Peter came storming out, his beautiful face full of rage, contorting it into something harsh. Yet when he passed me his face smoothed over. He was about to say something when Jane interrupted from behind me.

"Think about what you're doing brother!"

He looked to her again with annoyance but soon after nodded his head. He looked at me once more, then left without another word. I was still for a few moments before I turned back to Jane. Her eyes were filled with sorrow, cooling but dulling her green eyes.

"What was that about?" I demanded. She slouched into a chair and laid her head into her hands; and when she looked back up she looked weak. She looked weak.

It was strange to see her like that.

She sighed. "My brother is just bad at making decisions," she answered simply, as if that was all there was to it. Then she got back up without another word and left for her office. Leaving me confused and alone.

Again…

I went home more depressed than usual. The drive with my mother was more awkward than this morning. When we reached home, I turned to her and thanked her for driving me, but that I could drive myself from now on. Her face fell with disappointment, but she didn't say anything. I reached my bed and I collapsed onto it with a huff. I just wanted to fall asleep and never wake up. But my mind kept returning to Peter, his eyes, his smile. Just him. I've never really taken any interest in guys. I just focused on keeping to myself. I always wanted to be alone, that way I couldn't be hurt again. I pushed him from my swollen mind and undressed, burying myself within the covers of my cold bed.

The next morning, I woke up knowing I had the day off; this was the one day I got to sleep in. But the moment I closed my eyes again my mother burst through the door, eyes wide.

I groaned into my pillow. "What do you want Mum?" The grin on her face was quite funny.

"There's a young man at the door." I blew some hair out of my face and groaned again.

"And?" I started to drift off again. She lifted the blanket off my body. I shrunk back into a ball away from the cool breeze.

"He said his name was Peter."

I opened my eyes, my heart pounding. I jumped out of bed and rushed to make myself more human looking while she walked out of the door still smiling. I tried to walk as calmly and collectively as I could to the kitchen. When I reached it, I took a deep breath before stepping through. He was wearing a white plain T-shirt with black jeans, and he was holding a huge bunch of wild flowers.

"Hey."

He handed me the colourful flowers. I breathed them in as I held them. I filled a vase with water and placed them inside. He was close behind me when I turned to face him. And he didn't move away. But for my own sake of breathing correctly, I moved back.

"So, what are you doing here?" I said self-consciously while smoothing my hair down and straightening out my clothes.

His grin widened. "You have the day off today. Correct?" he asked while leaning against my fridge, arms crossed over his muscular chest, his eyes intense.

"Yes, why?" I asked curiously. I grabbed an apple and bit into it. The delicious juice dripped down my chin and I moved to wipe it away. Peter appeared before me and slowly lifting his hand to my chin, he used his thumb to wipe it clean. Never taking his eyes away from mine.

"I wanted to make it a fun day out," he answered. He smiled as he drew his thumb away.

"Where are we going?" I asked. Playing his little game. He stepped away and pulled his keys out of his pocket.

"Just dress for fun." He walked back out the door.

I was grinning like an idiot to myself when something came to me. "Wait… how do you know where I live?" I shouted, but I only got a chuckle in return.

He probably got my address from his sister.

I went upstairs to get dressed as quick as I could into my favourite outfit. Black skinny jeans and a soft pink jumper. I brushed my hair and left it down. I faced the mirror and smiled to myself. My skin looked healthy again, full of colour and pink cheeks. The freckles stood out and brought my eyes to life again. My eyes sparkled; gleamed. My hair looked smooth and shiny, like broken glass reflecting in the morning sun. I smoothed my hands over my dark jeans and took a deep breath.

Here we go.

I bounded down the stairs and shouted goodbye to my mother; her laughter rang through from the kitchen, including the sound of dishes and water. Warmth washed through me. She wasn't hungover and she was cleaning the dishes. A slither of hope ran through me and I didn't move to crush it so quickly this time. I let it fill me for a few seconds. I let it give me a little something to hang onto. I opened the door and stepped out of the house.

I slipped into his BMW and faced a smiling beauty, and I couldn't help but smile back. He had kept a single flower on his dashboard, and when he saw that I noticed it, he slipped it behind my ear. It was a large looking Daisy. He let his hand linger there for a few moments before muttering something under his breath.

"*Perfect.*" I thought he said when he leaned back to inspect his work.

"So tell me, what would you have been doing if I hadn't knocked on your door today?" he asked as the engine came to life. It rumbled through my body, almost purring.

"I'd probably still be sleeping," I said as we sped off out of my driveway and onto the nearest motorway. Then we began our journey to God knows where.

The morning sun was bright, so Peter let me wear his black sunglasses. They were a little big for my face, probably because he needed ones big enough to give his high cheeks bones room.

"Well it's good that I came along then isn't it."

As he focused on his driving, I leaned back and enjoyed the smooth ride. He drove with ease, and I was content with the silence, and he seemed so too. It was nice that we could sit without speaking and it wasn't awkward. It was a fulfilling silence. After a while, I looked over slightly and soaked the image of him in from the corner of my eye. The angles of his face were sharper in the new sunlight, but it was also very flattering, his hair shinned with flecks of bronze, as if it was melting. How could someone like him be interested in someone like me?

"Boo!"

I jumped in my seat as he laughed. My cheeks turned bright red. I covered them with my hands and I turned away embarrassed.

"Hey," he said while pulling my hands away. "I'm sorry, I just couldn't help myself," he said; he still had traces of laughter in his voice.

"Its fine, it was quite funny." I giggled along with him. He clasped my hand in his and laced our fingers together. I looked down at our entwined hands and noticed smudges of old paint, as if it had stained his perfect skin and made him more real.

"What were you looking at anyway?" he asked while watching the road again. He still held my hand on my thigh, and it was burning from his touch.

"I was just wondering that if you and Jane are siblings, why do you look so different." His eyebrows drew downwards. His face became harder, more like it was carved from ancient marble.

"I mean to start with, your hair colour is totally different." His eyes froze for a few seconds, then his expression showered understanding, and he stroked the top on my hand with his thumb. Such a simple movement, but it made me completely relax.

"We have different fathers," was all he said. His frame was lit up by the light outside the car, but his eyes were completely dark as he spoke.

I nodded and went silent, but I wanted to know more about him.

I took a deep breath. "Do you have any more siblings?" I asked.

He switched gears and took my hand again.

"I have a brother."

But he didn't look at me as he said it.

"Where is he?"

He kept his eyes firmly on the road, piercing the tarmac with his gaze.

"I've been asking the same thing for years…" I didn't say anything else.

He turned his head to look at me, eyes softer than they were a moment ago.

"Anyway, let's talk about you." He stroked my hand again. "I noticed that you were reading behind the bar. Who's your favourite author?"

I answered a little bit too enthusiastically, beaming as I sat up straighter. "Oh! I can't pick just one." He chuckled. "I love all of them." I laughed.

For the rest of the journey, we talked about anything and everything. It was easy to talk to him. The words flowed from my heart as I spoke about all the things that I've kept hidden for so long. My dreams, my regrets, everything just felt so easy saying it to him. He didn't really have any family, Jane was all he had. Other than his brother that he never sees. The last time he saw him was when he watched him set sail across the Caribbean. His father was a troubled man, and he doesn't see his mother. He told me that he spent most of his life either travelling, studying or with Jane. I told him about how I have never really been anywhere, and that one day I wish I could travel the world too. So he told me all about the places that he had visited, all the things he had seen. But we had arrived by the time he started to talk about Australia.

He parked the car and made his way around to open mine, and even in heels, he was still taller than me.

"Here we are."

We were at Sandlock pier. A quite but adorable little beach that held restaurants and a few rides for children along its neckline. He held my hand as we walked down to the path that touched the sand.

I groaned to myself. "I knew I shouldn't have worn heels."

He raised his eyebrow and without missing a beat of the waves before us, he lifted me into his arms and swung me over his shoulder.

"Its fine, I'll carry you down." I squealed in delight as he strolled down the beach. I could tell he was quite pleased with himself. "You should see the view, it's breathtaking," he said while taping my ass. I laughed as we reached the shore and before he placed me down, he took my heels off for me and offered to hold them.

"Thanks," I said as I pushed the hair out of my face. He winked and took my hand.

"No, thank *you*."

He laughed as I playfully hit him in the arm. We started to walk down the beach, watching the sun dance off the sand. There weren't many people left on the beach now, and the remaining were packing up to go home. Missing the best bit of it all. The breeze was gentle as it retreated from the Earth's face, all the colours of the sunset turning darker and richer by the second. I turned to look up at him, but he was already looking at me. A question lingered in his eyes, as if they were questioning *themselves.*

"Do you have any brothers or sisters?" he asked out of the blue, but I just gave a small shake of my head. There was a flutter of pain in the centre of my chest, so small and distant now that for a second I didn't even realise what it was. It was a reminder. A reminder that I got to live and they didn't.

"No, not anymore."

His eyes drew together.

"What happened? If you don't mind me asking."

I took a deep and steadying breath. "My brother and father died in an accident a few years ago."

He was quite for a few moments. "I'm so sorry."

My smile was weak.

Treading over the stones, he found a perfect spot for us to sit on. It was a soft patch of sand. The tiny gems that covered the beach shifting under our feet as we sat down side by side before the ocean.

"It's ok, it was a long time ago," I said, unable to give any more answers.

"Yet it doesn't make it any less painful," he said while leaning closer to me. I looked at him through my hair.

25

Grief. The purest kind of pain there is, yet it only seems real when it is said out loud. He pulled a lock of hair from behind me, watching the golden-brown colour reflect in the sun. He played with the lock of gold between his fingers and watched as the colours dazzled us.

But just as quick he broke out of his trance. "Are you hungry?" he asked while letting the lock of hair fall back into its rightful place once more. I nodded and he helped me up from the sand, his arms flexing as we arose.

We brushed off the rebellious pieces of sand and worked our way back up the beach. As I stepped on to concrete path, I turned to look at the dying sunset; it's strange how much time can pass by just enjoying someone's company. I left my shoes off until we saw lights further ahead, letting my feet enjoy the cool concrete. We walked down to the restaurants that were covered in fairy lights, and as we got closer I could see how they lit up the newly formed night. For the first time in a very long time, I was happy. I know its cliché to say that when I had only met Peter a day ago, but he drove all my demon's away just by standing beside me. He made me forget. I looked up at him as we strolled to the first restaurant door. His face looked carefree, radiant as the setting sun behind us. I remembered when I used to look like that so long ago.

"What about this one?" He pointed to the little restaurant with shells decorating the doorway. Little lights flickered through the windows casting shadows across us both.

I smiled. "It's perfect."

I thanked him as he opened the door for me. We walked in and passed cute tables and chairs. There were lights hanging from the ceiling all around us and there were shells in every available spot. I loved it.

Peter picked the table at the back next to the window, so we could see the entire beach fading into the night's darkness. The waiter came and took our orders just as soon as we sat down. I ordered some pasta and he ordered some chips with a cheese burger. When the waiter finally left, I could look around properly at the decorations. The walls were decorated with paintings of ships, mermaids and the sea. It was charming. A mythical era lived within these walls around us, and I wanted to sink myself into it and live with it.

As I turned my head back round, Peter was watching me. As if he was slightly puzzled by something.

"What? Is there something on my face?" I giggled a little nervously. He seemed to snap out of what he was thinking about and he took a sip of his water.

"Peter?" I asked again. He sat his glass down and smiled, but he still wouldn't look at me.

"Sorry, anyway, have you enjoyed your day so far?" he asked while bracing his elbows onto his knees. His puzzled look now replaced with his charming smile once again.

"Yes. It was wonderful, thank you."

"Can I ask you something?" he asked leaning back slightly in his chair. I nodded while taking a sip from my own drink. His eyes became serious; his calm blue eyes became *too* calm, like the sea before a war with the land. "When I walked into the pub yesterday, I'll be honest with you." He brushed his hair back with his fingers, taunting me to reach out and touch its bronze strands. "I wanted to approach you but I was a little nervous."

I sat my glass down and I knew my expression said it all.

"You don't believe me?" His eyes were still serious.

"I don't believe someone like you would be nervous around someone like me." I tried to laugh, but he just studied me; at least he had that in common with Jane. They always seemed to study everything they looked at. As if their eyes were the cameras to the face of the Earth.

"No, honestly. Anyway." He chuckled slightly. "I was thinking about how to strike up a conversation with you when I noticed something."

I stayed silent as he continued.

"It was as if you were waiting to disappear." I looked down, anywhere but at his eyes. "You just seemed in a whole other world to the rest of us, and I notice it many times with you." He lifted my chin across the table with his fingertip, and when I did look back into his eyes I didn't see compassion, but understanding. "Someone like you," he said, eyes piercing, "should never try to hide away." He let my chin go but didn't look away.

"Does it matter? When no one bothers to look for you anyway?" I tried to make light of the situation before me, but it didn't seem to work.

"It does because there *are* people looking for you." he said as he took my hand.

I didn't pull away from his touch as I did with everyone else's. I let him hold my hand, his skin warm against mine. We chattered through our meal, quite content with letting the hours disappear with the beach. But I needed to return home as I had work tomorrow. We made our way through the door and walked back towards his car; he had his arm around my waist the entire walk there. My heart didn't miss a beat of it.

The stars in the sky seemed to shine bigger and brighter the more I smiled and laughed. I seemed at ease with him. I wished for the night to last forever. But too soon we reached the car, and just as before he opened my door for me, I slipped in and turned towards him just as he got into his side. As the engine purred to life, sleep seemed to pull me into its hands and my eyes started to droop.

"Sleep Lucinda, I'll wake you when I get you home."

His soft voice hardly reached me as I drifted further away. I felt the car speed onto the road with ease, but before I could be completely taken, I thought I heard him mumble something into the darkness of the car.

"Dear god, what the hell am I going to do?"

Sleep wouldn't let me go. It held onto my flesh as I floated through dreams. I dreamt of speeding through darkness, flashing lights blinding me from behind my eyelids. Strong yet soft hands touched my cheek, tracing the skin that lived there. A door opened, warm arms encircled me and lifted me against a strong chest, but I was too tired to open my eyes. Voices, though hushed as they spoke, passed me as I was carried into a place of warmth. Then all too soon the arms that carried me laid me down upon a surface of comfort and content. Then with a gentle kiss to my forehead, the arms pulled away, the only evidence of them left was the smell of red roses.

We spent the next few weeks together. The days floated away into bliss, and I adored every part of it. I learned so much about him; not because he told me, but just from *him*. The way he pushed his hair back with his fingers, or how his eyes came alive as he gazed at me. Even the way he spoke about something he was passionate about became art to me. Everyone waits for the one moment that they touch someone, speak to someone, or even just see them out of the corner of their eye. Their heart starts to speed like a humming bird's wing, and it physically hurts to keep it in their chest. Don't wait for that. Wait for the moment where your heart is as steady as an aeroplane smoothly in flight. When all you need is a glance and you'll know when your heart is truly home. It will finally settle and start to beat alongside theirs. Now isn't that more beautiful?

Chapter 2

*"The only thing I know is this: I am full of wounds and still
standing on my feet."*

– Nikos Kazantzakis

Lucinda

I twisted and turned in my sweaty blankets. I was half-asleep and
half-awake. My mind was trying to drag me deeper and deeper
into the unknown of darkness and rest.

*It was dark, but light. A long road stretched out before me. But
that was all there was. I stepped over the glass that covered it,
their sharp edges biting my feet the more I disturbed their final
resting place. Pieces of once shiny metal rested everywhere,
claiming the places they weren't meant to be.*

Blood and silence was all that existed here.

*In the distance I saw them. Laying there, never to move again.
Never to blink, laugh, or cry. Both of them, not too far apart,
reaching for each other. But going still soon after.*

*Their bodies were twisted and bent in all directions that were
anything but normal. Blood covered them like how the night covers
the sky each night.*

Unending and absolute.

Michael.

His lifeless body twitched.

And his eyes were on me.

"Why didn't I get to live? Why just you?"

I screamed...

"Wake up Lucinda!"

I opened my eyes. A smooth hand was covering my mouth,
muffling my cries. I looked up and Peter came into my burly
vision, his eyes mere inches away from mine. He lifted his hand

away, hesitant in case I started to scream again. I tried to move, but I was pinned by him. Both of my arms were held down by one of his.

"It's ok," he said as he moved away. I sat up, unable to speak, blinking to clear my vision.

"Peter?" I asked confused. My voice was scratchy and sore. Like razor blades had been stuffed down my throat. "What are you doing here?"

His signature grin was soft but sheepish. "I wanted to see you."

I looked at my alarm clock on my bedside table. It was three o'clock in the morning!

I turned my head back to him. "In the middle of the night?"

"Yeah, I realise it was a bit stupid. I'll go." He stood up from the bed and moved towards the window.

"Wait!" I said.

He stopped.

"What is it?"

He leaned back into the room, a shimmer of something I couldn't quite read passed over his face as I sat quietly. Watching him watch me.

"Actually, would you stay with me tonight?" I felt incredibly small when I left the question between us. He studied me for a few seconds, then without another word he moved away from the window, took off his shoes and shirt, then climbed in the bed behind me. His arms snaked around my stomach and pulled me in tight. His hand stroking the flesh that was exposed. A small sigh escaped me and I knew he heard it. He body was so warm. I couldn't remember the last time I'd been this warm. It flowed through me, relaxing me against him.

And I didn't push him away.

I didn't want to.

And it felt good.

I closed my eyes and buried myself into the blanket. I could feel his breath against my hair drifting me to sleep, and this time I wasn't afraid of what awaited me.

"Lucinda?" he whispered into my ear.

"Umm?"

"What were you dreaming about?"

I opened my eyes. But I didn't turn to look at him.

"The accident that killed my father and brother."

He didn't say anything. I didn't think he could. So many people have said to me that it will get better, that the pain will go away. That it is even better that it happened when I was young, that way I wouldn't remember it. But I did. I do. It is as clear as the glass that covered the road. I remember it all. I don't think the pain ever goes away, I think we grieve for the rest of our days. I think the pain stays with us, reminding us how easy it is to be broken, that we are not the most powerful creatures on Earth, but the weakest. Because we are the ones that feel the most, therefore the ones that lose the most.

"Can I take you somewhere tomorrow?" he mumbled against my neck. I nodded. He pulled me close one last time before settling down for the rest of the night. I don't know how long it was before I followed him to the land of memories and dreams. I watched the beginnings of the sun rising through my window, the tempting pinks and yellows drawing my eyes to a close. And I was gone.

Chapter 3

"I close my eyes and let my body shut itself down and I let my mind wander. It wanders to a familiar place. A place I don't talk about or acknowledge exists. A place where there is only me."

— *James Frey, 'A Million Little Pieces'*

Lucinda

The morning was a blur, I was half drained from not getting enough sleep. But that was my fault.

I carried myself to the shower as Peter lazed around in my bed. He looked dazzling when he woke up. His hair was a mess as it shone in the morning sunlight, his eyes aglow as he smiled at me. His white straight teeth were gleaming too.

And I could only stare at him.

The hot water rained down on my body and brought it to life. I brushed my teeth, washed my hair and tried to make myself look a little bit more human. I jumped out of the shower and dried myself off before dressing. When I finally walked back into my room, Peter hadn't even moved.

"Peter?"

Nothing.

I dropped the towel and quietly climbed onto the bed. Letting my cold wet hair drag itself across his bare back.

He awoke with a yelp.

He looked up at me. I sat grinning down at him.

His smile was cruel.

He lunged for me, his strong arms pinning me against him. Our laughs mingled together. An endless bliss as he held me down on the bed.

"That wasn't very nice." He chuckled as he moved closer to me, our breathing now becoming one.

"What can I say? I like to see you squirm."

I couldn't help but giggle. His hands slipped from my arms, no longer pining me down. Instead he cupped my face, tracing my flesh with sweet delicateness. I could only look up at him, any words that I did have disappeared from me.

"Lucinda…" he said to himself, as if he was testing out my name. As if he was remembering how it had once sounded on his tongue. Yet that wasn't possible.

I didn't say anything. Instead I reached up and traced the skin under his beautiful eye. I loved them. They seemed to reach a part of me that couldn't be touched by hands. His eyes closed at my touch, his face filled with content.

"Peter…"

Our lips were inches apart. At my words, his eyes opened to find mine. There was nothing else to say. He leaned in the rest of the way and–

"Lucinda!" my mother yelled up the stairs.

We broke apart.

He stood up clearing his throat. But a smile still lingered on his lips.

"You should see what your mother wants," he said while leaning down to the floor for his shirt.

I nodded and climbed off the bed.

I walked into the kitchen and found my mother drying the dishes.

"When you bring a man home to spend the night I do expect to be told Lucinda."

"Sorry, it won't happen again."

She faced me and put down the last cup. But I could see her face light up.

"So do you both have any plans for the day?" she asked.

I sat down at the table.

"Peter is taking me somewhere. It's a surprise though." I couldn't keep the excitement from my voice.

"Ok, just be careful." She placed the cup away and I noticed how bright she was today.

Maybe this meant she was getting better.

I stood up and took a chance. I pulled her into my arms and gave her a hug for the first time in years. With a quite sigh she hugged me back, her little arms gently holding me to her as if I was still a child.

"Thank you Mum," I whispered into her hair, her smell was so comforting.

33

"What for?" she asked.

I kept my voice steady as a tear fell into her hair. "Just for saying that."

She buried her face into the crook of my neck and gave me a quick squeeze before we parted.

She had tears in her eyes too.

"Go on, go get ready. I'll have dinner done for when you get back."

I had no idea where he was taking me...

An hour had passed since we left my house, but all that was to see were trees and fields.

"Where in God's name are you taking me?" I asked while trying to keep the excitement from my voice.

He only grinned as he sped down the road.

"You'll see."

Another twenty minutes went by before we entered onto a dirt track. Dust flew into the air as we drove down into more and more trees.

He parked the car hidden within the shrubs.

He faced me, grinning ear to ear. "We're here."

I didn't say anything, I only climbed out of the car and looked upwards. The sunlight reached us through the thick shield of leaves. The day was warm, and I was grateful for the shade the trees gave me. I looked back to Peter, but he was already looking at me. His stood smiling like a child, his head cocked to the side, his hair slightly falling onto his forehead. His leather jacket and black jeans were dark against his white shirt, and he had his hands tucked into the front of his jeans. There he stood, eyes bright, glowing blue. The sun shining upon him like a halo gifted by the sky, and as he stood there, my heart didn't skip a beat, it beat on steady. Like the rays of the burning sun above us heating the Earth.

Peter

There she stood. Her long hair brushing her back gently as she smiled at me. I watched the joy on her face as she looked around, the fresh colours of the newly bloomed forest greeting her back. She wore black ripped skinny jeans and a cream jumper that once belonged to her father.

Her brown eyes burned in the mid-morning sunlight. The deepness of her eyes always captivated me, held me in place, showed me where I wanted to be.

It was a sight to behold, watching a human come alive.

She was beautiful.

Lucinda

I wondered what he was thinking as he stood there smiling at me.

"Come on, there's more to see."

He motioned for me to follow him, and so I did.

We walked side by side as we strolled deeper and deeper into the woods. The birds sang their songs, the deer danced their dances, the flowers showed their beauty. Vines covered in thorns climbed high on nearly every tree, and the centuries old trees hugged them back, as nature should.

It was like I was in another world. Completely separated from the one I was born in and placed in this fantasy of light and wonder.

Light. A pool of light greeted us up ahead, and as we walked closer I realised it was a small rounded plot of grass. The circle of light was surrounded by the huge Oak trees of the forest. The forest around it made the pool of light seem brighter than it really was, the dark woods stark against the circle of sunlight. I reached out my hand into the light; it warmed my skin. Peter walked in first, the sun blessing him as he walked to the centre of it all and sat down within the grass.

"Won't you come sit beside me?" he asked. The green strands brushed his jeans and held him in place. I swore I could hear something whisper around me, pushing me to join him, to be a part of this place.

I stepped into the light. I closed my eyes as I lifted my face skywards, letting the sun warm me, fill me.

It was so sunny, warm, comforting in a way. And as I sat down next to Peter, the world vanished. It became muffled outside of this bubble of nature and light. Purple and yellow flowers wavered in the gentle breeze; all beautiful.

It was a meadow.

A meadow that eclipsed everything else as soon as you entered its domain.

It was a home.

A home to someone.

I could feel the emotions flood through the grass, the love brush the trees, the sadness wallowing in the corners of the forest around me.

Something happened here.

Something graceful.

Something devastating.

This place was a fresh place ready for its perfect peak, but now…

"What happened here?" I asked as I looked at him.

His eyes traced mine.

"Many things…" His voice was quite, as if he was trying to shield it away from me.

"Tell me."

He let go of a deep breath as he tucked a piece of hair behind my ear.

"The story goes that two lovers came here once, many centuries ago, before cities and people emerged from the depths of creation. The man was darkness and the women was light. The world was new and this was one of the first places that grew flowers. So the man brought his lover here and picked her a single flower, and with that single gift, she used it to plant him a million flowers across the world."

"Then what happened?"

His eyes softened.

"One day, when he came here, he sat waiting for her, the flowers freshly bloomed, the trees growing their new leaves. Yet she never came. He waited for what seemed like days, maybe he did. But she didn't come."

"Why?"

"The Gods stole her away. They weren't meant to fall in love. Love wasn't allowed to exist. She was good and he was bad. They were the balance. The Gods couldn't allow that scale to tip. So they were separated. The meadow never saw them again. Yet the flowers continued to grow."

I was quite for a few moments.

"That's a beautiful story," I said.

"All things that end in tragedy are beautiful," he said.

The way he spoke, the words that flowed from him. It sometimes seemed like he was from a different time, a different world.

"You are so different from anyone I've ever met."

He cocked his head to the side. "Why do you say that?" He started playing with the strands of my hair.

"The way you speak," I whispered. "The way you hold yourself. It's like you're from a completely different world."

His eyes were like liquid sky. His soft thumb was stroking my skin, sending goose bumps across my entire body.

"I just see things differently, that's all." He leaned back onto his elbows and looked back up at me. "So, do you like it here?"

I turned away to the flowers, the trees, the soft whisper that the wind carried past us like an invisible ship taking its ghosts of the past across sea.

"It's beautiful. How did you find it?"

"My parents used to come here, and one day I followed them here. Then eventually when they stopped, I took over for them."

"Took over?" I asked. His dazed eyes captured mine once again.

His gaze held mine and didn't falter as he spoke.

"This place is the last reminder of my parents. I guess I come here to keep their memory alive. And on the plus side, it's a beautiful place to bring beautiful women."

He chuckled as I pushed him away, but I couldn't help but smile behind my wall of hair.

With a sweet hand he moved the wall of hair away from my face, his thumb stroking my cheek.

We looked at each other, our gazes locked as the sun blessed us with its arms of warmth. He seemed so at home here, like it *was* his home. He was at perfect harmony here, and so was I.

"You are beautiful Lucinda." His breath brushed against my lips; it smelled good. I wish I was the kind of girl that could believe those sort of words when they were spoken to her. Yet looking at this man before me, I felt like I could just this once. "And I know that you don't believe me, but it's true. And I hope one day you will believe it."

"Peter–" I didn't get to finish because small droplets fell upon us in silent warning.

We looked up and saw grey clouds creeping across the sky. How could it be so sunny one moment then dark and grey the next?

"That's strange," I said facing him again. But he was still gazing upwards, the grey sky making his eyes become darker. It was as if his eyes changed with the weather. He seemed closed off now as he faced me. His eyes no longer glowing, but hidden from me. As if he knew something I didn't. The world around us wasn't vibrant anymore; the flowers closed themselves and the trees shrunk back. Like the entire meadow was trying to hide itself away from the approaching storm.

Rain fell from the Heavens like canons from the clouds. It fell onto his face and into his hair and onto mine, but we didn't notice. Like a predator he watched me, the rain soaking us both, his eyes never leaving mine, and mine never leaving his. Yet I wasn't scared. Ever since I'd met him, I'd noticed the change that happened within him. When he can be smiling and happy, and a sudden change in the air made him go rigid, like he knew something was watching his every move.

I leaned forward. I was completely soaked, my bones crying out for a warm blanket. I touched his cheek with my fingertips, feeling the soft skin that was freshly shaved. And I noticed the slight grey skin around his eyes, the tinge of darkness that showed itself whenever the world showed its own.

Our lips were so close, inches apart. Then Peter laced his arm around me, pulling me flush against his broad chest. Our breathing was shaken, unnerved at our closeness.

I was kneeling before him as he sat before me. I was looking down at him as he gazed up at me. I held both sides of his face, needing to hold him to me.

I moved the rest of the way.

I brushed my lips against his, testing, taking my time.

But before I could kiss him, lightning struck across the sky, leaving a sound of thunder that left my ears humming. Then as swift as a humming bird's wing, Peter had me in his arms, carrying me to the safety of the trees. He stopped at the tree line, still holding me in his arms. He looked up to the sky with accusing eyes, as if his worst villain somehow lived within the world above us.

Then he turned away.

I looped my arms around him and hid my face away from the rain in the crook of his neck. He was so strong, to carry me with such ease through the thick forest that was now as soaked as us.

"Let's get you home before you catch a cold," he said. His eyes were no longer tinged grey.

"Can we come back?" My voice was nothing more than hushed words. He looked down at me then, his face utterly vulnerable to me.

"Yes." His own voice was quite. "We can come back whenever you want."

I was dripping wet, the rain marking me with its invisible brethren. But it didn't take him long to carry me back to the car.

He placed me down and opened my door. I climbed in and turned on the heaters for us both, absorbing the heat happily.

I looked back out of the window from where we came from. No one could find that place unless they knew where to look. It was hidden – hidden so carefully within nature like it was its only treasure. As if the trees concealed it away. It was easy to believe a story like the one Peter told me when it's about a place like that.

I hope we would get the chance to come back soon.

"Ready?" he asked me. I turned back to him, leaving the meadow behind for another day.

"Yeah, I'm ready."

Chapter 4

"Life will break you. Nobody can protect you from that, and living alone won't either, for solitude will also break you with its yearning. You have to love. You have to feel it is the reason you are here on earth. You are here to risk your heart. You are here to be swallowed up. And when it happens that you are broken, or betrayed, or left, or hurt, or death brushes near, let yourself sit by an apple tree and listen to the apples falling all around you in heaps, wasting their sweetness. Tell yourself you tasted as many as you could."

– Louise Erdrich

Lucinda

I awoke with a smile on my face. I shot out of bed to quickly find my clothes just so I could get to work just as fast. How could someone become your only source of happiness in just a few weeks? I was brushing my hair and placing it behind my shoulder. I liked wearing it down now. It was nice to see an old part of myself when I looked in the mirror now. I turned but stopped as something caught my eye. I turned to find the silver photo frame of my brother and father still turned around. The day they died I turned it around to face the wall, and I hadn't turned it back around since. The dust that harnessed no indents of fingerprints, the perfect layer of dust covered it, even spider webs had made themselves at home on it. I hadn't seen or tried to remember their faces since that day.

That was thirteen years ago.

I placed my hand on top of it, about to turn it when my heart stopped me. I thought back to the last few weeks with Peter. Did I deserve to be this happy when they had died so horribly? And more importantly, did that mean he would be taken away too? I lifted my hand away from the frame, leaving fingerprints indented in the dust.

I couldn't

I wouldn't.

I still couldn't look at their faces. I don't think I could really remember them anymore.

As I drove to work, I started to drift into my thoughts. I've taken my heart out of nearly every situation, and somehow, I'd distanced my very soul from the light of the world, hoping the darkness would hide it. That the darkness had enough of itself to share, to conceal my dying self from existence. Yet this man walked into my life and brought this kind of light along with him, destroying all the dark places where I would hide away. My heart was now exposed.

I arrived at work and walked through the door to screaming. I thought some customers were fighting at the bar when I walked in. But Jane and Peter were the ones screaming in each other's faces. Jane's face was furious, her hair wild and eyes blazing. Peter stood rigid, his eyes burning like hers.

They looked like they were in a battle between Gods.

"You're never going to learn, are you?!" Jane threw a chair at her brother's head but he dodged it swiftly.

"So I've got to stay miserable for the rest of my life just to keep them happy?" He threw a glass at the wall behind the bar, but I noticed he wouldn't throw anything directly at her.

"Yes!" she screamed. *"If you value your god forsaken life, and if not for that! Then for hers!"* Tears were streaming down her cheeks as she just stood shaking, looking at her brother with hate yet a deep protectiveness. As if something was going to hurt him.

"I can't do that," he said defeated. "Not anymore Jane, and you know it," he said calmly for the first time since I had walked in the door. I cleared my throat and they both looked at me with wide eyes, but Jane looked back to her brother also defeated.

"I won't hurt her," he said while looking back to his sister. "I won't."

"No…" she mumbled back. "You'll just break her, or yourself in her place." And she dismissed us both by walking to her office. I looked at him confused as he watched his little sister walk away. When he looked at me, his smile was strained.

"What was that about?" I asked with caution. He just shook his head and walked around the bar to pour a shot of whiskey.

"We've just had a disagreement, that's all." I scoffed at his words and took the glass from him. He watched me tip it down the sink without a word. And with a lot of guts, I wrapped my arms around his waist.

"I wouldn't know," I said into his grey shirt. He wrapped his arms back around me tightly, as if he thought I would disappear.

"Yeah, I know. I'm sorry you had to see that my little Lucinda." I lifted my head to look at him.

"Why do you call me that? Is it because I'm shorter than you?" I chuckled, but his eyes seem to hold something he would never share.

"You just remind me someone I once knew, that was what I used to call them." He sighed. He stroked my hair and laid his chin on top of my head.

"If that is just you and Jane arguing, I would hate to witness the both of you with your other brother." A laugh rippled through his chest as he held me. I finally let go to get ready for work, but Jane walked back through the bar. Her mascara was running down her cheeks and as Peter went to her, he wiped it away with his fingertips.

"Lucinda?" she called as she came out from behind him.

"Yes?" I asked, weary of what she was going to say.

"I can hold the fort today, take another day off."

She smiled before she walked back into the office. Peter and I stood alone, looking at each other in surprise.

"Well… I'm just going to leave you both to it then." I tried to slip out of the door, but his soft hands caught me first.

"Wait." I turned to face him. "Spend the day with me," he asked. His face was so hopeful, but for the first time since I'd met him, something was telling me to back away. Not because he was dangerous, because I already knew that. But because he was also the opposite, and if I lose that security again, would I survive that?

I took a deep breath. "I can't. I have things to do."

I yanked my arm away, and his face fell. I grabbed my things and rushed out of the door as quick as I could, desperate to clear my head. I didn't drive home that day. I went to Rock-bay beach. Hardly no one came to this beach as it was mostly huge rocks instead of sand. I had no idea what was happening to me. Instead of wanting the day to end as soon as it started, I wanted it to last forever, especially when Peter was in it. My heart rose from the deepest corners of my chest when he was near me. I could feel it when I wish I wouldn't.

When I finally reached the beach, I took my time walking down the hill. Then I climbed up the rocks and sat on the biggest one, watching the waves below crash against the smaller boulders. The wind was strong enough to bring tears to my eyes, or were they actual tears? Tears escaping after so long of being kept at bay.

The sky was darkening; patches of black in the clouds made the few people on the beach scurry away, but I stayed. Even when it poured down with rain. The storm passed overhead and rumbled with anger, lightning flashed brightly where the sea met the sky, almost as if it was stitching them together. I stood up on the rock and looked up towards the clouds, and something pushed on the inside of my skull... wanting to escape.

Everything was raging around me.

Then suddenly, pain unlike any other radiated through my skull. As if the crashing waves around me were filling my head with electric-fired water.

I screamed, gripping my head and digging my nails into my scalp. I wanted to tear my skull from my neck just to be rid of the pain.

Then it disappeared.

And in its place were fuzzy white walls, marble arms that reached up and up into the blinding beyond.

An angel on his knees before a huge white marble chair.

But the scene before me was blurry, and I couldn't make out any of their faces. I looked at the angel again and realised that his wings were black, yet other colours were mixed within the feathers too. His body was battered and wounds covered every part of his skin. I could see that scars would surely follow. He was bowing before her, head down. But as I watched him sob on his knees, he seemed almost familiar.

I knew him, but I couldn't quite remember who he was to me.

"Please don't take her from me!" the young angel begged. "Please."

Another voice reached us. It was cold and unfeeling.

There was no pity for him.

"She is the reason you are falling. But she also needs to be protected from you..."

Her voice was steady as she looked down at the broken angel before her.

"If you disrupt her life again, you will fall..." The woman on the marble chair stood silently, her one huge white wing spreading around her like a blanket. But the angel before her also stood, his wings demanding the space of the entire room. Even in his horrible

43

state, he stood with the power and dominance that could only be imagined. So much in fact that the woman fell back into her marble chair.

Eyes wide.

The space around us seem to shudder, shrinking back from him and hiding behind the woman in the chair.

"Then I choose to fall." His voice didn't stammer; it was strong and unbroken unlike his body. She glared at him and bent forward, her feathers ruffled like a cat's fur.

"You're a fool!" she hissed at him, but he stood by his choice. "Do you have any idea what this will do to the both of you?"

I was frozen as I watched them. He stepped back and bowed before her. But it wasn't a real bow. But a bow of mockery.

I could feel his grin. "I guess we will find out."

He turned and stalked towards me as the woman continued to yell from her chair. He walked through me and a cold shock of air ran across my body, immobilising my heart from beating.

Peter

I ran towards her. The breath in my chest hurt my lungs from the cold air, but I had to reach her. She was standing on top of a huge rock next to the crashing waves. They sprayed onto her face but she didn't seem to notice one bit of it. Her mouth was slightly agape, her eyes were glazed over white, and she was looking up to the sky as if she was in shock.

They had her.

"*Lucinda!*" I screamed her name. I was praying she would hear me before the waves took her down. "*Lucinda! Get down from there!*" I screamed again, I was nearly there. She seemed to snap out of her trance-like state and looked around confused through the powerful storm. She found me and shouted my name. She started to climb down from the rocks.

But she slipped.

The next wave towered over both of us and it swept her down from the rocks and out to sea.

I dived into the freezing water without hesitation and it seeped into my very bones. Pain screamed through my head like a knife, but when I saw her floating in the dark water unconscious, just a few feet away from me, I swam as hard as I could to reach her. Her skin was ice cold as I grabbed hold of her hand. I pulled her up to the surface as fast as I could.

As soon as I broke through the surface, I pulled her against my body so she wouldn't go under again. But the waves were too strong with the storm on its side and we went under.

The current was pushing us further and further down, away from the only light the sky seemed to give. I held onto her with the remainder of my strength, her hair spread out across the water around her.

Her eyes were closed peacefully, her skin white and cold. Beautiful.

She was beautiful to me. Beautiful in a way that a woman would be to a man. She wasn't my friend from my past anymore, not small and delicate. Now she was a powerful woman that was drowning before me.

Something deep within me awoke. It rippled through my back as the water around me moved away from it. It lifted us out of the water and into the storm filled skies. The rain washed the salt from our bodies, and washed our hearts clean as I laid her onto the sand gently, her skin still cold to the touch.

"Lucinda?" I stroked her cheek and she moved slightly. The strength inside of me was slipping away and left me struggling to sit up right. But with the remaining energy I had left, I dragged her up the beach and screamed for help. I was about to collapse when a couple came running up the beach, panic in their eyes.

I blacked out into the sand beside her.

Chapter 5

"People die of broken hearts. They have heart attacks. And it's the heart that hurts most when things go wrong and fall apart."
– Markus Zusak

Lucinda

The first thing I heard was shouting. The panic in their voices was obvious. But when I opened my eyes it wasn't me they were fusing over. I lifted my head and realised they were trying to perform CPR on a man. He was hooked up to so many machines and tubes. His skin was white and he was unconscious. Still as the dead.

I was in the hospital.

"Stop, it's no use. He's gone," one doctor said.

"Time of death?" another asked.

"The girl, 12:00pm, and the boy 12:15pm."

I laid my head back down and tried to be as still as possible. Someone placed a sheet over my head and I heard them leave soon after. When I was sure no one was coming back, I got up and took the sheet away.

Peter was laying on the other bed, still and cold looking. I shot to my feet and raced to his side, unable to understand what was happening or why he wasn't waking up. I pulled the sheet away and shook his shoulders. Tears ran from my eyes and down my cheeks.

"Peter! Wake up!" I demanded. But he didn't move. I was starting to panic the more I cried out his name. "Please Peter, don't leave me too." I sobbed into his chest. He smelled of the Ocean and blood, and it covered him like a red fog.

"Peter!" I screamed again, I pounded on his chest. He couldn't leave me.

Anyone but him.

I felt the sudden panic, the reminder of grief starting to greet me over my shoulder.

Then suddenly, he gasped deeply and his eyes opened wide. He struggled with the tubes attached to him. I cried harder as I held his face as I would an injured bird, and as soon as I touched his face, his eyes snapped to mine. Relief surfaced as he watched me cry harder. He cupped my face with his good hand and tried to speak. Yet only red sea water spurted out.

"Don't try to talk, save your strength."

I tried to calm him and my sobbing as he went silent, and he didn't try to speak again. Instead he stroked my cheek with his soft thumb.

"I thought I'd lost you," I whispered. Tears fell from his eyes as he looked at me.

"Never…" he struggled to say, but I heard him. I traced his face with my eyes and very tenderly, I kissed his cheek, then his forehead and then his nose. And then very delicately, I leaned forward, our lips inches apart. But I jumped back when someone shouted in the doorway.

It was Jane.

Yet again tears and mascara streaming down her face.

"Peter!" she sobbed as she landed next him on his bed. She looked over at me, hand over her mouth. But she held her arms open for me and I didn't hesitate to enter them. Her hug was warm and comforting, one arm around me, and her other hand holding her brother's.

"How dare the both of you make me panic like that! Don't ever do that to me again."

I was shaking as she held me. It was so nice to have someone worry about me like this, even if it was under horrible circumstances.

"We're sorry Jane," I said.

She sighed against my hair and pulled away. Her eyes were dry now but still red.

"I think I need a drink." She stood up and straightened her skirt. "But not the sober kind."

She laughed as she exited the room, but it was forced. She left me and Peter alone. My cheeks started to heat up as I looked over at him. He was taking his bandages off his body and I could see the bleeding had stopped luckily. But wounds covered his face and head, and the rest of his body was the same. He caught me looking and he held his arms out for me, his face vulnerable. I stepped around the bed but before I could enter his awaiting arms, doctors and nurses burst through the door, and I was pushed against the wall.

I watched as they all checked him over, stunned he was even alive. But he didn't take his eyes away from mine. I watched the wounds on his skin re-open as they pulled him around and sorted him out, and when they were satisfied with their care, they turned to me and checked me over too.

Then we were left alone.

I sat at the end of his bed, and his face became expressionless. Void of character.

For so many years, I wouldn't open up to anyone, terrified my heart would be broken again. I would watch the world pass me by from behind the bar, wanting to be like the characters in my books: broken, yet wearing the pain like a diamond encrusted crown on top of my head.

But that just doesn't happen in real life.

Who was I? When I was alone and the moon was my only witness, who was I really? The person I was as a child? Happy and content to play with my toys and listen to the world's music; or the girl I am now: broken and unable to join the world again. The girl I was just three days ago. I liked her; smiling and enjoying the safety of the man before her. I pretended to be stronger than I really am, but I needed to be honest with myself. I was scared to love again. To allow the young girl in me resurface, then watch as she disappeared in anguish because I was too wrapped up in my own foolishness.

That would kill me…

I wanted to be that girl again. That carefree. The open hearted. The girl that was whole.

I wanted to be able to go into life again with my heart on my sleeve, to not worry about being broken again.

Sometimes it all has to come down to one choice. Save yourself, or let yourself love while always having that risk of being destroyed.

I knew as soon as I let him in, like everything else, he would be taken away.

The room seemed to suffocate me as I stood. His eyes became intense as I looked down at him. As I looked into his crystal blue eyes, I realised how much they had claimed me. They were embedded on my heart now.

"I can't need you this much Peter. It's just too much for me to handle. When I saw you in this bed, not waking up, something in me broke." He tried to sit up, but I gently pushed him back down. He gripped my wrist with his good hand, confusion in his eyes.

"I don't have enough in me to allow another thing to break." I started to cry again. I couldn't help it. "I love entirely, and my heart is easy to break…" I stood and tried to push his hand away, but even in his state he was too strong. "Peter. Please let go." But he stood up unsteadily and shook his head. He placed my hand onto his chest where his heart was, just as I did. He didn't say anything. He didn't need to.

"Please. Stay." His voice a scrap of what it normally was. I couldn't look at him, and before I could pull my hand away, I was in his arms. He laid his forehead against mine, breathing deeply. I knew his chest was struggling to work. His eyes were closed, but tears still escaped them.

"Please," he begged. But I'd made up my mind.

I pulled my hand back and looked at him one last time. His arms fell limply to his sides. He didn't try to hold me again.

"I'm sorry."

I walked to the doorway and stopped for a moment more, my heart begging to stay while my mind begged me to leave. Then I went through. It took everything in me to walk away, especially when he started to shout my name. His shattered voice from the salty ocean water shredding his words.

But I kept walking. The more I walked away the more I felt like the girl I was before I had met him.

Non-existing.

I found Jane at the doors of the hospital, and when her eyes found mine, I knew she understood.

She took my hand and we made our way to her car.

"Where do you want to go?" she asked softly while I leaned my head against the window. The cold glass was equal to my cold heart.

"Home…" I answered weakly. Too tired to say any more.

She started the engine and played some music quietly through the car, but I didn't listen to it. I thought back to his face as I left the room. He looked as pained as I felt. I wondered if the world was laughing at me, laughing at the girl that loved too easily and with all her heart.

"Lucinda?" Jane's sweet voice reached me through my deep thoughts. I looked over to see compassion in her face, and that we were already at my house.

"I know what you are doing," she said. "And I respect that. But I just need to say something." I nodded and turned towards her. She took a deep breath and smiled, but it wasn't her usual smile. This one was forced, like the one she gave me in the hospital.

"I know what it's like to be brutally hurt, by a lover, friend, and family. And I've had to watch everything I've ever loved turn to ashes in my hands. But that doesn't mean I want to stop feeling that love, because sometimes it's the only thing that keeps me alive. And I will always be grateful to have that."

She squeezed my knee reassuringly.

"I understand. But I'm not as strong as you Jane. And today…today when he was just laying on that hospital bed…" Tears escaped my eyes, choking me up. "That day when I lost my dad and my brother, nothing has ever compared to that pain." I looked at her then, her eyes dying with mine. "Until today."

Her own tears fell. "I'm sorry Lucinda. But please–"

I interrupted her before she could get through to me. "I can't put myself through that again. Not with him." I turned away and opened the car door.

"What do I say to him?" she asked gently.

I paused.

But I couldn't say anything. I had no answers for her. So I climbed out of the car and into my front door. I closed the door and kicked off my still sea drenched shoes. Then I heard my mother bounce through the hallway.

"And what time do you call this?" Her voice held some authority, which was a big change.

"Sorry," I mumbled through my still sore throat. She crossed her arms over her chest.

"Don't you think I deserve more of an explanation?" she asked again. I wasn't in the mood to ague tonight. I walked passed her and started to climb the stairs.

"Lucinda!" she said a bit too forcefully. She came after me as I started to pull my coat off. She walked in my room with her arms still crossed over her chest.

"Where have you been?" she asked again.

"In the hospital," I said finally. She acted shocked and tried to check me over for scraps; if only she knew.

"What happened?" she demanded. I literally just had one of the worst days of my life. I didn't want to talk to anyone, especially her.

"I am your mother, I have the right to know!" Her voice scraped at my head and I snapped. After years of holding it all in, I finally snapped.

I spun around and faced her fake concern.

"You forfeited your right to know anything about my life a long time ago!" I hissed as I threw my wet jacket across the bed.

"How dare you, I'm your mother," she shouted. I laughed in her face which made her turn red with anger.

"No. A mother is someone who doesn't abandon their child when they need them most! When I screamed your name during the night, you would never come as you were too out of your head! I never got a cooked meal unless I made it. I had to walk miles to school every day by myself while you dealt with your hangover! I pay for the bills, I pay for the food in this house, I pay for the car, and I've been doing it since I was a child!" I started to pace across the room, everything just spilling out of me, years of hurt.

"I picked myself back up, and I tried to do the same for you!" I stopped pacing and pointed my finger at her accusingly. "All those years has ruined me, I was the child. You should have been the one there for me, to pick *me* back up." I lowered my arm and just stood there, glaring at her. My mother was clutching the kitchen towel to her chest, sobbing into it.

"I was grieving, I didn't know how to deal with it. It was all too much for me to bare Lucinda." She begged for me to understand. But I couldn't. I didn't want to.

"Yet... A six year old child could," I calmly said. Her face broke as soon as I said it.

"I lost my husband and my son! What did you expect to happen?" she screamed across the room crying, but I only stood watching her.

"And we both know I lost a lot more..." We both fell silent, she crying and I glaring. I turned my back to her and faced the window. She sighed and closed the door as she left.

That night, I couldn't sleep. I just kept returning to Peter's face as I left; it was like I ran a dagger into his stomach and then smiled sweetly to him as I twisted it.

I wondered if my heart could hold that, that expression along with all my other grief without collapsing someday.

Everyone watched as I was slowly fading, as destruction slipped into my life, and I was left to deal with. But now, through so many years of it, I realised that it was better than falling apart all over again.

Chapter 6

"You are so brave and quiet I forget you are suffering."

– Ernest Hemingway

Lucinda

Months have passed since that horrible day. My mother never really speaks to me, and I don't try to speak to her. But I was more miserable than I'd ever been before. The days dragged on and faces passed through the days at work. Jane didn't really smile anymore, but she was still a comfort to have nearby. But today made the rest seem more horrid, but also not so. It was a dull, rainy day.

I was cleaning the glasses behind the bar when a young man approached. His hair was like captured sunlight placed upon his head, his hair wavy but a little wild. His eyes were a smooth, creamy dark chocolate. He was muscular and much taller than me, but he wasn't intimidating at all. Even when he was dressed in a long black trench coat. Well he was in all black anyway.

"Excuse me? Could I get a drink please?" he asked from the other side of the bar. I cleaned him a glass and poured him what he wanted, but I didn't speak as he passed me the change. But it was a few minutes of him starring that I snapped at him.

"What the hell are you starring at?"

He seemed shocked that I would talk to costumers like that, but like I said, I wasn't having a good few months.

A good life to be honest.

"Sorry." He held his hands up. "You just remind me of someone I used to know." I relaxed a little and apologised. His eyebrows drew together and he leaned onto his elbows.

"Bad day?" he asked. I laughed slightly and shook my head.

"You could say that." I looked at him again and saw something strange in his face.

"Do I know you from somewhere?" I asked. He seemed unsure if he should answer truthfully. He watched me, steady eyes looking for something.

"I wouldn't think so. I've never been here before."

He took another sip from his beer and smirked. It wouldn't have worked for anyone else but he seemed to make it work in his favour.

"So, what's your name then?" he asked.

The last time someone asked my name from behind this bar, it ended badly to the point of where I just wanted to let the world kill me.

"It's not that interesting," I said quietly. His grin only grew wider.

"I bet it is," he pushed again.

I sighed and told him, but his face fell like a stone as soon I did. And as soon as he noticed that I noticed his expression, he faked a smile again.

"Well, is there anything around here that's even slightly interesting?" he asked a little bored.

I sniggered and turned around to put the clean glasses away.

"Not unless you like bingo."

His laugh reached me and made my heart stop. I turned around slowly to face him. He was still laughing.

"You're him aren't you."

He stopped laughing and took another sip.

"Who?"

"Peter's…" It was still difficult to speak his name aloud. "…Brother," I finished. We watched each other. His face was as smooth as stone.

"How did you find that out?" His voice was cautions as he spoke.

"You both have the same laugh," I said honestly.

He swirled his drink and sighed.

"So, he came for you then. He finally found some balls to come for you," he said almost to himself.

"Excuse me?" He looked up almost surprised he had said anything.

"He hasn't told you yet?" he asked surprised.

"No, we haven't spoken in three months," I said with a little hurt in my voice. He looked even more shocked at my words.

"What happened?"

"Honestly?" He waited. "I was just scared." His eyebrows came together at my words. He leaned closer for me to continue. And for some reason. I did.

"We were in a really bad accident." He started to get up from his chair but I reassured him his brother was fine, and he sat back down to listen. I told him about my dad, my brother, even my mother. He listened to everything I said without interruption, and when I finished he nodded his head and took another sip of his drink.

"I see," he said finally. I leaned forward as he sat his drink back down again.

"Really? What do you see?" I asked.

"You're afraid to get hurt again. I understand that. But I know my brother, even if I haven't seen him for so long, I know he wouldn't hurt you."

I was silent, because I knew it too.

"You're actually afraid to love *too* much," he explained. "I've been there myself once too. I've loved too much and at one point, it broke a big part of me. But it was the best thing I have ever done." He shifted in his chair before continuing. "Lucinda. You don't get to choose who you love, no more than you can control the gravity of the Earth. It's something that will continue to happen around you, even if you allow yourself to be a part of it or not. It will still affect you. All I see is two people who had something special, and one of them didn't know how to deal with it. And that happens all the time." He finished the rest of his beer before handing me back the glass.

"What do I do?" I asked a little desperately. He smiled slightly, and I saw a little of Jane in his smile.

"No matter what you do in life, you'll get hurt. But it might as well be by the thing you love most." He slipped a cigarette between his lips, but didn't light it.

"I don't love him," I said defensively.

He just grinned. "I've just met you and I can already tell that you're a bad liar."

He stood up and pulled out a lighter from his pocket. But he still didn't light it.

"What's your name?" I asked before he turned away. He looked at me again and grinned.

"Kyle Hellfire," he answered. I nodded and he stepped away from the bar. "Lucinda?" I looked back up at Kyle.

"Yes?" I asked.

"Good luck."

He turned, leaving through the door. When he left, I missed his company oddly, like a friend almost.

"Who was that you were talking to?" Jane asked coming up next to me, and I smiled a little, which surprised her.

"Your brother Kyle." Shock crossed her eyes and she looked like she was about to jump over the bar after him, but something seemed to stop her.

"Aren't you going after him?" I asked, but she smiled instead. Did he make everyone smile wherever he went?

"No. He'll be back. He always comes back." And I was happy at her words.

I found Jane at her desk a few hours later. She looked tired, and not in just one way. I knocked before entering and smiled as she looked up. She rubbed her eyes and still managed to smile back.

"It's time to close up," I said as she stood up from her chair.

"Thank god." For some reason she flinched as she cursed. But I acted as though I hadn't noticed and turned away.

"Lucinda?" I stopped and faced her again. Her face seemed older.

"What is it?" I asked.

"He's not doing very well." Worry showed itself through my eyes as I couldn't hold it in.

"What do you mean?" It even showed in my tone.

"He's not eating or sleeping. He hasn't left his house since…" Her face broke. "That day."

I closed my eyes as I remembered the crushing water, his arms around my cold body as we shot out of the water.

"What can I do about it?" I said a bit too harshly as I opened my eyes. She was clutching something in her palm. It shinned in the lamp's light.

She was looking at it with memories behind her eyes, and when she looked up again, something was missing in them, as if *she* wasn't all there.

"He saved your life, and he nearly lost his in doing so. The least you could do is talk to him. Help him as he did you." Her voiced aged as she spoke, as if she was ancient. I nodded and left swiftly through the back door to my car. And I sat for a few minutes, debating whether to go home or do as Jane had asked.

I realised that time doesn't heal us. It just shows us what is worth grieving for, what is worth loving.

I went back in for his address and left soon after that.

He lived far out by the coast, vast and alone by the cliffs. Right at the top of Rock-bay beach sat a huge house among some trees. The house was white and looked abandoned, but Jane told me that was the house he would be in. I drove up next to the front door, and just stared at the house. Many years ago, I would've loved to have lived in a place like this.

I stepped out of the car and knocked on the door, but there was not answer. So I let myself in. Inside, it was huge. The walls were painted white like the outside, the furniture was all black, Victorian style. There was a crystal chandelier hanging from the centre of the ceiling. But all the mirrors were covered up. Strange.

As I was gazing at the décor, the sound of glass shattering came from the other room. I ran to see Peter holding the top of a whiskey bottle. The rest was broken across the marble floor. He threw the remains of it onto the floor and got another bottle from the cupboard. He forgot the glass and just took a swig straight from the bottle. He was shirtless and I noticed small, thin trails of scars across his back and biceps. They covered his entire top half of his body, and I could see the fresh scars from our accident also covering his flesh; just as mine did now. He turned to find my shocked expression mirroring his own. He still held the bottle in his hand before he let it go. Yet again glass shattered across the floor along with the alcohol. He seemed to snap out of his shock to realise what he had done.

"Again? Really?" I asked sarcastically. He looked back at me with annoyance. But I could also see relief.

"What are you doing in my house?" he spat. His whole body was shaking. I shrunk away from him a little. He looked… Powerful. But he looked slightly hurt as I moved away.

"I…I…I'm sorry, I just came to see how you were doing."

He glared at me, but it held something else too. As I could now see all of him, I saw how painful it must have been for him to have saved me. His wounds, which were now scars, were a nasty red colour and there were yellow and purple bruises across his skin.

A mismatched puzzle of suffering I left him alone to face.

"I'm sorry," I said.

He could see I meant more than just walking into his house uninvited.

But for everything.

"Get out!" The hurt must have shown on my face as his softened, but stayed defiant. I nodded my head and turned to leave, but tears ran down my cheeks. What had I expected? To fall into his inviting arms? *I'd* hurt him. So why was I crying? I never should have come. I opened the front door and was about to step through when soft hands grabbed my jumper, pulling me back in. I was pinned against the wall with Peter inches away from my face. And he only pulled away to take another sip of whiskey from yet another bottle. He still glared at me with hate, yet also longing.

An odd combination.

"I thought you told me to leave?" I asked. I couldn't help but tease him. He leaned even closer so I could smell the alcohol on his breath.

He jerked away and took another sip. He walked into the living area and laid across the leather couch.

"So you thought you would just come and check up on your hero?" he asked me as he chuckled to himself.

I walked in with my arms holding my sides, completely out of my comfort zone for the first time while being around him. He looked over to me with a smirk. He was sprawled out, and even drunk he was just as attractive as before.

"I guess so…" I sat across from him and watched as he drank some more of the whiskey. He looked as I felt inside, lost and confused.

Rain started to batter against the house, and in an odd way it was comforting.

"Well how lucky am I?" he said in fake excitement. "The very girl that deserted me wants to see if I'm holding up ok! Bless your dear old heart Lucinda."

He toasted with the bottle before gulping down the rest of it, then threw it onto the other side of the sofa. He looked over at me and sighed.

"You think you're the only one in the world that has been hurt?" He shook his head. "You have no idea that losing the people you love is nothing compared to some of the things I've been through." I stayed silent as he stared at me. I had so many things to say, but I couldn't find the proper words. "I wanted to heal you Lucinda. Not hurt you." He spoke softly for the first time since I'd been here.

Tears streamed down my cheeks as he watched me.

"I know." My voice cracked. His eyebrows drew together in confusion. "But that day in the hospital showed me how much I already needed you." He sat up and faced me properly, his expression even more confused. "Peter, for a moment I thought I had lost you and the same pain came back as it did that day I realised my brother and father weren't coming home. And that nearly destroyed me. So I did what I thought I had to do to save myself from all that pain. I tried to let you go."

Understanding crossed his face as he leaned his elbows onto his knees.

"And I'm so sorry. But I was scared that if I did let you in, I would've lost you too."

He covered his face with his hands, shielding himself from me. But finally he looked up and something I did not recognise rimmed his blue eyes.

His face was as beautiful as the surface of a star.

"When I dived into the water, all I could feel was the crippling temperature of it. It blinded my sense that I nearly blacked out. But I saw you only a few feet away, drifting through the dark current unconscious. And something awoke in me, and all I wanted was to save you. I didn't care what happened to me." His eyes were intense as he remembered. "And the same ice cold feeling broke me as you left me in that room," he said as I looked down defeated. "I hope that shows how much you mean to me just as much as you say I mean to you."

He got up and went up the stairs into the hallway. I didn't know what to do. I have walked alone for so long. More alone than a spirit invisible to the living world, but I realised I was no longer so alone while I had him. It had been so long since I had felt like this.

He walked back into the room a couple of minutes later with damp hair, a black jumper and grey jogging bottoms. He sat down beside me but didn't touch me. He seemed more sober now that he had showered.

"I have been hurt too, and Jane, more than anyone I have ever known. My brother, he doesn't even live in the world most of the time from how much he has endured from it." He gently took my hand in his own and stroked the top of it, just like he used to. "But you don't have to deal with it alone anymore." He gazed into my eyes, inches away. "I'm here now. I want to help you." His words whispered against my ear as he leaned forward. I closed my eyes to the sensation of his touch. I turned towards him to trace his face with my fingers. He closed his eyes to the feeling of it. He looked so tired and beaten down since I'd last seen him.

58

I placed my hand across his chest, right were his heart lived; the heart I had now damaged. He tucked the hair out of my face. Since I'd arrived his eyes were hard, distant. But now they were bright blue and shinning, open to me.

"Stay? I've missed you so much," he asked with a little hope in his eyes.

"Of course I'll stay," I whispered.

I did stay that night. We listened to the rain outside batter against the house. But he was still drunk, so he fell asleep not long after. I helped him upstairs to his bed and began to leave for the sofa downstairs, but he pulled me down on top of him.

"Don't leave me…" he mumbled into my hair.

"Ok, but I need to change first."

He climbed up from the huge bed and gave me one of his shirts to wear. It smelled of him, of red roses and dusty pianos. I couldn't stop smiling as I tied my hair at the nape of my neck. He reached out for me and I climbed into his strong arms. He settled against my back, spooning me in warmth and security that I hadn't had for such a long time. He fell asleep before me, but I was thinking about my father and my brother, and I knew that they would want me to move on with my life and not waste it. We were both collaterally damaged, and for once I wanted to be the one to fix someone, instead of someone fixing me.

Chapter 7

"The greatest human quest is to know what one must do in order to become a human being."

– Immanuel Kant

Lucinda

White. Blue. Him.

It was all I could see. Everything was burly again, but I could tell I was surrounded by sky and clouds. Blinding blue and faded clouds that surrounded me like a cocoon. The angel from before was looking down towards Earth. He was dressed in armour of shining light, and each feather on his wings was suited by metal coverings. Symbols of ancient history were engraved within the rare metals. The sky around us seemed to chant as his eyes seared the planet before him. Asking, wanting, daring him...

He looked over-powering.

Too powerful.

Determination was placed in his face as he stared downwards, something bothering him deeply.

"Wait!"

Another angel shouted while running towards him, his face panicked. When he reached him, he clasped his silver shoulder, his grip unrelenting.

"Please my son, don't do this," he begged, but the silver angel stepped away from his grasp, and faced the Earth once again. It seemed he was unable to look away.

"I have to, I have to know her."

The other angel looked defeated as he knew there wasn't any way that he could change the young angel's mind. He nodded and stepped away.

The silver angel took pity, and gripped his shoulders, smiling.

"Gabriel!" His voice held undeniable anticipation. *"If you would have just taken the time to meet her, then you would understand why I have to do this."*

The angel named Gabriel gave him the kind of smile that a father would give his son before he left to make his own adventures. Sad but proud. An unending love that would link them together for eternity.

"I know," he said. *"But in love, you make stupid choices. I just hope you're making the right one."*

They embraced one last time before Gabriel walked away.

He faced the Earth again and smiled to himself. He turned around to face me, and before he fell, everything cleared. As if the world brought the veil away from my eyes.

Peter stood before me dressed in a white silver battle suit, his eyes glowing a luminous blue. I thought that, for a moment, the world up above must've blessed them with the purest of summer skies. His wings were black, but each wing held all colours of the rainbow. Each of them shimmering like the reflections of the Ocean against the sun. Every twist and turn of them showed where the colours hid and where they were born. As if they were forever trapped upon him.

He was breathtaking...

Everything about him glowed and shimmered. The sky reached out to touch him, to behold what they had created. I wasn't scared. I wasn't shocked...

He fell backwards and I seemed to fall with him, the sky passing us so fast I couldn't breathe. The air never reaching me, I was unable to take a breath.

We passed a barrier of some kind and the world slowed down. And as he passed, it rippled like water, swallowing him in and then spitting him back out through the other side. When he resurfaced, he fell quicker, screaming in agony as white fire engulfed him. His wings were burning and breaking away into ash. They fell around him, with him, the colours vanishing with such destroyed grace.

He fell faster than any star, and he was just as bright. But the only thing that prevented it from being entrancing was his chest ripping screams. As if the fires of Hell were escaping him in invisible fumes.

I've always tried to imagine what a fallen angel would look like.

I awoke with his arms around me, everything silent but his breath warming my hair. I untangled his arms from me and gently climbed out of bed and wandered about the house. The rooms, the walls, they were beautifully crafted. Patterns covered every bit of the décor. Like many things, the house was nothing to admire on the outside, but inside; it was a treasure. From room to room I looked, and I came across what looked like a small library. Books covered the floor and shelves. Paintings hung from every available part of the walls, and as I looked closer I could see they were paintings of angels, some fighting, some helping other angels, and others were simply paintings of white buildings. I traced them with my fingers and felt the texture of the dried paint.

I felt something as I touched the paint, something pull at me.

Like the sand calling out to the Ocean.

Or the air calling out for the birds.

The floorboards squeaked from behind me, but I didn't turn around. Because I was staring at the painting on the other side of the room. It took up the entire wall as it hung from the floor to the ceiling. The man in the art was standing upon a dark cloud and he was looking slightly over his shoulder. His attention seemed to be somewhere else, but the only thing that really got my attention was that he was the silver angel from my dreams.

"Who is he?" I asked, my voice slightly unnerved. Because I already knew the answer.

He walked closer, and placed his hands on my hips and leaned in to rest his forehead on the back of my head.

"It's not important Lucinda. Please just come back to bed."

I stepped out of his arms. I couldn't look at him.

"Tell me."

"Lucinda…"

"Tell. Me." He sighed from behind me, but I wanted an answer. My life was such a mess and I needed some truth in it. So I answered for him. "It's you, isn't it."

"Yes it is…" he whispered.

He held my hand and made me face him. And when I did, I saw nothing but his eyes.

Clear and crystal blue.

"Before you panic or call me a lair, I will give you the chance to leave, to leave all this behind. To leave me behind…" He looked down as he said those final words. "But if you stay, I'll tell you the complete truth. Everything, no matter how crazy it will sound to you, I'll tell you," He stepped away and held a hand out to the way of the front door. "I'm giving you the chance to walk away from this, and I'll be honest. If you do stay, your life will be turned upside down. It will crash and burn. So I'm giving you this chance to spare yourself so one day, I can say I gave it to you."

He didn't take his eyes away from me as I looked to the door, then back at him.

"Who are you?" I asked, he didn't speak. "*What* are you?"

Then he spoke. "I'm an angel."

We fell silent.

"What is this? Do you think I'm a fool?" His face fell at my words.

"Of course not. I'm telling the truth."

My legs moved on their own accord.

"No, there is no such thing as angels! You're lying to me and I've had enough of it."

I ran out of the room and out of the front door, the bitter wind of the late night biting my bare legs. All I had on was his shirt. I reached the car and reached into the pockets I didn't have for the keys I'd left behind.

"Shit!"

"Lucinda wait!" He came running out of the front door and stood before me shirtless in the bitter cold.

"Leave me alone Peter!"

"I can prove it!"

"What are you talking about? There is no such thing as–"

My words were blown away by a sudden gush of the cold wind. The night seemed to become darker, the first rays of sunlight that started to escape the horizon disappeared. The wind picked up. It blew my hair everywhere, as if it was trying to take it for itself. There were no stars, no light, there was nothing.

Only him.

He stood with his thick taunt arms at his sides. His entire body became rigid and strained as he hung his head low.

And I realised that the night was shrinking *away* from him somehow. Like it was *scared* of him.

And there they were.

Two mighty wings.

They curled around him, holding him, protecting him. Even without any light I could still see how every colour that could ever exist reflected off each feather. Each feather was sleek and smooth, so much so I could cut myself on one. They were huge! They towered over us. He stood at six foot, but his wings stood taller.

The tips reached passed his head and the bottom tips were gracing the floor slightly. They were thick, intimidating and just as beautiful as they were in my dreams; maybe even more so. I could feel the ground tremble before him. I knew there was a part of him that was different from us all, a part of him that wasn't meant to exist in a normal man. A darker side, a side that wasn't born from this world, but another.

And it was true.

It was true. It was true. It was all true.

I kept repeating to myself, and I didn't know if I was talking out loud or not. At this point I didn't care.

He finally lifted his head to me. The skin around his eyes was dark, grey and…and just *dark*. Like the darkness inside of him could only escape through his eyes. But they were open as he watched me. They weren't evil; they were vulnerable and completely open to me yet again.

Waiting for me to react.

To turn and scream as I run down the cliffs and away from the creature before me.

But…

But he wasn't a *creature*.

He was a man.

An angel.

With surprisingly steady feet I approached him, the wind dying down as I moved closer to him. His eyes never left mine and mine never left his.

With shaking hands, I lifted my fingers to his face. Carefully, as if not to startle him, I touched the grey skin around his eye. The blue shimmered and shifted as I traced them. And they glowed ever brighter by the second.

I took a deep breath.

And lowered my hand to his right wing.

His breath hitched as I graced his feathers with my touch. They were so soft, not sharp or cutthroat as I first thought. But incredibly soft. Their colours seemed to trace my own skin as I moved my hand across them.

I could feel his eyes on me, his face so close to mine.

I looked up to him. We were inches apart.

"You're an angel," I said.

The corners of his lips lifted.

"I'm an angel."

Chapter 8

"For he shall give his angels charge over thee, to keep thee in all thy ways."

— *'Psalm' 91:11*

Lucinda

He sat at his desk, his head down and his hands clasped on the desk before him. The window behind him showed us the early morning rays of the sun. His wings were gone; he was normal again. But I still couldn't get that image of his wings out of my mind.

"There isn't just one God," he spoke up. "Well there is, but every few million years, a new one is elected. The ruling God at that time chooses an heir. And it's very rare."

He stood up and faced the window. "Our ruling God now is my mother. Yet she has never acted like one. And I was born a very long time ago—"

"How long ago?" I interrupted, void of emotion. He turned and watched me before answering, his strong arms bracing him against the desk.

"I stopped counting over ten thousand years ago."

My heart skipped a beat.

"Wow…"

"Do you want me to carry on?" he asked, his face impassive.

"Yes."

He studied my face before continuing. "Gods are not meant to have children, yet she had me. She had three. Me, Jane and Kyle. Normally the previous Gods wouldn't allow it. But somehow my mother got away with it. When I was born, I was handed straight over to my father. Then, when I turned five years old, I was given back. I don't quite remember the details. My tutor Gabriel became the only parent I can really remember." He looked down, no longer able to look at me. "As I grew older, my wings turned black and my powers increased, so much so that they started to rival Gods.

Everyone was terrified of me. They shied away from me as I passed in the halls. At one point even my own siblings feared me."

He walked over to the huge painting of himself.

"And as I grew into a man, the power became unbearable. I couldn't control it. So my brother thought about maybe putting them to use. That's when my mother used us for her wars against the Devil. I relished in it, the bloodshed, the void of battle. I could finally let it all out. But when I finally looked around at the chaos I caused…" He took a deep breath. "I stopped. I left war behind me. I needed to put my powers into *good* use. So then I joined the flying squad, an elite group of trained angels that protect Earth and the Heavens. It was good for me."

I stood beside him, watching him look at his artwork.

"Earth was so different back then, so new, so fresh. It's devastating for someone like me, someone that is forced to live this long. I've watched history destroy itself, change for the worst. In the beginning, this world was beautiful, peaceful. But now it has been torn apart. My existence has always been a battle, a war I'll never win."

"Surely there have been moments where it hasn't been all bad, moments that kept you going?" I asked.

He looked down at me, his eyes coming back from the past.

"Yes." His eyes were gentle as they watched me. "There have been a few."

He didn't take his eyes away from me as he continued.

"One day, when I was coming back from Earth, I came across a small child. Innocent and quiet as she played with her dolls. Humans cannot see us unless we allow them to, yet she could anyway. I'd never seen anything like it. And to top it off, she wasn't scared of me."

"Who was she?" It was a few moments of him watching me, unable to answer me. Then I realised. "She was me…"

"Yes, she was."

Suddenly I saw it all. Black wings that visited me every day. A shadow that never left my side. A cast of dark clouds that always seemed to find me, a storm behind the sun. He was there, watching me. The way he studied me, the way he watched me, I always felt like it was familiar to me. As if I that look he always gave me awoke something in me I never even knew I had.

Something powerful.

"Why did you leave?"

His eyes grew sad.

"Your parents thought you were talking to yourself, but it was me you were talking to. I would visit you all the time. I would be by your side all the time, yet you were quiet about it. It was like that for about two years, and you became my only friend." He said it like it was the most pathetic thing in the world. "But when the Heaven's court found out, they thought what I was doing was wrong. So they tried to stop it, and I knew it was wrong to be friends with a little human girl, but you were all I had in the world. So I came to visit you one last time and told you I was sorry. You didn't understand, so I made you forget…

"So, after that I tried to carry on doing other things, like reading, studying, but I didn't carry on with the flying squad. Over time, I realised that I just didn't belong there. I didn't want to. So I fell. I lost my angelic essence. Everything. And I got over it." He rolled a piece of charcoal in between his fingers. "I didn't think about any of it for thirteen years. But then I walked into my sister's stupid pub. And boom." He laughed sadly. "I saw my best friend behind the bar, sitting as if she wanted to be anywhere else, or *be* anyone else. And I didn't lie when I said I didn't know how to approach you. I had no idea what to do, or what to say to you. I just watched you go about your business, and I finally saw that you weren't the little girl I had once left behind. You were a woman now." He finally looked at me, intensely and as if looking for something. "I never saw you as anything than just a friend. Of course you were just a child. But the more I watched you, the more beautiful you became to me that day. The more I saw you for what you really were, the more I wanted to know this new girl that now stood where that young girl once did."

I didn't say a word as he looked at me.

"So I finally gained the balls to talk to you, and you sounded the same. Your smile was the same, your eyes sparkled the same. But you seemed so broken. You were the same on the outside, but completely different on the inside. I felt so sad for you. I wanted to help you, to be a part of your life again. I had no idea what I was doing. I still don't. A human and an angel? That just doesn't happen. I can't. It's wrong."

He moved away from me to stand before his window.

"Yet you came back for me," I stated.

He was quiet for a few moments.

"Yet I came back for you…" he said to himself.

It was morning. The light shone through the window, casting such a glow upon Peter that it could have been pouring from the centre of him. I moved to stand next to him. His body was tense as I touched his arm. His eyes snapped to mine, and I saw an ancient soul stare straight back at me. Such history hidden within his beautiful eyes. I could see how they beat down into my own, studying me, holding my young soul in place.

"Are you afraid?" he asked, his eyes never wavering from mine.

I took a deep breath.

"I've never been afraid of you Peter. And I'm not afraid of you now."

His face softened, yet he still kept a part of himself locked away from me. Unable to let himself fully hope.

"How are you not scared? How can you believe me so easily?"

I had to turn to myself for that answer. "I think I've always known what you really were, that you weren't a part of this world." His skin was warm and safe. "I know who you are Peter. I see who you are and who you pretend to be to protect the people you love. I see that now. And I have no reason to be scared of a man like that."

His face crumpled in relief, but he made no move to reach for me. So I took my hand away, letting ourselves take our time with each other.

I could see it as easily as a figure before a mirror. The wall he tried to keep between us. The cold stone. He tries to protect everyone by pushing them away, by keeping them at bay. I understood that better than anyone. But I wouldn't let him do that to me.

"What is this Peter?" His brow creased in confusion, but he said nothing. "Why am I here? You claim that you want to protect me, but that means by staying away, yet here you are." My voice was smaller with my next words. "Yet here I am."

He turned to face me fully and with gentle movements he cupped my face. His soft thumbs made my skin tingle.

The way he looked at me, the rolls and swirls of answers in his eyes that he couldn't speak out loud. I could see them there, floating within the blue. He only stroked my cheek, his eyes never leaving mine.

These eyes that always seemed to capture my darkness and seal it back into its cage.

He couldn't say it.

For years he has been alone, utterly alone. As have I. We have both lived within the dark, unable to reach out and live with the rest of the world without being scorched by the light. Our hearts doomed to burn. Too scared to even let ourselves to just exist. But then we found this, this thing between us. Wrong as it seems to others, to the divine up above us, here we are. Unable to walk away even when we know it is the easiest, the best choice.

I reached up and placed my hands over his on my face, our fingers entwining. And slowly, the corners of his mouth lifted, not quite a smile, but something close.

Hope.

"Stay with me Lucinda, stay for a little longer," was all he said.

"Why?"

He took his hands away from my cheek and rested them in my own.

"Because I've waited a very long time for this, for you. And I just want to enjoy it."

It took me no time at all to answer him.

"Ok, I'll stay."

And I did.

We laughed and enjoyed each other for the rest of the day, but eventually we fell asleep again as the orange streaks of sunlight made their way through the window. The Ocean was gold from the sunset, and it reflected against the cliffs, as if the world really did have a heart of pure gold.

I wanted to stay in this spot. I wanted to be wrapped up in his arms until my very last day. Then I wondered to myself: how long *has* he been alone? Compared to myself, I wasn't always alone. My mother was at least in the house with me, but *this* house was huge for only one person. And to have lived for as long as he has reminded me there are some people that could be more broken than me.

I turned in his arms and faced him. He stirred and pulled me tighter to him but didn't wake up. Looking at him this closely I noticed thin yet delicate white lines across his skin. They followed the trail of his veins on every inch of his flesh. From what I could see, his arms, chest, back, neck, and very lightly, even his face. They all held these scars. He was a masterpiece that no one wanted to see all because he was slightly damaged.

When I looked up he was already smiling down at me. My hair coated my shoulders and his with its length. He twisted one of its strands and his eyes shined.

"Still just as soft," he muttered as he let it fall to its rightful place. His hair shone in the golden light from the sun, making him look even more angelic.

"Why didn't they like you?" I asked. He'd closed his eyes but he still answered.

"No one likes me, but which ones particularly are you talking about?" he mumbled.

"The other angels."

He opened his eyes but didn't look at me. He only looked at the ceiling.

"They just didn't like angels with black wings," he simply answered, but I wanted to know more.

"Who are your parents?"

He shook his head, and climbed out of bed.

"Asking all these questions will get you hurt," he said with a vicious edge, as if he was angry with himself.

I climbed out of the bed and stood before him.

"You said you would tell me everything! Now you're going back on your word!" I shouted in anger. He just shook his head again.

"And I have told you that they will take you away if they find out I am involved with you again!" His eyes were begging me to understand.

"What is so bad about me knowing who your parents are?"

"Well firstly," he shouted straight back at me. "My father will kill you because I chose you."

I fell silent and he stared at me with unwavering eyes. And as he spoke his truth, I could feel the house shudder in fear.

"And my mother will kill me," he said defeated. "But my real concern is my father."

"But why? Why do they hate you so much?"

He opened his mouth to speak, but something crashed through the front door. We looked at each other before running down the stairs. Peter stood in front of me, his arm holding me behind him.

We slowly climbed down the stairs, his hands behind him gripping my waist to make sure I was still there, and my own on his strong back. We came to rest at the bottom of the stairs to find a panicked and bloody faced Kyle leaning against the doorframe. Peter rushed to his side and pulled him onto the living room sofa.

"Well, if you're here brother that means I'm already too late," Kyle said while looking at me and nodding his blood-soaked head.

But Peter wouldn't even turn his head my way. "Have you told her?"

"Not everything. It's too dangerous," Peter answered, his back to me.

"It's more dangerous if she knows nothing," Kyle warned as he held his hand out to me to shake. I shook it and smiled a little. "It's good to see you again little human." He smirked as I blushed at the remark, and I took my hand away.

"Likewise," I replied.

Peter still had his back to me. He stood with a lot of tension, as if he was a taunt elastic band ready to snap. And Kyle noticed.

"You need to tell her all of it Peter," Kyle pushed on firmly.

But he only shook his head.

"If anything happens to her, you know what I will do brother."

The air seemed to freeze around us.

"I know," Peter's brother said softly. "I've seen it happen before."

They both went quite.

"Can someone please tell me what is going on?" I snapped at their silence.

Peter turned, his eyes burning. His wings burst from his back and darkness exploded through the room. The world around us held its breath as his eyes gripped mine like a prisoner in its darkness.

"*I will not sit here and watch your eyes turn to disgust before me!*" Kyle grabbed my arm and gently pulled me back. "If you want to know so bad at least I can say I warned you!" he said with a softer tone as he realised Kyle had to pull me away from him, but his eyes still blazed. He tucked in his wings and walked through the back door and took off into the sky, like lightning and thunder dancing across the Earth.

Leaving us alone.

Kyle rubbed his eyes, then leaned down and closed them.

"Don't worry, he's only like that when he cares," he mumbled. I could see the exhaustion eating away at him.

I sat on the other sofa and took a well-needed deep breath.

"Why did you pull me back?" I asked.

He hesitated before answering. "Because when we have our wings out, we can't be controlled. And he would hate himself if he ever hurt you."

"Why does that happen when they are out?"

"An angel's wings link them to God, and she created emotion, so we were created with very heightened emotions. Everything we feel is intensified a thousand times more than yours."

"Oh," I simply said.

"Yes, oh." he simply replied.

But I needed to know more. "Who is your father?"

He opened his eyes and slowly turned his head to look at me.

"You should be careful on how many questions you ask, little human."

I just waited in silence.

He just sighed and sat up straighter.

"I'm guessing you already know who our mother is?"

I nodded.

"My father is the angel of life, Haniel. He has guarded the tree of life since the very beginning. I get my need to protect the innocent and my raw power in battle from him. I've only met him once. I was training for the army, and he came to watch me. He never said a word. He only stood there watching me knock down every male in my path like how lightning strikes the surface of the Earth," He spoke with a contorted face. "We looked nothing alike. But I knew it was him."

"How did you know?" I asked.

His eyes pierced mine.

"It was the way he looked at me. It was the same as my own. There was nothing there. Just a void of duty before the heart…"

Just a void of duty before the heart.

"That's not true Kyle."

He didn't comment; he just carried on with his story.

"He watched me, judged me, then left. His mighty sword, that I will one day inherit, placed between his shoulder blades. And I never saw him again."

"How long ago was that?"

There was no pause.

"Over five thousand years ago."

My eyes widened.

An ordinary person would think this man was only in his early twenties. Yet he was thousands of years old, maybe millions. His eyes were a deep creamy chocolate, a shade darker than my own in this light. But they were dull, beautiful. But somehow it was like the world had just sucked out every inch of the angel he once was. Like there was no light left in his body to shine through his eyes.

Is this how I've looked for all these years, void of life?

72

"Still want to know more?" He grinned at my shocked face.

I could only nod.

His grin grew. "We are the first children a God has ever given birth to. Each of us has great power, but Peter's are limitless. So much in fact that he is said to be the most powerful creature in all of existence." His face softened with a slight sadness. "So he holds the most burdens. He can barely control it all sometimes. He says it rages through his body like a storm. And he hates himself for it. But when he met you, he felt as if he wasn't all that bad."

I could barely speak. "What happened after he couldn't see me?"

He face became grave, but he continued with the story.

"In the bible, it is said the great war between Heaven and Hell was created by the Devil. It was wrong. When they hid you from him, he nearly went mad with rage. He lost control of his powers and destroyed nearly all of Heaven and Hell."

"How did he stop?"

"Jane and I tried to stop him, and were almost killed trying. Even the Devil tried. But it wasn't until Jane suffered the most that he finally saw what he was doing."

"What happened to her?"

He opened his mouth to speak, but was soon interrupted by a sweet voice from the doorway.

"A troubled man at that time tried to find Peter through me."

Jane stood leaning against the wall.

"It didn't work. But I lost a lot for it." She embraced her brother and sat down next to me. "Everyone lost something in that war, but Peter lost the most." She clasped my hands in hers and kissed my cheek.

"He did that over me?" I asked. They both nodded.

I couldn't wrap my head around it. Why would he fight so hard for me? I was just a human.

"That is what he did for his friend," Jane said. "He never asked for anything in his whole life. He always gave and never asked for anything in return. And now he has finally asked for something. You were the only thing that he had ever wanted, yet for the universe? You were the one thing he couldn't ever have."

Pity for her brother was laced into her voice as if it was born entwined with her. Jane stayed for a while longer before hugging us goodbye and leaving. Kyle fell asleep in the spare bedroom soon after, so I brought him blankets and pillows before walking out to the cliffs.

The moon was huge and bright in the dark sky, and the waves crashed against the cliffs below, bowing to power of the moon.

I walked along the cliffs and enjoyed the gentle breeze. It made my tears disappear so I didn't have to wipe them away. But footsteps followed me from behind. I turned to find no one there. But the footsteps still followed close to me until they stopped.

"Are you ready Northern star?" a voice spoke out to me. I wrapped my arms around myself as the wind got colder and colder.

"Who's there?" I asked, my voice uneasy. But I only received a frozen chuckle in return. It was soft, soft as the inside of a snowflake, but ancient like the stones of Egypt.

"I am Phanuel, the angel of truth." It moved closer. "Do you want to know what you do not?" Its voice seemed to travel through me.

I had no control over my words.

"Yes."

I could barely move my lips as ice started to cover the cliffs, then the Ocean started to freeze over as fast as I was blacking out.

"Very well," it said.

The air seemed to stop moving as I fell to the ground, frost covering my body. I had no idea how long I was unconscious for.

I awoke to the sound of screaming. The bitter sound of wailing women and men. Black smoke was rising into the never-ending sky, and white and red was all around me. I stood and witnessed destruction unlike any other. Angels of all kind were running in every direction, while others were in battle armour. Some in black and others in a shining silver.

But one stood out among them all.

I ran to what looked like a battlefield made of an outstretched cloud, and there stood two sides of angels.

One of light and the other dark.

But between them stood a battered and bleeding Peter. He had no amour and no weapon but the raging storm in his eyes. He stood facing an elegant woman in silk and silver armour. She wore a crown that seemed to be made of light in her white blonde hair.

"Before you make the biggest mistake of your entire existence, think before you act son." She seemed calm but her body was ready for war.

His body shook with rage. "The biggest mistake I ever made was calling you my mother!" he hissed with his fists clenched against his sides.

"You knew the rules! You only have yourself to blame!" She seemed to be begging him just as much she was trying to scold him, but he just smirked in her face.

"So because we broke some rules, you thought you had the right to destroy your children?"

He stepped around her as if she was the prey and he was the predator.

"I did what I had to do." She wouldn't look at him as she spoke, but rage boiled in Peter's face.

"Have you even seen the state of Kyle? The scars you have left on his body and mind?" She kept her head high but her bottom lip wobbled.

"He got what he deserved..." Her voice shook as she spoke, her chin held slightly too high.

He snarled in her face.

"And I bet," his smile was cruel, *"you weren't the one to do that to him. You had to get someone else to carve his body and break him. They burnt his wings and burnt his mind, just to get to me."*

Tears fell down her cheeks as he spoke, and he gripped her face with his hands roughly.

And she didn't try to pull away.

"And what about poor little Jane? Innocent little Jane..."

"She survived, didn't she!" His mother hissed back at him.

"Kyle survived. He took away whatever piece of sanity he had left. But you ordered to have her wings ripped from her back. She was tortured for months. She was your little girl, and she suffered the worst out of everyone. All because she knew the meaning of family. When you didn't."

He pushed her face away, and blood trickled down her cheeks from where he'd dug in his nails.

"They knew what they were doing," she screamed. *"They were traitors!"* She wiped away the blood from her face and continued to stand tall.

His words were calmer, softer, more forgiving. *"She was my friend. Kyle, Jane and Lucinda were the only good in my life. But now they are gone. You lost us. You lost me."* She didn't say anything.

"I will fall. I need to protect my family from you." He turned to face her one last time. *"But one day, I will return, and I will destroy you and everything you hold dear."* Her face became like

stone as Peter's army vanished. He stood alone with his sword to her throat.

"And just so you know I'm not bluffing…"

All I saw after that was the clean swipe of a sword and the blood curdling screams of his mother.

I was ice cold and couldn't move as I watched my breath become mist. I was back on the cliff and under the moon light. But soon after I awoke, I was lifted into warm arms and carried back into the house. The stars passed me by like the mixture of night and frost. We went up the stairs and he gently placed me onto the bed, but I was too cold to speak.

"I'm going to kill Kyle for leaving you alone!" he said, but he seemed too worried to really care about his brother as he pulled off my soaked jeans and replaced them with a pair of his jogging bottoms. "Shit, you're so cold." He swore.

He pulled off my top and replaced it with one of his shirts. He lifted me back into his arms and placed me under the blankets on the bed. Once I was covered he slipped in next to me and wrapped his arms around me.

"Peter?" I whispered. He leaned over me, his breath sweet and warm on my cheek.

"Are you ok?" Worry was still there within his eyes, but he seemed to relax as he heard my voice. So I curled against his chest. He wrapped his wings around us both and it was comforting.

I was home.

"I'm sorry I left," he whispered into the darkness of his wings. But I just pulled him closer.

"I think I saw your mother." I had more strength to speak better, but he didn't say anything. "She's a bitch," I said, and the familiar sound of his laugh burst from him as he pulled me closer. It was wonderful to hear him laugh again.

"Yeah, she is," he said.

I smiled at the relief in his voice. I was starting to see how much he had lost and that he was terrified if I was going to be taken from him too. I knew the feeling, I knew how scared it was to wake up and wonder who was next in your life to go, and if finally I would be left on my own. But I wouldn't let that happen to him. I wouldn't let myself be taken from him. Even if it killed me.

Chapter 9

"There are always two deaths, the real one and the one people know about."

– Jean Rhys

Peter

I stood invisible to her. Watching her weep over her lost family members alone in her room. Her mother was downstairs crying, and ignoring the child that she had left. The tears fell slowly down her puffy cheeks and she wiped them away roughly with her small fingers. I wanted to wipe them away for her, but she couldn't see me; she won't be able to ever again. It hurt to see her hurt, but not being able to do something about it hurt more.

I walked over to her bed and sat down next to her, but she didn't notice. The look on her face was torturous.

It wasn't the kind of expression that should be worn by a child.

Lightning flashed outside the window in the dark skies above, and it reminded me of the pain that I would forever feel now, and it struck my heart every time I moved. She whimpered and gripped her pillow to her, her little hands turning white. Her entire body shook, her pain escaping her and filling the room.

A look came across her face.

She threw the pillow aside and climbed down from her bed. She pulled her drawer open and gently pulled something out. And there, sitting between her fingers was one of my feathers, the feather I gave her for her last birthday. She brushed it against her neck, its softness taking away the tears that ran down her skin. And for a moment, as I watched this little girl, this human, my friend, I knew that there was no doubt in my mind that one day she would find her way back to me. That one day I would find her. But for now she would have to be alone, she will have to find her own way through this mess. I could not help her through this.

I moved from the bed, my own tears falling, and stepped towards the window. Today was another day that I had to say goodbye to a member of my family. Again. Because she was.

I opened the window and pushed it up so I could escape. But he little voice caught me in its thread.

"Angel?"

I turned back, afraid and hopeful that she could see me. But her eyes didn't. They wandered around me, trying to see something that she knew was there, but that the world would not allow her to see. And more tears fell from her eyes because she knew *I was here, she knew I stood here somewhere. But she was not allowed to see me. So I turned away and climbed through the window. She did not move to it. She stayed away, her big eyes shining as I slowly lowered the window. The glass now separating us, ending our friendship like the severing of a thread.*

I took off into the skies above, my wings thrusting me higher and higher into the black clouds. Hiding me away from the cruel eyes of the world. I always kept her close to remind me that I wasn't all evil, that if an innocent human could be around me, then maybe others could too. Eventually. She taught me how to be kind, how to stop hating myself. To see something other than hurt, hate and grief. She didn't see me. *She saw someone else, someone who I wish I could be. She didn't see a monster. And I will miss her for the rest of my life, I will forever miss my friend.*

I woke up. My breath was hard to catch as my lungs squeezed painfully. My skin was wet from sweat, the covers twisted around my legs.

But I reached across the covers, warm skin met my own, a warm hand. Her hand.

She was here. She was beside me now. I wasn't alone. I closed my eyes and wrapped my arms around her yet again, relief filling me as her breathing laced itself with mine.

Lucinda

Peter had woken me with his nightmares, but when he found me beside him he finally relaxed and fell asleep once again. I watched him sleep, my eyes watching the rise and fall of his scared chest, the faint white lines that were in the place of his veins. I wondered how someone could live so long, hold so much grief, and not break with it. How much can a simple heart actually hold?

The world was still dark outside, the stars were gone; they must've fallen asleep among the morning. The sky above us was as old as the angel next to me; maybe he was older than the darkness outside. I couldn't rule out anything like that anymore. And it was driving me crazy.

I heard a faint clash of pots and pans downstairs, so I crept into the kitchen. I saw Kyle frying some bacon and eggs in the pan, his back bare to me. He had two scars down his back. Peter didn't have anything like that. They were the length of his back, but they didn't look just like scars, but something deeper; more traumatic. He had the same little white scars that Peter had across his skin. I stood there watching him, admiring the warrior before me, the power he must hold.

"I'm surprised my brother let you escape his bed so easily."

"Whatever do you mean?" I asked innocently.

He turned around from cooking with a cup of coffee. He drank his fill of it without taking his eyes away from me.

"Well, if I had you in my bed, I'd take my sweet time with you. And I'd certainly need more than one night to get my fill."

He spun back round after he gave me one of his playful winks. He was so charming when he was playful.

"Kyle?" I walked in a bit further so he could see me better. The shadows of the doorway receding from me.

"Hungry?" he asked to ignore what I wanted to ask. But I continued anyway.

"What are those scars on your back?"

His hand stopped moving, but he didn't turn around.

"Just battle wounds, nothing to worry about." He brushed it off as if they were fleabites.

"They don't look like nothing," I said wearily. I forgot they were all warriors of god. He handed me a plate full of food and sat next to me with his own.

His face was soft, yet completely worn from war.

"I'm sorry," I said. "I don't mean to pry." I looked away and dug into my food, but he grabbed my hand and I looked back at him startled.

"You should pry. You deserve to know everything about what you're getting yourself into."

His eyes were serious, too serious before they lightened again and filled with sarcasm and joy. Then he let me go.

"Ok, so what happened?"

He shovelled bacon into his mouth before answering. "It was just before the great war ended. Jane was just released from prison. I will never forget the state of her. In human holy history, the punishment for angels betraying their god is stripping of wings. But that isn't quite true. It wasn't practised because it was too dangerous for the victim." His eyes were grave as they focused on mine. "Jane was the first angel to be stripped." I sucked in a sharp breath and waited for him to go on.

"We never found out who did it to her. She knows, but she also knows we will rip Heaven apart to get to the bastard that did it, and we won't care who gets hurt in the crossfire. So she never told us and I don't think she ever will."

"Why is it dangerous to have your wings stripped?"

He took another piece of bacon into his mouth and leaned back in his chair.

"Our wings are directly connected to our spines, our minds. So imagine me spending hours ripping your limbs off with hooks, the bones splitting apart. Your flesh tearing. All you could think about would be the pain. Wanting it to end. But we are immortal, we can never die unless another angel drives a sword through us.

"And we feel everything a million times more than humans. She became insane, she became the angel of insanity."

I became confused.

"What do you mean? How can she become the angel for insanity?" I asked. His lips were in a tight line.

"Just what I said. Every angel to ever exist has a purpose, is the master of something in existence. And she is the angel of insanity."

He stood up and took our plates to the sink.

"What are you the master of?" I asked softly. His shoulders seemed to slump, but he turned with a smirk on his face. I could see the strain it took for him to put it on show.

"Hell fire, little human, hell fire." He lifted his hand and it was engulfed in black fire, and he walked to me with his hand outstretched. "Don't be afraid." He spoke quietly as he watched me. I looked up and his eyes seemed to hold the same fire as his hand did. With his engulfed hand, he pushed the strands of hair out of my face, and trailed his fingertip down my cheek while never taking his eyes from mine. The fire didn't burn me. It seemed to flutter against my skin with a sort of protectiveness.

"We will protect you, you are a part of us all now." And he pulled his hand away, the black fire gone.

"Thank you," I simply said in return for his vows.

He nodded and started to wash the dishes. It was after a few more minutes of chatting with Kyle that Peter walked in still half asleep. He saw me sitting at the table and smiled sweetly. His hair was sticking out in every direction, his clothes rumpled from his sleeping. He was a sight to behold first thing in the morning.

"Morning brother," Kyle said without turning to face him, but he only greeted Kyle with a nod and went to the fridge. "Why are you in a mood now?"

Peter's voice was curt. "Next time you leave her on her own like that again, I'll break your leg." A little mockery was laced into his voice, and Kyle saw it and only barked out a laugh.

"I would love to see you try." He placed the plates away in the cupboard before turning back to us both.

The air was calm, soothing. The brothers grinning at each other and me. A simple human enjoying the first morning that, in a very long time, I was glad to greet.

Peter turned his attention to me. "I've got a few things to do today, so you must suffer without me. But Jane will be round soon."

Kyle pushed off the counter. Peter nodded again and his brother walked out, not even looking at me as he went. Kyle does the same thing his brother does. He sometimes forgets to hold onto his emotions, his heart, his humanity. But when he does forget, I can see the man beneath the holy flesh. I see how he tries to hide it, as if he is scared the world will see him as he is, and try to trample upon him. Even with his own siblings, he keeps them at arm's length. But with me, he can let himself forget because I am at no loss to him. I am nothing but a small piece of company that shares his morning's burdens. Nothing more.

He was made into a man way before his time.

Peter watched me from across the room, the sun finally rising across the sky outside the house. His eyes were bright, refreshed.

"Did you sleep well?" I asked, not able to keep my eyes off his angelic face. The angles of his face were so sharp that they seemed to reflect the morning sunlight with ease.

"Indeed I did. How about you?"

I was about to speak when Jane's voice rose through the house.

"Peter?"

Peter rolled his eyes and we both made our way into the living room.

"What are you doing here so early?" He faced her annoyed. She just grinned and plopped down on the couch while twisting her red hair between her fingers.

"Kyle needs your help today, and you know I can't go. So you will be leaving Lucinda with me."

"Is that so?" he said. Her eyes grew serious as she looked at him. Daring him to argue back.

"Yes, he shouldn't go alone, and you're…" She looked at me before looking back. "You know who he's dealing with, knows what he wants. So it's better if you both go."

He didn't argue back. He nodded his head.

"Very well." He turned to face me, eyes worried, but he smiled all the same.

"I know this is hard on you, so thank you," Jane said looking up at us both before walking into the kitchen.

I wanted to touch him, help him somehow; but did he want me to? Every time I felt the urge to move to him, I felt like I was in an entirely different world to him. To them all. Maybe all I was to him was a friend of the past, maybe that was all I ever was.

Why would someone like him ever want something like me? Why would someone trade the Heavens for a small pathetic human?

"I'll be gone for most of the day, will you be alright?"

His voice was rough with concern, concern for his friend. Yet somehow I knew he'd just shut himself off from me. Was it always going to be like this between us? Cold one moment then warm the next?

"I'll be fine, don't worry."

My smile was strained and he noticed. He stepped towards me but stopped before he touched me. Instead he just nodded his head and walked upstairs.

Kyle and his brother stood at the door, both dressed in black, a while later. Kyle seemed ready for whatever was coming. And Peter said nothing. He only watched me as if he would never see me again.

"Peter…" I began to say but he turned away and ignored me. Kyle shot him a dirty look but also said nothing.

"Jane." Everyone was silent as he looked at his sister with a hard stare.

"I know," she said softly.

"With your life," he answered, and he walked out the door with his brother. Kyle didn't say anything else as he followed him out. But I couldn't help but slam the door after them.

"So," she said as if she was talking to a ticking time bomb. "What do you want to do for the rest of the day?" I only shrugged. "Well I actually have a few things to do, but I'm not leaving this house. So if you need me, just yell." She embraced me and kissed my cheek before disappearing into the kitchen again.

But I just wanted some time on my own. I haven't had any time to think for myself in days. So I wondered about the house, looking at thousands of years of history on the walls dance before me. Paintings and clothes, pots and vases that carried lives of millions of people that were now gone.

And I couldn't help but think to myself, would I eventually end on these walls one day too?

I ended up at the study and it was the messiest room I'd ever seen. I picked through the books that were laying across the floor and stacked them high in the bookcases. Some were extremely old, and others didn't even look like books anymore. When the floor was cleared, I moved to the pile of sketches on the desktop. But as I moved through them, I realised they were mostly of me. Surprise ran through me so much I leaned down to sit into the chair behind me. The charcoal was perfectly smudged as it flowed across the old paper. It was beautiful. In some of them, I was a small child, one showed me crying in my room…

And I realised it was the day my family died. But with Peter sitting beside me on the bed.

Another one was of us both in my garden, each of us smiling as he handed me a feather.

The feather I still had…

More and more fell from my hands, each of me throughout my life until now. One showed the day we first met, myself being behind the bar. Another showed me sleeping in his car the day we went to the beach. The next was of me drowning, with a hand outstretched to me in the murky water. And finally, the last one showed me standing, or almost hovering high in the sky. I was surrounded by glowing stars, but the sun was still setting behind me, and the earth was far underneath my feet. My hair flowed around me, almost framing me. But the thing that caught my attention the most was that my eyes were glowing, as if light and crystals were animating from inside my eyes.

I looked powerful and untouchable.

Just like any other angel.

I pushed the drawings away and placed them in his drawers. I didn't want to look at them anymore.

Once the desk was cleaned of clutter, I picked up all the paintings that were in each corner and hung them up all over the walls.

All artwork should be seen.

A few hours later Jane stood leaning up on the door frame smiling.

"What are you smiling about?" I laughed. I placed the last picture frame up on the wall.

Done.

"Am I not allowed to smile?"

She bounced into the room, but her face fell as she walked up to one particular painting. It was of herself and her two brothers.

They were all standing in shining armour on the clouds. Kyle was standing slightly in front of his sister, that protectiveness showing again through the black fire that was all over his body. But in this artwork, it included his wings and they were made up of it. A never-ending hell fire at his back. Jane stood defiant with her chin high. Her red hair was even longer in this painting; it reached her mid back, like flowing lava. Her face was different too. It looked less worn, more innocent to the horrors of this world. The paint showing me the version that hadn't been torn down and battered by the world around her.

The warrior sister.

Jane lifted her fingers to trace her painted wings. They were a bright white, but had red feathers randomly placed across them. Unique like herself. She snatched her fingers away as if Kyle's fire had somehow burned her through the painting, and smiled at me as if nothing was wrong.

"Don't we look good in this snapshot?" Jane giggled a little bit too long, but they did. They looked like the kind of angels that would defend their God, who would defend each other.

"You all look powerful." It was the only word that came to mind as I looked at all three of them.

But Peter looked *too* powerful. He was the only one that was dressed like the others, but was completely apart from them. He stood beside his brother on the left, his armour a shade darker than theirs; and his wings were much, *much* bigger. Black with all the colours of the rainbow included. His eyes were bright, a shining blue, like the clearest oceans of Earth. He seemed to overwhelm the sky, as if it wasn't big enough to hold him quite right. All three of them had glowing swords and daggers, but they didn't look like they needed the weapons.

They *were* the weapons.

But as I looked at Jane, she didn't look like the angel in the painting, but a broken version. Just like her brothers.

"I see what you see Lucinda," Jane said quietly. "I see this painting and then I look at myself now. And I see a shell, just like my brothers. But being as old as we are, life has caught up with us. It catches up with everyone. Just because we are angelic, doesn't mean we do not suffer."

I laid my hand on her shoulder and squeezed it slightly.

"I know," was all I could say.

"We were warriors. The most powerful angels in all the skies. Our enemies would turn to dust at the sounds of our battle cries. We loved war, lavished in fighting and protecting each other. But we didn't see how it was destroying us also. How it broke Peter more than anyone."

"What do you mean?"

Jane finally looked at me, eyes hard and distant.

"Peter can sometimes be cold and he hides his emotions well; but he struggled to hold his power in those wars. He could have killed us all." Jane walked to each painting and stared for a while as she spoke. "And we were selfish enough to forget how much he had to fight for, that we didn't."

"Angels were created to defend and fight for God, and in battle we lose ourselves in the combat, in the feeling of victory. We give ourselves over to our full power. But Peter can't *ever* lose himself to his power, can't *ever* lose his grip on that side of himself. Or we will all cease to exist. Slowly, it ate away at him. Some even said he should be stripped and have his power taken away." Her eyes were grave. "Even killed."

I couldn't speak. I could only try to push that thought away.

"But his father wouldn't allow it. It wasn't until our final battle that everyone saw what he really was."

Jane's eyes dazed off as memories of war resurfaced in her face.

"What did he do?" I asked. Jane snapped her eyes back to mine.

"He changed after I was stripped. He only lost it for a split second. If it wasn't for Kyle, he would have killed every angel in that sky at that very moment." Jane touched one of the many scars on her arm. "So he cut off one of our God's wings instead."

We stood in the study in silence for a few moments, just letting her words sink into my ears.

My vision.

"She deserved it," I said, my voice steady as I spoke. Jane smiled wide and her eyes sparkled.

"Oh I know, and she will be in for much more than just one severed wing when I get back up there." Jane tucked my hair away from my face, just as a big sister would. "You are no longer alone Lucinda, you have us. And we protect our own."

For the first time in years, I was the first to pull her close for an embrace. She was shocked but hugged me back.

"Thank you Jane." I could feel her smile against my cheek.

"Right." She lugged me into the living room. "The boys will be back soon, so what do you want to do before they come back?"

"We could watch a movie?" I suggested as Jane switched on the TV.

"Sure, but just to warn you, he doesn't keep up with the times." I laughed as she looked in the pile next to the TV. She picked up a chick flick. I nodded and she slipped it in. We watched movie after movie, but Jane jumped up and stood in front of where I was sitting abruptly a few hours later.

"Jane? What's wrong?" She said nothing, and I heard the door slam open with the boys coming through, shouting at each other.

"You have no idea what that took of me!" I heard Peter yell as he walked into the room. Kyle followed while shoving his brother hard.

"What about us? Do you ever stop to think about what we have to give for your mistakes?" Kyle yelled back. "Do you ever see how much we all bleed for you?" They stood looking at each other harshly, as if they wanted hit each other. But Kyle was the first to move.

Kyle pinned his brother against the wall, but Peter shoved him away harder. They weren't using human strength.

"You are a burden on us all!" Kyle hissed, but Peter only laughed.

Kyle lost it.

He punched Peter hard in the stomach and he toppled to the floor. He was still laughing, so Kyle kicked him in the face. Blood poured from his lips and nose. Anger blazed in the angel's face as he swiftly rose. And with a wave of his hand, Kyle went flying into the walls, again and again until Jane started crying.

"Peter stop!" She pulled at his arms but his eyes stayed on his brother, who was still flying into the walls.

So I tried.

"Peter! You're hurting him!" Yet he didn't listen. It was as if he didn't know I was here. Kyle was covered in plasters from the walls and his own blood. And as he hurtled towards me, I gripped his hand and tried to pull him down. But Peter was too strong, and I went flying with him.

I smacked against the wall, my head crashing through the plaster. Jane's scream rang through the room as I dropped to the floor. Warm liquid ran into my hair and down my neck. I sat up and pulled my hands away to find my own blood shinning back up at me.

I looked up to see shocked eyes staring down at me, but Kyle stood in front of me before I could even think.

"See what you do Peter?" Kyle stood shielding me from his brother. But Peter only watched me, his eyes wide and his face white.

"It doesn't matter who it is, you will hurt anyone to get what you want. Even the very *thing* you want!" Kyles tone was slightly lighter as he spoke to his shocked brother. "Some bargains are just not worth the price brother!"

The room was silent as I looked at him from across the room, blood dripping down my face. The blood started to drip down my forehead and onto my lashes. I blinked as my own blood found its way into my eyes. My legs were weak and I held onto Kyle for support. His hands reached back and steadied me against him. But when I looked back up, he had walked into his study and slammed the door.

Kyle turned to me and examined my injuries, and so did Jane.

"It's just a cut across your hair line. It just looks bad from the amount of blood."

Jane whispered so Peter wouldn't hear. Kyle sat me down and dressed the wound for me, I just sat quietly for the entire time.

"He didn't mean it," Kyle spoke as he finally packed the first aid kit away.

"I know, I just wish he knew that too," I finally said. But I looked at his cuts and began to worry.

"What about you?" I asked concerned. He only shook his head and smiled a little.

"I'm an angel. I'll heal in a few hours."

I nodded and didn't say anything else.

"We fight all the time, but he never hurts us the way we hurt him. He never uses his full power on us, but we do. He's a good person. The world just portrays him as bad," he reassured me.

"Who is his father?" I asked. Kyle's hands slowed on their work, but carried on nevertheless.

He said nothing.

"Why won't you tell me?"

His eyes became afraid.

"There is a reason why all of Heaven and Hell fear us Lucinda, and like us, we got a part of our power from someone. We got ours from our mother. But he didn't." He stood and smiled one last time before walking out the door, leaving me to my demons. I took in a deep breath and walked to Peter's study door. I knocked but no answer. So I walked in.

Peter stood with his wings taut and his feathers on edge, like a cat's fur. He was leaning against the window, whiskey glass empty in his hand.

"Get out before I hurt you again Lucinda."

His voice was rough and he didn't turn as I walked up beside him. When I touched his arm, he didn't look at me. His eyes went straight to the cut on my head.

There was a twinge of self-hate in his eyes. It was stirring in his face like the blood under his flesh.

"Dear God!" he cursed as he shattered the glass into pieces in his hand.

"Stop it!" His eyes snapped to mine in surprise at my harsh words. "Stop hurting yourself. I know you feel bad but please…" My voice was hushed. "When you are hurt, it hurts me *more*."

He took a deep breath and dropped the remaining pieces of glass from his hand.

"But are you ok?" he asked. He was so close to me now and all I wanted to do was step closer.

"I'm not fine china," I snapped while looking away from him.

He looked down at his hand. Glass protruded from his already scared skin.

"But I did that to you," he said mostly to himself.

"I'll get even with you, don't you worry about that."

He laughed at my promise, his eyes becoming a little brighter. And that alone made me feel better.

"I'm so sorry Lucinda." I didn't say anything, neither of us said anything. But I could see that yet again he was drawing himself away from me. Every time I felt him open to up to me, show me his heart, firm walls shut down before me. Cold and made of the harshest stone.

But it was me that stepped away this time.

"My mum is probably worrying about me. I should go home."

He nodded his head.

"Sure, I think all of us need to get out for a while."

He held my hand as he led me out the study to the living area. Kyle and Jane were watching the movie I never finished. Jane looked up and smiled, but Kyle ignored us.

"We are all taking Lucinda home." Peter grabbed his coat and Jane bounced to my side.

Kyle stayed on the couch.

"Have fun." His voice scraped against my skull, and Peter narrowed his eyes at him.

"We all need to go brother."

"You brought her here, you wanted her, you deal with her. She's your problem."

"That's fine Kyle, you don't have to come just to drop me off."

He looked at me from the corner of his eye, but said nothing.

"In fact, I have my car. Why are you dropping me off when I can get home on my own?" I stated a little confused at their worried glances.

"You can drive home. But we will be flying over you until you're home safe."

I looked at Jane and she smiled brightly. It filled her face beautifully.

"He carries me. It's nice to focus on the world around you instead of focusing on flying straight all the time." She winked at me. "You should let him show you sometime." I blushed, thinking about him showing me something like that and how extraordinary it would be.

I turned to the blonde angel one last time. "Ok, goodnight Kyle."

He didn't take his eyes away from the TV. So I walked out the door without another word.

I opened my car and got in without looking back and I sped down the road, not caring who was behind me.

I reached home soon enough. It was pitch black and silent outside the car. I stood in the darkness and saw no lights in the house.

She must be sleeping. I walked up to the door, but I couldn't feel the door handle. I couldn't feel the door at all.

It wasn't here.

"Mum?" I stepped into the house. It was freezing, colder than it was outside. Fear settled into my bones as I heard nothing in return. "Mum?" I yelled a little louder, my voice shaking. But something moved behind me. I spun around, but I couldn't see anything from the dark.

"Is it time for their destruction to take flight?" a voice called out in the darkness. I could hear the smirk in its tone, the mockery twisted within it.

"It has finally begun…" another voice answered. This voice was clearer, clear as glass, but as harsh as ice.

Their unnatural laughs crawled across my skin like insects.

"Who's there?"

Their laughs stopped dead.

"Oh dear little Lucinda. We are your friends," the clearer voice called out. Then somehow, I could see him. There wasn't any light, but he became the only visible thing in the room.

As if the darkness made him real.

"Who are you?" My voice was steady as he stepped forward from the darkness. His hair was black and so were his eyes, but his skin was a murky grey.

We locked eyes.

The void I had always imagined to exist in the vastness of the outer universe stared back at me. Darkness filled with every spec of distant stars that were not wanted, thrown away by all the suns in the sky. Stared at me. Watched me. I could see a slight sadness in them, a sadness of not being wanted.

And yet I knew those eyes would be here long after the last sun dies.

"You have a lovely home here Lucinda."

He seemed to roll my name out of his mouth like the purest acid there was.

"Where is my mum?"

He didn't blink. His eyes were unnaturally large and round, like a doll.

And he never took them off me.

"We will get to that." He waved his hand as if she meant nothing.

"What do you want?" I was starting to sound desperate, and he noticed.

"I want my weapon back. I want what you stole from me!" His hiss rang through me and brought me to my knees.

"What are you talking about? I haven't stolen anything!"

But he just chuckled to himself.

"Such a silly little human. You have no idea, no idea that you stole the most dangerous thing known to the stars."

He bent before me and with a black claw he lifted my chin upwards, our faces inches apart.

"When I look at you both, it reminds me of something that shouldn't be remembered. Something that should stay out of the minds of men."

His never-ending eyes seemed far away from where we were now. But they soon snapped back to mine.

"What did I steal from you?" I whispered as blood dripped down my chin to my chest from his claw biting my skin. Even his smiled was unnatural, as if it didn't belong on a face, but something of another kind of nature.

"You have stolen the Devil's son." Shock ran through me. He couldn't mean Peter, could he? I couldn't see any part of him in this creature before me. "Ah, you don't believe me, do you?"

His teeth were white and straight, but pointed into mini daggers.

But I did believe him.

Kyle had said that all angels gain their own power by building on a piece from what their parents pass down to them. But for Peter to be the most powerful angel in history, more powerful than his siblings combined even when they all come from the same mother. His father would need to be just as powerful as his mother.

The opposite.

The equal.

The Devil.

"I didn't steal him."

His eyebrows drew together. "Stealing someone's heart is the equivalent of stealing the entire person my dear." His voice oozed like black tar.

"Where is my mum?" I asked again, but he ignored me. But he seemed to be inspecting me, like a butterfly he was about to de-wing. "Who else was here?" I asked again.

"My other son."

Other?

"Don't worry, you can meet him, when the time is right."

"I don't want to." I could feel his claw dig deeper.

"You won't have a choice. You don't see it now, but you have a big role to play in the wars to come. You may very well play the role that starts them."

He let me go. He stood up and turned his back to me.

"She was a defiant woman. I could see why your father wanted to have you with her. No matter what we did, she wouldn't tell us where you were. Pity to waste such promise."

My voice shook.

My words were unsteady. "Waste?"

He turned to face me again.

"I didn't want to do this. Peter forced me to do this really. He got his stubbornness from his dammed mother. But the best way to get their attention is to create some trouble." My lip wobbled.

"Have a good night Lucinda."

His chuckle rang through the house as the darkness swept up with him. The lights switched on. They blinded me for a few moments as my eyes adjusted.

The first thing I saw was the blood.

It was everywhere.

It covered every wall, every piece of furniture, the floor, the picture frames. The brilliant colour gracing the wallpaper like historic tapestries.

Footsteps ran up the front of the house and stopped behind me, but I didn't turn to see who it was.

I already knew.

I crawled to the sofa chair in the corner. Her face was slashed and burnt; bones from all over her body were mangled and sticking out in all the wrong places. Skin was missing, and her stomach was hanging down her legs. But I ignored it. My mind didn't want to see it.

"Mum?" I spoke softly and I held her hand. "Mum please answer me."

Nothing.

Tears ran down my face as my mind screamed what my heart didn't want to know.

"Please, please wake up. I'm back now," I begged into her stained red jeans. "Mum! You can't leave me again!" I yelled, but she didn't move. Her eyes were glazed over and non-seeing. "I'm sorry I didn't come back in time. I should have been here. I should have been here for you long ago. But I'm here now, I'm here now, so wake up."

"Lucinda?" his voice came from behind me.

"She is going to be fine," was all I could say, but she wasn't. She never would be again.

"Lucinda, she's gone."

Jane's sad voice also came from behind me. Her skin was so cold, so white. I couldn't hold it in. I screamed.

I screamed loud and brokenly. It ripped from my throat with sorrow and pain. I shook her hard.

"*Wake up!*" I screamed again and again, but still she never stirred. The very same pain that awoke in me that day my brother and father died awoke again. I felt something in my chest collapse in on itself. It stopped moving, it ceased to live and work properly. Everything stopped.

I think it was my heart.

"Pick her up, he could come back at any time."

Strong arms caged me to a strong chest, but I didn't notice as I couldn't stop crying. I couldn't feel anything but the blinding pain that was circling in my chest.

Bright orange lights engulfed around us. I looked up and saw Jane looking down at me, her red hair framing her pretty face. Her own were eyes crying, and she was the one holding me.

The fire still raged around us, and I was slipping in and out of consciousness. Everything blurred and blended into each other.

I fell asleep in the red haired angel's arms.

Chapter 10

"If you know the enemy and yourself, you need not fear the results of a hundred battles."

– Sun Tzu

My mind cleared and awoke, but I refused to open my eyes. Pain flashed through my entire body, like a bitter sea crashing and pulling me underneath its waters. I heard the TV in the background, its sound grating on my very existence.

But I couldn't hide from the world. I had to face it.

I opened my eyes to find myself on a sofa. Everything hurt, but I opened my eyes wider.

Kyle had my legs over his as he watched the TV, and Jane was sleeping on the other sofa on the other side of the room. Her body was rigid and covered in ash.

I moved a little and Kyle's eyes snapped to mine. They were red and puffy.

He'd been crying too.

He didn't say anything, but kept opening his mouth to speak, trying to find a way to explain it all, to explain himself. Explain why he should have been there. Yet it wasn't his duty to be there for me.

It wasn't his father that killed my mother.

"I know Kyle, I know," I soothed him.

He thought he should have been there, to have helped. To have stopped it.

But that's what I thought about myself too.

My throat was red hot and burning. "Where is he?"

He was about to answer, but the door crashed open and then was slammed closed. I noticed we were back at Peter's house suddenly. Its white walls were a slight comfort to me.

He walked through, his wings out and clenched to his back in taut knots. But he paused when he saw me awake, his eyes hard and sad at the same time.

He didn't move and neither did I.

We just watched each other. Because we both knew that I knew what he really was, *who* he really was.

So he focused his attention to Kyle instead.

"I couldn't find him. He's hiding from me now."

His wings vanished and so did the extra darkness in the room. The room cleared and settled.

"We will find him and we will make him suffer," Kyle answered.

But his brother only nodded.

"That was him, wasn't it?" I asked them both. They looked at me, but I already knew the answer. "That was your father," I said as I finally looked back to Peter.

He was as still as a statue. His eyes were unreadable, locked away from me. I knew he wasn't to blame. He hadn't chosen his blood. But I couldn't keep my eyes on him. I had to look away. I walked out of the room, and locked myself in the bathroom. I heard them talking through the walls, so I turned the shower on, undressed and stood under the hot water letting it wash away my tears down the drain.

I had no idea how long I stood in the shower crying. No one disturbed me, I didn't want them to.

Her blood and empty eyes just kept running through my mind. It was agony. Yet again I lost somebody I loved, and yet again I never got to say goodbye.

I'd spent almost three whole hours in the shower, and when I finally dragged myself out, no one was home.

I was so grateful.

I tied my hair at the nape of my neck and dressed in warm jeans and a jumper that were left outside the bathroom door. It must've been Jane.

I had no idea what to do with myself. I was empty. Maybe that's what happened to the heart after it grieves too much; it shuts down, buries itself. When I was a child it was easier, all I had to do was cry. I didn't really think about it. But now…

Now everything was caving in on me, the same pain but also somehow worse this time came flooding around me.

Striking my heart every time I moved.

Some of us are good, and some of us are bad, and the rest are just aware. Peter came from somebody bad, but chose to be good. Yet the bad will forever follow him because a little of it resided inside him, in us all.

And because of this darkness, a darkness that I welcomed into my life…

My mother was now dead.

Weeks passed. Kyle and Jane kept me company for most of it. Yet since the day I woke up on the couch, Peter had been absent. He left and never said a word to me.

The house seemed so empty without him, like he took the heart of it when he left.

The sun would rise, then it would set. And I'd hear nothing from him.

The night my mother was killed was the last time I'd spoken. I couldn't bear to bring forth any words. I didn't know what to say, to myself or the angels. The siblings would talk to me, try to comfort me, but I gave them nothing.

Today was the same. The sun was setting, the rays of sunlight were retreating from the curtains, and no one was back yet. I grabbed my jacket and went out the back door. I wanted to walk down the cliff's edge.

Yet again the world around me seemed to glow gold from the dying sun. I stopped and looked out to the Ocean. The waves were strangely quite as they crashed against the cliffs below. The soft breeze blew against my face. I closed my eyes, letting it remind me that I was still alive, that I was still here. And that my mother had finally been reunited with her lost family, even if that meant I had to stay behind.

Something appeared next to me with a soft thud.

Peter stood by my side, looking out to the same sea, but I knew we both saw completely different things.

"A few hundred years ago, this was just a huge lake. Now it's grown and built itself over people and cities."

He sounded the same, yet he stood with such a weight upon his shoulders, like God above was pushing her almighty power down upon him.

I looked up at him. I looked up to his golden face, and thought it was breathtaking. As I gazed up at him he looked down at me, his eyes sad and dull. I lifted my hand and traced around his eyes. They never left my face.

I'd never had a favourite thing before, but his eyes seemed to fit. They were a bright crystal blue, as if they were crafted from the purest stones in the night skies across every universe.

Sometimes words were not the correct thing for these kind of moments. These moments can be so intense that words aren't even possible; it's like they become stuck in the throat. Everything that needs to be known in that very second is more deep, raw and most vulnerable place known to man.

The eyes.

Because once someone hears words, they can easily forget or mishear what was said, but with the eyes it is seen. And you can never un-see emotion, not when it is showing itself in the very place it was born.

"How can you bear to touch me?" he whispered.

I placed my hands on each side of his face. I could see him now. Not the angel, not the son of the Devil, but the *man.*

"I need to apologise," I said. His eyes grew confused.

"For what?" His voice was equally as quiet as mine.

I took a deep breath. "When you walked in that day, I couldn't bear to look at you. I only saw the man whose father had just killed my mum."

Tears fell down my cheeks as I let the pain slip in again. He looked down.

"But I am, it's my fault."

He looked anywhere but at me, so I drew his face closer. His eyes were rimmed with un-shed tears. Tears for me, for my mother, for the blame he held for himself.

"No. No it's not." I needed him to understand that I did not blame him. "You cannot blame yourself for something that was committed by another."

He looked at me then, and his tears fell. Then I realised something.

Peter never showed his emotions to anyone but me. For centuries he sealed himself away from the world, from people, even his own siblings. I was the only person that saw this side of him, the side that allowed emotion. Around other people he was closed off; he shied away. Separated by thousands of years of pain and rejection that now…now he even rejects himself. And that's why he's been absent for the past few weeks. He blamed himself. He thought I blamed him too.

"I understand why you wouldn't tell me who your father was, but you are not him!" I pulled my hands away and placed them across his chest, right over his beating heart. It beat faster than the average human's did. It was steadier, as if it was confident in the body it powered. "When I look at you, I see a man that fears being who he really is, just in case he hurts those around him. When I look into your eyes, I see pain beyond this world. I see these scars across your skin and see a battle yet to be won."

He said nothing as I traced the scars up his arms.

But I continued.

"I have felt grief. I'm feeling it once again. But I know you have felt it more than anyone else. You see yourself differently than I do. You see a weapon. A monster that came from an even bigger monster. But you're not. You have become the only light in my dark life, the only person that is keeping me from breaking." I traced the scars on his face now, so very faint against his skin.

My words were quiet but not weak. "The only crime that you have committed is that you are the thief that stole my heart. But you are also the one that has saved it—"

He kissed me.

He cupped both sides of my face and held me to him. The stars started to shine as they witnessed us. He was much taller than me, much broader, but he fit against me perfectly. His wings spread out around us, wide and black against the ocean. Our lips danced like two ballerinas finding their perfect routine; the sea was our music and the setting sun was our spot light. His lips were as soft as they looked, and every now and then he would slow his pace and just gently trace his lips across mine.

I gasped and pulled him closer, gripping his shirt in my shaking hands. His lips left my mouth and trailed smaller kisses down my neck, setting my flesh alight.

But he soon abandoned my neck to kiss me again. It felt like the stars were engulfing me. His hands moved down my waist, holding me to him so I would never leave him again.

But too soon he pulled away, stroking my lips from our kiss with his thumb while leaning his forehead against mine. I felt like I was free falling.

"I've wanted to do that for years." He was breathless as he placed a kiss on my nose. He turned his head to look out to the ocean, then back to me with a twinkle in his eye.

"Do you trust me?" He grinned as he waited for my words.

"Yes." I smiled, my cheeks grateful for the joy.

He said nothing else, only wrapped my arms around his waist, his smile warming my heart.

I'd never seen his look so happy before.

Slowly, as if he was taking his time, he grazed his fingers across my arms, my neck, and finally rested his hands on both sides of my faces. Cupping my cheeks like his hands were a puzzle piece to me. He leaned down, brushing his lips across mine, then kissed me again. This time it was slower, as if time was slowing down for us, our lips moving in tune to each other like a paced melody.

We took our time. Small pecks and long strokes of our tongues swept me up into him.

I held onto him as if he was my only lifeline to this world, and he held onto me as if I was all he had to live for.

He stepped backwards, his grip never loosening, our kiss never faltering. He moved back to the edge, where the cliff ended and the sea began. I didn't struggle against him. Instead I moved with him. I trusted him.

Our kiss ended.

My eyes never left his as he held me, as he led me to the cliff's edge. His hands still cupping my face, my arms still holding his waist.

And we fell…

Chapter 11

"What's the difference between the love of your life, and your soulmate?
One is a choice, and one is not."

— *Tarryn Fisher*

For a moment we were standing on solid ground and the next we were falling back off the cliffs. We were falling so fast I forgot to scream. He held me tight and steady. The water was racing up to meet us, then he spread his wings wide.

They seemed to never end, they were strong and broad.

The wings of a warrior.

One curve of his wings and we were gliding across the sea's face. He moved sideways and his wing sliced through the top of the water, pulling a wall of water upwards behind us. The wind rushed passed us. My heart was beating so fast it could break my chest wide open. I looked up at the angel holding me, but he was already smiling back.

With the powerful sweeps of his wings we flew harder and we started to leave the ocean behind. We soared upwards to the shining stars. We moved so fast, but I wasn't scared.

I felt everything.

Then he levelled us out in mid-air.

"I'm going to turn you around so you can see it all ok?"

I nodded and I unwrapped my arms from his waist. He turned me around so my back was to his chest. He wrapped his hands back around my stomach then leaned his chin on my shoulder.

There weren't any true words to describe what we saw. People got to see this every day from planes, but to be in the middle of it; to have the fresh wind ripple through my clothes. To feel the empty air beneath my feet, and to be able to reach out to the clouds around us.

It was exhilarating to my human soul.

The dark waters reached out across the Earth for miles, the lights from the cities lit the skies above; and it was like I was in another world. Apart from all the suffering of my life, somewhere no one could reach us.

The stars shone like diamonds. They seemed to reach down to me; but they were also around me, under me. I could see more stars than if I was on the ground, and I felt comforted by it strangely.

The clouds hovered around us, and we were careful not to disturb them on their journey.

He whispered into my ear, "I have always wanted to share this with you, to do this with you." I turned my head towards his, and somehow his eyes were glowing luminous blue.

"Your eyes are glowing," I gasped, but he only grinned.

"It's because I am closer to Heaven right now. It happens to all angels."

They were more beautiful than any star, brighter than any sun to me. I kissed his cheek and turned back to watch the world, the skies, the entire universe. His hands were warm against my belly. His entire body was a warm beacon for mine. A comfort I now know will always be there for me, a man, an angel.

"I am so sorry about what happened Lucinda. If I could take it back, I would."

I reached back and laced my fingers into his hair at the nape of his head.

"It wasn't your fault."

He buried his face into my hair, his nose gliding against my sensitive skin.

I could feel them then, the hidden eyes that followed us everywhere we went. Their power beating down on us like a hammer to a nail.

But they saw power in everything but us, and soon they will see how dangerous that is for them to think.

We stayed in the sky for a few more minutes, but soon we had to return before his siblings noticed we were missing.

We gently flew down for the cliffs and he landed us onto the grass outside his back door.

"That was amazing Peter. Thank you for sharing that with me."

It had distracted my mind for a while.

He held my hand and kissed the top of it.

"I'm happy you loved it as much as I loved taking you up there," he said as he opened the door for me. It was pitch black, but my skin crawled as if it was covered in millions of insects.

Peter froze in front of me.

"Something is wrong." His voice was low, his wings shaking under my hands; he wrapped his left wing around me. To protect me.

He reached out a hand to turn the kitchen light on, and as the light flooded into the room we found Kyle across the floor unconscious. Peter dropped to his knees and shook his brother's shoulder.

"Wake up brother."

Kyle's eyes fluttered open and Peter lifted him to his feet. He steadied him but didn't let him go.

"What happened?" Peter demanded. Kyle held a hand to his head, coating his fingers in fresh blood.

"Lucifer," he said. He seemed to come back to his senses and looked at me with grave eyes. "And Damien," he added, and Peter's face fell like stone. He looked at his brother as if he just told him he was going to die; and he looked like it too.

"Where's Jane?" Peter's voice became panicked.

"She wasn't here, she's safe."

"What's happened here?" I spoke for the first time since coming through the door.

The two brothers looked at me.

"I think it's time we all tell you everything," Kyle said.

"Well it's about time, it's all I've been asking for." I exhaled. I helped Kyle get to the sofa chair in the corner of the living area, and after we cleaned him up I sat on the couch next to Peter.

Ready to listen.

Chapter 12

"But the thing about remembering is that you don't forget."
– Tim O'Brien

Lucinda

"You know that Lucifer is my father," Peter began, yet he didn't look quite himself as he spoke. "And Kyle has told you his and who Jane's parents are. But there is a lot more to this story than a struggle of angelic power."

Peter cleared his throat before continuing, like he was choking up the truth for me.

"There can't ever be just *one* God. It's like an election; the perfect angel will be born and God will pass on her power to them. They rule for a few million years and then they give up the holy throne for the God after that."

"Why? Why can't there be just one?" I asked intrigued. He wouldn't look at me, or answer, so Kyle carried on for him.

"Having that kind of power drives the host insane. They cannot hold it for forever. But only the strongest angel can withstand to have it and to handle that kind of power; they have to give up so much more in return."

He rolled his shoulder back and I heard it click.

"Like what?"

His eyes grew hard. "Our mother broke many rules that cost her nearly everything. She had children. Even had one of them with the Devil. God and the Devil must keep apart to keep the balance from tipping; light must stay pure, untainted from darkness. But she fell in love with Lucifer and nearly tipped that balance, but what else do you expect from an insane woman?"

Kyle smirked at his words, as if it was all a big joke to him.

"Can't they say no to becoming God?"

"No, since the day of their birth, they were chosen by the first ever God." He leaned back in his chair. "The God we have now is called Lola. She is our mother. She has been God for many

103

lifetimes now. Some say too many; but her time is nearly up. Lucifer is the same; a new Devil must be elected."

He looked at his brother and back to me.

"When Peter was born, everyone in Heaven and Hell knew what he was going to become. So Lucifer chose him to be his successor, but he will not accept the role. This started the war between our nations, and a part of it led us here."

Peter still wouldn't look at either of us, his mind was elsewhere, most probably returning to unwanted memories.

"When both nations rejected him, they rejected me and Jane too as we wouldn't leave his side. He never wanted the role, he never wanted to be a weapon to anyone–" Peter then chose to speak up.

"So I chose my mother." His voice was void of emotion. "She was better than being with that monster. We made a deal to be her generals in her army. We would use our powers at her mercy. But then I met you when you were six, and everything changed." His eyes burned as he watched me. "My mother didn't like it, so she hid you from me, and I lost my mind. And the grip on my power. I nearly destroyed Hell and Heaven in the process, along with millions of lives."

I sucked in a breath; he really did do all that for me. I should have been disgusted with him for what he had done, but I wasn't, and he knew it.

"I hate myself for it, you should hate me for it too. Everyone suffered at my hands, even my own brother and sister. So to end it all, I fell to Earth with my family. Lucifer became mad with rage at what I did. And because I chose to become a fallen angel, I couldn't be his heir. So he had another offspring with one of his demons, something that was completely demonic and pure evil. Damien. But he was too savage to be his heir."

It all made sense.

Is it time for their destruction to take flight?

"That was the other voice I heard when I first met Lucifer," I realised.

Peter didn't say anything. His face was like stone, no expression.

"You don't understand what you are, *who* you are. You are power itself, you are the Holy Spirit. When you drowned, your angelic power finally awoke."

Kyle spoke up again as Peter didn't seem like he could.

"When Lucifer turned his back on her and made the wedge in Heaven, God created a weapon, just as powerful as Peter. Maybe more so."

They both looked at me with admiration and fear in their perfect eyes.

"What? What am I?" My voice shook.

Kyle took a deep breath before answering. "I helped Lola create the first star. She wanted to keep it far away from her enemy. So she placed it in the sky, but it still wasn't safe. So a few million years later, she placed it in the eyes of a human, a small little human. It was genius. Who would look for such a weapon in a weak human?" What was he saying? "But who would have thought that the most powerful angel in all of history would fall in love with the most powerful human?"

Kyle seemed to be hiding a smirk as we both looked to Peter. But he wouldn't look at me. He stared his brother down, his face distant and cold.

He loved me?

"You are what brought us to this." Kyle leaned forward and braced his elbows on his knees.

"Are you telling me I'm a star? An actual star?" I felt a little weak. Sick even. Peter stood and kept his back to me.

So Kyle nodded his answer for him.

"I don't believe you," I whispered, but Kyle only laughed.

"But you believe everything else?"

I said nothing.

"There is so much that you don't know. Your father is archangel Azriel. He came down to Earth to be your father, to protect the star. But Lola didn't interpret that he would fall in love with your mother, and so Archangel Michael was born. Also half angel and half human, like you."

We were all silent. They allowed the words to sink in to my confused mind.

"I thought half angels and half humans were called–"

"Nephilim?" he added.

I nodded my answer.

He sighed before speaking, letting out a well-used breath. "If an angel of the Devil has a child with a human, then yes they are then called Nephilims. But your father was an angel of God."

"So what are my kind called?"

"No one knows. You and your brother are the first of your kind…"

For a moment the air was cold in my lungs. It was getting harder and harder to take all this in.

"So that's why Lucifer killed my mother? He did it because you refused to be his pawn?" I turned, accusing the dark winged angel before me. But he wouldn't turn to look at me. "What about my father and brother? Did he kill them too?"

Kyle's eyes said it all. I couldn't breathe properly, my heart was beating too fast.

"Peter tried to save them, but he was too late. He saved your mother, but he couldn't save the rest."

The Devil had killed my entire family out of spite, all because his son refused to be as evil as he was.

"What happened to them?" My voice barely rose above a whisper.

"When an angel is killed on Earth, they are sent back to Heaven. They are alive, they are safe. But they couldn't get back down here for you."

Kyle eyes were soft for me.

Shock and pure happiness ran through me. I lifted my head to look at them both.

"They are alive. All this time they were alive?"

They nodded their heads. Peter turned to look at me with pale eyes.

"Why didn't you tell me sooner?" My voice arose with a rough edge to it.

"Secrets weigh more than a grieving heart Lucinda, and they would have crushed you," Peter finally spoke.

"You still shouldn't have kept that from me," I shouted at him. "All these years I shut out the world, I never stopped grieving, I never healed. And you could've just told me the truth." I stared him down. I started to pace the room, fury raged through me. I couldn't be still, years of anger pumped through my body all at once.

"I trusted you, and all I have gotten in return is more heart ache. And now the loss of my mother."

I stopped pacing and faced him, glaring. I could feel my eyes burning. He looked completely breakable as he looked at me. As if I was the only one able to shatter him and that he would gladly let me do it.

"I didn't want to hurt you!" He begged me to understand, but I couldn't. All I felt was hurt, rage, and more hurt. "You could never see them again. How would knowing that they were alive have helped you? That they left you! And *never* looked back!"

"I deserved to know…"

"I was trying to protect you!"

"Oh ok, so you broke me instead," I answered calmly.

He just stood there watching me, then his wings fell a little.

"I did it to protect you," he said defeated, his wings now slacking. "Every angel would have come after you. I could not let that happen. But now it has. You know what you are; and now they will come for you. I may have all the power in the world, but it only means I have a weakness just as great. You."

I said nothing, but tears ran down my face; yet it wasn't because I was angry with him. It was because I wasn't *truly* angry with him. I don't think I could be angry with somebody that destroyed the world just to have me.

I was more disgusted with myself *because* I felt like that. I should hate him; I should want to beat him to the dust and spit on his remains. But I didn't, and I hated *myself* for it.

He stepped towards me. He placed my hand across his heart and placed his own on top.

"As long as I still breathe, I will put you above everyone else. I will put you before any nation, and you can hate me for it. But I'm the son of the Devil. I've been hated all my life. I can deal with it; just as long as you are safe."

He kissed my forehead and walked away into his study.

I was alone with Kyle, and he had no grin on his face as he looked at me. But his eyes held compassion. For a moment, Kyle's eyes became thoughtful, as if he was sorting through both sides of the argument in his head, but soon his eyes grew thorny.

He had made his judgement.

"My brother has done many horrid sins in his existence, but he tried to be good for you. You are a part of something bigger than all of us, and he has always tried to shield you from it. Take it from someone how knows more than most people, pain makes you stronger. But love?" I looked at him, his eyes shone like his brother's did. "Love makes you *powerful*."

He stood and went after his brother, leaving me confused and aggravated with everything.

All through my life I had carried a hidden anger for the world, and maybe some anger for everyone in it. Time altering doesn't bring pain, but the fact that we must change too; meaning we have to leave the past behind us and everyone we've ever lost with it. That is what makes it all so painful.

Kyle

I would never lie to Lucinda, and I didn't understand why I couldn't. I lie to everyone; it's a habit almost. I just know I will always tell her the pure, blood-soaked truth.

Humans are brave. I don't think much of them, but in some points in history they have proven to me how brave they can be. It's been many centuries since this thought has crossed my mind, but meeting Lucinda again reminded me of that.

I have loved once before. It was so long ago now that I can't even remember what she looked like. I just knew that I loved her.

But love was labelled to be a sin in Heaven. It is said to play tricks on your mind to drive you insane.

So I lost her. And I never allowed myself to feel any kind of emotion again.

But maybe, feeling love makes you human; and maybe pain is what makes humans so strong.

Do we feel pain to reassure ourselves that a part of us is still human after we have loved and lost?

I pray to God that it does…

Lucinda

I could hear the brothers mumbling through the walls, but their words never made it past the ringing in my ears.

I was still standing in the middle of the room, hands in fists with my nails puncturing the flesh on my palms. I welcomed the pain; it's what I deserved. Blood dripped down my wrist as Jane burst through the front door. I rapidly wiped the blood away so she wouldn't worry.

She stepped into the living room and paused. Her eyes were red rimmed and her skin was pale as white ice. I could see scars covering her skin too, but they were worse than her siblings. They looked as if someone had carved indents or chunks into her flesh. They weren't white and pale trails like Peters; they were like human scars.

The kind of scars that would kill us.

She knew what I was staring at. She ran her hand over her arms and neck, as if she was ashamed they were a part of her.

"You're beautiful Jane."

She didn't smile, but we sat next to each other on the couch, sinking into the pillows.

"I know I'm not Lucinda. You don't have to lie for me."

Her eyes were dull as she fiddled with the rings on her skinny fingers.

"Believe me Jane, you're beautiful physically and mentally." She looked over at me with tears rimming her eyes. That was why they were red. "Beauty comes from your strength, and you're the strongest person I know."

Her eyes grew a little brighter and so did her smile. It was a joy to see her smile. If you've ever wondered what an angel would look like when they smiled, just look at Jane. She was the definition of the divine. We both looked up as the boys walked back into the room. Kyle wore his smirk and Peter's face was unreadable.

"It's too dangerous here." Kyle was the first to speak. "We have to get you away to somewhere safe Lucinda."

His eyes were stone, but I nodded my agreement anyway.

I cleared my throat. "Where are you taking me?"

Peter wouldn't look away from me, but I couldn't bear to look at him.

"We are going to visit the Pope in Rome, the Vatican City." Kyle sat down and clasped his fingers together. "He can help us contact our mother."

He sounded like he was going to his own funeral. His eyebrows were drawn together in deep thought.

"The Devil is coming for you Lucinda." Peter finally spoke up. I looked up and his eyes were harsh; as if every pain the world had ever experienced was cramped into them. "So the only person that can protect you now is the one that made you. Lola will protect her weapon. And I will protect you."

I didn't answer him; we just watched each other. He had his arms crossed over his chest. It seemed he was trying to keep his heart from falling out.

"I know you will." I sounded too tired for someone who was awake.

He opened his mouth to speak, but couldn't find any words. So he stayed silent. His hair was wild, dark hair falling across his eyes; his skin was paler than usual and his eyes were dull. The overwhelming power that normally rolled off him was dimmed. The once choking smoke of fire just seemed to be disappearing.

"When do we leave?" I asked.

Jane stood beside Peter and gripped his hand before letting go. It was strange how Jane looked at her brother in that moment with regretful eyes and how he returned it with a sad warmth. Two utterly broken souls still holding on.

"Immediately," Peter answered me when he looked away from his sister. "It's too dangerous here, even with us here to protect you. And we can't take the cars. We have to get to Rome without being seen."

His eyes went away in deep thought, but Kyle soon interrupted his thinking.

"We could fly there."

Peter's eyes widened as if Kyle just presented him his liver right from his stomach.

"It's not a terrible idea," Jane agreed.

The blue-eyed angel threw his arms up in the air in a childish huff.

"Am I the only sane person in the room right now?" he exclaimed.

"Think about it brother," said Kyle. "Lucifer is betting we get Lucinda to Rome, but he won't be betting on us taking her there in the most vulnerable way possible." Kyle stepped towards the distraught angel and placed his hands on his shoulders, his grip strong but reassuring. "We have laid down our lives for each other for thousands of years, and for however longer we live, we will continue to do just that."

They embraced, their white trailed scars moulding together through their flesh.

"It's not me I'm worried for."

Peter glanced at me from across the room with terrified eyes. The emotion was brief, but it was there.

We decided to leave early the next morning. If they were flying and carrying me across the world, they would need to sleep and gather strength. Yet I couldn't sleep, not even for an hour.

My mind was wide awake running through thoughts and memories; my mother's eyes glazed and un-seeing. My father and brother, laying in their coffins white and still as pearl statues. Could I still care for Peter after he had betrayed me so badly? My heart had bled for years at a time. For as long as I could remember, the grief would cut me each and every day while I wouldn't get the chance to heal. But if you live with something like that for so long, how can you tell if you've healed or not?

The pain becomes natural to you.

The grief had deformed me so badly that I could never hope to regain my hearts natural form ever again.

We were all sleeping in the living room, except for Peter. He went away to his own bed. Jane slept soundly next to me. So I crept upstairs and inched open his white door. He laid on top of the bed tangled with the pitch-black blanket. His chest was bare except for his imperfections, his white scars that I loved.

The moonlight streaked through the curtains onto his sleeping, calm face. His head was turned to the side slightly and his arms were gently laid over his wings on either side of him. He always seemed to be ready for someone to paint him; he was the perfect muse for any artist. Many might think it was creepy for me to watch him sleep, but it fascinated me to be able to see angelic beauty so close and so at peace.

"Lucinda?"

His sleepy voice startled me from my deep thoughts so much that I tumbled into the doorframe. With cheeks flaming deep red I looked up to see him leaning up in bed.

"I'm… sorry." I stumbled over my words as well as my feet. His eyes watched me slightly concerned. I couldn't help but stare back, my heart reaching out for him to wrap me up in his wings; but my mind was not so forgiving.

Yet the words came flowing out like burning lava.

"I'm sorry Peter."

He leaned up further and braced his elbows on his knees.

"Lucinda–" he began to speak but I butted in before he could continue.

"Please wait. I must say this or I never will." He nodded and sat silently. I took a deep breath. "I understand why you chose to protect me instead of my family, and I shouldn't have judged you for it. I understand why you didn't tell me who killed them. To have to look at you while knowing the truth is a crushing burden to have." His expression became hurt, and he didn't bother to hide it. I stepped towards his bed and sat at the edge, the bed dipping for me. He never reached for me or tried to move closer.

"You bring destruction with you wherever you go, and my greatest sin–" He braced his body for my next few words, but in that minute, I had to brace myself too. "Is that I will never hate you for it. I couldn't, no matter what you do, no matter who gets hurt. It will never effect my feelings for you. And that will be the greatest sin in my life, putting myself before the needs of the world."

He didn't speak; he seemed to have lost his voice.

"I haven't loved in a very long time Peter." He sucked in a breath as I spoke. The moonlight traced his features like a paintbrush, paint streaks of beauty that shone in the purest darkness in the most tainted of light. "But it's happening, though you must give me time. My heart is only just starting to beat again. But if you want it, whatever is left of it, then I couldn't trust anyone but you to have it."

He was speechless for a few moments, but he soon pulled me into his arms and wrapped my body into his soft wings.

"I would be honoured." He smiled; his eyes grew bright once again and it warmed my heart. I was sitting in his lap with his arms secured around my waist.

I was home.

He kissed my cheeks, my eyelids, my neck. I dragged my fingers into his soft hair, and I felt him grip my hips to him.

His wings curved around me, warmth engulfed us as I leaned in to kiss him. Our lips danced as his hands graced the skin on my back. I bit his lip, but he only kissed me harder. I was grateful for the shield of his wings; the world shouldn't see our mischief.

The button on my jeans opened and he pulled away, both of our lips swollen, both of us breathless.

And we only looked at each other.

His voice was soft as he spoke. "You need to sleep for tomorrow."

I nodded and started to climb off him, but he only pulled me in for another kiss. It was softer than before, but I could feel he was trying so hard to be soft with me, and not give in to what he really wanted.

Us.

He pulled away and we were both grinning.

Two shining stars in the dead of night.

He pulled me down beside him and wrapped his arms around me sweetly. I could forgive him for everything he did. Every crime. Every sin. He hadn't done anything wrong to begin with. He just gave in to his deepest sins.

Love.

Chapter 13

"The best thing about bravery is even a little is enough."
— *Beau Taplin*

Gabriel

50 years later.

"It wasn't a particular moment," I said while looking at them. "That made them fall in love."

They danced with different people, but always had their eyes on each other.

"It didn't take a moment for her to love him; it was more complicated than that. It was the way he smiled, traced her skin, watched her from afar, and how his eyes sparkled for only her. So many things twisted and entwined between them."

The music spun the room around them, a constant rhythm of chaos and peace. Everyone shone, their clothes reflecting the stars from the outside world. But they did not notice; they only noticed each other.

"How can the court expect her to completely forget a love like that?"

I looked down at the little broken angel, her eyes coloured with judgement and sadness, an undying burden in those irises.

"He's her life line, the cord that she holds to this world. They must unwind her very soul to rid him of her heart."

We were quite as we watched them dance their sad song, forever cursed to play the same steps without each other.

"How can she survive that?" she whispered from beside me. I swallowed the lump in my throat before answering.

"How could anyone survive that?"

Jane

The pain rippled through both sides of my back, as it does throughout most of the day and night. I awoke from blood-covered dreams of war to the darkness of the living room. But I could only control my sobs when I could hear my brother's steady breathing from the other side of it. I always felt as if the darkness was watching me, or if something from inside it was; judging me. I was never afraid of the dark.

Just of what was in it.

Everything watched me. The walls, the floors, the sky.

Everything. Always watching me, waiting for me to slip up enough to fall back into their clutches.

But I've learned that if they were going to watch me, I might as well look back…

Kyle

I didn't try to sleep again until Jane settled back down.

The night was disappearing from the skies outside of the house. I could even hear the birds start to sing gently to the sun. The floor was hard and cold. I rolled over to try and find a comfy position but came face to face with a pair of feet.

"Good morning Lucinda," I groaned. She sat down by my head and she looked tired. Very tired. "Why are you awake at this hour?"

Her sweet voice reached more than my ears.

"I've had trouble sleeping for the past few months."

"Oh," was all I said.

"Why are you helping me?" she asked again, her voice a little sad.

"Why wouldn't I? My brother loves you, and I love my brother."

I kept my eyes closed, shielded from her.

"I've had visions, dreams of the three of you before you fell from Heaven. But I've been having this one where I see a man holding a ball of fire. And there's this woman holding me." She took in a shaky, deep breath. "But it's the only one that doesn't make sense," she said almost to herself.

"They're memories." Her wide eyes found my dark ones. "Memories that your angelic soul is trying to show you," I whispered against the darkness. "We have a saying where we are from. 'Quae tamen ut pervenire possimus terrs memorias.'"

"What does it mean?"

"Memories are lands that are unseen." She was quiet, her breathing the only comforting thing in this room. "It means memories are never lost, they live around us as another world."

I could sense her smile. It was delicate and sweet. Like a Bambi facing death without knowing how much danger it was in.

So I added with a small voice.

"It was me."

"What was you?" She moved closer to catch my words.

"The man with the fire, it was me."

She froze. She didn't move closer, but she didn't move away either.

"My mother knew she had to hide you." My voice shook. "But she didn't know how to mould a star into a fragile human body. So she entrusted me to build her one that could withstand its power."

She didn't say anything. I could only hear her calm breathing.

"I made you, I spent years on you. Making sure you were strong enough to hold a star."

"You made me?" Her tone shook slightly.

"I made your body. But you are who you are today because you are your own person."

It was lighter in the room now. I could see the outline of her body next to mine.

"I met you first?" Her question was small and innocent, but I didn't answer.

I couldn't.

"Who broke you Kyle?" she asked out of the blue. My eyebrows drew together in surprise, but she couldn't see it. No one had actually asked me that before. They knew, but they have never asked me to my face. It took a few moments for me to answer without stammering.

"Why is it important?"

"Why wouldn't it be?" she questioned in time with my answer.

I rolled away from her. "It was a very long time ago."

"Yet it still weighs heavy on your heart," she said again, I faced the ceiling and chuckled to myself.

What was it with this little human and asking so many questions?

"She was a demon. A beautiful, wild, evil, brave demon. And I fell for her instantly. But the war between Lucifer and our God was still very fresh. Peter was gone, Jane was gone. I only had her. I first met her while I was still building you. She even helped me a little."

"Did they take her from you?"

I shook my head.

"No." The word was bitter on my tongue. "She chose Lucifer over me. He wanted you, your power. And he sent her to gain my trust. I wouldn't give you away, so they took my wings in revenge." The anger rose in me again, after thousands of years it rose in me again savagely. "They couldn't have you, so they tried to take my fire. The only thing they got were my wings." Memories choked me from the inside out. "I never trusted anyone after that. I buried every emotion I ever had. I have no choice in loving my siblings, we're family. But everyone else? I will never allow myself to care for anyone ever again. I will kill myself before that happens."

My tone was so sharp. Lucinda flinched slightly as if I had cut her.

"Remember when you told me we have no control in who we love?" she said in a soft tone, as if she was talking to a wild animal in a cage. Frightened and enraged.

I guess that's how she must see me.

"Yeah I do," I said.

"It was true Kyle, we don't have any control over it. But that doesn't mean it's a bad thing. You were hurt, but you survived. We all did," I could finally see her eyes in the dim early morning. "Love takes every bad thing from our soul and leaves it clean." She took my hand into hers. "And you will love again, maybe not tomorrow, or in a year." She grinned. "Or maybe not even in my own life-time… But you will, and it will set you free."

My chest warmed at the sound of her voice, my eyes even softened towards her.

"Lucinda–"

"Brother?" Peter's voice floated into the room, stopping me from exposing my true self. I lifted myself up swiftly and pulled my hand away from hers, pretending to forget Lucinda was in even in the room with us. He looked between us both and gave a lope-sided grin. He then slipped his hand into hers, as if it always belonged there.

I never despised him for loving a human, or judged him for nearly destroying Heaven and Hell for her. Because I've been there once too. I have felt that burning love slip into my veins like lava.

I have loved, but the difference between me and my brother was that I have loved and lost.

While he had gained.

Through my many years of roaming this planet, I trained myself to ignore emotions, to forget what is was like to care. I have become a living statue of stone and I am perfectly happy living this way...I am...I am...

I was.

Chapter 14

"In this universe we are given two gifts: the ability to love, and the ability to ask questions. Which are, at the same time, the fires that warm us and the fires that scorch us."

– Mary Oliver

Lucinda

Everything was ready. We locked down the house and all huddled together at the top of the cliffs at the back.

The sky was an angry grey. It flowed across the ocean until they touched in the far distance. As if they were sharing a kiss.

The ocean was as black as Peter's wings, and as wild as his eyes. I looked away from the sea and up at him, and he was already looking back at me.

"Are you ready?"

There was something hesitant about him as he spoke. He sounded like he wasn't ready *himself*. But his eyes were empowering as I stared into them.

So I nodded for us both.

"As long as I'm with you, I'll be ready for anything," I said. And I took his hand. I tried to smile bright for him, but he only watched me; his eyes were trying to hide something from me.

"Kyle. Jane," he spoke up while keeping his strange eyes on mine.

"Yes brother?" they replied in unison.

"Stay safe."

As soon as the words left him he lifted me into his arms and shot into the sky like a graceful dove. His siblings couldn't follow; it was just us in the vast skies ahead.

When we were high enough, we started to fly across the ocean, using the strong wind currents to glide next to the clouds. Something was bothering him. I could feel the unusual beat of his heart against my side.

"Peter?" I breathed against his ear. He turned his head to look down at me, yet again his eyes troubled. "Is something wrong?"

His voice even sounded too distant. I lifted my hand to the side of his perfect face. I touched the skin under his perfect eyes. Then his cheek, and finally his full lips. He sighed against my touch and kissed the ends of my fingers delicately.

"I'm sorry, I'm just lost in thought. I've got a lot on my mind." He sighed.

"I know, as do I."

"Through all of this, I haven't even asked you if you still want to be a part of it." His face was cold to the touch from the harsh wind. "I'm dragging you across the world, ripping your life apart, and I haven't even asked you how you're feeling about it," he said with disgust. And I couldn't help but laugh about it; he thought all this was his fault.

But I was the one they were trying to protect. The one who was changing *their* lives for the worse.

"What's so funny?" he asked, annoyance on his face. But I only laughed harder. I wrapped my arms around his neck, twining my fingers together hoping I never had to let go.

"You will never see how much you have made my life actually worth living will you? Never understand how you freed me from the cage I formed around myself, or how you gave me the strength to fight for what I wanted."

His eyes were full of surprise. They glowed even more as we flew closer to Heaven, but I liked to think it was because he was with me.

Maybe it was.

"But I destroyed it," he said.

I kissed him, our mouths dancing as one, like the moon and the sea when it was full. I pulled away and placed a smaller kiss upon his cheek, and he held me tighter. I cupped both sides of his face and held him to me. I could live in this moment forever.

But we started to fly off course.

He drew away and steadied us again on our correct route, and when he looked back to me, we both burst into a fit of laughs that shook the skies around us. It was refreshing to hear him laugh again.

"Stop distracting the driver," he said still chuckling. I leaned my head onto his shoulder and smiled wider.

"Well it's not like we're about to be pulled over and fined, are we?"

We were silent for a second longer, until his chest rippled with more laughs, setting me off again too. I wasn't until we finally settled down again that he spoke up.

"That is what I fight for Lucinda, that's what I *have* fought for."

I lifted my head back up to look at him. His eyes were bright but hard.

"What do you fight for?" I could only bring my voice to a whisper. Barely audible over the wind. But I had to hear it, even if it was just once.

"To hear that joyous laugh," he said. "For the rest of eternity." His eyes never shook from mine, and I didn't look away from them.

"And I will fight alongside you…forever," I replied, my voice determined, and the corner of his lips lifted.

"I know. I always did, and I never doubted it."

Pride laced itself into his words, and I rested my head against his warm chest, listening to his soft breathing and to his heart that would always be mine.

Peter

For many years, I have watched humans fall in and out of love. I gazed down many times when no one was looking, and saw tragedy, exquisite tragedy.

People killing their own hearts for something that created sin.

Yet here I was. Flying across the world with only a shred of battered hope that I could save the one I love.

I never understood the emotion. It was described in poetry and music for millions of years; but I only chose to listen when I saw Lucinda for the first time.

She had fallen asleep in my arms hours ago, but I couldn't stop watching her. Her hair was matted by the wind, her nose was red and cheeks were pink.

But she was beautiful.

Every angel, God, Demon and Saint… Everything was turned to dust when it came to her.

My love was a burden on her, but she opened her arms to it like it was a million flowers. She believed anyone could be saved, and I admired her for it, adored her for it.

But it was her choice to follow me into Hell, and I couldn't take that decision from her.

I knew I was flying to my death. Everything I had done had led me to this moment. But I was dying for love, and to me she was worth dying for.

Lola

6 months later…

I stood looking down from the balcony, watching my daughter. Her red hair shone in the clear, sun-filled day. She was strong; many said she was too strong for how weak her mind had become.

She held the bronze sword in her hand with a mighty grip, her face alight with a wild fire of power. She fought like the warrior the world knew her to be, like how the world made her.

Her ablaze eyes met mine, and her face twisted into a sneer of an animal corrupted. She still hated me. She would forever hate me. They all would…

For what I did to *her.*

My advisor came and stood beside me, his arms strong at his sides, ready to defend and conquer for me.

"She is strong," he said.

I nodded my head. "I just hope she will be strong enough to defend herself and the others when I am gone."

"She will. I have every faith in her… And the others."

We fell silent, watching the princess of Heaven teach the next generation of warriors. Her body was swift and lean as it flashed from one end of the battle ring to the other. Her haunting scars out for the world to see. Yet there was no hint of hesitation as she took off her fighting leathers, no show of shame as she held up her powerful arms to fight.

A memory reached me then, a distant and old memory.

My young daughter, only a few years old, a small and dainty thing. Always swapping her pretty dresses that I'd made her for old fighting leathers that hung off her.

She was always climbing into the fighting rings.

"Jane darling, you know you can't fight. You are a princess, not a fighter." I bent down to the floor of the weapons room, trying to find her little feet.

Her little voice called out. "But mimi, why can't I be both?"

And there, huddled in the corner I saw her little eight-year-old feet. Her shoes I'd spent hours making muddy and torn.

I stood up, she stood holding over-sized fighting leathers in her little petite fingers. She was so small.

"Because only boys fight. They are meant to protect and fight for us. Our purpose is to rule them, and in return they protect us."

Her eyes were huge and beautiful. My little doll.

"But mimi." *She stood straighter, holding her chin high.* *"I want to be the one to protect you."*

I stood there, watching my little girl gripping those fighting leathers to her little chest. And I stood there remembering all those times she fell down over the frills of her dresses, how she hated having her hair brushed and tied up, how she always wanted it down and wild. When she always ran down the halls and never walked. How she always got into fights, and how she always, without fail, fought for those that couldn't fight for themselves.

And when she was born, the world filled with storms and screamed her name across the skies for all to hear.

Her very first battle cry.

"So you don't want to be a princess?" I said finally.

She shook her defiant little head. Her small and delicate red and white wings were tucked in tight to her little back.

"Well if you don't want to be a princess, what do *you want to be?"*

And without missing a beat, she spoke for the first time not as a child, but as an angel.

"I want to be a warrior."

So that very night we tided away her dresses for shirts and trousers, let her hair run wild and free, put her little shoes away into the wardrobe and placed boots in their places.

Then lastly, she placed her small crown into its box and gave it to me for safekeeping.

I watched her walk down to the fighting rings, my daughter defiant that she make the journey on her own. And I stood smiling as she climbed into the ring with the boys.

Dressed in her very own fighting gear that fitted her perfectly, and that brought out the warrior I knew she would become.

There she stood, fists held up and ready. Ready to fight and defend the world she would never inherit, but would always protect.

One punch to the face and she went down, blood pouring from her mouth. And the young boy was standing there smug.

I stepped forward but was soon held back. I looked down at the arm that was holding me.

"Let her learn," Gabe said. "The more she falls, the better she will rise."

I turned back to her.

Tears streamed from her eyes and her lip was split. The boys were laughing at her.

But she did what no girl had ever done before.

She wiped the blood away, no longer crying, no longer showing any pain.

Then stood up to fight again.

And there, for the first time in history, arose a warrior.

Peter

I rested her down on the bed and brushed the soft hair away from her peaceful face. I couldn't help but watch her eyelids flutter for a few more seconds before I turned away. The room was an ugly yellow colour, like dried sunflower petals.

There was a desk in the corner, a television on a rustic nightstand, and a window where I could see the ocean we had just flown over.

I sat down at the desk and rubbed my eyes roughly with my fingers. My wings ached with a burning sensation; hours of flying and holding Lucinda had taken its toll.

But I wanted her to sleep, to forget the nightmares around us for a few more hours.

Buzz, buzz, buzz…

I looked down on the desk and saw Kyle's number pop up on my phone.

I answered. "Brother?"

He was breathless on the other end, but I could hear the rumble of an engine.

"Are you there yet?" he asked. I looked out the window to see stars starting to rise in the sky.

"Yeah, we are at the hotel, Where are you?"

"We've landed, but it's going to take a few more hours before we reach you."

I could hear my brother speed up his car.

"How is she?" he asked with a slightly warmer tone.

I looked over at her sleeping soundly across the bed. Her hair spread across the pillow, like a hallow of golden and brown shades.

"How am I meant to do this?" My voice shook. Kyle sighed on the other end of the phone. "How am I going to manage to let her go?" I could hardly force the words from my mouth. They seemed to blister my lips as they passed through.

"Remember that time I fell in love?" Kyle spoke up, his voice calm and collected.

"How could I forget? It was the first time I'd ever seen you cry."

He chuckled over the static.

"She showed me something Peter. She may have broken my heart, but she showed me that I did have one."

"Is this leading to a point?"

I hesitated before walking over to the bed and sitting down beside her, tracing the face I have loved for many years.

"If this love breaks you, breaks you both, then let it be so. There is nothing better or worse than loving someone and having them break your heart at the end of i–" Kyle took in a deep breath before continuing. "It's going to kill you both, but it will be worth it when no one else can own her heart."

"I don't want this to hurt her," I whispered in defeat of my heart.

"That is not your choice to make. It's hers."

We were both silent for a few moments. The waves outside were in rhythm with the empty static of my phone.

"I have only one more day with her, one more day. Before the world around her changes forever." I slumped to the foot of the bed.

"Then love her. Love her with everything you hold in your body. Take this last day and make it last for forever in your heart." I could hear the pain in my brother's voice for me. "And when the day is finally over and the stars shine brightly for her to return to them, look at her one last time. Take her all in, and then let her go…"

My sharp intake of breath caught his attention. I couldn't speak; my throat was swollen with the struggle of keeping back years of unshed tears.

"It's the only way you will both survive what is to come," he said finally. He hung up the phone and left me to the silence of the ugly yellow room.

Only her gentle breathing stopped me from having a panic attack. This could be the last time I ever saw her like this.

You'll never know real loss until you're picking up whatever pieces are left of your heart from the floor, and you have no hope of putting them back together.

I held my head in my hands, my body slumped on the floor while the helplessness surged through me like cold iron.

I envy people that could move on unexpectedly. When they wake up one day and they don't even think about their grief once. They forget about the very thing that destroyed them.

How lucky they were.

I looked up and saw the moon through the window now; it was as pale as Lucinda's skin, but just as beautiful.

I thought back to all these years that I watched her from afar; watched her laugh, watched her cry, watched her love, and watched her grieve like how my siblings have grieved.

I loved her more each and every day. I loved her the way I should have loved myself.

I remember walking into that pub and being frozen to the floor. As if the world stopped spinning and gave me that moment all to myself. My heart breathed in her face, her sad frown, the brown eyes. I hadn't seen her in years, but the sight of her, all grown up, no longer the sweet human friend I once knew.

It had blown me away just like the first time she had ever seen me. It was strange; no human could see angels, but she had actually *seen* me. It was the first time in my whole life that I didn't feel so alone.

But she had shown me who I was, who I wanted to be; and for that I would be forever grateful.

Lucinda

I opened my eyes from hours of blissful sleep. The room was dim and only the light of the white moon was evidence that the world around me was real. I lifted my head to see Peter laying across the bottom of the bed. I sat up and brushed his face softly; a light stubble was forming on his perfect jaw.

He'd set my heart on fire and didn't even realise how I would forever burn from it. These were the best kind of moments, when you could steal away a second or two of perfectness, no matter how shameful.

His eyes fluttered open. "Lucinda?"

I snapped back to reality and looked down at the angel before me. His head was lifted towards me, his eyes laced with sleepiness and a strange vulnerability.

"I'm sorry, I didn't mean to fall asleep. I was just trying to rest my eyes a bit," he defended himself as he sat up and rubbed his eyes, then gave me a startling smile.

"I'm glad you got some sleep. What time is it?" I asked while sitting up against the headboard of the bed. I started to knot my hair up, but Peter's hand snatched my wrist.

I looked up in surprise.

"Don't...please, just leave it down." His voice racked my chest.

"Ok," I said lowering my arms. He didn't take his eyes from me; they were unblinking and truly open.

"What's wrong?"

I touched the side of his face and he turned his head and kissed my palm sweetly.

He looked so tired; not from lack of rest, but lack of peace. As I looked closer I saw bags under his eyes, and his smile was strained.

"I'm fine, it's just still a shock that you're here, next to me and not a dream of my cruel mind." His voice cracked as he spoke, as if he couldn't inhale through the words.

"I'm here and I will be here for as long as you want me to be."

I drew his cheek to my lips and kissed him. His sharp intake of breath gave me goose bumps across my neck.

We were still for a second, both of us not daring to move in just in case we would shatter against each other.

He looked at me, his eyes warm and a bright blue. They seemed to glow in the dark just for me. He leaned forward and carefully, so very carefully, as if he was afraid of breaking me. He kissed me, gentle and slow at first. I couldn't move. I could only sit and feel his lips against mine. Then he kissed me harder. I could sense desperation on his mouth like fatal poison; but still I kissed him back with everything I had and everything I ever was.

He paused and leaned away a little to look at me. Taking me in.

"You are everything to me," he said. "Everything." He touched my bottom lip with his thumb before he kissed me again. Holding my face to him as if he thought I would be taken away.

I wanted to show him that I would forever be his, that I wouldn't be taken from him. So I locked my fingers around his neck and pulled him closer, our lips never breaking apart. I leaned down onto the bed, pulling him down with me, his body covering mine against the world. He gasped against my mouth. He nestled between my legs, and I wrapped mine around him like a vice. He watched my face, both of us breathless and our lips swollen from our kisses.

"What?" I asked while trying to catch my breath. He only grinned my favourite grin and kissed my nose.

"You're just so beautiful," he said.

He gaze travelling across my face, I never believed that I was beautiful, but by the way he was looking at me now...

I finally believed it.

We kissed again, our moans mingling together like a song. He lifted my shirt.

His scarred hands ran down my torso in lazy streaks. I gripped his narrow hips to me. I couldn't get enough of him. I tore his shirt away to discover the scars that I loved so much; they were painted all over his magnificent body like a puzzle I was meant to piece together.

He kissed my neck, his fingers tangled in my wild hair like thorns. The only sound in the room was our gasps from holding each other so tightly, and I didn't realise how hard I was digging my nails into his shoulders until he pulled my hand away. He sat up with me still pinned beneath him, his wings spreading out and making the room darken even more from it.

They stretched out like a storm cloud.

Those beautiful eyes were striking as they looked down at me, powerful and *empowering* as he pinned me down.

He looked at my bloody fingernails with an animal like aura, then back down at me.

I was trapped under his gaze.

"I'm sorry," I breathed.

He didn't say a word. He just watched me, a wolf stalking what was his. Then he bent down and kissed me again. But it wasn't desperate, it wasn't passionate. It was a sweet kiss; simple, a peck.

Then he pulled away.

Before I could respond, the door burst open.

"Brother, guess what I found–" Kyle looked up to see Peter covering my half-naked body with his own. "Oh–oh right. Jane back up, back up. Shield your innocent eyes."

He covered his eyes with his bag of candy and Jane's lovely voice came around him into the room.

"Whoever said that I was innocent?"

Both Peter and Kyle turned flabbergasted to their little sister. She came bouncing into the room to stop dead in her tracks.

"What?" she asked looking at us.

"What do you mean little sister?" Kyle's warning voice broke into the silence in the room.

"I've existed for millions of years, brother. Do you really think–"

Peter voice interrupted their arguing before she could finish her confession.

"I do believe we were in the middle of something?" Their eyes snapped back to us. Peter was still trying to cover me.

"Oh right," Jane said. "Well wrap it up. We have things to do." She clapped her hands together like we were in a classroom.

Kyle and his sister left with a click of the door.

We looked back at each other, trying to hold in our laughter.

But his eyes were still hungry. "We will continue this later."

I nodded and he pulled me off the bed. He handed me my shirt and kissed me once more before pulling away. Once we were dressed and had tamed our wild hair, we called his siblings back into the room.

Kyle leaned against the wall by the window with his arms crossed, the new morning sunlight splashing colour across his golden hair. Jane sat on top of the bed side table, her small feet hanging down and her red hair tucked behind her pixie like ears. While Peter sat behind me on the bed, he rested against the headboard and had his hands wrapped around my tummy. I sat between his legs and held his hands.

I needed the comfort of his touch.

"We need to be smart now." Kyle spoke first. "He could have his spies everywhere. He knows we will try to get her to the only place that she would be untouchable to him. And I will be extremely surprised if we get her there without a fight."

"She needs a disguise," Jane spoke up from her small corner.

"We need a miracle," Kyle said as matter of fact.

"I can fly her there," Peter added while holding me closer. "I am the best flyer."

"Exactly." Kyle turned to him. "That's why they'll will be ready to shoot you down the moment you take flight."

"I'm too fast for them."

"Or." Kyle scratched his chin. "I could disguise myself as Lucinda and distract them while you get her to the palace?"

"No."

"Why not? Scared I'll look too much like her and you'll find me attractive?" He smirked.

Peter didn't say anything in return. I looked around at each of their faces. They were all ready to risk their lives for me, and I was just sitting here quiet.

"I have a plan…"

They all looked at me. I sat forward and crossed my legs under me.

"Your all thinking of ways to get me there with at least one of you attending me. But it's not going to work," All their attention was on me now. "Lucifer won't count on me getting there on my own. He will be looking out for at least one of you, an angel. He won't expect that any of you would let me get there by myself. I will be vulnerable, but that's also how I will get there the safest."

None of them spoke, but I could see the wheels in their minds working.

"No, absolutely not." Kyle spoke first, his voice final.

"Why not? It's the best way. I can wear a disguise. Technically, they will be looking out for you. Not me." I raised my eyebrows at the plan, but his eyes were dark as he spoke.

"It's a stupid plan that will get you killed," he hissed. He actually *hissed* at me.

"Why do you care what happens to me?"

Everyone looked to him, his arms were tense like barbed wire.

"I don't care about you, *human*." His tone made me flinch. "I care that if you die, it will destroy my brother. I've seen him destroy Heaven and Hell just because you were separated from him. Imagine what he would do if you actually died?"

I felt Peter lean his forehead against the back of my shoulder. I reached back and gripped his shirt.

"Then trust me when I say I will get myself to that palace. I will get myself there not for me, but for him."

Kyle's eyes held a little surprise at my harsh words, but then he also held a little pride too.

"It doesn't matter anyway."

Peter finally spoke up. I turned around to look at him. He looked defeated and tired. Drained.

"What do you mean?" I asked as I cupped the side of his face.

"You are going nowhere without me, and *that's* final."

I took my hand away, surprised at the darkness that covered his face as he looked back at me.

"It's the only plan that will work."

"And it's the only plan I will not accept if it means you have no protection."

"No, you don't get to make all the decisions here Peter!"

Anger rippled through his body.

"*You're going nowhere without me Lucinda, and that's final.*"

He roared and his wings burst out behind him. Jane and Kyle shrunk back, almost as if they were trying to hide from him.

I just looked at him, his glowing eyes locked to mine, but I didn't say anything.

So I stood up and walked out of the room.

"Lucinda!" Jane's voice called after me, but I kept walking.

"Well done brother," Kyle said.

"Prick."

Chapter 15

"I will never say the things that I want to say to you. I know the damage it would do. I love you more that I hate my loneliness and pain."

— Henry Rollins

Lucinda

I sat at the bar down stairs. I'd had a few drinks and I wasn't ready to face him yet. The sun was high in the sky; its golden rays warmed my back through the window.

"Can I sit down?"

I looked over and saw Jane sitting down beside me at the bar.

"It's not like you need my permission," I said while taking another sip of my wine glass. She gave me a sheepish smile and ordered her own.

"Are you ok?" she asked. I sat my glass down and turned to her.

"Honestly? I'm terrified."

She rubbed my shoulder, doing her best to comfort me; but just her being here was enough.

"I feel like no matter which way I turn, someone I love is going to get hurt. And I can't watch that again. I can't stand there helpless while one of you goes down for me. I've seen it happen to my father, my brother, and now my mother. So if anyone is going to put themselves in danger, it's going to be me, and Peter is just going to have to deal with it."

I drank the rest of my wine and pushed the glass away.

"When the war ended," Jane spoke as if she was breathless. "I was an empty shell. I still am. They were all I had, and even they were shells of their former selves. Peter was the worst. He lost everything. All he did each and every day was watch over you. Silently he watched, but he was there. But it was killing him, so he vanished. For over a decade I heard nothing from either of them.

Then you came back into our lives." She looked at me, her eyes painfully sad. "I remember the day you came into the pub, asking if there was any places available for work. And I'd never met you before in my life. I'd only ever heard stories of a little girl from Peter. Yet I knew it was you. I felt it in my heart." A small tear escaped her. "You must forgive me Lucinda, but to us angels all humans are just specks of life floating under us. I never understood why my brother did what he did for you. For a human. But when I finally met you, I understood. You were so alive, even though you were so broken. Like us you have endured, endured countless sufferings. But you soon became not just a light for Peter, but for all of us."

She cleared her throat of possible sorrows.

"We live for millions of years Lucinda, and even then some of us never die. There are so many people out there that want immortality, and it can be the greatest gift at the time. But there are burdens to it my dear, trust me." She touched the scars on her arm. As if over the years it had become an impulse. "Some of us got caught in the cross fires, some of us died from it. But Peter suffered most of all. No one knows that he has the purest heart, but the darkest soul."

"What happened to you Jane?" I asked quietly as if I was soothing a wild animal. Her eyes snapped to mine abruptly; fire burned in them. A deep fire that was so old, *too* old to possibly still be burning. Yet here it was, here she was.

She was claws, talons and a place for death to reside while it calculated its revenge for her. She had been through so much, things that I could never comprehend. Things I don't think I will ever want to know. But in the place of this woman that was once a sweet girl was a warrior of blood and war, a woman who would tear down whoever and whatever dared to challenge her.

I wanted that.

I wanted to be that strong.

And I hope one day I would be.

Unless it broke me first.

"Many things, sweet human, many things." She still had her hand over her scars.

"Why won't you speak of them?"

She placed her hand on the side of my face, like an older sister would when her younger sibling had bruised their knee.

"Because there is no point in burdening you with what is in the past." She smiled once more and jumped down from her stool.

Peter stood behind me then.

He had his hands in his pocket and his head was down. Jane left the bar and us alone with each other.

"Lucinda?"

He sat on the stool that before held Jane. I didn't look at him. I couldn't, not without thinking about all the ways I could lose him.

"Please look at me." He placed a finger under my chin and made me face him. Tears fell from my eyes; but he kissed them away. "I'm sorry I snapped." He leaned his forehead against mine, and closed his eyes.

"I'm not angry about that," I whispered. He leaned away, eyes confused.

"Then why–"

"I'm scared I'll lose you, just as you fear losing me."

Understanding crept into his face, like a gas lamp lighting up a dark room.

"Then tell me what to do, tell me how to make all this better without putting you in danger or without losing my god dammed mind."

He sounded hopeless, but I couldn't give him the solution that he wanted.

I didn't know how to pull myself away from him, to untangle myself from him. But why would I want to? Why would the world want to tear the stars away from the moon?

"You have to trust me," He shook his head. "You have to let me do this. You couldn't bear to put me in danger, yes?" I pulled his face to mine; we were inches apart. "Well I couldn't bear to do the same to you."

He looked at me when my voice cracked. When my entire soul shattered for him onto the very floor.

Our broken eyes met each other, one begging for the other to stay and the other to let go. I tried to put his face to memory, all the angles and sharpness of his beautiful features. I needed a piece of him to take with me.

"Make it back to me Lucinda." His own voice was weak. "Please. Make it back to me." The lines on his face were tired, too exhausted to carry on the fighting.

"Always."

That night, Jane disguised me as best as she could. The wig I wore was coloured black, the fake hair chopped to the mid-shoulders. She painted my lips red and gave me green contacts for my brown eyes. I wore a black trench coat with a hood to cover my face, but I couldn't recognise myself in the dirty looking mirror in the bathroom anyway.

I stepped out to show the brothers. Kyle wolf whistled but Peter didn't say a thing.

"Looking good little human." He twilled his finger to get me to spin. Which I did.

"Kyle, let's leave these two to it for a minute." Jane opened the door to the room and stepped out. Kyle followed soon after.

The room was deadly silent. He just watched me, his fists clenched, his knuckles white. His entire frame was tense, slightly shaking with fear and anger.

"The plan will work," was all I could say, yet his eyes stayed like stone.

"Will it?" His face was angry and dark, but he sounded like he was going to fall to his knees.

"Yes."

He stepped forward and brushed my red bottom lip with his soft thumb, but I soon turned away. I turned away before I knew I would lose the strength to leave. I stepped towards the door. I opened it and was about to leave; but his warm hand enclosed mine on the handle, his breath brushing the skin on my neck.

His whole body was pushed up against mine. "Please return to me," was all he said. Shudders ran down my back, then he let me go.

I didn't look back. If I did, I wouldn't have been able to leave. So I forced my feet down the stairs, one step at a time.

Leaving everything behind.

I pulled my hood up and over my wig, my black trench coat floating behind me. I knew somewhere Peter was lingering – watching me, my every move. And that thought kept my heart from escaping my chest.

All three of us knew the route I was taking. I had to get through the city to the Vatican palace.

The Apostolic Palace.

There was a priest there that would help us. I was meeting him at the entrance.

I just had to make it there alive.

I kept my head down. It was getting dark now; the streets were lit with windows and the stars of the night. Everywhere were stone buildings and stone walls, stools selling all kinds of trinkets and foods were piled on the path ways. I didn't look at anyone, but I didn't rush my pace either.

I walked down all the alleyways, out of people's sight. I made myself one of the shadows. But then the hair on the back of my neck stood on end. I walked faster, my feet nearly tripping over each other. Footsteps followed behind me like a mimic of my own. I could see the pillars of the courtyard of the palace, but I could feel in my bones I wouldn't make it unless I ran.

So I ran.

I pushed my feet as fast as I could. I passed buildings and stools in a quick flash. But the footsteps kept up with me. A burning dug itself in my thigh, but I kept running. I made it to the pillars, but a hand gripped my wig along with my real hair pulling me back; a lock of my hair was ripped from my scalp. Blood dripped down my neck. But I kept running.

Then my feet were knocked out from under me and I landed on my side. My head smacked onto the centuries old ground. I looked up and saw one of the monsters from my nightmares.

I screamed…

Peter

I heard her scream.

I jumped to my feet and pulled the door off its hinges.

"Brother!" Kyle called after me. I didn't stop. I flew down the stairs and rushed out of the door. My wings stretched out as far as they could and lifted me into the sky above.

Please let me make it in time.

I prayed for the first time in five hundred years.

Lucinda

I kicked at the creature. Black blood dripped from its yellow stained teeth as it snapped at my legs. It looked like a giant-blind bat. I hated bats.

"*Get away from me!*" I screamed as I tried to crawl away. And it did.

"That's enough, Vespertilio."

I looked back and saw a lanky, sickly looking man approach. He bent down beside me and seemed to study my every intake of breath.

"Who are you?" My voice shook.

His skin was grey just like Lucifer's. Even his eyes were unnaturally black and wide. He was dressed in divine fighting leathers. His face was drawn down, as if all the gravity around the Earth was pulling his body down to it.

"I am Belial, one of the three princes of hell. You may know my boss?" I was speechless. He didn't blink; he just watched me with his pointed toothed smile.

"What do you want?"

"Don't ask questions when the answers are obvious." He shook his finger at me, like he was teaching me something.

"Let me go!" I pushed myself further away, but it didn't help much.

"Sorry sweet pea, but I'm the delivery boy today, and you're the gift."

He reached out for me, but a horrible gurgling had us looking at each other in confusion.

He turned around and stood up straight. Peter stood with the bat creature's heart in his hands, dripping black blood from his fingers. The dark clouds made him look terrifying. His eyes glowed blue and his wings looked enormous. He stood as he was. No armour, no weapons. Just his eyes piercing the prince like daggers. He dropped the heart and took a step towards the prince.

"Uncle Belial," he simple stated. They circled each other, both predators.

Peter stopped when he stood in front of me.

"Peter." The prince looked shaken, terrified even though he tried to hold his ground. "You know why I am here."

Peter nodded.

"Sorry, but it's going to be a wasted trip for you."

I stood up behind Peter's back. I held his shirt and he reached behind to hold my hand.

"Why?" The prince looked at me in disgust and confusion. "For a human? *She's just a human.*"

Peter's grip tightened on my hand.

"She's *my* human," was all he said.

"And are you prepared to die for her?" The prince smirked as hundreds of bat like demons crawled around the pillars.

"Are you?"

Kyle came forward to stand with us along with Jane. I looked at all three of them, and the portrait of the three warrior angels in silver came to mind. They looked wild and unpredictable. Jane gripped my arm and pulled me away from Peter.

"No, I can't leave him!"

But he peeled my hands from his shirt and pushed me towards Jane.

"Jane! Take her and go."

He turned away towards the battle.

"The only fallen angel that refused to fall."

The demon prince chuckled, but the two brothers never faltered as they stood together. They didn't say anything as the prince sent forth his demons. They didn't need to. You can say many things, and they could be meaningless; or do nothing and say everything. Jane's grip was strong; too strong as I knew she would leave bruises as she yanked me away from the battle.

We ran.

The sound of demon bats from behind us made it feel like my feet were moving in slow motion, as if no matter how hard I pushed my feet forward they would always be too slow.

"Hurry!" I looked towards the doors to see a hunched over priest at the opening way. He ushered his arms to us. We ran up the stairs hand in hand.

"What about Peter and Kyle?" I asked breathless. Jane didn't say anything; she just pulled me harder.

We reached the doors.

"No Jane! I can't leave them!" I ripped my arm from her and turned to the fight. It was pure chaos, black bat blood covered both the prince and the brothers like their very own trench coats. Kyle had a bow and he was victorious in his every shot he fired. His hair stuck to his forehead and neck with blood and sweat. He looked like a force to be reckoned with.

"*Peter!*" he shouted as he fired another arrow. I looked for him, and amongst the chaos he stood with no weapon, his hands lose at his side. The brothers glanced at each other in silent agreement, then the world seemed to shift under us.

Peter turned his head slightly to the side and clicked his neck, then his defiant wings appeared behind him again like their very own army. They were dark and each of the feathers looked glossy, like polished knives. The clouds above darkened to his will, lightning struck the Earth every time he took a step towards the prince. His eyes glowed like two blue stars colliding with each other; a spectacular thought, but a terrifying reality.

"God bless us." The priest sucked in a breath.

Everything. All the buildings, stools, walls, the palace, the people. They all started turning to dust around us. The bat demons screeched as they too disintegrated. The ground peeled away like the skin of diseased man, yet the world was quite as it watched itself be destroyed. Kyle ran to our sides and stood between us and the devastation, like he was our shield from it.

Stars, planets, the universe surrounded us like a warm and breath-taking blanket. The prince was on his knees with his head bowed low to the ground.

"Forgiveness! I beg your forgiveness."

He sobbed into the floating dirt around him, but Peter didn't move, he didn't speak.

"He's gone too far, he can't get back!" Jane's panicked voice rose through the stars around us.

"Then we run!" Kyle pulled her away and turned to leave, but I couldn't move. Peter's strong, winged back was to me. He looked beyond dangerous; he was destruction itself. But I couldn't turn away. Instead, I walked up towards him. His brother's voice screamed for me to return, to run away and be safe.

But I kept walking.

I placed my hand on his shoulder and traced the feathers on his gigantic right wing. I circled around to face him. The skin around his glowing eyes was grey and they were still fixed on the prince that was grovelling on the dirty ground.

"Peter?" He didn't move. "Peter!" I said again with more force. Nothing.

"It doesn't matter what you do." The prince spoke up. I looked down and stood between them.

"What do you mean?" I demanded, and he still had the bravery to smirk.

"Do you really think the sound of your voice is enough to snap him out of his evil trance?"

He chuckled as blood dripped from his mouth. His fingers were slowly turning to dust just like the rest of the world around us.

"He isn't evil, you are!" I stepped back closer to Peter, yet he didn't even flinch.

"It flows through his very veins, silly human!" I gritted my teeth at his snapping tone. "It is his very DNA. Did you really think that our Devil fell in love with Lola and didn't gain something out of it?" Blood poured from his eyes, deep red like the colour of a new morning.

"I know him and he is good!" I shouted at his accusations, but his blood-soaked eyes only danced with amusement. "I see who he is."

His eyes grew still. They became fearful, but not for himself.

"Not now you do, but someday you will. One day, when you find out who you truly are. Take this warning with an open-heart Lucinda Sky." His face grew grave. I held my breath and felt for Peter's hand.

"You may love him. You can for forever; but your heart will not survive it. So many obstacles stand against you both. Even the universe stands between you and him. The son of the Devil against the weapon of God?" He reached for my hand and held it, like he was giving me his condolences. "Now have you ever heard a more tragic love story than not quite doomed love?" I pulled my hand away from his grey and clammy hands.

He didn't say anything else. He couldn't because Peter's hands were suddenly wrapped around his scrawny neck. He lifted him off the ground as if he was lifting a bag of sugar.

"Doomed or not," Peter finally spoke up. The prince started choking on his hard grip. "I will protect her with my last breath, even if that means I break myself to do it. I am not my father. And I am not a Devil. Now take my warning in with a *fearful* heart, uncle." The prince's eyes bulged from his hollow face with terror. "I will gladly destroy the world and everyone in it if that means she is safe. And if *that* makes me the Devil, then so be it."

"And do you think that gets you into Heaven's good graces once more?" Blood poured from the now gaping holes in his neck from Peter's savage grip. "Do you really think that makes you a hero?" His smirk was mocking Peter to harden his hold. The prince seemed to like playing with fire. "Heroes never get a happy endi–" His words were cut off abruptly from the crushing of his neck. Peter had collapsed his windpipe and now he was dead. He then turned to me with his glowing eyes. He didn't blink; all he did was glide towards me as I backed away. I kept my hands lowered but between us like a shield, a barrier of force against the angel before me.

"Peter stop!" Kyle's voice rang across the chaos. He was running towards us, bow and arrow at the ready.

Suddenly, strong and deeply scared hands were wrapped too firmly around my neck. I tried to claw at the fingers on my skin, but to no avail.

"Peter – listen to me!" I choked as his hand tightened. "This isn't you, this will never be you." His vacant eyes seemed to truly lock to mine. His face contorted as if two people were battering each other in his body. "I have seen the power that resides in you. I understand the struggle you deal with each and every day. And I know you can't control it, but don't let it control you in return." His eyes softened, and so did his grip. "Let me go."

Slowly his gorgeous eyes lost their grey shadows, and once again grew calm and controlled. He gasped deeply as if in shock, and let go of my throbbing neck. As his shocked eyes fell back to me, he looked traumatised and disgusted as his widened eyes looked down at the hand that had just held me captive.

"It's ok," I tried to sooth as I reached for him. He didn't flinch away but he didn't reach for me either.

"I can't believe I just did that to you." His usual strong voice cracked.

"I'm fine, that wasn't you. That wasn't your fault." I wrapped my arms around his waist before he could step away from me. I leaned my ear into his chest to listen to his damaged but still beating heart. Then, he too, wrapped his arms back around me. Caging me in his warmth.

"I'm so sorry."

His words blew against my hair, I looked up and he lifted his hand from my waist to touch the delicate skin on my neck.

"I'll be ok."

Something in his eyes shattered, obliterated in his wake.

"But I won't–" he said into my hair.

I kissed him before he could finish those toxic words. He wielded to my mouth, struck down under my power. I couldn't stand him blaming himself over something that was beyond either of our control.

"I forgive you. I forgive and you will forget…" His hands clung to mine as he laid his forehead to mine. And our eyes only left each other's when Kyle appeared next to us, his breathing sharp.

"Peter, you need to fix this." He indicted to the mess around us with a tilt of his golden head. The bow and arrow still in his hands, knuckles white as they held the deadly weapon. My angel nodded and closed his eyes.

The dust of ruin steadied around us in mid-air, then all too quickly every atom and particle once again began to take form. They became the darkened skies above us, the hundred years old Vatican walls, the stone pillars of the courtyard. Everything moulded together to create what was just lost as easily as the stroke of a pen. Even the people took no notice as their arms and legs were still taking shape as they walked down the dusty paths and roads. They had no idea that their world had just exploded, that they had just been wiped off the face of Earth. But for that single brief moment, I understood the true meaning of naiveté.

"We must go now." The priest had finally crept up behind us. "It is still not safe here, come."

He rushed back towards the newly formed palace doors where Jane stood gaping, white faced and nearly crying. Peter sighed and walked to his sister's side. They embraced, the brother whispering sweet nothings into his sister's ear and the sister sobbing into his shoulder. He walked through the doors with his arm wrapped around his little sister's shoulder. Kyle and I followed.

Gold, silver, all colours of the rainbow claimed the walls and ceilings around us like a cocoon. It really was a palace. The lights above reflected off the golden walls and then bounced off Peter's wings, making the colours in his feathers even more vibrant and luminous. If it was even possible. He looked over his shoulder at me, concern and…something else in his bright eyes that I couldn't quite figure out before it vanished. Then he turned away.

"The Pope is busy at the moment, so you can freshen up and I will send someone to tell you when dinner is made. But please do not make any noise, or break anything."

He looked at Kyle pointedly, but he only smirked and flicked a bit of dirt from his shirt at the priest. He held his arm out to three doors on the left of the hallway. Jane took the middle door and Kyle took the end. Peter didn't t even look at me as he opened the first and disappeared into it. I looked at Jane, her hand still on her door handle. We didn't speak, but I believed she knew what I was thinking. Her face was still white as nearly formed ice crystals, and her cheeks still damp with now cold tears. She nodded once and went through her door.

I stood alone in the beautiful hallway. Even the priest had somewhere else to be. Raw emotion racked my chest at the thought of going through that door. Was he mad at me? Did he finally realise that I wasn't worth all this trouble? I guess I wasn't…

The hallway suddenly became cold and dark, an invisible loneliness engulfing its beauty. The door was slightly ajar, as if beckoning me to push it open and face the angel inside. I wasn't afraid of him. I couldn't be even if I tried. I was afraid he resented me now; if I had finally lost him.

I took a deep breath and slid my hand across the door to push it wider. The room was almost pitch black, but I could see the outline of a huge bed in the centre of the room. A wardrobe was on the right side of the room next to what I assumed was the bathroom door. The walls were equally as startling in its décor as it was to the hallway, or from what I could see of it.

I could see his outline on the edge of the bed, his elbows on his knees, his face covered by his hands. His wings were gone, so he looked like any other fallen soldier. I was about to speak, to slice away the silence of this room; but he beat me to it.

"I need to talk to the priest, freshen up and I'll meet you for dinner."

He was so blunt, like the end of a broken pencil. I only nodded and moved out of his way as he passed through the door. I stood for a few moments to collect myself, to gain back some of my thoughts. When I looked to the bed I saw something shimmer in the dimness.

I grinned.

I met Jane in the hallway soon after. She looked exhausted, yet her eyes bathed in excitement for the promise of food. When was the time last we ate anything? I took her in and smiled; it seemed she got a little something shimmery too.

"Ready?" she asked literally bouncing on her feet.

"For food? Always." I was starving.

We followed the ancient walls through this golden temple until we came to stand at two double doors. Both crafted from the purest specks of gold.

"How do you know your way around?"

She looked at me from the corner of her eyes. "It's a long story. I'll tell you after dinner."

And she opened the doors.

The room was bright, giving out hues of gold that could only belong to the setting suns. Elegant pillars with flowers of gold wound themselves together like a chain. And in the very centre sat a table with every kind of food that I could imagine. Fruits, roast chicken, vegetables, fish, and every kind of sweet that could grace my lips. My sweet tooth began to ache. I looked on and found Kyle, his long strong legs hooked over the other on the table. The gold in the room made his hair glow, like the sun had chosen his head to sleep upon. His eyes met mine, and they held mine, as the sun and moon push and pull at each other to stay in the sky. His eyes mirroring my own, like two shattered mirrors trying to piece themselves back together over a too long of a time. Jane and I stepped into the room. I felt the light warm my face, but I never looked away from him. I couldn't.

His face held no expression, nothing. He turned the empty glass in his hand over and over again with his beautifully crafted fingers that any artist would be proud of.

He was dressed in a smart and crisp black shirt that was stark against his skin. His equally black jeans made his legs seem longer as they lounged on the beautiful decorated table.

And Peter was nowhere to be seen.

My heart sank a little. I wanted him to see me. I'd never worn anything like this before, and he wasn't here to see.

I sat down at the head of the table and poured myself a large glass of wine. I guess the only thing you could drink here was the drink of Jesus.

The dress I wore was a soft silver shimmer material. It hugged my body perfectly. My leg escaped the slight slit in the dress that ran up my thigh. I quickly covered it, but I was not quick enough for Kyle's wandering eyes. Our eyes locked yet again, but he looked angry. As if he wanted to tear me apart, or himself.

His eyes rimmed with it, not quite hate, not quite lust. Something deeper and self-hated. As if he was battling with himself. His eyes slipped behind me, as if he was looking through me.

"Kyle?"

My voice seemed to snap him back to us. We looked around and found everyone watching us. Jane, the priest, and all the servants.

"You look beautiful," he said before his eyes closed off to us once again. He cleared his throat. "Both of you," he said again while turning to his sister. And he was gone.

"Where is my darling brother?" Jane asked while reaching for the food and piling it onto her plate, breaking the awkward silence.

"He had a meeting with the Pope, he shouldn't be long." The priest filled his plate too, but only with the sweet fruit that was laid before us in piles.

"Why weren't we invited?" I asked while digging into the chicken.

"It is a private matter, my dear. Something that only he can face."

No one mentioned him for the rest of the meal.

Instead we dined and ate our fill. I sat back while the man of God laughed and argued with the children of his master.

"So how have you been dealing with all of this?"

I snapped out of my daze and looked up.

"What?"

"How have you been dealing with the truth?" the priest asked.

I had to take a few moments before answering, trying to figure out the best way to answer. Kyle and Jane's eyes waited for my answer, curious to see what I would say. How I felt.

I took a solid breath before I spoke. "I didn't believe it at first. Peter had to show me his true form before I could even consider it. And even then, it was hard to stomach. But all my life I've never felt normal. I never felt like I fitted in anywhere. But when I found out the truth, everything clicked into place."

"How so?"

"I think a part of me always knew there was something else, something more to what I could see. As if the life I was living wasn't really meant to be *my* life. And those feelings clicked into place when Peter told me the truth. I was never scared of him. I never ever saw him for anything else other than who he was."

"And who is he?"

The air was so thick with judgement, with chaos that was lurking just before the pillars. Ready to strike.

My eyes hardened. "He is–"

"Evening everyone."

We all turned to find Peter finely dressed and sitting down at the table. He was dressed like his brother was: crisp white shirt and black jeans. Two opposites dressed the same. Peter didn't eat anything; he only sat beside his sister, as far as he could get from me. I tried my best to not show the hurt in my eyes, but I knew Kyle could tell as he was the only one that would look at me.

I pushed my plate away. I'd lost my appetite.

"How was the meeting?" the priest asked Peter while placing a piece of apple into his mouth. Peter leaned forward and clasped his hands in front of his rigid body.

"It was fine."

"Did you find what you were looking for?"

I could cut the tension in the air with a butter knife. Peter stared at the human man, and the human man did not buckle under his weighty stare.

"Anyway." Jane broke the heavy silence. "Who's up for dessert?"

The holy man was the first to look away. Only then did Peter look away, but he did not look at me. Anywhere but at me.

So I ignored him in return. And that's when I noticed that the priest's glass was empty.

"Priest, do you not drink?"

"Never. Drinking is a sin. The Devil made it."

Silence yet again. Silence until Kyle, with feet crossed on the table, a glass in his hand and a smirk on his lips, spoke up. "Servant?" A young man hurried to his side, fear clearly plastered on his young face as he stood before the mighty angel. "I'll take a bourbon."

The priest choked on his apple.

Jane nearly fell out of her chair with laughter.

Peter covered his mouth with his hand trying to hide his smirk.

Even some of the servants turned away hiding their grins.

"Of course sir." The young servant boy scurried away to fetch the angel's sinful drink.

"You are a disgrace." The priest threw Kyle a distasteful look.

Kyle only grinned more and gladly took his drink when the young boy returned.

"Well." The human man stood and cleaned his mouth with his napkin. "I will take my leave. Enjoy the rest of your evening." And he left the room.

The room began to darken, so the servants moved quickly to light candles for us as we dinned further into the night.

"So what's the plan?" Kyle asked his brother. "How are we getting Lucinda to Heaven?"

"I've spoken to the Pope, and he seems to think we need some sort of book to call our mother."

Kyle stuffed more meat into his mouth. "Why a book?"

"It holds a prayer of some kind that my father used to call upon her when he wanted to see her. He said we can use it."

"When do we leave?" I finally spoke up.

None of them looked at me; instead they glanced at each other, eyes regretful. Kyle placed his drink down and now even he wouldn't look at me.

My body started to shake. I gripped the tablecloth. I needed something to hold onto.

"Lucinda–" Kyle's voice was soft, too soft that it made my body shake harder.

"You aren't coming with me, are you," I said to all three of them.

Jane's face broke.

"You have to understand Lucinda, we cannot return with you because we are needed down here."

My chest began to throb as if it was breaking through my bones.

"You lied to me…" I whispered.

I looked down at my white knuckles gripping the tablecloth. I could feel their vibrant eyes on me. None of them dared speak, not until I let the fabric go. Finally… Finally I looked up at them all. My human eyes holding theirs. Yet Peter *still* couldn't look me in the eye. And now I knew why.

"You all lied to me."

"We never lied to you. We never said we were going with you," Jane said, her face begging for my forgiveness.

"You let me think you were, and that is just the same as a lie."

"That's not fair." Kyle pointed his finger at me, accusing me of not being fair. My heart began to burn; it began to rage through my body. Inside I was screaming. Not again, please… Please don't leave me alone again. I was begging them, hoping one of them at least would hear my silent prayers. But they didn't hear me. We stared at each other. Human against angels.

I can't believe they lied to me.

I reached over the table and took Kyles bourbon. And without dropping their gazes, I swallowed the rest in one flick of my wrist. It warmed the fire in my body, the burning that was slowly consuming my heart.

"That was mine."

My eyes looked to the blonde angel.

"So was my life before you deemed it fit to destroy it."

Peter's head snapped up at my words.

"How dare you say that!" His fists clenched together as I faced him. I could feel him grind his teeth together. "All we have done is try to keep you safe, to *save* you."

"I didn't need saving until you came along!" He flinched. "I didn't need any of you! All of this mess happened *because* of you. You go on and on about how much you have sacrificed for me, but you are the reason for *everything* that's happened to me. You are the reason my entire family is *dead.* I was fine before you showed up, I was coping fine on my own."

"Lucinda–" Jane tried to sooth me.

"I was perfectly fine with being broken!" My voice cracked. Peter tried to reach across the table for my hand, but I snatched it away before he could touch me. *"I didn't ask to be fixed! I never*

146

asked to be! But yet you came along and did it anyway, and now you want to leave. You want to leave me…"

"We have *no choice.*" Kyle tried to reach for me too. But I stood before anyone could.

I knew tears were streaming down my face, but I didn't care. I could feel it all again, the darkness, the sorrow, the past tapping me on the shoulder. That pain resurfacing.

I could no longer look at them. I couldn't bring myself to do it. I was going to be left again. I was going to be alone.

"Please." I looked up at Peter. He'd stood up with weak legs, his hand outstretched for me. I could see his fingers tremble, as if a mountain was about to fall upon us all. We watched each other, waiting for one of us to fall. His face was open once more to me; he was letting me in to see his entire self. I could see the heart he was ashamed to bare, the heart that held so much love, and it made me sad that he felt unworthy to share it. To lock it away. To hide it away from me.

I looked around at them all, and I could feel it. I could feel that tug I had once felt as a child. A small and barely-there tug. A pull that was trying to take me somewhere where everything was better. I was here. But I knew that I'd ran out of time.

But it was Peter that I settled my eyes on when I spoke.

"I didn't get enough time," I whispered. "I want more time."

Peter's eyes broke and I saw it all. He wasn't quick enough to hide it from me this time. He sat there frozen, staring at me as if I just drew his very own sword through his heart.

"Lucinda please…" Jane stood on unstable legs.

But I turned away. I couldn't bear to stay in that chair for another second. I gathered my shimmering dress and ran from the room, my heels clicking through the empty halls of this cursed palace.

The night was quite as I laid curled up in our huge bed. Hours passed before the door opened. I willed myself to stay as still as possible, to make sure he thought I was sleeping. I didn't have the energy to talk. I didn't want to.

He settled beside me on the bed, the mattress holding his warrior body. He stayed there, his breathing deep and steady. I could feel his eyes on me, the weight of them heating my skin.

I couldn't say how much time passed as I laid there and he watched me. But I knew I was between the two worlds of dreams and reality when I felt a touch to my cheek, it being so soft that I swore a whisper from Heaven had landed on me. Luring me to sleep. The simple touch trailed itself down my cheek, down pass my neck, and brushed my collarbone.

"I'm so sorry," he whispered. "I'm sorry that I've made such a mess of things. I never wanted to hurt you. I never wanted to bring this chaos into your life." Soft fingers stroked the hair away from my forehead. "But I am the son of the Devil and I am the home for all that is selfish. I am selfish. I am selfish for wanting you all to myself. I was a young angel that finally found someone that wasn't scared of me, someone that could look me in the eye and call me by my true name. You gave me hope, freedom, love… But I never thought about how this would affect you. How it would hurt you. And I can never take back all that has happened to you, no matter how much I pray I could. I am not a good angel, but I will try to be a good man for *you.*"

The sweet touch vanished from my skin.

"You deserve better, you deserve a man that can love you without letting that love put you in danger. I have fought so many wars for you, for this, moments like this. I have watched my fellow angels die on both fronts, I have ended empires, destroyed armies, watched families die. I have stood back and allowed it all to happen… For this. And I know that would disgust you. I know it's wrong." He took my hand into his and kissed my knuckles. "And I will hate myself for it for the rest of my existence. But I would do it for forever more if it meant that you were safe. That you get to live. So that I can hold you, kiss you, and watch you be the woman I know you to be.

"I was never stupid enough to think that we would ever make it through this, to succeed in these horrors. I just thought that when the Gods up above saw how much I fought, how much you made me better – oh I don't know. I just hoped that one day you can forgive me. I hope one day we get to have more time."

I couldn't hold on anymore. I fell into the darkness that surrounded me like a blanket of snow. I knew this was all a dream; at least I thought it was. I couldn't tell what was real and what was fake anymore. Everything swirled together.

My body was sluggish when I awoke; every part of it was heavy. I lifted my head in the thick darkness. I was alone.

I swung my feet over the bed and crept out of the room. The hallway was dark, yet the moonlight gave me enough guidance to see my way. I walked through the palace, passing hundreds of paintings and works of art that I couldn't name. The walls were filled with it. Covered with faces that have come and passed.

Some were filled with clouds, angels, temples, places I'd never seen before, but knew better than my own room. I saw my angels many times, more than any others in fact. They looked so whole, so powerful, so at home among the other angels of Heaven and Hell. I could understand why they wouldn't want to stay with me, not when they had lost so much because of me.

A huge wooden door that looked too old to hold anything precious stood before me. I twisted the door handle and pushed. Again the room was dark, but not as dark as the hallway I was just standing in. The ceiling reached up and up to the stars. As if they wanted to fuse and form together with the darkness. Statues surrounded me, their silent faces watching me from every angle.

But that wasn't what held my attention.

At the very end of the room, a magnificent statue kneeled with her head bowed, her hands clasped before her and her heart open to the world. There also kneeled a statue; no, a man. His head was also bowed, his hands clasped in his lap before him.

"Please," he whispered. "I'm begging you, don't make me do this. I need her." He lifted his head. His back was bare, his wings nowhere to be seen. He seemed to be so focused on his prayer that he didn't notice me approach him from behind. "I know I have done unspeakable things, and I know they can never be forgiven, but please." His voice was broken, as if he had no more pleas to give. "I'll do anything, I'll give you anything–"

"Peter?"

He stood abruptly, almost losing his footing. His face was wet in the moonlight, his eyes were shocked as they gazed at me, not truly believing that I was there.

"Lucinda? Why are you awake?"

I stepped closer and he didn't pull away. "I could ask you the same thing."

He didn't say anything at first, and neither did I. Instead I stepped closer, taking my time so I didn't push him too far. He studied my every move, but when I finally reached him I couldn't help but lift my fingers to his cheek, gently wiping away his sorrows. He closed his eyes at my touch as if it soothed his inner demons back to their cages for another night.

"Peter," I said, my voice hushed between us. "Talk to me, please."

"There is nothing to talk about."

"Don't lie to me."

No one else was in the room with us, no one but the cold dead statues. So he let his eyes open to me. In front of everyone else they were stone cold, dead to the world. But for me and only for me, he allowed them to open up, to show his true self. Emotion in its truest form. I cupped his face, my hands shaking while trying to get through to him.

"I don't have anything to say," he said, but his eyes were saying something different. He pulled my hands away from him, pinning them down.

He turned away.

"Peter!" Nothing. "Why do you do this? Why do you push me away?"

He stopped, turning his head slightly to the side as if he lost the words I had just spoken.

He sighed. "Lucinda–"

"No!" My breath shook as it left me, my voice struggling to keep quiet in this stony room. "You can't keep doing this to yourself! To me! You push me away because you think it is the only way to protect me. But it isn't. I am *here,* I am here for *you.* I always have been. You saw me when no one else did, you fixed me when no one else could. Yes you have done wrong. You have been a terrible person. But the only way you can be forgiven is if you forgive yourself *first…*"

The silence stretched out between us. I stood waiting for his answer. Finally he turned to face me.

"That is not why I do what I do, I know I have sinned. I know that I am a horrible person. But I know I would do it again and again because I didn't do those things for a bad reason. I did it for *love*."

I felt so small when I spoke. "Then why? Why push me away? What are you so afraid of?"

The room seemed to shudder at my words, as if I had just unleashed the truth like a canon aiming for the sky. His eyes were trained on me. I knew the darkness that lived there. I was the only one that would gaze back when it set it itself on me.

He thought that he was the only one with darkness. The only one with something dark in their soul. I felt it every day, the claws, the talons that clung to me. I wasn't of this world. My body was of human flesh, but my soul, my heart, my whole self that lay hidden in my bones. That was of the stars above.

"You," he said simply. "I'm afraid of you."

It was a few seconds before I could answer. What did he mean?

"Why?"

He took a deep breath, steadying his thundering heart.

"I am the most power creature in existence. Some say I am more powerful than my father and mother combined. But you–" His words broke on him. "You are my greatest weakness. And for someone like me, that is…" He struggled to speak. He roughly brushed his hair away. I could easily see him shaking. "My tutor once told me that the greater the power, the greater the weakness. I never knew what he meant, but now I do."

"Peter–"

"If anything ever happened to you because of me, I don't know what I would do. But if the only way to keep you safe is to let you go, then so be it."

He turned and slammed the great wooden door, leaving me to face the stone angels alone.

He thought he was the reason I was in danger. But he wasn't. I was a weapon, a star that was created from the flesh of Gods and the fabric of the skies. I was in danger the moment I took air from this world and the next. Before we had even met, before we both became who we are, I was in danger. The only difference he ever made was that he made me want to fight, to live… To love.

For the rest of that night I prayed. I prayed for my salvation, for Peter's, for Jane's, for Kyle's. It wasn't until the birds outside this cursed palace started to bring my ears to life. I arose from the floor, hearing my bones crack from being in the same position for so long. I left the room and returned for my own.

"The bath is ready, you can have it first."

His voice was as rough as broken seashells. He was sat on the edge of the bed with his head bowed. Yet he still couldn't bear to look at me.

"Are you sure?" was all I could muster; but nothing.

Silence.

I walked through the door and wonderful steam and fruity smells of shower gels reached my nose. I stripped my clothes and kicked them aside into a pile in the corner and stepped into the bath. The water was warm and the bubbles comforting. The steam awakened my pores and seemed to clean my bones. I lowered myself under the water for a few seconds, the world muffled and my thoughts wholly mine under the clean water.

I resurfaced to find Peter leaning against the doorframe with his arms crossed. His face stormy, as if troubled thoughts feasted there. We didn't speak, but his eyes devoured the parts of my body that weren't concealed by bubbles. My breasts, thighs and legs free for him to roam with his intense and predatory eyes. I sat up, not bothering to cover myself. I wanted him to see me. No one else had ever seen me so vulnerable. I had never wanted them to, but this angel before me, who could easily kill me with his little finger. I needed him to see me, shattered soul and all.

His eyes softened and calmed as if he had just finally found his way out of a storm at sea. And without saying anything, he moved to the edge of the bath and sat upon a stool. He grabbed the shampoo and squeezed it into his hands, then washed my hair. I leaned into his touch as his fingers worked my scalp, the tension leaving my body all at once. He took the showerhead and rinsed the bubbles from my hair, then started to condition it after. His hands were delicate as they moved from my hair to rub my neck and shoulders. I couldn't stop the little moan that escaped my lips at his touch.

His fingers stilled…

I turned to face him. His eyes were blazing blue, like shattered church glass.

"Peter?" my weak voice asked, but his mouth stayed silent, and his eyes continued to burn. But slowly, his hand cupped the back of my head and his face lowered to mine. The kiss was so feather like I almost thought it never happened; a brush of lips and that was all. I pulled him down, but I couldn't get him close enough, so in our clumsy stumble he kneeled half in the bath and half out. His hands were moving downwards and gently he cupped my breast. His damaged hands were soft on my sensitive skin. And I couldn't help the small moan from escaping me. Our breaths mingled. Becoming the same.

"Peter…"

He pulled away with a pained expression and his eyes sealed shut, as if it was painful to look at me. When he did finally open his eyes, he stood up and walked out of the bathroom. But I finished my wash even though the bath water was now cold without him.

I inched out of the door. I was freshly dressed in a set of pyjamas that were laid out for me, but I left my hair wet. He was sitting at the end of the bed, and as I stepped closer I could see he was holding a small dagger in his hands. He spun it around his fingers and I could see there was symbols carved across the metalwork. I stood in front of him, but he didn't look up from his dagger. I bent down and lifted his chin so he would look at me. His eyes seemed to be the only thing in the room that was alight. A constant burning blue flame, struggling to keep the body it was captured in warm and alive with life.

"I have always believed you were good," I whispered as his eyes watched me. "Even when I was little and knew no better. But you were, you *are* a good man. And I know no one has ever told you that and maybe that's why you don't believe it. You are the best thing that has ever happened to me, and I understand why you are sending me away. You are doing what you think is right. And I know that my forgiveness is not the forgiveness that you need, but I give you mine anyway. I just hope one day you can forgive yourself."

He opened his mouth to speak, but only a void of quiet came instead. I kissed his cheek before standing and leaving him to rest. I knew he was angry with me. Fury radiated from his very flesh. I didn't want to further that hate. I let the door click behind me and tiptoed towards Jane's room; maybe she would let me stay for the night. I slowly opened her door. Muffled groans came from inside. I opened the door fully and found Jane thrashing and tearing at the sheets. I ran to her bed and shook her shoulders.

"Jane!" I continued to shake her body, but she continued to cry and thrash.

"Please stop!" her voice cracked as she pleaded with the monster in her dreams.

"Jane wake up!"

Her eyes opened, wide and glazed with trauma and sleep.

"They took my wings. They took my wings. They took me," she said over and over until she finally settled down.

"I know, I know," was all I could say. Her eyes locked to mine and calmed when I sat her up against the pillows.

We sat together for a while, her breathing slowing as mine did. The room was the same as mine and Peter's; gold and dark from the night. I had never seen Jane look so scared, so vulnerable before. It was as unnatural as putting a fish on the moon.

"Thank you."

She spoke up with a weak and croaky voice. She seemed calmer, at peace amongst the pillows.

"I'm sorry I snuck in. I just wanted to give him some space."

Her eyebrows grew together at my soft words. She laid a hand on mine.

"Why? What happened?" Concern was there, not for her brother…but for me.

"I think he's mad at me, or…"

I thought back to my bath, how he had touched me, kissed me. How could someone do that to another they were disgusted with?

"Lucinda…" I looked up and her warm eyes met mine, understanding showing itself fully in them. "I know how confusing he can be. We have been together for over ten thousand years, and Kyle and I still can't fully understand him yet." She smiled, as sweet and gentle as ice cream and cherries. "But ever since he has met you, he's changed. Changed from the cold, unfeeling, son of the Devil. To who he is now. His own man. You don't seem to see it because when you look at him, you see coldness in him. Yet when you turn away he continues to look at you. The only difference is, his eyes soften. They finally brighten after centuries of darkness."

I smiled. "I do see it. Most of the time I do. I just feel like I'm a burden on him sometimes, like I am a burden to you all. I don't want to be the reason he breaks…"

My voice trailed off in silence as I spoke those terrifying words. But Jane only squeezed my hand in comfort and promise.

"You were never a burden, but a gift. A gift to us all. If you would have seen the way you have changed him for the better, how you haven't broken him, yet how you have saved him. You would understand how much he loves you. It's hard for him to admit. Not because he doesn't want to, but because he has never loved before. He doesn't realise that what he feels for you is love. It is the very definition of it. But he will, and when he does it will set you both free."

I smiled down at her sleepy eyes. I admired the fierceness of the colours in them.

"You are the perfect storm Jane."

"Why? Because I'm such a mess?"

I shook my head.

"No. You're not a mess, you're chaos. But it's only because you have a heart of a lion, and no one has been able to tame it." I pushed the hair back from her forehead and she closed her eyes. "No one can withstand your storm Jane, be proud of that…"

I left Jane to sleep and crept back into my own room. Peter was sleeping on the bed with no blankets to cover his body. He still wore his jeans, but his shirt was gone to the wind. I slipped a blanket over us as I crawled in and eased next to his back, entangling my legs with his as he lifted them for me. Then I wrapped my arm around him, resting my hand next to his on his stomach, but he was the one that entwined our fingers together.

He sighed, his chest warm against my hand.

I started to fall asleep next to him, his stable heart beating through to mine, as if they were having a secret conversation. My skin was always too cold and his was always too hot. So we entangled ourselves and seemed to stitch our cells together; and it was our relief when our flesh touched, cooling and warming the other's skin.

Chapter 16

"The Earth is littered with the ruins of empires that believed they were eternal."

– Camille Paglia

Lucinda

Gold radiated off the walls. I opened my eyes further to see the room glow like a sun engulfing me with its light. And for a moment I forgot that my life had just gone to shit. I rolled over to find the space next to me empty, but the sheets were still slightly warm. I jumped out of bed to dress. I left the golden room to follow the golden halls.

Paintings covered the walls like a signature; angels, clouds, temples on clouds. All beautiful, scary and bright. All different. I passed many through the never-ending halls of art, until I passed a slightly ajar door. It was heavy looking, carved with many different selections of symbols. I crept through to find a huge room full of statues. On the left side of the room was a wall covered with white marble, life-sized angels, wings huge and made of perfect crystal marble. The room was so tall and wide it must have hundreds of statues decorating it. On the right side, the wall began to turn to black marble. Black, shinning marble statues stood, defiant and broad. Their wings all different and ruffled like a cat's fur. And I understood. The left side was the angels of God and the right side was the angels of the Devil.

"Over-whelming, isn't it?" I jumped at the voice from behind me, I turned to see Kyle strolling up next to me, hands clasped behind him and his shoulders back.

My voice shook a little as I spoke. "What is?" He looked down at me as he stood beside me, his hair a golden halo of light.

"All these statues, everything that's happened." The corners of his mouth turned up. I looked back to all the figures around me. Some were praying, others were in a battle stance. Others in an eternal state of screaming…

I was breathless as I replied, "It's hard to keep up with it some of the time, if I'm being honest."

"I know, we all know what it's like. We have been at it for thousands of years. Some of us millions. And it still doesn't get any easier." He took a deep breath, like it took everything he had these days to speak the words. But he pointed to the biggest statue at the end of the room. It separated the white angels to the black ones.

"That is our mother, that is God." He lowered his arm and we stood starring up at her. She was about fifteen feet tall. Her hands were held out before her, as if she was holding it out to be taken by her angels.

"Were you really going to fire that arrow on your brother?" I spoke up. His eyes snapped to mine and I swear he could sense my heart pounding for his words.

"No." He didn't blink and he didn't move his eyes from mine. But from the unruliness in them, I knew his next words were the complete truth. "That arrow wasn't for him."

His eyes softened for a slight moment before they hardened again to brown ice.

I knew he would always put his brother first. I was just a human that was plaguing his life right now. And Peter was his blood. But I knew my face showed him the hurt I was feeling nevertheless, and I could see he saw it too from the regret in his eyes as he spoke again. Yet I would have done the same.

"This may sound cold, but Lucinda..." He inched over and laid his hand across my shoulder, and squeezed it gently. "That arrow was for you. I was ready to shoot you and take the burden and the hate of my siblings. To ensure my brother wouldn't. I knew his grief of hurting you would destroy not only himself, but the world too. So yes, I was going to kill you if he had slipped too far – but not out of spite, but out of respect for my brother. Rather he blame me than himself."

He leaned forward and kissed me briefly on the forehead before leaving me alone with his stone mother and my cold thoughts.

I roamed the halls, uncovering all the hidden corners and rooms. Pictures and visions flashed through my mind nearly every few minutes, leading me here and there. Voices racked my mind with each step I took...

Their tones seemed to shatter the inside of my skull.

"She will steal my empire..."

Another and another, one after the other…

"But you will love again little sister, someone like you is unable to stop loving."

Some of them were pure, gentle as they spoke through my ears. Then others were cruel, unfeeling as they blasted their hurtful words at me.

"Let me invade your empire, let me walk through its gates with trust. Trust that I will walk its streets with ease. Allow me to bring it to its knees. And with your consent I will make it cower, and rip its heart through its rib cage as I watch it gasp for mercy. Give me the influence to take over and become its ruler. I'll wear the crown like I was born for it…and finally I'll raise this city out of the ashes and into the stars. With you as my ruler."

I recognised this voice. Its dark and timeless intrigue echoed through the emptiness of my mind. I turned a corner and ended up in a dark corridor. There weren't any windows; no light except from the melting candles. But a door was visible through the dim light at the end of the hallway.

I inched closer, griped the door handle and opened it.

The room was brighter than the hall, but it was covered in years' worth of dust. It floated in the untouched air around me as I entered. Beautiful artwork hugged the walls. There wasn't a space left without at least one painting or sculpture gracing it with itself. All were bright and colourful. Each showed angels; some ready for battle, others praying. There were so many…the room was big, almost the size of a grand hall. The walls that showed were crystal white, carvings and symbols followed each side of the walls around me.

But one in particular caught my attention. I walked towards a painting that was miles high. It leaned against the farthest wall on the left-hand side of the room.

At the centre of the canvas was a glowing, white marble throne. Hundreds of angels of all kinds surrounded it, bowing to whoever sat within it. Beside it stood a broad angel; he had black hair and a strong jaw. But I couldn't see any of his features. In fact, I couldn't see any features on any of the painted angels in the paintings.

"Intriguing, aren't they?" I jumped back from the rugged old voice that suddenly appeared beside me.

I turned to see an old man looking up at the huge canvas, his face damaged from years of life. He was dressed in white robes and appeared to be wearing a silver chain across around his neck.

I asked, "Who are you?" He looked at me; piercing grey eyes worn from old age stared me down.

"The Pope, the master of this house. And you are?"

He stood staring at me. I straightened my back and held up my chin.

"Lucinda Sky."

He blinked in surprise.

"The star," was all he said before turning back to the painting.

"Why are all their faces blurred away?" I whispered into the awkward silence.

He cleared his throat before answering. "The artists that were gifted with the sight to see the angelic world painted these for *our* world. They believed they could guide us towards the light if we could actually see it. But there was a price. They weren't allowed to see the faces of the angelic beings."

...*We are all pieces of what we remember*...

One of the voices whispered beside me. I looked up and I noticed that it was a woman sitting on the throne. She was wrapped in a dress that flowed across the floors. It seemed to glow, like millions of white suns lived in the fabrics of her ruffles. Her face wasn't blurred out like the others around her, but her features weren't clear either. I could see her sharpened cheekbones and her razor-sharp jaw line; yet her chin was soft and her hair was piled and twisted around her huge crown. But her eyes couldn't be seen because blinding white light was shooting out of them across the canvas. Her eyes were glowing. Like two stars were born there and were finally escaping their nests.

She was God...

"We will never know them," he spoke again and drew me out of my daze.

"Who?" I asked a little too innocently.

"Them, the angels. God." He touched the cross on his chest. "They're something that will always be apart from us. Above us."

"I don't think so." He looked at me with slightly wide eyes.

"Why don't you think so?"

"I understand them," I said calmly as I stood gazing at God. "I've lived with them my whole life. They created me as a weapon. But they are not my superiors. I own myself." I finally looked back to him, his grey eyes hard. "I love them, but I do not bow to them."

"No, she does not."

That familiar soothing voice travelled to us from the door. We turned together to see an angel leaning against the doorframe, arms crossed and a foot crossed over the other. Peter smirked at me, his eyes bright and his smile dark. His hair was falling slightly into his forehead, and it was intoxicating to watch him smile at me like that. His wings were nowhere to be seen and he was dressed in black from head to toe; so completely out of place in this white painted room of pureness.

"Pope."

He inclined his head as he approached us. He stopped behind me and wrapped his arms around my waist; then he kissed me beside my ear, tickling me and making a giggle escape from my lips. I looked up and saw the Pope's face cover with disgust as one of his priests entered soon after Peter did.

"How dare you bring these riff-raff into the house of God!"

His priest flinched at his tone as he came to rest beside the Pope. He had hissed like he had his own venom.

"Careful there." Kyle smirked as he entered along with Jane. His face was a mask of deadly sarcasm and golden beauty. "Or you're going to make us blush…" I had to bite my lip down to keep from smiling.

"Brother," Peter mockingly scolded, but he was smiling too. "Show some respect to the man of God."

Kyle looked up at his mother in the painting, his face falling a little.

Then he looked back to the Pope.

"There was only ever one man of God, and look at what happened to him."

His tone was icy. He stared down the little man. The Pope was small in comparison to the angels around me; not in size, but in soul. Even Jane held herself better than he did, and she was delicate looking and petite. Like a china doll.

The Pope watched me stand beside them, watched me hold Peter's hand. The Pope's eyes were unrelenting. He was the most powerful man in religion, yet he was powerless against us. Against me.

"The great Lucinda, the human that stole the heart of the Devil's son." He tried to stand taller than he really was, but he was trembling in the presence of my angels. I stepped out of Peter's arms, but I never let his hand go.

"You worship God, yet you insult her children?" His face fell, but he said nothing. "You understand why we're here?"

"Of course. I've been waiting for the day the Devil's son would come to me. The day he would try to save his lover." His face contorted as he spoke of the man beside me, as if it made his stomach cramp.

"His name is *Peter*!" Everyone jumped as I snapped at his holiness. I was being protective over the most dangerous man in history. How ironic.

He regained his composer. "Why should I? It's the truth. Do you even know the man whose hand you're holding?"

He sounded so disgusted that I chose to even be in the same room as these siblings. I looked around at them. Kyle was standing with rigid wings, yet he seemed unfazed by the comment. Same for Jane; she just looked back at me with an apologetic smile, like I was the one being insulted and not them. And finally I looked behind me at Peter; his eyes were raging, yet contained. His thumb stroked the skin on my hand, soothing my inner rage. And I realised something. They weren't fazed by any of it because they were used to it. Maybe for thousands of years they have been used to it. The unfair hate, the judgement they must have received for their mother's mistakes.

I turned back to the bitter old man. He must have seen the anger in my eyes; because he backed up a step.

"I hold the hand of a man who thinks his only purpose in life is to save a simple, useless human life." His hand tightened on mine, but I continued before he could say anything. "All three of them have spent their whole existence to serve and protect me and I would gladly lay that life down for them in return." The Pope didn't answer. No one spoke. They just looked at me. Until Jane stepped forward.

"You know who we are." She sounded like a whole different person. Her face was hard and shielded from view. She wasn't the screaming, panicked girl I'd comforted from last night. No. she was the warrior armies trembled before on the sky's battlegrounds. "You will help us, you will serve us just as you serve our pathetic mother. You will get Lucinda to Heaven." The Pope faced her, hands still on his chained cross.

"And if I don't?"

She stepped towards him. He didn't back down. She showed no emotion. No inch of the Jane I knew was present.

Her voice wasn't her own.

"If you refuse, I will nail you to your very own crucifix. I will cut down every priest in this temple. Then I will burn down this palace around you like firewood. And smile as you burn."

She didn't blink, didn't move.

"You wouldn't dare!" His voice trembled.

She only grinned as if she was showing him her blood-covered teeth.

"I've already done it to Heaven's temples, I can easily do it to yours."

He gulped down his words and bowed down before her. She was a queen of fire. An angel of Heaven and Hell. And as I looked at her, defiant and truly insane, I tried not to think about the kind of torture it must have taken to bring someone like her down to their knees.

"There are archives under the palace. There is a book. The grand grimoire." The room was silent. Peter tensed beside me.

"That book belongs to Lucifer," Peter spoke up, his hands gripping me tighter.

"Yes, it can summon him."

"Then how is that useful to us?" said Kyle.

"Because it doesn't just summon the Devil. It can summon an angel of God, and sometimes in great need, God herself."

"How is that even possible? If an angel comes to Earth, they fall." The Pope only shook his head.

"They only fall to Earth if they go against the law of Heaven and Hell. But if they are summoned for a course for their court, they get to go back."

"I'm guessing this means you are willing to help us?" I asked. He looked briefly to the red headed angel, then back to me.

"Do I really have a choice?"

It was Kyle who answered him.

"Not if you want to keep your holy balls un-nailed *and* in between your legs."

I smiled then.

Chapter 17

"She who has been a Queen of England on Earth will today become a Queen in Heaven."

– Anne Boleyn

Lucinda

Hundreds of steps took us down and down under ground. Dark and mouldy walls closed in on us as we followed the Pope.

Kyle followed behind him, then Jane, then me, and Peter was last. Guarding my back from the eyes of the darkness around us.

"I could just kick you down these steps. It would make this journey a whole lot quicker," Kyle sniggered cruelly.

I could hear the old man gulp from the back of our little walking train.

"Kyle!" Jane hissed at her brother, but he only laughed back.

"I'm joking," he laughed. "I wouldn't have told him. I would have kicked him first."

"We are here!" his holiness stammered, trying to distract Kyle away from his horrid ideas.

We came to stop at an old wooden door. The front had twists and bolts engraved into the woodwork. Like a puzzle ready to be pieced together.

"May I have the key?" The old man looked over my shoulder, I turned to see Peter pick around in his pocket. He pulled something out and with warning eyes, handed it to the man's wrinkled hand. He placed it into a small slot in the centre of the door, and with a click of the bolts the puzzle pieces started to move and unlock its secrets.

It swung open.

There was only darkness as the candle went out. Then suddenly, light was born yet again. The room before us brightened, as if ghosts had lit a million candles all at once.

"Magic," Peter whispered down into my ear for only me to hear. I griped his hand and entered first.

The room went on for what seemed like eternity. Bookcases beyond bookcases of old and new books, scrolls and tapestries.

"The most important objects reside here Kyle Hellfire," the Pope warned before entering alongside us. Kyle's smug eyes snapped to his. "So try not to touch anything."

Kyle only winked and walked past us and disappeared through the mountains of books.

"So where is it?" Peter demanded, but the man ignored him and walked before Jane.

"You know what is down here, but out of respect would you like to see it?" Her lip trembled. Her eyes were yet again the eyes of the Jane I knew.

"I don't think I'm ready for that," she whispered. He only nodded and walked back towards me.

"Are you ready?" he asked, his mouth a thin line.

I nodded.

He looked at the angel beside us, and his eyes began to sadden.

"It was hidden down here somewhere long ago, but no one knows where. It was for the world's protection. And only the blood of the Devil can find it."

Peter nodded, yet his smile was strained as he looked at me before moving away.

"He is more broken than we are able to fix." Jane's soft words hung heavy as we stood watching him walk away, his shoulders slumped.

"How?" I questioned. She sighed and twisted a lock of my hair around her slim finger.

"Because he has to fight a war that isn't his…"

He was gone when I looked back, lost among the books.

I looked back up to her. "What did the Pope want to show you?"

Her eyes looked to mine, but she didn't see me.

"A feather, from my wings," she said. The shock must have shown on my face.

"When I fell to Earth, the angel that took them from me threw them out with me. They were destroyed from the fall, yet a single feather survived. A Pope from a few centuries ago found me. I wanted to destroy that single feather like the rest of them. But he wouldn't allow that. He said I would want it again one day…When I was ready. When I was at peace."

I didn't speak. I only clasped her hand. She smoothed down my hair, smiled and walked away after her brothers.

I followed the invisible steps after Peter. It smelled of unread pages and forgotten faith. The further I walked down the aisles, the darker it got. I found him leaning against one of the bookcases, hands in his pockets and his face looking defeated.

"I can't find it, it's useless."

His face was nearly concealed with darkness. Only a dimly lit candle showed any of his features.

"We will, just take a moment." I stepped closer, He looked down at me and his eyes were the only bright thing in this basement of lost memoires.

"What you said to the Pope, in the art room. Did you mean it?" he asked. I moved closer, almost touching him.

"Which part?" I questioned. His eyes studied me.

"When you thought your life basically wasn't worth saving." His tone was hard, judgemental.

"Yes…" I whispered.

He didn't move towards me. He never said a thing. I only looked at his chest, unable to look at him. We stood, the air around us thick with emotion. Until he lifted my chin up with his soft finger.

His face was once again gentle, but only because we were alone.

"Yes, you have brought all kinds of Hell to my life. And believe me, I could live without the extra stress." I tried to look away but his fingers held firm. "But I wouldn't want to live in the kind of Hell where you aren't a part of my life at all." I looked back, tears shimmering down my cheeks; the corners of his mouth turned up.

"If you weren't a part of my world, I would create another one just to have you in it." My blood roared in my ears, my heart pounded through my chest to try to reach him. He held my face and gently turned it upwards so he could kiss me, his hand framing my jaw as his lips moved with mine. Kissing him was like finally being able to breath after years of drowning, unnerving relief filling my lungs. His fingers brushed away my tears and he pushed me up against one of the bookcases. His tall and broad body covered mine. He was the only thing I could see, the only thing I ever wanted to see.

My mother once told me: Love is when you're blinded by everything else but that one person standing before you… And I was going helplessly blind.

"Sweet Jesus!" Kyle cursed from a few rows over. "They're back at it again. Jane! Cover your innocent eyes."

"For the love of God! *I am not innocent!"*

"You're my sister, you will always be innocent!" he shrieked back.

"You have obviously never met any of my guy friends…" she uttered back.

"Excuse me?"

We chuckled against each other's lips, but continued and ignored their bickering.

All too soon he pulled away and looked further into the darkness. Grabbing my hand, he closed his eyes and the room somehow became darker.

"I've found it."

His wings stole all the space that the room had to spare. His eyes no longer glowed. They focused on me, and for a moment I thought I saw worry in them. And when I looked again, they did. And I understood. He was worried I would fear him, fear this side of him. But I didn't, I never did. There wasn't anything to be afraid of, except losing him.

Further and deeper into the suffocating darkness, the only security I had was his soft feathers as I let go of his hand and held onto his beautiful wings instead. It wasn't because I didn't want to hold his hand, but because I wanted to show him how safe he made me feel. How much I trust not just him, but his wings too.

I couldn't see anything, there was no light left. Everyone else's voice vanished. It was only us.

"I can feel it," he whispered back to me.

His wings fell from my hands, and when I reached back out to them one of his hands replaced them. I breathed my relief.

"I've got it."

His words breathed through my hair. He pulled me to his chest, his heartbeat steady against my cheek. And it made my own calm in return.

"I knew you could do it. I never doubted you."

He kissed me again, and the darkness around us didn't seem so scary anymore. But more like a soft blanket that gave us privacy; our own separate universe.

A gift from the Gods.

We placed the book on the old dusty wooden table. Candles hung around us like the eyes of the ghosts that lit them. The book was bound in black leather and only a thin string kept the pages at bay. I reached out, my fingers steady as I traced the covering that shielded these deadly words we so desperately needed.

"Your father's grimoire," the Pope said softly behind Peter's shoulder. He kept away at arm's length, afraid of approaching such an unpredictable animal that was trapped in a human body.

Peter swallowed before speaking. "What am I looking for?"

The room was silent.

"I don't know," was all the old man said, "I've never read it."

We all spun around to face him.

"What do you mean?" Kyle demanded while bracing a hand on the table. The Pope's eyebrows narrowed at the threatening move.

"It is not for the eyes of men."

"Then how are we meant to know what we are looking for?"

The golden-haired angel's eyes flashed with warning. The Pope just stared at Peter, eyes steady and unblinking.

He looked once to me, then to his siblings.

"I'll find what we need."

"How?" Kyle bellowed.

Peter crossed his arms over his chest and an unreadable mask plastered itself across his strong face. "You are starting to sound like you care brother…"

We all looked to him. Jane went to place a hand at the base of his back, but he stepped away before she could even make contact. There was a look of hurt on her face; it was brief, but it was there. Then as quick as the changing of a second to another, it was gone. He stood straighter, like a steel cord was rammed up into his spine. His face became colder, almost untouchable. Since I had known him, he had always been distant, cold, unfamiliar, as if he trapped himself in a whole different world to us and we would never be invited to enter it with him. But how he held himself to us now, eyes closed completely, his lips a thin line. He wasn't the man I sat with before dawn.

"I don't care about anything!"

I noticed Jane's eyes flicker to me before quickly looking away as he spoke.

His voice was low, too calm, a viscous calm that shook my ribcage.

"I care for *no one*." His sister flinched behind him. "I would let you all die if it means I get to live my life in peace for once. But oh no *brother*!" He hissed the word. "I have to come and clear up all your mess yet again. I have to put my life on hold for you." He then looked to me, eyes full of the calm storm I had only ever seen in Jane's eyes. "And *you*." His voice was less harsh, but full of something else entirely. "This is all because of you. All this shit, all this suffering." He looked to Peter, then to me once again. "I would gladly watch you perish. But if that happens, my dumb ass of a brother would destroy the world. And I still have places to see, things to do, many more wars to fight and women to fuck."

We all flinched at that.

"So no brother." He looked one last time to Peter. "I do not care." And he left.

No one moved, no one breathed. I couldn't explain the need I felt to follow him. I didn't want to face that male of fury and thousands of years of deadly power up those dark stairs. But I did. I left the rest of the angels in the light and disappeared into the darkness of voices and murmurs.

Peter didn't say anything. He didn't call out my name as I climbed the stairs.

There are some kinds of love that can overcome lifetimes.

The whisper was soft, like the inside of a healing heart. It was a single voice, like the voice of a child. And it vibrated through my head like a humming bird, lulling me to sleep. My eyes started to drift close and my body started to fall. But a strong, warm arm caught me by the waist. I couldn't see my saviour. I could only hear his bright heartbeat through his thick chest as he hauled me into his arms and took me away into darkness.

Chapter 18

"If you have it [love], you don't need to have anything else, and if you don't have it, it doesn't matter much what else you have."
— *J. M Barrie*

Lucinda

Something brushed against my forehead, so light it didn't feel real. Then again, light and reassuring, sweeping the hair from my sweaty skin.

"Wake up Lucinda." An equally soft and contented voice reached out to me in the void around me. I battered away the thing touching me and rolled over into the warm blankets.

"Go away Michael…" I groaned into the pillow. The hand stilled.

"Lucinda, it's Kyle."

I rolled back over and opened my eyes.

Kyle sat on the side of the bed next to me. His hand reached across the blanket next to my head. His eyes were dark, and like his brother's they seemed to glow in the dark. But they weren't bright and vibrant like Peter's. Kyles glowed like a different shade of darkness in the night; not scary, or intimidating. A warm glowing brown that cocooned you in stars and chocolate.

"Kyle?" I said while sitting up a little.

I felt groggy, my bones heavy and my blood slow in my veins. He didn't smile, didn't move except for the incline of his head for an answer to my question.

"How long have I been here? Where is everyone?"

"They're still down in the archives. I didn't tell Peter you fell. He needs to work."

He bowed his head, his golden hair shielding his guilty eyes.

"I'm sorry for what I said, it wasn't the truth. None of this is your fault," he admitted.

I didn't speak. I couldn't form the words.

"Why did you follow me?" he asked. He lifted his head to look at me, his question hanging in the air like an axe over my head.

I thought about what I wanted to say before answering.

"Why did you bother to catch me?"

The silence stretched across us like a battlefield after the bloodshed.

He only shook his head and asked hesitantly, "How is your head?"

"Fine. How did you know it was my head though?"

He smiled; it was almost a smirk.

"Because the only other thing we fall from is our heart, and yours has already fallen."

I sat up fully and realised how close we were, our faces inches away. Brown eyes mirroring each other.

I whispered, "Who made yours fall Kyle? What was her name?" I wanted to know who broke this soldier of Heaven.

He blinked a few times to clear his mind, then he looked down. Anywhere but at me.

"Lilith."

His face became drawn, older than it normally was. Like the thousands of years he has lived just crashed all around him in heaps of rubble.

"She wasn't just the love of my life, she was everything that *made up* my life. She made me uncover real emotion. Love, hate, sorrow, jealously, anger…lust." He drifted away to the land where memories are stored and kept safe. "And she betrayed me, betrayed us all." And his face transformed back to being hard rock. He was the perfect cold stoned statue.

I laid my hand on top of his. He snapped his eyes to our entwined hands, but didn't move his away.

"I'm sorry," was all I could say.

"We are angels," he declared. "We endure what we have to, survive when we need to, and love who we want to."

"That doesn't mean you should *let* that stop you from loving."

He stared at me. Eyes like cold fire.

"I'm not sure I even know how to anymore." He got up and with his rough scarred hands, he gently pushed my shoulders down into the pillows.

"Get some rest Lucinda."

The way he said my name, like it was secret only the two of us could know. His lips again in that hard line, but his eyes were softer than before. He turned and placed his hand on the door handle. He was in a void of duty before the heart I realised.

I said my final words before drifting away to let sleep take me.

"She didn't deserve you."

I heard the door open, but it was a while before I heard the door click shut again. The room was silent, the only proof that the world was still around me were the whispers and the songs from the stars outside my window. But even then dreams floated around me like blood coated sweets ready to choke me.

"That was interesting."

An old but stern voice called out to me in the darkness. Nothing. There was nothing but a void around me.

"Hello? Who's there?" My own words shook as they left my lips.

Something drifted past me, a breeze of promise of someone else being trapped in this dark place with me.

It chuckled. "You know who I am, young star."

I could feel it settle in front of me. Its eyes drilling into the spirit that was hidden in my own eyes.

I shook my head. "No, if I knew who you were, I wouldn't be asking..."

A cold invisible finger reached out and stroked the length of my cheek. I could feel its sorrow like the marrow in my bones.

"Sweet star, you are destined for so many great things." My brows lifted in confusion. "Your name will be the battle cry for armies. Your face will be the symbol of freedom and death. Your very existence will be their gift."

It spoke almost to itself, as if realising something.

"Who are you? What do you want?" My own voice was strong and firm.

I stepped back and its attention seemed to bounce back to me.

"You don't understand what you are. You aren't just a weapon, you are *the universe. Its stars race in your blood streams, your heart beats to the explosives of planets."*

It started to circle me, its gaze never leaving me.

"You're a God..." I realised.

Shock ran through me like cold dread and wonder.

"Congratulations, you've figured it out."

"Why are you here then," I asked. "To destroy me?" I held my chin higher, not letting it see my fear.

"Hold your chin any higher and I'll see your brains through your nose," it snapped. I lowered my chin again. "I'm not here to destroy you. I'm here to save you." It paused, then added, "If you'll let me."

"Why? Why would you want to help me?"

"You are a part of a game so much bigger than any God or Devil. And it's been in play since the very first God. Peter, Kyle and Jane are here to guide and teach you how to do your job."

"And what's that?" I pushed.

It smirked. "I cannot tell you your future. I can only warn you of it."

"Then deliver your warning and leave me be."

Its smirk grew wider.

"You will be destroyed in every way humanly possible. They will take your little human heart and shape it to their desire. But you will raise empires and destroy nations." The emptiness around us started to grow. "You will love with everything you have to give, and still…you will somehow give more than you actually own. He will break you. And yet you will continue to love him. And that will be the end of you. You have been warned Lucinda Sky. Turn away now and save yourself. But go with them and there won't be another chance to turn back."

I could barely drag a murmur from my throat. "Who are you…?" I asked one last time.

But it disappeared. Its everlasting echo was the only sign that it was actually here with me.

"I was Baraqija…"

And I woke up.

Frozen statues surrounded me like millions of dust particles in the air. I was in the angels' room.

Their gazes pinned to my face, and God's hands reached out to me like they were my only salvation.

"Lucinda?"

Peter stepped out from the many statues, a shadow among the moonlight that shrouded us.

"How did I get here?" I croaked. He held a hand out to me. I grabbed it, and he pulled me up to face him. His eyes were unreadable, like a book for the blind that was given to the seeing.

"I don't know," was all he said. I brushed my clothes off from any dust. But when I looked up again, I saw the sadness in those eyes that he had been hiding from me.

"Peter?"

His smile was weak.

He stroked my bottom lip. "I'm ok, I'm just tired." Should I tell him about my dreams? Should I place yet another burden on him? "Are you ok?"

No, no I couldn't.

"Yes, I guess I was just sleep walking," I lied.

"I found the spell."

He took his hand back and turned away. He walked over to the statue of his mother with shoulders tense and his head hung low.

"Oh, well that's good news isn't it?"

I tried to sound more enthusiastic, but I was sure he could hear the cracks between my words.

He shook his head. It was such a small movement, but I didn't miss it.

"I guess…" His voice was empty.

Silence.

It was more silent than the emptiness of space. He kept his broad back to me, the muscles strained from the tension in his coiled body. It must take a strong back to wield those kinds of wings that hid away in the flesh of his back.

"Then why do you sound so sad?" I spoke with such gentleness, like I was coaxing a small Bambi out of its home.

With his back still to me, he admitted, "Because this is where we have to say goodbye…"

I couldn't say anything. I didn't want to. I think in the back of my mind I always knew we weren't going to Heaven together. That he would be staying behind, that I would be going on alone. But I didn't comprehend the kind of hole it would leave in my chest as he actually spoke the truth.

"What?" My own voice was weak, weaker than his had ever been.

My body burned like wood being turned to ashes, the panic that settled into my stomach. How he just wouldn't look at me.

I stalked over to him and pulled his arm round so he would have to face me. But I wasn't prepared for the look on his face.

Broken. Simply broken. Like a mirror that was shattered from a battle of lovers, shattered and was never glued back together.

"You would give me up that easily?" I started to tremble as I spoke, and my chest started to ripple in pain.

He stepped forward with his striking yet sad eyes. They kept my soul captive in an undying trance.

173

He cupped my face and traced my skin with his thumbs. "I would easily give up the privilege of having you in my life if it meant you could keep yours and be safe." The pain on his face ripped at my heart like the claws of a wolf. "I'm giving up the love of my life to *give* you a life."

He turned away so I wouldn't see the most heart-breaking expression that ever lay across a face. And it shattered my entire being.

"I cannot forgive you if you do this," I sobbed as he walked away. He paused briefly for only a second.

"I can live with that…" And he left the room.

I fell to my knees. How could he be so cruel? Why did he always want to push me away? I knew he didn't mean what he said, but it still hurt all the same. He needed me to want to go, to leave him. Yet how could I. When Heaven was just a place with no Heavenly grace without him.

'*It was not enough. Our love was not enough.*'

'*Do not lie to me. What you really mean is our love was not enough to make you want to stay.*'

I ran after him. He was walking the length of the hallway when I opened the door back open.

"Peter!" I shouted, but he didn't stop. "*Peter!*"

He never slowed.

So I ran up behind him and pushed him as hard as I could. He turned with burning eyes, like glowing sapphires in darkness and moonlight.

"*What are you doing?*" he shouted straight back at me.

I was breathless at how hard I had to shove him.

We stood, staring each other down with fury in our faces.

"You don't get to throw me away like this!" I shouted. I didn't want it to end here.

His face hardened and it reminded me of Kyle`s expression that he wore most of the time. "You can't just make me feel all these things and walk away! You can't just leave me!" My voice broke and his eyes softened.

He let out a defeating breath. "I'm not throwing you away. I'm trying to save you."

"No you're not. You're just handing the burden over to someone else."

We stood there glaring at each other. Our fists clenched in anger. Our hearts beating for each other.

"Oh my little Lucinda." Tears fell from my eyes at his soft tone. He pulled me into his arms and wrapped me up with his wings. They were strong as they held me, and I instantly felt stronger. "You were never a burden. You are everything I've have ever wanted." His wings held me tighter, as if I would melt through his feathers. "I never asked the universe for anything. I always gave and never asked for anything in return. But now I have, and maybe it's because you're too good for me, too pure. But for the universe? You are the one thing I just can't have... And I curse it every day for it."

He kissed the top of my head.

"I want to spend each and every day with you. I want to build with you. Learn with you. Grow with you. I want it all with only you. I'm selfish enough to want to claim your future and place myself in it. But I can't. I can't ruin it all for you." He lifted my chin so I would look at him, and slowly he brushed away my tears like he was brushing the powder off a moth's wings. "I want to give you the world and all its stars. I want to worship you and walk through life with you. But being in your life means putting it in danger. And if anything ever happened to you–"

He didn't finish his sentence. His air seemed to be cut off from him. He only stood with his wings around me, eyes locked to mine. And I prayed with all the power in my soul that the Gods above would seal this moment away for us to visit again one day.

"How am I going to live without you?" I spoke up.

It had been years since I opened up to anyone like this, to admit that I couldn't live without them. To confess how much someone meant to me. Over the last few months, before I met this man, I never would have dreamed of saying these kinds of words. That without him, I would have nothing and no one. That he somehow, in this short space of time, became a part of who I was... How do you let that kind of person go?

"The same way I will have to live without you..." He leaned down and kissed my forehead, his lips imprinting their mark upon my skin. "We will live in the hope of seeing each other again one day, even if it's for just for a second. That's how we will live with this..."

His voice trailed off like a long-lost love story. His lips trembling as he lowered them to mine, savouring the taste of them to his memory. The kiss was slow, as if he was drawing out history for it, showing it we fitted together like the perfect puzzle.

"Come," was all he said as he pulled away and held onto my hand. "I just need to hold you one last time…"

I nodded and followed him down the hall and into our room. I couldn't see him. I could only feel the soft touch of feathers as his wings appeared. Then I was wrapped up in his strong arms and placed gently on the bed. I searched for his glowing eyes in the dark and found them in no time. I reached up and touched the skin beneath his lashes. They closed at my touch and a low moan escaped his lips. As if my touch was making love to his skin. I pulled him down with me and slowly he wrapped his arms around my waist like I was made of fine china. And by his simple touch, he would break everything that I was.

"I just thought we would have more time."

His vulnerable words floated around us like a thick fog, and his arms tightened. I stroked his soft hair and placed the feeling to my memories.

"We have this, we have tonight," I whispered into the dark. He buried his face into the crock of my neck. "And you will forever have my heart." He lifted his head and kissed my forehead, his breath soothing my skin.

"Then how can I let you go?" His eyes were the only light in this dark room.

"Come with me…" I whispered.

"I can't." He sat up and pushed the fallen hair from his forehead. And in that moment, with his shoulders slumped, his head bent, and his eyes silently closed.

He really did look like a fallen angel.

"Tell me why, tell me why you cannot come with me," I begged as I placed a hand on his. He turned his head to look at me from over his shoulder, then he took a deep breath.

"When we fall, only God can invite us back again. But we are her children, her blood. And we left her. She deserved it, but we hurt her. So she will never let us return home for it is our punishment."

He smiled a little and it made my heart warm at the sight of it.

"But I would never choose differently Lucinda, I would never regret falling to Earth for you. From the very beginning you were all there was. And for the rest of my life there will only ever be you."

"But you have lost so much."

"Yes," he sighed lovingly. "But I have gained so much more." And he kissed me.

I leaned down against the pillows, his beautiful face in my hands. He hovered over me, his wings splayed out around us. He held me to him like I was his set of armour and he was my weapon against the world.

I pulled away slightly. "When do I leave?"

"Tomorrow morning…" His voice was weak, as if he didn't want to believe what he was saying.

"Then hold me until then."

He only nodded.

He pulled me into his embrace and wrapped me away within his huge wings. I gripped his hand to my chest, begging the world to not rip me away from his hold. We stayed awake all night, just gazing at each other. Holding each other's hearts in the other's hand, waiting to see who would break who's first. And too soon he pulled my arms off him and his hands shook as they held mine. He forced himself to let me go and I was sure I could hear the clouds begin to weep outside the palace walls.

The morning was dreadful. The air hung low over our heads like an axe waiting to drop. Everyone, even the Pope held dread and regret in their hearts. Peter and I walked hand and hand to the great hall in the centre of the palace, his grip tight but soothing, as if he was caring for a lamb before its slaughter. I kept looking up at him, but his eyes were unreadable. He was wearing his mask again. And the only indication of affection I received that grey morning was a slight brush of his thumb to my cheek as we came to the doors that opened to my fate. He said nothing and neither did I.

The doors opened.

Chapter 19

"So here's my question: when you lose the most important person to you in the entire world, where is all the love – love you never even knew you were capable of – supposed to go?"

– Ted Michael

Kyle

They walked in slowly but surely. It was like they wanted to slow down the world just enough to freeze this moment to push away the goodbyes they would have to make in a matter of minutes. But too soon they stood before the pentagon in the centre of the marble floor; yet their grip on each other never faltered. Never loosened.

"Are you sure you want to do this?" the Pope asked as gentle as he could without coming to a whisper.

Peter only nodded his head.

"Very well then."

He bowed his head, picked up the old book and began to chant. Strange words that were not even familiar to *me* flowed from his lips. And with each word the statues around us seemed to move and breathe with each pulse of his chanting.

"Amen…" he finished.

Silence.

"Is that it?" I asked, my tone not at all kind.

His eyes hardened as they hooked themselves on me.

"Sorry if I didn't bring candles."

His raspy voice could have made my feathers stand on edge, if I had any left. So I only glared in return.

"I have called them. It is their choice if they want to answer."

"You better hope they do," I hissed.

He swallowed and stepped back. I looked to Jane and she shook her head with the smallest of movements. Then he looked to her.

"This is your last chance Jane. Do you really want to leave it behind?" He spoke softly, but his voice was unfeeling.

"It took a long time to make these walls around myself," she said with the vulnerability of a child. "They won't come down easily, not even by my own hand."

I held her hand, and she squeezed mine back in return.

Then suddenly, the pentagon started to glow. The symbols were alight against the hard centuries old marble floors. They threw shadows against all our faces, but it was scary when I looked upon the human and my brother.

The shadows on their faces made them look anything but normal. It made their eyes look darker, stranger. Deadlier. Caved in like a hammer to metal. They looked like something from a different kind of Hell. And in that moment, she looked perfect for him; just as dark, just as secluded as he was. Holding each other like that, I could really see how they were two peas in a pod. Two sides to the same coin.

And God help anyone who tried to rip them apart.

Jane

I can't believe I'm finally going home. All kinds of emotions rushed through me in waves. Happiness, revenge, dread, fear…Regret of leaving my brothers behind. I looked at all of them around the room. All their shattered pieces of souls around them, floating around them like particles of dust. And distantly, I could feel a gaping hole form in the centre of my chest.

I looked at Kyle first.

His golden-sunlit hair curled around his ears, the base of his neck and his tanned forehead. His brown eyes, which were a shade darker than Lucinda's, were closed off to us like they always were. I put his features to memory; all his scars, all his imperfections that actually made him perfect. I burned them into my mind like a burn to flesh. I remembered so long ago, when he was so heartbroken he could hardly walk, couldn't talk because if he did he would scream of his pain. How, when he finally did let us see the real him, his true eyes, they held pain of endless centuries. The kind of sorrow that festered under the skin of the heart. It had forced him to never love again, never to feel true emotion. He had tried for so many years to hold himself together, trying to show us a mask of strength, a non-caring man. But I knew him. He hadn't truly cared for anything in so long that I believe he couldn't now even if he tried.

And I knew that without me here with him, he would lose everything he had left of himself. And that broke me the most.

So I looked away to Peter. Our older, more crippled, damaged brother. He had sacrificed so much for us; so much we have given for him. His blue, crystal eyes were fixed on the pentagon before him. And to others they would look like hard, cold crystals that were formed in the loneliest of caves. But not to me. I saw the desperate, loving man underneath them. The man that was fighting the entire world for the woman he loved, and he would fall for her. He would take down Heaven and Hell for her. But the hardest thing he would ever have to do was let her go…

The light reflected off his bronze hair like a mirror, and I placed that to my memories. Every angle, every feature to his angelic face, every single one of his scars through all his wars he has fought. I stored them away along with Kyles. I watched as he tried to stop his expression from breaking. He didn't want to show his pain in front of Lucinda. He has always tried to spare her. Shield her. And it has cost him deeply.

I took them in like a drug, a drug I would never have again. And I placed them into the dark, distant corners of my broken mind, and there they would forever stay safe; they would forever stay with me. And maybe that way I could survive what was to come…

A life without them.

Then an image came to me.

I stood watching them, a young woman with an old heart, her weary eyes staring into his. A man with a strong body, tainted with the darkness, his eyes filled with sorrow as he looked at her. I stood watching them both, and they held each other as if a huge crack would form between them and separate them on opposite sides of the Earth. Yet I couldn't help but think of how perfect it was how creation could make such a love like that.

Lucinda

No one spoke. Maybe it was because the light around us was growing brighter, or that it was nearly time to say goodbye.

I looked up to the angel next to me, and found his eyes already on mine. And it felt like it was just us.

I hadn't noticed before. I hadn't noticed his smallest details until now, in our last moments. He only showed his true self to me. What would become of him when I was gone? What would happen to me without him? He saved me, everything that was left of me; he picked up all my shattered pieces and handed them to me. He didn't keep them for himself, but gave them back so I might heal once again. And there would never be enough gold, money, or hearts in the world for me to repay him for what he has given back to me.

But the universe had decided that our lives were not meant to be linked. That we could have one last look at each other…And be forced to say goodbye.

He cupped my face one last time and wrapped us up in his majestic wings.

"Don't be afraid, don't let them see your fear…"

"I'm not, I won't." My voice was too weak for real words. "I promise."

His eyes burned a soft golden flame. They were so warm and inviting. I traced the soft skin under his eye. And I silently said goodbye to my favourite part of him. Silence hung in the dark air under his wings, and it was beautiful.

Then he let the world back in.

"I don't get paid enough for this shit!"

An old, yet also young voice rang against the walls around us like the bells of Heaven.

"Oh look, it's God's lap dog," Kyles said sniggering.

I looked to the pentagon and in the centre was an angel with purple wings and silver amour. As I looked closer, I could see through the glowing light that he had black hair and it was cut short to his head. He had an early stage of a beard growing across his sharp jar. But it was his eyes that startled me the most. They were very old. I could see history pool out of them like a tidal wave. They were a bright violet that swallowed up everything else in the room. It was like seeing all the different shades of purples and violets that swirled in the universe all at once in just two irises. He was tall and muscled, coiled and lean. He was a taut elastic band ready to snap at any given moment.

"Kyle, always taking the pride from our Lord's name, aren't you." His tone rocked my core. If this angel was this over-powering with his angelic power, what were Jane, Kyle and Peter once like? Would I have even survived their presence?

Kyle only shrugged. "It's my only past-time."

Then the stranger smiled.

His white straight teeth shone against even his whiter skin.

"Peter."

He bowed his head to him, but his eyes were weary as he watched the man beside me.

181

But before he could reply, I spoke up.

"Gabriel," I said. His eyes widened slightly, but collected themselves just as fast.

"Lucinda," he said. "Look at how you have grown…"

I blinked.

"Do I know you?" I asked,

He chuckled. "I knew your father."

I went quite as he turned away to the Pope.

"Why was I called here?" His full lips went into a thin line.

"We are in need of God's help, and it would be for her complete benefit."

He seemed so small as he spoke. A man amongst angels.

"You want us to save the human?" he said while looking back to me before looking back to the Pope.

"Yes."

"No."

"*What*!" Kyle bellowed.

"Why?" Jane gasped.

"Why would we? She is the reason the great war began." He rose his voice over everyone else's. "She is the reason the greatest angel in history fell to Earth." He looked to Peter. "She will bring the world to its knees, and she will drag you down along with Heaven and Hell."

"Please…" Peter begged, his voice strong, but thoroughly exhausted.

Everyone stared at him. Shock rose up on their skin.

"I am begging you Gabriel. Save her, and I will do anything. I will disappear off the face of the Earth." I gripped his arm and panic filled me. But he only stepped out of my grip. "I will bow down to God, I will give her my *wings*. Even kill myself if I have to…"

Jane started to cry; silent tears slipped down her face. Kyle looked like he was about to fall part on the spot. I didn't want to know what I must have held in my own face.

"Just save her…" His words rang in our ears, his everlasting plea.

Gabriel's face softened for a second. "Sometimes Peter, sometimes the bargain is just not worth the price."

He didn't blink.

"She is. She will always be worth every scar, wound, war and every loss that I must endure. She will always be worth it. Now save her."

Gabriel didn't say anything. He only opened his arms out. And the room began to throb with angelic energy.

Peter turned me to face him.

"Jane is going with you."

Tears welled up in my eyes. I gripped his arms with desperation.

"Don't do this, we can find another way!" My voice started to break. None of my words came out as I needed them to.

"She will protect you," he went on.

My knees began to wobble.

"I've just found you," was all I could muster to say, even though all it was just a whisper.

His eyes broke.

"And I will find you again," he lied as he pushed me towards Gabriel. Light surrounded me as his strong arms held me to him. I looked back to my angel, his eyes rimmed with tears.

"Peter! Please!" I screamed as blinding light engulfed us. The world slowed down as I began to rise into the air. This was it. Heaven was taking me away.

His voice was gentle, a broken instrument that was trying not to sing a goodbye song.

"I love you," he said low enough for only me to hear and hold dear. Then the world filled with blinding light, and the last thing I saw were his blue tear filled eyes.

Then the world went dark.

Chapter 20

"How do you ever know for certain that you are doing the right thing?"

– Anthony Doerr

Lucinda

Nothing made sense.

My mind was a jumble of pictures and thoughts that were scattered to the wind. I laid upon a soft object of nothingness, whispers all around me like the feathers on a bird's wing taking flight. I opened one eye, then another.

The world around me blurred with white. Brilliant whiteness that stunned me as I sat up.

"I don't want to see her! And I don't want her anywhere near Lucinda!" Jane hissed while pacing around my oddly shaped bed.

"Jane?" I croaked out.

She turned, startled, then rushed to my bed side. She held my hand and helped me sit up.

"Where are we?"

"You are in Heaven Lucinda. Welcome home…" I looked around, and I realised that the pure whiteness was the walls around me. Everything was made out of perfectly carved marble; swirls of grey decorated the marble too. The Vatican palace was nothing compared to this.

Then I realised I wasn't in a room at all; but I was sitting on a marble floor that was surrounded by pillars and sky. I was in the sky. And all that was stopping me from falling out of it was a huge cloud holding the floor I was currently on.

"Jane?" My eyes widened as I gripped her hand with terror. There was no wind, although there was a gentle breeze that brushed my hair. But no rushing winds that were meant to be up here while being this high.

"It's ok, you aren't going to fall. I'm here."

"Where is he?" I turned to her, eyes wide and ready to spill.

She sighed and stroked my hair back from my face. My heart started to pound against my ribs.

"He's isn't here. He is still on Earth with Kyle. He is safe, but he is gone."

Sobs racked my very soul as I collapsed against her. Her thin but strong arms held me. I couldn't fully understand why he wasn't here; he had always been by my side, always there.

His last words rang through me like knives flowing through my veins.

I love you.

I spent the next few hours crying on Jane's shoulders, then her on mine.

We sat for hours. Talking. Crying. I poured everything that I was into her hands, and strangely I felt safe doing it. Peter had been the only person I could ever really be myself with, the only person I could talk to, give myself to.

And now he was gone.

I shut the thought out, pushed it away.

Because every time I think about the circumstances of what's happened, when I let the truth settle in. My heart cuts off. And I feel like I'm about to die…

"Ladies." That old yet young voice filled my ears yet again as I turned to see Gabriel stand at the edge of the pillars. His voice, a deep rumble with a sweet edge to it. It could only belong to a man that has seen every horror and gift the world could offer, and still be able to walk without buckling from the burden of it.

"What do you want?" Jane said while clearing her face of tears.

"She wants to see her, wants to see you…"

Her eyes hardened more. "She can go to hell."

"She has already been there, may I remind you."

Jane's laugh was bitter. "Yeah, she dated it too."

I don't know if it was real, but it seemed that the male angel flinched at her words.

"Nevertheless. She demands to see you both. *Now.*"

And he flew away, powerful wings lifting him into the skies around us. And he was gone.

"Are you ready for this?" I asked.

She looked to me, eyes still red and puffy. Centuries worth of panic and hurt came to rise in her eyes. And looking at us both, I realised how much a parent can either rise up a child, or tear them down before anything else can.

"No," she sighed. "Let's go."

We were carried to our destination; soldier angels held us as we flew across the sky. The clouds had started to turn to a yellow, golden colour. And the sky was a perfect reminder of Kyle's hair, so I looked away.

We reached vast white buildings. I looked down and I could see that most of them were temples, their style reminding me of Roman buildings. Strangely human for such a divine place.

Ancient temples for Gods and humans alike.

The biggest was like a palace that sat on top a huge mountain made from more cloud. It was mighty to look upon. All around it stood pillars that I realised were holding up the gigantic roof. From up here it shimmered against the sun as if it was made of diamonds. Or maybe stars. Its towers reached up into the sky, as if it was trying to beg the universe for a single touch. Windows reflected the light like mirrors across its stone work, making it seem brighter than it truly was.

Smaller buildings surrounded it; small homes for the lesser angels maybe. Because what surrounded this magnificent palace was a city. Miles and miles of lights and souls walking its streets. And off into the very distance, I could see an ocean…

There was an entire world up here. Just above my own world, there was a completely different one.

"Land in the flying gate!" one of the angels ordered.

We lowered to the palace, and gracefully they landed gently on their feet. The flying gate, as they called it, was a huge archway in the left side of the palace. And as I looked inside the palace before me, I could see white walls and thin pillars that held up an extremely high ceiling. Although the room was bare, it was breathtaking. The angels moved towards an exit at the far end of the room. I turned to Jane.

"I'm with you Jane, you are not alone."

I held her hand. And she gave me her weakest smile.

"I know."

We followed the male angels through halls grander than any castle, palace or temple I had ever seen before. Art of all ages and history were engraved into the marble around us. I knew I was gaping at it all. But I couldn't help it. I was a human that had made it to the place of angels. The most vibrant flowers covered every inch of the walls, over every piece of furniture. They seemed to grow as the light grew, moving with our footsteps, watching us as we passed.

Finally, we reached a set of even grander doors that were at least ten feet high, white and gold decorated everything we passed.

The door opened.

"Here we go," Jane whispered to me, or herself, I couldn't be sure.

We entered hand in hand.

"I've got you," I said again to reassure her.

The hall was vast. Huge pillars held this ceiling too. They stood in rows on either side of us as we walked in. I couldn't see where this magnificent hall started or where it ended. Marble flowers, small cupids and other intriguing creatures of art covered the pillars. The artwork reached up and up to the ceiling made of the finest of diamonds. They glistened off the dying sun's rays outside the walls. I looked ahead and came to find the throne I had envisioned for so many years.

And there she was.

God.

She sat upon it like she was the one that had created it. Her throne sat upon three almighty steps. Her long lean legs showed through her silken gown that flowed down those steps. But the layers of ruffles and clean-cut crystals that were so clearly sewn into the fabric could not hide the fact that she was responsible for so much pain. As I took her in I noticed how white her skin was; it was as white as the walls in this beautiful Hell. Her slim arms laid across the arm rests of the throne, her sharp nailed fingers tapped repeatedly against the cold looking stone. She wore no jewellery, only a huge crown that I believed no one was meant to fill but her. It was made of bright silver, and it held three diamonds. One in the centre, and one on each side of it itself. Other smaller jewels encircled them, framing them. But the crown only made the angles that made up her beauty sharper. As if the skin was pulled too tightly over the bones in her face. It made her look less natural. And strangely, the most beautiful woman I had ever seen.

Her lips were rose coloured and perfectly plump. Her chin was sharp, as was her strong jaw. Her cheekbones framed her shinning green eyes. Her hair was like spun white silk wrapped and entwined in that almost disturbing crown. And only a slim long neck held it all.

We both came to rest at the bottom of the steps.

The rest of her angels bowed, but we did not.

I looked up at her. Her back was straight and her one huge white wing was wrapped around the throne like it was showing me who owned it. Light seemed to create itself from her presence, seemed to flow from her every pore. She leaned forward and the stone cupids on the pillars started to whisper.

"Welcome home daughter."

Her voice froze every muscle in my body. To herself she may have spoken so very quietly, but to a simple human…I could have fallen to my knees and wept at the sound of it if Jane wasn't holding my hand.

"This is not my home and I am not your daughter," Jane said calmly and composed.

Her back was straight, yet she bore no wings to behold. Her face was even more angelic up here; I hadn't noticed from the pain we were enduring. But her skin glowed, her red hair was like wild fire sprouting from her scalp. But her eyes didn't glow like Peter's had when we went flying; like the rest of the angels did in this throne room.

"Why are you here?" God asked. Demanded almost.

"Peter sent us."

"Yes. How are my sons?"

"My *brothers* are fine."

Her mother's eyes narrowed. And finally she looked to me.

Her eyes saw through me like shattered mirror pieces. Reflecting my soul to the world as they passed through me. They were the same shape as Kyle's. They shared the same coldness in their eyes too. Though they were different colours, they shared the same essence. Jane had gotten her coloured eyes from her mother, and Kyle had her heartlessness. I could see so much of them in their God, but I could not see Peter at all. Was I glad? That for however long, maybe for forever, I wouldn't have to see any reminder in my maker's eyes of him? He was everywhere I looked, just not in his mother.

"Lucinda." My name echoed off her lips to the walls around us. "Or should I call you by your real name? *Astralis.*"

I sucked in a breath. That name, it hummed through my body. As if my very being answered to the sound of it.

She chuckled.

"You recognise it? You should. It is the name of the star that lives inside of you. It has been dormant for too long now, but it has returned to its master now."

"You are not my master," I spoke with steady words.

"*I am everyone's master.*" Her own words rattled my teeth from their power.

I shook my head. "Not ours."

Her eyes blazed, but stayed contained in their sockets. She leaned back and lounged in her chair, her stare still on me.

"I admire your bravery, your guts to give cheek to your maker. But mind yourself human. I can unmake you as much as I have made you."

"To my memory, I believe Kyle made me. And be my guest my Lord, strike me down. I'll pray for you when your son comes for you."

In the corner of my eye, I saw Jane's lips turn up, a smile she was trying to hide.

"*I am God, he cannot harm me!*"

Her voice was warning me to back down, but I couldn't. Not when I had seen so much pain conflicted by her.

"Then where is your right wing my Lord?"

She went silent. And then she started to laugh.

"I will never understand why Peter ruined his life for a speck of dust like you," she hissed down to us from her throne.

I spoke the truth. "Neither do I." My voice was lower than before.

"I will protect my star, my weapon." Jane looked to her mother at that. "I will teach you how to use it. Who you use it against is your choice Astralis. But I will not leave you defenceless."

"Thank you," Jane said softly, God looked back to her, opened her mouth to speak, but thought wiser of it. And turned back to me. "I hope you know Lucifer will come. I will try my best to protect you, but he will come."

We nodded.

"Jane," she said. Jane's eyes became harder than before as she looked up to her mother. "How have you been? Well I hope?"

I could see that she was trying. But for what she had done, there wasn't enough time in the world to find out all the sins she must have committed against her children.

"How have I been?" Jane scoffed. "Do you really want to know?"

God said nothing as she looked down at her child, her eyes emotionless.

"My life has been wonderful mother. For most of it I have lived alone, separated from my family. Partly because Kyle was always off hiding from the world and Peter was hiding from himself. But we all know who is to blame for that, don't we?" Her mother was about to speak before Jane continued. "I have learned the ways of humans. Their anger, hatred, and pain has rubbed off on me slightly. I still have trouble sleeping, as you have probably guessed by now. The flashbacks still haunt me. Each and every day. The sound of the tearing flesh, the feel of maggots under my wiped flesh."

Jane's eyes drifted away to the land of madness.

"That is enough–" God spoke up but still, Jane carried on like her mother hadn't spoken at all.

"I can still feel the breaking of my spine. The sores on my throat from the screaming of weeks at a time. I can still hear the laughter of other angels as they took in my decapitated stumps on my back as I walked past them. I can still remember how I cut away the remaining parts of the infected stumps. It was brutal, blood everywhere. But all of that was nothing compared to seeing what has happened to my brothers. Centuries of pain and torment has corrupted Kyles mind. He cannot feel anymore. Just like you mother. I suppose you should be grateful for that. At least you have one thing in common with at least one of us. Then there is Peter…"

"Jane–" she tried again.

"Sweet, loving, innocent Peter. He has broken himself in so many ways now I fear he is lost. There might not be any way of getting him back, now that you have taken Lucinda away from him."

Jane looked up to God, only to find an expressionless face looking back to her.

"You brought her to us," God said.

"Only because you wouldn't allow him to be with her without war."

"I did what I had to do. I did my duty to the world."

Jane laughed. It made the hair on my arms stand on edge.

"So doing your duty, did that include nailing my poor wings to a crucifix for the whole of Heaven and Hell to see?" Jane's voice broke.

"You had to pay for what you did."

"*It was a mistake!*" Jane screamed.

"Yes!" God stood abruptly, her only wing spreading wide in warning to her daughter. "Yes it was a mistake, a mistake that cost you everything!"

Jane went silent.

190

"So some of us, your *children* make some mistakes. And you think it is perfectly fine to destroy them in every way possible? To bring an empire to its knees to stop a love because you couldn't keep your own?"

God's sharp nails began scraping against the throne again as she sat back down.

"You have no idea why I had to do what I had to do back then. The sacrifices I had to make for the good of the empire. No one understands what being a God truly means. What it takes from you, what it asks of you. I have saved you more times than I have hurt you Jane. The least you could have done was forgive me for the sacrifice I had to make *you* give."

Jane stepped forward.

"Maybe if you would have just visited me in my chambers, spoken to me at least once in the years after the taking of my wings. If you would have just helped me wrap my back just once, like a true mother should have. If you could have spared just a few moments to help me bind my whiplashes instead of letting me struggle in pain doing it myself. I might have forgiven you. But now?" She paused before continuing. "You lost one wing, I lost two. You lost your children, we lost our minds. We are nowhere near even, but it's a start."

Silence followed until Jane added.

"So to answer your question mother, I have been very well…"

Jane stared at God, waiting for her answer that we all knew would never come. But her face stayed cold; no emotion let alone any love was there. If being a God meant being alone, apart from humanity, then I was happy to be human. But looking at Jane now, in her element, in her home. All I could think was how entrancing it was to watch her destroy herself.

"Gabriel," God called out looking away from us. The angel climbed the steps to stand beside his master.

"Yes my Lord?" His voice soft.

"Take them to their chambers. I'm done with them for today."

And with a brilliant flash of light, the throne became empty. Gabriel turned to us with shinning violet eyes.

"Really Jane?"

His words would have been like a slap to the face if they were directed to me, but Jane only grinned.

"Is it still hard to hear even now Gabriel?" Her eyes become as frozen as crystals.

"I will take you to your rooms," was all he said. He walked out of the throne room.

"Jane?" I tried to touch her shoulder but she moved out of my reach.

"Lucinda, I'm fine." And she walked after the angel.

We followed him through the winding halls, past hundreds of doors and rooms. And finally he stood before a smaller version of the throne room doors.

"Both of you will share a room. I'll take a guess and think you both would want to be close."

We said nothing.

"We will see you at dinner."

Jane took a deep breath and pushed the doors open. But I didn't follow her in. I knew she needed time to herself. Even if she was too strong to admit it. Sometimes we don't realise that when we are trying to save the ones we love, we are actually the ones who are killing them.

"Lucinda?" His voice stopped me from walking away. "Can I talk to you?"

My eyes were blunt as I looked up into his violet ones.

"About what?"

He was silent for a moment.

"Do you not understand how much you have to lose here?"

"I have nothing to lose anymore."

I moved to turn away but his hand on my arm stopped me.

"You humans will never understand how much you really have. All that freedom to love who you want to love, hurt who you want to hurt, live however you want to live. I have fought every war that has ever been waged. I have seen every star fall. I have served *every* God. But you humans, you get everything served to you on a silver platter. And you never have to fight for the freedom that you are given."

"What is your point?"

I heard him sigh. "To love so innocently, without a drop of sin is the definition of humanity. Don't trade that for the love of an angel. Because you will be given nothing in return."

I turned away. "I don't get how loving someone could be so bad."

"That's what the Devil said right before he fell."

I had nothing to say to that. So instead of answering, I pulled my arm out of his vice like grip and vanished through the halls.

I went exploring. I know it sounded like such a childish thing to say, but if I stopped for even a second, Peter would flood my mind and it hurt too much. So I distracted myself.

Room after room, painting after painting. Thought after thought. Many different kinds of angels watched as I passed them. Some with disgusted faces, some with fascinated faces, and some were even scared. They moved out of my way like the sea parting for Moses. I had never felt so alone before. Even when I was on Earth before all of this, I had myself, my heart. But now the most important thing of me was millions of miles down under me. Gone. He had stolen my heart, and now he was gone. And I had no one.

I entered a room with no doors and before me stood a huge statue. What is it with the angelic world and its statues?

It was delicately carved and designed. It was a woman with no wings, her long hair covered her shoulders as if that *was* her wings. She held smaller versions of humans and angels in her hands. They sat on her legs, knees, shoulders, in her hair; they were all over her. But it was her eyes that struck me most. They looked so sad. So broken.

"Astralis."

I jumped back from the sad woman sculpture and found God standing before me.

"I'm sorry, am I intruding?" I asked, but she only studied me, stared me down. At least that is one thing Peter has in common with her.

"This is your home. You may go anywhere you like," she said without taking her eyes from me.

"What is this place?"

"Do you mean Heaven? Or this room?" she questioned.

"Both," I answered.

She nodded. "This place has been here since the very first Devil. God wasn't the first one here. All this." She held her hands out to the world around her. "He created this home for himself to rule, a master piece of art and power. Then he created the first God. To revel in his power. He created Hell to make Heaven shine brighter. To make good look better than evil. The first God didn't agree with his plans. She believed there should only be goodness, no evil to make it look better. She believed light should shine bright on its own without the help from something else. She fought him. She won. She gained the Heavens, but it cost her everything else."

You gave everything to everyone. But you took what little I had away from me to do it!

A voice screamed through my mind, a voice that had been locked away and forgotten for too long.

"There has never been a God that has sat upon that throne and that has ever felt happiness…" God said to herself.

"Your children could have been your happiness," I spoke up.

Her striking, hard eyes pierced me as she looked to me.

"No. Maybe once they were. But Gods cannot have children. To pass down that kind of power…It goes against nature itself."

"And yet Peter exists," I challenged.

Her eyes narrowed. "Yes. He exists."

We stood in silence.

"He isn't evil," she spoke up again. "He never was…" She looked out to the forever-roiling skies, an endless painting of clouds. "The darkness surrounds him, but he didn't *choose* to surround himself with it."

"If you let yourself truly see him for who he is, you would see he is the purest darkness that was mixed with the most tainted of light," I said as I tried to block his face from my mind before my tears fell.

"How is he?" she whispered.

"Honestly? I don't know. He doesn't like to share his burdens with me."

"Why?" Her voice, for the first time, was gentle.

"I believe it's because he's scared they will become my burdens too. He tries so hard to protect me. Even from himself." Traitor tears fell from my eyes. I wiped them away before she could see. "He is a good man who is forced to wear a mask of a villain."

"Are we telling the truth here Astralis?" she asked while lifting her eyebrow.

"My name is Lucinda."

"Lucinda…" she tried out on her tongue. "It suits you."

She looked at me the way a human would look at another human. "I have sacrificed so much, but that is what a God does for her kingdom. For her people."

"But why do you prosecute us? While you were with the Devil?"

Her face froze. No anger, resentment was there in her eyes. No emotion at all. The God of no emotion.

"Because I have been there," she said in a hush voice. Maybe she was worried the spirits around us would hear her confession. "I have tasted the sweet toxins of the Devil's honey. And I was poisoned by it. It nearly destroyed me. I know it doesn't look like it, but I am trying to save you both."

"It's too late for that."

"I know," she said with a slight smile.

"What made you fall in love with him?"

Something flickered behind her eyes. Not warmth, or love, not something breathing or living in any way. But the essence of a past memory.

"No one will ever understand why we fall for the people we fall for. Only but ourselves. And sometimes even then we cannot fully understand why. He wasn't always the man he is now. He has changed from what he was…And it breaks me every day."

"What changed him?" I questioned.

"Love…Power…They are the most dangerous things of all. So to mix them together… It created chaos." She stared at me before continuing. "We will always have to pay a fortune for the poorest kinds of love."

"Then how could you still love him?"

She thought for a few moments before answering. "No matter what it is, you can never stop someone from doing something in the name of what they believe in. And even if it is wrong, we have the responsibility to love them for it."

"This is all very touching, but it is kind of dragging."

A wicked voice froze us both, like its grip was deep into our bones. We turned.

The Devil stood clapping his hands, striding slowly towards us.

I could see him clearly now that the mists of darkness were nowhere to be seen. He wore black shining armour that made my skin go numb. A metal covered cape embraced his brood shoulders, and his grey skin and his unnaturally wide black eyes made my skin burst out in a cold sweat. A small but dominating crown of dark stars encircled his black hair. He looked just like his son. I didn't know if I wanted to run to him or away from him.

God stood in front of me.

"Lucifer…"

He greeted her with the kindness a disease would show a healthy host.

"Lola." He bowed his head to her in mocking respect.

"Why are you here my love?" she asked.

"You know why my Lord."

His smile showed perfectly pointed teeth.

"You cannot have her," God Lola said.

"Yes I can, and you will not try to stop me."

"And why is that?"

He was close to us now, but he hadn't looked at me once. He eyes stayed on his Lord.

"Because if you do not surrender, I will kill Jane. Your sweet daughter now sleeping in her chambers. Another guilt you will have to live with."

Her body tensed, but she did not back down.

"Then I will kill your son, your heir." He only grinned back to her.

"No you won't." He chuckled.

"And why is that?"

He came to stand inches from her.

"Because he isn't just my son, now is he?" His breath was on her face. I realised that Peter didn't have anything in common in his mother's looks. He looked just like his father; but the Devil's build and face was harder, broader. While Peter was leaner, sleek. His face sharper like his mother's. While he didn't look like his mother, he had her personality; her power, her strength of the heart.

"Tell me my Lord." He circled her once before facing her again. "Does it stir inside you every time you see me?"

"Are you here to end this or blabber on?" she said. Through the terror, I hadn't noticed the black horns that protruded from the Devil's head. They curved forward at the base and then they reached back towards the back of the head. They were huge, yet beautiful. Horrifying.

His eyes softened for the briefest of moments.

"I'm sorry…"

And he stabbed her in the gut.

I stumbled back in shock. Shock as Lola doubled over and held onto the stone-faced Devil. Her white face was a mask of pain and gasping. He said nothing as he pulled the dagger out, picked her up and handed her over to one of his soldiers that appeared out of nowhere. He handed one of them the dagger, the dagger that was covered in God's blood. And I couldn't help but admire how the red reflected of the sun's rays like shattered rubies. Rubies melting in the burning sun.

"Take care of her," was all the Devil said. The soldier nodded once and left us alone. The Devil pulled out a handkerchief to wipe away the blood from his hand.

"How could you?" I gasped as I fell to my knees in shock. He looked to me, his face bored.

"Do not worry human, she has done worse to me. But she will live. I would never kill her."

"Because you love her?" I forced out over my harsh breathing. He said nothing.

"You are my prisoner now. Do as you are told. Or regret it deeply."

He threw the ruined handkerchief to the perfect floor, her blood ruining the white marble.

"You are evil!" I hissed as he approached me.

"That *is* my job darling…" he said chuckling. He gripped my arms and lifted me onto my feet with ease. "You don't understand this world. But here is a summary. Sometimes demons do more damage than angels ever could. All because we mistake destructive creatures with being misunderstood. And sometimes angels do more damage than demons ever could. All because we mistake beauty for innocence."

"That doesn't make sense." I struggled against his grip, but it only tightened.

"One day it will." He grinned and turned to leave. He waved his hand for me to follow. I hastily did.

"This temple is under my control now, so keep your mouth shut and you may survive long enough to see your family again."

"My family?" I asked confused. I could feel his wicked smile even though his face wasn't in view.

"Michael? Your brother? And your dear old father? Azriel? Do as I say and I won't kill them."

"You've done it before. How can I trust you not to do it again?"

The now empty halls made my skin tingle with the bitterness of absence.

He came to a sudden stop and turned to me, those wide black eyes somewhere on my face.

"Excuse me?" His voice was laced with confusion, but my eyes only narrowed at it.

"You killed them to try and make Peter agree to become your heir."

He was quite for a few seconds, his eyes zoning out.

"Lucinda. I don't care if you believe me or not," he said carefully, slowly so I wouldn't lose any of his words. "But I didn't kill your parents."

No. I didn't believe him.

"Then who was it?"

He watched my face like a hawk and I stared right back.

But I did not expect his answer.

"Peter."

Chapter 21

"You can't unchain a soul that refuses to be free."
– JH Hard

Peter

The room settled. Everything became as still as the stone walls around us. My lungs seemed frozen, unable to draw in any air. My brother's eyes locked to mine with sadness that he had not shown me for centuries; yet he didn't move. Neither of us did. I knew the men that were left here with me were waiting for me to explode with unrelenting power. But I wouldn't. I couldn't. I had nothing left to give.

But she was gone…

My mind went blank. No words of comfort made it past the roaring in my ears, no thought made it past my walls of despair.

I'd let her go.

But I always knew I would have to let her go eventually. I braced myself for it every minute of every day. Yet now that had it finally happened, I couldn't have anticipated how empty I now felt; that I had just let my heart be taken away…

"Brother?" Kyle approached me. I looked at him and saw that even his own eyes were red. But I couldn't say anything. She was gone. They both were.

I felt it all in that very moment. Every single thing that I'd kept buried, buried so that it wouldn't affect my choice to send her away. The room still hummed from the Heavenly presence. But now it shuddered from me.

My body shook with temper, rage that I'd hadn't felt since the Holy war. It crept up through my veins and burned my heart.

She's gone.

She's gone.

She's gone…

My wicked mind kept repeating to me.

Kyle stood back, his hand held up in mercy as my frame vibrated with anger. Anger for the Gods, anger for my parents, rage for the whole damn universe. My fists clenched together as my darkness surrounded me. I could feel it claw at me, holding itself to my skin as my eyes grew grey. It whispered to me, curling around my ear like the snake of Edom.

Her face, her smile, her eyes…

It all filled my mind like a never-ending sea.

Suffocating me under its waves of salt and tears.

She's gone.

She's gone.

She's gone…

The world exploded.

I let it all go. Everything that was filling my chest with poison. I let it pour out of me with a roar.

My throat burned as my voice escaped me, the palace becoming deaf with my roar of pain, of sorrow, of anger for my lost love.

My body was concealed with darkness. Not an inch of me was open for the world to see. The windows shattered from my power, the pillars fell to the ground in heaps, the floor cracked in tune to my screams. I could hear the city around me fall. All its houses, temples, palaces. They all fell to me. I could feel it all rush through me like a high from drugs. The feeling of something mighty bowing to me, from my very will. My darkness reached out across the city and destroyed everything it touched.

But for the grace of my Lucinda, I left the people alive.

When I finally settled and let my power return to me, I risked a look to my brother and the Pope.

They were horrified, but the only difference between them was that my brother held some understanding. The world around us was scattered, placed at random in this newly formed chaos. And I was glad. I hoped my mother witnessed it all. My hurt. Our pain. She knew this pain, this horror. And yet she forced it upon me, she made me feel it. She did to us what happened to her.

Her heart was broken, so she broke ours too.

"Peter."

I heard my brother call out for me. His voice was the only thing that reached me through the dust that now surrounded us like a cloud. But I didn't answer. I couldn't. I felt so empty. So hollow. I just wanted to vanish, to have the entire world swallow me whole and consume me into its core. But instead I stretched out my wings, braced my knees and with an echoing cry I lifted myself into the sky, letting the ruined ancient city die away under me. I flew as fast as I could, forming a storm around me and letting my power fill the skies. It needed to breathe. I needed to breathe.

My wings screamed at the joy of flying. They stretched out to their full length, the tips touching the clouds on every side. The lightning struck the Earth all because I could not reach Heaven.

She saw every part of me. The good and the bad. Even the rusted pieces in my hidden corners that I have tried so long to forget about…

She saw the man hidden within me that I never even knew was there.

And now she was gone.

The sky was black, as black as my wings, the inkiness clinging to me like a second skin.

I made the choice to love someone, to love them more than I could bare, more than I could cope with. Yet it had made me stronger on every level.

I thought back to all those blood filled moments of war. Of all the bloodshed. Every scream, every hurt, every life lost.

And yet her face was all I could see.

She was all I could see through the dark skies, the lightning, through the rain that now battered my wings.

I let the storm drag me away. I let it rip me apart and scatter me across this world like the remains of bodies on a battlefield.

I was gone…

Lucifer

The look on her face… If I owned any emotion at all, I would have felt sympathy for this little human. But alas, I am the Devil for a reason.

Lucinda

I couldn't breathe, couldn't move, couldn't think. It was like my body was shutting down. I could only look at the creature before me, my eyes unblinking in case I missed any lies that snuck past his face. But there was only the unbending truth that lurked there.

"What?" I muttered.

He did not grin, he did not chuckle.

"Peter killed your brother and father."

We stood together in the hallway that was growing colder by the second.

"There are many things he has not told you Lucinda." I looked up at him again, but he was already walking away. "But that was the biggest of all his secrets."

"How could he?"

The Devil laughed. "He will destroy everything that makes you who you are. But you will love him for it anyway."

We reached the throne room doors, but they were already caved in. Shattered wood was visible across the ruined floors.

I stepped over them as I followed him in. "Is that what you did to Lola?"

He didn't miss a beat as he replied.

"We did it to each other…"

He climbed the three broken steps to the untouched throne. And when he sat upon it, the white stone darkened. Grey cracks formed as his hand laid on the armrest. I stood alone at the base of the throne, arms around myself; but I noticed how wrong the scene looked. The temple shook slightly with a sickening feeling, as if it was trying to throw up and get him off its throne.

"We are powerful beings Lucinda. But the difference between you and I is that I am not bound by love anymore. I do not let myself be pulled and broken down by emotions. I am free to be who I am destined to be. You could be too, if only you'd let basic human habits go."

"What are you going to do with me?" was all I asked.

"Nothing at the moment." I didn't move. "I am going to wait to unleash your power when my son gets here."

"What makes you think he can get here?"

His smile was disgustingly handsome.

"Oh he will. He loves you, he will come…"

"And if I don't want him to?"

He stared down at me for a few seconds. Playful intent smoked around his eyes.

"I will not confine you. You are free to go wherever you wish. But do not try to escape. Or I will kill Jane."

"I wouldn't have guessed you could be so merciful," I joked, but he did not hear the humour in my voice. He only rolled his eyes and huffed.

"Me neither. It's exhausting." He laughed as he roughly rubbed his eyes. "I don't know how you do this all the time…"

He sat with his eyes closed, head resting on his hand. His wings slumped against the throne, darkness rolled and slivered through each of his feathers.

His only company in the world.

I turned to leave.

"It's called being human," I said as if it was the simplest thing in the world to be. He opened his eyes to look at me, but he said nothing, did nothing. So I left.

He killed my family. He blamed it on his father. But he did it. He lied to me. He made me care for him. I allowed him to heal me…But who do I believe? The Devil? Or his son? My head throbbed with my pounding blood.

How could I ever forgive him?

I trusted all the wrong people. And for that horrendous mistake, I've lost everything. But I healed from it. And I realised other people cannot truly heal you; they can only start you off. Make your heart beat that first beat. But it is your choice to make it continue fighting for each pounding struggle after that. Peter found me… he helped heal me. But in truth, I healed myself fully.

In this world, you will experience life and death in equal measures. There is no changing it, or persuading it otherwise. And there is no escaping it. But that's what makes the scale fair.

"Lucinda?" Jane's scared voice crept up from behind me. I snapped out of the daze I was in to find ourselves standing alone in one of the hallways. Why were there so many hallways?

I turned to find her tear stricken cheeks and red eyes looking at me. She was concealing her mouth with her hands as if a waterfall of tears would spume out. She looked human for once.

"I'm so happy you are ok…"

She opened her arms out to me and moved to hold me in her embrace.

"Did you know?" I asked with hollow words. She stopped dead in her tracks, arms still out.

"Know what?" She hiccupped from crying.

"That Peter was the one that killed my family?"

She slowly lowered her arms as if she didn't want to scare me away before she could attempt to catch me.

"Lucinda–"

"Did. You. Know?" My voice broke on me.

More tears fell from her eyes.

"Yes."

I ran away as fast as my simple little legs could carry me. This was too much, I couldn't process any of it. I ran to any room I could get into and slammed the door. I shut it so hard the shudder was felt across the temple. The room was dark; the statues around me were cold and distant as I circle them all. Each had unique features. I released a strangled breathe as I came to realise I was in the prayer room and that I was finally alone.

I could feel the rhythm of my heart thump throughout my body like a broken clock. Time didn't feel right anymore, the tears that ran down my face didn't feel right. I'd always been scared to love anyone or anything because I knew I didn't deserve it. I got to live, but my family had to die for that to happen. How could I ever forgive him for that? For making me live with that? How could I ever forgive myself?

My heart now belonged to the man who broke it…He had turned it against me, used it to his advantage.

But he had also saved it.

I leaned against the stone wall that faced all the angelic faces. I couldn't hold myself up anymore, my knees were too weak. I wrapped my arms around my middle, hoping to hold my insides from falling out.

And I fell to the floor.

The room was bitterly cold and lonely, as if the air in here hadn't been disturbed for centuries. My chest rocked with sobs, each clawing at my ribs each time I drew in any air.

His face, his eyes, everything about him kept flashing across my mind like a record on repeat. And I could hear my heart scream every time.

"What is wrong my dear?"

Someone called out to me from the dark. I lifted my wet face to see who it was. But no one was there.

"Who's there?"

"I am Phanuel…"

"Oh."

"Why are you crying?" Its voice was soft and almost caring.

"Peter killed my family." I choked on the words, like bile on my tongue. Phanuel went silent for a few seconds. But then I could feel its essence move closer to me.

"Poor child." It seemed to settle near to me, kneeling before me.

I took in a rugged breath.

"We are angels," it said. "We endure when we have to, survive when we need to, and love who we want to."

Kyle said that once.

"What does that mean?" I blinked through the tears.

It sighed deeply, then laid an invisible hand on my knee.

"The most important thing about love is that it escapes its chains…Even when we tighten them to the point of snapping and breaking off. It slips free as easy as the sunlight chasing away the darkness."

I went quiet, and so did the invisible creature.

"Why can't I see you?"

It lifted its hand away, but didn't move away from me. "I don't have a face of my own. I am a spirit. An idea. A state of mind for others that need it. I could be whatever you need in the moment. And right now, you need a friend that will speak the truth."

"Tell me the truth then," I said. "Did he kill them?"

"There are many truths to that, but also twisted lies. But to understand it all, you have to understand the past of *them*."

"Explain it to me…"

"As you wish." The creature moved and sat beside me. I leaned my head back against the wall and I could feel the last of my tears roll down my face, then disappearing down my neck.

"After the white days, when Lucifer and Lola were officially at war, the three siblings of Heaven and Hell were placed in the middle. Pulled apart from each side, loyalties were tested, families shattered. Hearts broken. But the Holy war wasn't between God and the Devil. It was between Peter and his parents. And it nearly destroyed everything we have come to know. Jane… She was the daydreamer of Heaven. A body that carried all the damaged goods of the skies. And because she was so carefree, such a wild spirit, nor Heaven or Hell could contain her. So they tried to break her. But instead they created a wild beast of rage, a fiercer warrior than the whole world will ever know. But she holds no reason for anything. She destroyed herself for those she loved, and in return she became the heart of them all…"

It sucked in a breath that rocked the room.

"Kyle…The soldier of angels. He battles through history for a simple moment of peace, and he loves those who sought to hurt him. His heart is of pure iron, surrounded by the black fire of Hell. He won't give himself to anyone. Too afraid it would be the thing to break him. But when he finally does love, the universe will feel it a thousand-fold."

"Lola. The God of no emotion. She is unfeeling, and at times unloving. She has been broken in so many ways it was almost impossible for her to feel emotion. She has never been human or angel, purely God. And it has left her alone. Many have tried to love her, a few have even succeeded. But her heart isn't her own. It is owned by the Devil. She has always wanted to be normal, to have a simple day. It is the only thing she has ever wanted…To love who she wanted without consequences. And because she can't, she won't allow herself to feel anything at all. Lucifer. The Devil. He is the evil in the world. He has only ever bought destruction and misery with him wherever he went. But he was created from good, by loving God, and giving the world a son of proof; proof that not everyone is their parents, that not everyone is who they claim them to be. He has become the evillest creature in history, the darkest man in the world…All to make the only thing he ever loved shine brighter than himself."

"Peter…" it finally said. "The good Devil. He is the son of everything evil. He's been claimed to be more so than his father. The world shies away from him when he approaches. The world would bow before him he if wished it. Yet he does no such thing. He is the most powerful being to ever exist. Yet he can't bring himself to use any of it. His heart belongs to only a simple human. He would sacrifice the world and everyone in it for the woman he loves. He fought all the wars, sacrificed his undying soul for her. He chose to be the very thing he hated for her to live… His love is purely good and bright. It shines in every corner of the universe for her. And it may break them, but the sacrifices they will make for each other, their love will be payment enough…" It sat breathless as if the truth was too much for its little heart.

"The human. She will break herself in every single way possible. She will be the most damaged woman to ever exist. She will love the wrong man, yet she also loves the *right* man. Her heart will shine bright like all the stars in the sky, lighting the way for the world to see; while her soul will be consumed by darkness. She will sacrifice herself in every way she can. She will save the Devil's son by loving him more than the world she is meant to protect before him. She is power itself. The universe will be at her fingertips. And even though she loves the Devil when she shouldn't, the world will forgive her for it; because it will be the only thing that keeps a part of her alive…"

"I don't understand. What does that have to do with what he did?" I asked frustrated.

"There is always a reason behind everyone's actions. No matter what the deed is, who we are as a person, a soul, God or Devil or angel. We must understand them before we can judge them." It touched the dried tears on my cheeks before continuing. "Lucifer knew how important you were to his son. And he knew that Peter would never be his heir, so he used you against him. He said he had a choice. Kill your father and brother, or kill you. He knew he would win from whatever he chose. You would either be gone, or you would suffer from the loss of your family and forever hate him for it. Lucifer wanted his son's power for himself, for his legacy. And your father and brother knew that. They knew of the Devil's plans and agreed to it. Peter refused, but they insisted…" My entire body began to throb.

"Peter. Kyle. Jane. Michael. Azriel. And many more. They have all done these horrible things all for you. Because they love you. All in their own way. They all have a past with you. And now they fight for a future *for* you."

I held my hand up to silence him.

"They agreed to it?" I whispered against the darkness around us.

"Yes," was all it said.

I knew then. I knew that they would never have left that day if even a small part of them wanted to stay. But I understood. Heaven was too much to pass up. Yet Peter did. He gave up a kingdom. A throne. All that power for me.

"Love is a dangerous thing. It decides the course of nations. It destroys the most powerful of monarchs. But it can also save it all. Forgive him. So he can finally forgive himself…" And Phanuel disappeared after giving me its final words.

Peter

I sat upon Mount Everest, the wind harsh and below freezing on my skin. Everything was white, not a soul in sight. Here, I could hide away here for the centuries to come.

I zipped up my jacket and tucked in my black wings. I could feel every feather that froze to the winds howling.

I looked upwards. The grey skies haunting me. Taunting me. Smiling at my pain.

I would never see her again.

My Lucinda.

My little Lucinda.

The world screamed at me. Its voice as harsh as a clash of swords. I was so close up here, so close to her. It was like I could reach out my hand just above me and I could pretend I was touching her…

"Gabriel? What are you doing here?" I demanded.

I turned and took in the blood covering him like war paint. Panic seeped into my bones.

"Lucifer…" was all he said before he started to collapse.

I hurled him up, swinging his arm over my shoulders for support.

I gently laid him down on the snow, him flinching as he went down.

"What happened?" He cracked open his eyes to look at me in pain.

"Lucifer… and his armies broke the wards…around the temple." He gasped as his chest rose and fell. "He wants to unlock her power…the power of the star! Offer yourself in her place. Your mother will let you in, just save them!"

There was too much blood. It poured from every inch of him.

"Rest now general, rest."

And I stood to face my brother.

"How did you get up here?"

He had his hands tucked into his front pockets of his jacket.

"I may not have my wings, but I do still have *some* power."

We stared each other down. Two brothers agreeing and going off to yet again another war.

"Looks like we are going home after all," he said. That smirk doing its job.

"So it seems."

"So you *are* going to sell your soul to the devil…" He smirked.

"Oh shut up Kyle." Gabriel managed to grunt out.

Chapter 22

"That's the funny thing about time: it's born every second, but as old as the hills."

– 'Stories by Sam'

Lucinda

I awoke to metal arms grabbing my own. Armoured angels in black pulled me to my feet. I looked around to find the sun had risen and that I had fallen asleep against the wall.

"Where are you taking me?" I struggled in their fierce grip. There were two of them, one on either side of me…As if I was capable of escape at this point.

I was dragged into the throne room before the Devil yet again. He lounged himself across that chair while smirking down at me, smirking at me with his son's smile. I was shoved to the floor. My body may bow to him, but my heart never will.

"I want what I came for human," he said quietly. It was just us two left in this vast marble tomb.

"And what's that?"

His eyes grew darker as they prowled at mine. His black sharpened claws racked the side of the armrest of the throne.

"I want the power that lays dormant in that little heart of yours."

He pointed a claw towards my chest and I could feel a stabbing along the side of my heart.

"Then take it," I said.

He rolled his black eyes. "I can't. You have to awaken it before I can seize it."

"How do I do that?" I asked, but his attention wasn't on me. It was on the object in his hand.

I couldn't see it because it was concealed within his grey fingers. But there wasn't any emotion on his face; no anger, hurt, love or curiosity…Just nothingness. I wondered how empty someone would be if they couldn't feel any kind of emotion at all? Even pain is better than nothing.

His eyes snapped back to mine.

"Figure it out." And he hid the secret object away. "Or I will kill one angel for each time you fail me."

Then he stood, his dark cloak concealing his wings away from view. Then he vanished into thin air, a whisper in this dark room and nothing else.

I sat in the throne room for what seemed like years. Starring at the marble walls and pillars that surrounded me as my prison. I tried to make something happen, but nothing did. I had no power. Whatever was in my chest was dead. Gone. Ashes to the wind.

I was nothing more than a simple human that had nothing to offer but my mortal life. And because of this stupid belief that I contained a star, I had lost everything.

Including myself.

I looked back on everything that had happened, and all I could see was suffering. Pain coursed through me.

"You must be Lucinda." A honey smothered voice reached out to me in the darkness. I turned to find no one in here with me.

"Why do angelic beings have the need to sneak up on me?" I asked no one in particular.

"Why do humans have the need to crowd our throne room?"

"I didn't ask to be brought here!" I turned towards where the voice was coming from.

It scoffed. "Yet here you are."

I fell to my knees.

"Yet here I am…" I said in defeat.

It was silent as a cemetery. "Get up!" it said. It sounded like a woman's voice. A powerful force, that was nearly always hidden among our words, came through, a storm that was always ready to either bring destruction or new life to the world. It was defiantly a woman speaking to me now.

"Why?"

"Because you have lives on your hands right now. You can't give up." She moved closer, but I still couldn't see her. "You will get up. And you will fight for them. Learn to control your power, learn how to use it against *him*…" And she was gone. I could feel her presence leave the room like the after-effects of the storm.

Something awoke at her words. Something deep inside me that has slept far too long now. Something that was ready to wake up.

The doors opened.

"I should hope you have made some progress by now?"

The Devil walked through in his cloak of slithering darkness. The room became darker, like his eyes, as he saw me defeated on the floor.

"How do you expect me to find something when I don't even know what it is?" I begged for leniency. But he was the *Devil*. I shouldn't expect mercy.

He leaned down before me, eyes hard and sharp. "I expect to get what I want," he hissed.

"Then you will be bitterly disappointed won't you?" I spat into his grey face.

He wiped the spit away with a single claw. Then quicker than a flash of light that same claw left a gash along the side my cheek. It throbbed as I held myself away from him. My palm was warm with blood as I held my cheek together. I could feel it run down my jaw. He sighed and straightened, then waved his hand to one of his soldiers, who bowed and walked quickly out of the room.

I kneeled in silence as Lucifer sat himself in God's chair.

"The star has always been a part of you. It is a living, breathing thing that can wield worlds. And I want it. So if you try to keep it from me, I will destroy everything around you before I destroy you." His voice was stupidly calm for a man who was so full of rage.

Anger coursed through me like fire. "How can I give it to you when you won't tell me how!"

His eyes snapped to mine. "Figure it out."

Again, that was all he said. It was the most basic, human thing I had heard him say.

Then the solider came walking back in, dragging a small little angel by his hair after him. The poor angel looked so small under the grip of the man before him, tears streaked down his red little cheeks. His arms and legs were skinny and dainty. He only looked about nine years old, yet he could be millions of years old. Ancient yet still vulnerable as a child.

"Please!" His sweet but panicked voice ripped at my heart. "I haven't done anything!" The soldier shoved him down to the steps before Lucifer. Yet all the Devil did was smirk as little trickles of blood weaved through the little angel's hair from the horrid grip of the lap dog.

"You have either two choices human," Lucifer said while still smirking. "You either give me what you want, or I kill this angel."

The child like angel's eyes finally looked to my torn-up face.

211

"Please help me!" he begged. Sobs escaped me. I couldn't help him. I didn't know how. What he was looking for in my face I didn't have. I lost the fight when I lost my heart all those years ago.

"Please don't do this!" I begged the grey man on the throne. "Please find some mercy in your heart. Please don't hurt him. Punish me! Punish me!"

He shook his head.

"I know you Lucinda." He nodded to his soldier. "You won't give in if I hurt you. You will fight on. But if it is taken out on the innocent, you will yield…"

The soldier approached the young angel and pulled his beautiful face back by his raven black hair.

"Please!" we both screamed together. I tried to run for him, to shield him. Hold him. But cold hands held me back. Pinned me like the pathetic human I was.

His gurgling was all I could hear when the solider slit his throat with a small knife from his belt. Such a small object that did so much harm. Blood poured from his white skinned neck, so vibrant against his skin. So eye catching against the marble floors as his body fell to the floor with a thud. His mouth opened and closed like a fish. Until he fell still and silent.

From somewhere in the palace I could hear wailing, so many voices rising up to scream. But the sound that followed was unbearable, cruelly broken. I couldn't see who was screaming. I couldn't understand anything. I couldn't feel anything as I was hulled away. It was as if a crazed animal was trying to escape someone's throat, begging to be free from all this chaos.

They threw me down in a bright cell and slammed the iron bars behind them before leaving me alone. But as I looked around at the dense light that pinned me like an ant under a piece of glass, I saw that I was truly alone. And that the screams were coming from me…

Chapter 23

"This is the strange way of the world, that people who simply want to love are instead forced to become warriors."
– Lauren Oliver, 'Requiem'

Lucinda

"Astralis…" A gentle voice called out from the blinding light. But I didn't move. I didn't flinch. I wanted out of this world now. I wanted to be free of it all.

My heart was spent…

Phanuel

She laid across the cell floor, her haunted face now haunting my mind. It was so sad to see such an innocent creature be broken so easily. It is a tragedy when the darkness can trample the light with such ease.

I couldn't help her now, now when it was a fight against her own mind.

Lucinda

Images floated across my eyelids. Faces I have known all my life. Faces I've never seen before, yet recognise better than my own. Shinning flowers, blue skies, golden clouds, a time before chaos. They all danced around me. I knew I was delirious. Slowly going out of my mind, it had finally snapped and I hadn't even realised.

"Hello little one…" Someone again reached out from the darkness. I turned, but no one came to greet me. But then out of the swirling shadows, I saw a girl. She only looked about six years old, so small and delicate. Her blonde hair flowed down her little

back like a cape. I couldn't see her face as she was turned away from me. But a part of me knew her…

"What's your name?" the same voice asked the little girl.

"What's yours?" She giggled. She reached out a hand to touch something, as if she was stroking something invisible.

"My name is Peter." Then he appeared.

He was bent before the young child, a bright smile plastered on his beautiful face. I stepped closer, but they didn't notice anything but each other. His face seemed younger; angels don't age but his face seemed more innocent. More naïve.

Then I realised the girl was not just stroking mid-air, but his wings.

"I'm Lucinda."

He chuckled a little with her. "You're very small for such a big name," he said as he plucked a perfect feather from the same wing she was stroking. She took it with a bright smile and tickled her neck with it, then his in return.

"Little Lucinda," she said.

"Little Lucindas," he repeated after her. And they vanished.

I've never seen him smile like that before, so bright, so open, so carefree.

So happy…

I turned again to another image.

"Why do you think I threw you out of Heaven then?"

A woman dressed in white and pearls came into my view, her eyes full of ice blue fire that would make any creature beg for mercy. I couldn't see who she was talking to, but there was a deep pain in her eyes. Even too deep for me to understand.

"Because my views will never be the same as yours."

Someone of shadow answered her. And she vanished just as quick as she had appeared.

"I have no home anymore…" A younger version of my beloved Jane now sobbed before me. Then Kyle appeared by her side like a knight of Camelot. His hair lighter and his eyes brighter than I had ever seen them before.

"I'll be your home then." He kissed his sister's forehead and lifted her into his strong arms. Then they too vanished, and the only thing that remained of them was Kyle's sweet echo.

"I'll be your home…"

"Are you ok?" someone else called out.

"As much as I can be," my voice called out to answer, yet I hadn't open my mouth to unleash it.

There I stood before something only the other version of myself could see.

"These paintings of you both are so beautiful."

But it was only her and me.

I heard myself sigh, that empty and broken sound was all too familiar. "Yes," I said. "Burn them all..."

"My daughter."

I turned to find my mother standing before me. She had no bruises, no cuts or wounds. Her stomach was intact and her clothes were free of blood. She even looked sober. She looked like the mother I once knew as a child.

"Mum..." My heart wanted to run into the safety of her arms, but I didn't know any safety when it came to her anymore.

She smiled like a weak kitten. "I'm here now darling. Everything is going to be alright." She stepped closer but I stepped away. Her face fell. Did she expect me to act like the defenceless child she always thought I was?

"What do you want?" I said bluntly, even though I knew her death was my fault. I still couldn't show her any love. Even when she wasn't real.

"To help you, comfort you. That's what I–"

"Why now?" I asked. She only looked at me in confusion. And I hated it. "I needed you long before now. I needed your comfort years ago. I needed your help years ago...Not now." She stood flabbergasted. "I needed my mother when I was a child. Not now when I'm an adult that has lived through life and is now at the end of it. You should have told me the truth about who I was, what I was. Maybe then we wouldn't have ended up where we are now."

Tears ran down my face, tears that I have held back for so much of my life. Hurt and anger I have felt for the world, but also for my own mother.

"Lucinda...Please..."

"Why? Why didn't you tell me?"

"It was the only way I could protect you. If you knew who you truly were they would have found you."

"But that wasn't your choice to make..."

"I know." She sniffled. "I know I made mistakes, I know I should have told you. And I'm sorry. But I couldn't see another way. But that doesn't mean I don't deserve forgiveness."

We watched each other.

215

I knew deep down I forgave her. She was my mother. And she thought she was protecting me, even if she made mistakes along the way.

So I stepped towards her, and for the first time in a long time, I opened up to her and pulled her into my arms.

She was shocked at first. But soon after she wrapped her arm around me too. And I kept my face hidden, not allowing her to see my tears.

"Goodbye Mum."

And I was the one that turned away. And so I slipped back into the slide-show of memories and nonsense.

I didn't think about the many hours that must have passed me by, or how many angels must have walked in and out of my blinding cell. Time wasn't real here. Not in the land of memories.

But there he stood.

So light.

So...

So free spirited as he looked down at me.

I was laying on my back on a warm marble table, draped with a silk sheet. We were in a small room; no pillars and thankfully no thrones. No one here but us. It was quiet, apart from the gentle laughter of children from outside filling my heart. His blonde hair tickled my nose as I slept, tickled my skin as he worked over my mechanics. He stitched my flesh together with such delicacies, such focus so he wouldn't make a mistake. And even though he pierced my skin with a fine needle, I didn't feel any pain. I looked around me. The windows were crafted from fine glass with a tint of crystal blue. It reminded me of something, something important.

I turned back to the male working on my newly made leg.

I doubted he even realised I was watching him.

His shining hair fell into his face many times over, and every time he pushed it back. Like an artist who was so involved in his work that he didn't have time to tie it back. But it was longer now, still slightly curled, but it was long enough that it reached his shoulders. Shinning curls of sunlight that framed the face of Heavens representation of perfection. There were no scars that reigned his tanned skin, no indents that showed the bitterness of Earth's reality. Here he was his pure self. The man that I should've have met on Earth. The man that had not yet sacrificed his innocence for a corrupt nation that did not deserve it. Here, he was Kyle. Brighter, lighter, and completely and rightfully whole...

I don't think I had ever seen his eyes so alight, so wide, so allowably open before. They were always beautiful, a deep chocolate brown that warmed you in a bowl of sweet dessert. But they never actually moved me before. To know now that this is the real Kyle, the real man that had once existed. This is who should be standing where Kyle stands. This is who Kyle should really be.

But to know...to know that this is him, the innocent, caring, vulnerable angel. It broke my heart to know that this is the man that was destroyed and broken by everyone he loved most.

"You're awake!" I came back from my thoughts.

I found him beaming down at me. His smile. It blew up my chest with sorrow...

It was such a beautiful smile, such a young smile.

He grinned down at me. He had finished my stitching, yet there was nothing on my skin.

"Amazing, isn't it?" he burst with excitement. He looked down at my patch of skin and marvelled at such a simple thing. "You can never be scarred, never be marked by anything."

He held out for my hand and helped me stand upon my feet for the first time. I never let go of his hand. I held on for his touch, his security.

"Who...what..." I spoke, and it sounded like as if bells rang through our little room.

He was still smiling down at me. "You are whatever you want to be."

"Why am I here?" I asked.

"That is for you to decide, and only for you to figure out."

"Will you help me?"

"Of course. I just need to fetch a friend. Will you wait here for a moment?" His words were like soft musical notes to my ears.

"Will you come back?" I asked.

He smiled once again.

"Always."

She was beautiful. A captivating creature that laid broken across the cold dirty ground. A huge cavern surrounded her. And she was at the centre of it all, the focal flower, her self-portrait. Her body was useless now. Blood coated her like her hero's cape. The sky was dark and rain gently fell upon us, upon her. The world's fallen princess.

Her long braided hair framed her head, flowing like lava against the wet muddy ground.

She didn't move; she couldn't. Her bones were shattered from the fall.

Her once perfect silver armour that displayed her triumphs of war was now dented and laid in tatters in the mud.

It was the perfect picture for a fallen angel. Yet she had no wings, or any scars or stumps on her back from what I could see, to show if she ever did.

She laid there. Every part of her broken and bruised. Looking up at the sky, as if she was waiting for someone, anyone to help her, to save her. Those shinning eyes. They did not flinch as the rain fell on her skin, mixing with her blood and becoming her war paint. The rain wasn't cold; it didn't sting as it fell on me. Was it sent to soothe her dying skin? To help ease her pain if nothing else could? I did not know.

A shadow flew over us, and it was only then did I see her move her head slightly and let out the smallest of moans. It landed a few yards away, a powerful creature covered with armour that seemed to be made by the stars. It did not belong on Earth.

"Lilith," it said as it approached her. It bent down and brushed back her blood-soaked hair from her forehead. She only looked at the creature, which I now realised was a male. A handsome male that held wings of the purest baby blue. As I looked at him more closely, I realised that he was blind. His eyes saw everything but what was before them. But they were just as beautiful. His hair, cut short and tied back with a piece of leather, looked so soft I wanted to reach out and touch it. He was blinding, but also, too captivating to turn away. As he moved her a little, she cried out in gut-wrenching pain. He lifted her into his arms so he could cradle her, to hold her as she died.

"Orion," she managed. She gripped his hand to what was left of her breast-plated armour. And as their tears fell, so did mine.

"I'm so sorry," he cried as he kissed her tender fingers, leaving red on his full lips. She gently wiped it away as if she knew that his beauty should not be tampered with.

She cupped his cheek. "Take my body home my love. Take it back to Edom."

She was only strong enough to give him the sweetest of smiles.

He said nothing. He only kissed her on her blue lips and gently swept her up so he did not hurt her further. And lifted her into the grey skies above.

Another...

I was speechless. Somehow my heart knew something that I didn't. Something I wasn't allowed to know.

"I know you don't remember anything or anyone anymore. But you were loved." His voice cracked like old glass under the weight of the world. *"So loved. And I'll never forget you, none of us will..."*

And another...

"I fell in love with him because no matter how much the world hurt him, took his strength and snapped it in half, or when it beat him down to the point where he couldn't stand back up, he never let it change him. Never let it change who he was. Never let it tell him who he was. And in a world like this that is a beautiful thing. And I fell in love with it. I fell in love with him for it."

Lucifer

I stood behind her door. A coward. A coward for not being man enough to face her. I placed my hand on the door handle and turned it. When I entered, the first thing I could see was Lola chained to her bed, her glorious wing strapped down by chains. I knew she was drugged with heavenly fire. It was the only way to keep her down. But it was the look on her face that reached the deepest parts of me.

It took me back to my trial, the day of my fall. I remember the courtroom as clear as if I was standing in it now. And I remember Lola sitting in the centre of it all. Angels of all kind battled for their say on my punishment. My future. While she only stared me down. Her piercing eyes holding me in place. But I didn't care about the opinions of lesser beings. I didn't care that I would fall. It didn't affect me that all their faces held hate. But to look at Lola and see her like that... She didn't hold any hate, or anger, or even disappointment...

I was the only one that has ever brought emotion out in our God, so I was expecting anger or hate at least. Not for her to look at me like every other being in here. With no emotion at all...

"Come to grace me with your presence Devil?"

Her hissing words ripped me back to reality and away from memories.

"We are alone now Lola, you can call me by my name." I pulled my cape from my shoulders and bent down next to her.

I didn't move to touch her, but I needed to be near her for only a moment. Just a single moment.

She looked up, her skin wet with sweat from battling the poison rushing through her pale body. Her eyes still burned though; they always burned with such intensity. They were one of the reason I had fallen so hard for her.

"I hate you," she hissed.

I tucked her sweat soaked hair behind her little ear and sighed.

"No you don't," I whispered.

Her eyes softened for the briefest of moments. Sometimes words aren't enough for these kinds of moments. These kinds of moments can be so delicate and precious that words could never be enough. Everything that needs to be known is in a deeper, raw, most vulnerable place known to man. The eyes. Because once someone hears words they can easily forget or miss-hear what was said. But with the eyes it is actually seen. And you can never un-see emotion, not when it is showing you itself in the very place it was born.

"I wish I did," she said as her tears mixed with her sweat. "Sometimes I do, but it's never enough."

Her voice trailed off into a half-felt whisper, and she turned away. There was nothing else to say, nothing I could say to calm her raging heart. Nothing to say that will earn my forgiveness. And so I stood and walked away. Maybe one day she would understand, but not today.

I left the room and gently shut the door as if I was sneaking out of her room before all this happened, pretending I could hear her laughter ringing from the inside.

Lucinda

"What's the best way to die?"
"Knowing you are loved."

The images were blinding me, the voices made my ears bleed, and the pain of it all was suffocating me. I couldn't bear it all. I had to wake up.

"She sees power in everything but herself and that is dangerous for her to think." My father's voice made it past the others. Then slowly faded back to the place of whispers and mystery.

I started to scream. I screamed and screamed until my throat burned with a thousand words. They flowed from me like blood from an open wound. I fell to my knees. I pounded the floor, the pain ripping at my flesh. All the grief and guilt from over the years came at me all at once...

I opened myself to it. I let fill me to the point of breaking; and then I let it all go. Like the tide coming in, then going out again after washing you clean.

I had forgiven everyone for breaking my heart, shattering my soul. Yet I hadn't forgiven myself. I hadn't forgiven myself for living on when my family couldn't. I hadn't forgiven myself for loving the Devil's son. Of how much of a sin that is in the eye of God.

I love him.

I loved him for who he was, who he could be, for who he is now.

And that was my biggest sin.

For loving evil. For forgiving him when he couldn't forgive himself.

But was he really, truly evil? Did darkness flow through him to control him, or to shield him from the judgement of others? For some reason I had always believed he was good, even before I knew him. And he proved it when he chose my safety over our love. He was willing to let me hate him in exchange for me to live. He may be the son of the Devil.

But he was also the son of God.

So what is true evil? Darkness is associated with it, but the kind of darkness I see around Peter...it was gentle, protective, understandable...

I could look into it and understand it.

Because the same darkness lives inside me too.

I remembered all the faces I have come to love in such a short space of time. To Jane's wild red hair and emerald green eyes, to Kyle's warm chocolate eyes and the cold heart he pretends to bear. Then to Peter...His beautiful blue eyes that captivate me every time I glimpse into them. Or his bronze hair that seems to melt in the sunlight, or how the colours in his wings make me feel so safe.

My heart has held so much over the years, yet it was nothing compared to what my new family has dealt with; but nevertheless, pain is pain, grief is grief. And heartache is heartache.

I could try to move on from Peter. I could try to save myself. But I knew that if I would attempt to move on, he would be *standing there, blocking my path with that smile made of stars and those eyes that held the universe.*

Yet how many times would I allow my heart to forgive him? How many times would I forgive myself for forgiving him? Is this what love is meant to be? It's strange how these feelings can creep up on us. How one person can make you ready to destroy yourself and the world along with it.

I guess you know you love someone when they have wronged you in the worst possible way and you are still willing to forgive them.

"What do you mean?" A little girl cried out from the darkness. The young girl came back into view, but she looked slightly older compared to how the first young girl did.

But it was still her.

"I have to go away now," Peter said with his back turned to me. He was bent before the child. Tears ran down her cheeks, and she was clutching his hands like they were her childhood doll.

"Did I do something bad?" she whimpered.

He shook his head and pulled her into his strong arms. Cradling her to his chest as a big brother would comfort his little sister.

He kissed the top of her head. "You didn't do anything. All you have ever done is bring me happiness. But I can't see you anymore…"

The little girl cried on.

"But why?"

"Because I'm no good for you my little Lucinda. You need to grow up with other children and enjoy being a child."

He pushed her back gently to arm's length and tucked her long hair back for her.

"But I don't want you to go away. I want you to stay."

The ache in her little voice tore at me.

"I know." His voice broke. "I know."

"Then stay…"

"Lucinda. Maybe one day you will understand. But I'm doing this for you. I know it's hard, but you have to trust me." He wiped away the tears that were running down her red cheeks. "I'll always be with you," he said as he pointed towards her heart. "I'll always be watching over you because you are my best friend. And that's what best friends do." He kissed her forehead and stood up,

his wings nowhere in sight. Just a boy saying goodbye to the only thing he ever had to call his.

"Goodbye my little Lucinda." And they vanished.

Everything shone once again. A deepness, a void of light that was quiet and soothing.

It was the throne room. But it was different. More settled, almost peaceful, as if all the power that kept it running died away and just the left the marble structure behind it.

I stepped forward, raising my hand to shield my eyes from the light that was letting me pass. And as I did, I saw a woman kneeling. Her gentle hands were clasped before her, her head lowered and eyes closed. Her pale yet glowing skin covered with shimmering robes, her hair spun into a simple crown upon her head. I stopped before her.

She was kneeling before the throne.

She looked up at me, her eyes burning, raging with something I'd never seen before.

I'd never seen her before in my life, yet the woman kneeling before me…I knew her better than I knew myself.

There was no expression on her face, just that burning nothingness. We existed there for a few seconds, watching each other.

Her eyes mirroring my own.

She had no wings, no divine power radiating from her except for the power that she was born with and not given. She didn't blink once. Just that steady gaze that ripped me apart and spilled the blood from my heart and onto the floor before us.

We were linked. I could feel a pull between us. A chain of private understanding that completed us both.

We've been waiting for each other.

She's been waiting for me to return…

"What a sight to behold, a woman kneeling before her throne instead of a man."

I turned away from the kneeling saint to the voice that called out to us.

I was alone.

No more voices.

No more visions.

"Who's there?"

Nothing.

I turned back to the woman. But she was no longer kneeling. I was. She stood before me and I kneeled before her. Her hands were still clasped before her, as if she was a centuries old sculpture that was crafted from the hands of the finest artist.

Chapter 24

"Whatever beauty you have known, you will know a thousand times more."

– Haffiz

Kyle

We made it to the Vatican City in less than two days. Peter was beyond himself with worry that I could hardly get him to focus. His eyes were crazy with war and destruction every time he looked at me. I could understand why others thought he was the end of everything. The end for the world. Each moment that passed I could see his heart darken with rage that was ready to explode at any given second. I worried about him. I have known for thousands of years that he could be the end for us all, but I never tried to stop him. Restrain him. End him in any way. Because he was my brother. My blood. But I know that there will come a time where I will have to step between him and the world; but I just hope he will be the one to take me down instead of it being me taking him down. Because I'm so selfish that I don't want to have to live with his blood on my hands.

The city was still in ruin. Everything destroyed. The palace was still slightly intact, so much so that we still had to knock on their door.

"Kyle!" he snapped as we stalked towards the Vatican palace. I sped up. Everything looked the same as before, when we came here to send Lucinda away. But the air was heavier, sadder.

Like the world understood our loss too.

"He should be here by now," he said again as we neared the doors. And he started to pound on the door.

"Open up!" he bellowed, but it did not open.

"Brother." I stepped forward and tried to place my hand on his shoulder, but he pushed me away with his gigantic wings.

I stumbled back onto the steps.

"Peter stop!"

"We can't!" he screamed as he turned to me. Fury laced in his features, so much that I could see his father hidden there in his face.

The rainbow in his feathers disappeared, his eyes darkened and so did his entire heart in that moment.

I held up my hands in surrender. "Just stop. *Breathe* Peter."

He closed his eyes. And took a deep breath.

"I can't lose her, I just can't."

"You won't. But if we carry on like this we will make a mistake that could hurt her. Remember, he has both Lucinda *and* Jane. He won't kill Lucinda, but he could kill Jane. We have to think. And stay calm." I clasped his shoulder and squeezed. "We will save them. But if you carry on like this you will lose control and then we are all lost."

He nodded. And then knocked on the door. And it opened.

The Priest from before opened it.

"That's more like it. You used some manners."

Silence.

Then I heard a horrible crunch and the priest was on the floor holding his bloody nose.

He'd punched him. Then, without a word, Peter simply stepped around him and walked down the grand hall.

I helped the stupid human up to his feet.

"Next time, you'll know to keep your mouth shut." He gave me a glare, then stumbled away.

Lord give me strength.

Chapter 25

"Forgiveness is a slow trickle. Like a heartbeat, like rain."
– Alison Malee

Lucinda

I looked up from where I was curled up on the floor. Light. Bright and blinding light concealed me in this white cell. Nothing else existed.

Then footsteps sounded from the other side of the door.

"He just said to bring her to him. We follow his orders."

The sound of jingling keys made its way into the cell.

"But what is he planning on doing with her?" another deep voice asked.

The lock turned.

"Who cares? It's not our problem."

They made their way in and stopped before my cold body. I didn't have the energy to move. I could only stare up at them.

"Are you sure she is even going to survive the trip to the throne room? She looks like Death gave her a good slap in the face," one of the guards said.

The one that spoke had soft eyes, eyes that held concern as they looked down at me. His hair was pure white, like snow graced his beautiful head. And his eyes where white too, like he had no irises. His skin was sun-kissed and made his hair and eyes stand out like he was the only star in the sky.

They pulled me to my feet and carried my useless body before the Devil's newly stolen throne. He raked his long talons across the marble again. It seemed to be his habit. His eyes were yet again harsh, like a soul that has seen all the horrors of the world and couldn't recover from it.

His smile was cruel. "Come here," he commanded. But he wasn't looking at me. My heart froze.

Then out of the new shadows that now covered every corner in this old temple, a familiar shape emerged.

227

She was the same.

Older. Older than she was when she had died.

But she was the girl I had always imagined her to look like if she had survived, if she had gotten the chance to grow up *with* me.

She wore a black gown that shimmered as she moved, as if diamonds were sewn in with the fabric like how the clouds perfectly sat with the sky. She naturally made the room bow to her. Her pale legs dominated the floor she walked on. The walls surrendered to the sound of her footsteps; the world shrunk back in retreat. She looked like someone who had bowed to men before and she had to learn the hard way that men should never be bowed to. She would bow for no one. Not even herself.

She didn't look at me. But I still saw how black her eyes had become. They sucked in the world and gave nothing back. Like black holes, they held secrets that were not meant to be in a woman's eyes, but in her heart. Her light ginger hair was cut shorter than I remembered, just above her shoulders now, beautifully curled. It bounced with each footstep, the dance of a now darkened beauty.

Her wings were matte black, each feather as sharp as any blade. I could feel a sting on my skin just by looking at them. They towered around her, framing her. But the most remarkable thing about them was that in the perfect lighting, the feathers shimmered gold, as if the edges of them still showed us that a part of her will always belong to Heaven, not just Hell.

She stopped before us, no emotion showed on her beautiful face as she finally looked at me.

I choked on my tears.

"Arianne."

Chapter 26

"Be careful in the world of men, Diana. They do not deserve you."
– 'Wonder Woman'

Gabriel

"I have a plan," Kyle said with a bounce in his step as he circled the map of Heaven.

Peter arched an eyebrow at his brother.

I rolled my eyes.

"Kyle, I don't plan on dying today."

I stepped forward to pull the map away from him, but he placed his hand down before I could even lay a finger on it.

He smirked. "Oh don't you worry general." His smirk grew. "Your day of judgement will not be today. In fact I can guarantee that everyone will get out alive."

Peter jumped in. "How so?"

The blond angel looked between us as his smirk grew even bigger.

And he told us his insane plan.

Chapter 27

Jane

My head throbbed. My back screamed in pain, the kind of pain that I have tried so hard to forget. I felt sticky. Cold and sticky. I opened my sore eyes to the blinding light around me.

I was in a cell.

Its walls were all too familiar to me.

Like an old foe that had once presented itself to be my ally, it had finally come back to mock me while I bathed in my despair.

"You are awake."

My mother's voice echoed against the white walls that were now stained with blood, probably my blood. She sat against the wall opposite from me, her pale arms chained above her sweaty head. Her pretty white dress was ripped and hung around her in tatters; the white blond hair that was once curled around her crown, that now no longer sat upon her head, fell around her like disrupted waves of an ocean. She looked broken, almost broken enough that I felt bad for her.

I sat up straighter on the cold floor.

"What happened?" I demanded. I tried to move my arms, but soon realised mine too were chained above my head.

She sighed as she watched me.

"He has her," was all she said.

I pulled and pulled on my chains, but they didn't budge. They should have broken off easily but-

"We have been injected with Hell fire. It's no use," she clarified.

That's why she couldn't magic herself out of here. He dampened her powers. And mine.

I leaned back.

"Then how do we get out of here."

She shook her head. "We don't."

"You're optimistic," I grunted as I moved to get comfy.

"Are you ok?" She tried to move forward as if she wanted to hear me better.

I narrowed my eyes.

"Don't act like you care."

"Jane," she sighed. "I've always cared. You've just chosen not to see it."

I looked around at the cell and came to realise why it seemed so familiar to me. Every inch of the once crystal white walls was nearly all red; a burgundy red that had haunted my dreams every night for the past thousand years.

The red hand prints on the door.

The old rusted chains on the far wall.

The echoed screams of long ago memories was as soft as the inside of a broken heart.

This was *my* cell.

Everything came crashing back. Everything I had buried in the deepest corners of my mind came creeping back like the waves of a storming ancient sea.

I could remember my bony wrists that were chained to the walls that now surrounded me. How my skin was so bruised and beaten I could hardly move. And when I *could* move, even just a little, I could remember the sound of my wounds tearing open again and again. All because they were too infected to heal properly.

They kept me in constant darkness, yet it became my only friend.

They wiped me until my back was nothing more than torn flesh that showed only my spine and split muscles.

The pain was unbearable.

But I never made a sound.

I wouldn't give them that satisfaction.

"If you don't tell me where he is, I *will* kill you," the man had hissed into my face.

I had been starved for weeks, beaten for weeks, but because of the angelic essence that clung to my soul, I wouldn't die. But still I had the energy to spit into his face, grinning as the saliva dripped from my split chin. He lifted his hand and wiped it away. Eyes burning with anger – anger and terrifying viciousness. He turned his back and braced his hands at his sides, knuckles turning as white as the walls around us. Yet I stood tall and proud. I would never give my brother away…

He clicked his fingers and two guards came in through the blood-stained door. He faced me again with chewed lips and a grim expression.

"It's such a shame," he said as if he really meant it.

I knew what he really meant, what he was really about to do.

"What is?" I leaned my bleeding back against the cool and soothing stone wall. "That your precious God isn't brave enough to do it herself?" I couldn't help but scoff at him.

The chains begun to dig into my wrists again. I could feel the bitter metal bite my flesh once again.

"Why are you doing this for him? We all know he wouldn't do this for you or Kyle, so why not just give him up and we will let you go?"

"No!"

"Why!"

"He is my brother!"

"And you are his sister, yet here you are."

I only grinned.

"I always wondered how our God could create an angel like you," he said while shaking his head in wonder.

I began to laugh, screech, scream as my throat burned from my laughing. It was uncontrollable. It wasn't until the tears were rolling down my dirty and pale face did I stop. And after all this time of being trapped in here with the darkness, I used the light from the door to really look at myself. My clothes were ripped away to show my poor, naked body. Deep wounds covered me like tattoos humans liked to get. I could see how red and raw they were; gaping open like the mouth of fishes struggling for air. I was filthy. Blood, fresh and old, seemed to replace my skin now. Blood was all I could see now. It was all over the walls, all over the floors. I knew maggots had made their home in the ripples of my broken flesh in my back. I could feel them every day and night as they moved and ate away the rotting skin that was still attached to me. It was so painful. Yet I never made a sound. The only thing they never touched on me were my wings.

I looked back up at him.

"When you are on your knees begging for your life when my brother finally rises, then you will understand why God gave birth to someone like me." I sat back, no longer strong enough to move. "A perfect angel like you will never understand what it's like to survive in a world like this. What I have had to give up, what I have had to do."

But he didn't care for what I had to say.

By my hair, he pulled my head forward to unlock my neck chain that bounded me to the wall. Then he did the same to my wrists and the rest of my chains. When I was free and laying on the floor, the two guards grabbed my arms and held them up and locked new chains to my wrists. They pulled my hands forward and flat against the floor before me, leaving my battered back exposed.

He leaned down to my bloodied ear. "May God have mercy on your soul."

Finally, he stepped away. The look on his face was of pure regret and sadness. As if he thought he had no choice in what he was about to do. Yet he didn't look away.

The two other men pierced my wings with two rusted hooks.

I did not scream at the pain.

The blood fell onto my face. Drop by drop. Blood painted my face anew.

Yet I did not let out a sound.

But when they started to pull, when the torn flesh that now made up my back started to tear open again. When the maggots started to fall out of my decaying flesh. When my spin started to separate from my wings, when the sound of bones cracking vibrated through my body.

That was the moment I screamed.

That day, millions of angels heard my screams. Even the kingdom of Hell heard me. But it wasn't until weeks later that I was actually released from that cell I now call home. I was left with scars across my body that were spoken about for years to come. The angry and ugly scars that now decorated my body, they asked me about them all the time. But I didn't have the heart to answer them. I couldn't. But they noticed how I changed. They noticed how I went from my carefree, loving self to the distant, hateful person I was now. I couldn't bare the touch of another, to look another angel in the eye. Or even to speak. I shut myself away, locked everything I was left under lock and key.

And I never regained my sanity.

I had to give everything I was to overcome what they did to me.

And the biggest price was my sanity.

They made me a wild creature, then tried to put me down for it.

But they only made me angry, savage…And broken.

Being insane isn't the thing that makes me insane. But having that small piece of sanity left, to understand that I was losing myself.

"Jane!"

I snapped back to reality.

I was wrapped up by chains I could feel the rusty edges bite my bruised skin. I couldn't see the angels pulling me away because of the beautiful metal helmets they wore over their faces. I looked back towards God. She struggled against her own chains. Tearing at her own flesh to get free. The look of panic on her face pulled at my heart.

"Don't hurt her!" she screamed. "Jane!"

"I'll be ok," was all I could say before I was pulled away from the cell completely.

And all I could hear was God screaming my name, before she came to an abrupt halt. And went silent.

Chapter 28

"The Romans feared her [Cleopatra] as they has feared only Hannibal, and they created a legend that survives to this day."
— Sarah Pomeroy

Lucinda

I stood completely frozen.

And she just watched me, tears rolling down her beautiful face. Her glorious wings were shaking as I watched the emotion rush through her. The room around us seemed to close in, like how the volcano Vesuvius enclosed Pompeii with millions of tons of ash.

She stepped forward on trembling legs. "Lucinda," she whispered.

We ran for each other and collapsed into each other's arms. We fell to the floor in a pile of cries and laughter.

The laughter of two little girls.

The sound echoed off the grey stained walls. Echoed memories that had long since died.

Relief filled every corner of my soul in that moment. It was a feeling that I thought I would never know again. The feeling that you were no longer alone.

She felt the same, so warm. So light.

She held on to me.

And I to her.

And she said the very thing that I had waited so long to hear.

"I'm here." She hugged me harder. "I'm here…"

But the moment was ruined by the man in the big chair.

"Yes, yes, this is all very sweet but we have things to do Lucinda." He called for me and I stepped forward, angling my body so I was just before my friend. If anything happened, I wanted to be her shield.

"What things." My tone was hard, distant.

His eyes narrowed, "Have you done what I have asked?"

I was silent.

"Lucinda!" his voice warning me to give him the answer he wanted. But I couldn't. And I knew that if I couldn't defeat him, then I would do everything in my power to keep my star away from him. I may be just a human, a structure kept up only with bones, blood and flesh. But that in itself was a powerful thing. And I was brave. I was brave to stand here and defy the Devil himself. To stand up for what I believed in when I knew it could be the end of me. The end of everyone I loved. Peter. The great love of my life. He stood against his own parents for me, for what was right. For what he wanted, even though he thought he would parish from it all. He stood defiant and strong for me, for his siblings, for the world he loved so much. So I could do the same. I would *be* the same.

Arianne stepped forward and gripped my hand.

And I knew she would stand by me, go down with me, die with me if need be. Because we are the heroes behind the scenes. The ones who would sacrifice themselves even if that meant that our names disappeared from history.

I held my head high.

"No."

"No?" he hissed.

"No," I repeated.

"How dare you!" he roared as he rose from the mighty throne.

"No. How dare you."

He blinked.

"You think that because our views and opinions aren't yours, you can try to destroy us for it. You think that just because you have been scolded by a woman, you can stop love flourishing between the entire world. But that's not the way things work." I let go of my friend's hand and started to climb the steps. "Don't you see Lucifer? You will never win because what you are isn't what the world is meant to be. Yes, there will always be good and evil. But neither will win because both need each other." I stopped before his burning face. "You won't ever win because you are all alone. You can kill me, you could kill everyone. Yet you wouldn't prevail because even if there was only one person left. They would never bow to you."

I smiled at my brave words.

"You cannot have my star. It is mine, it is a part of me. As much as a part of me as the blood that runs through my veins. Kill me, it returns to the skies. Or even let me live for the years to come, you will never have it. Never."

He was silent, his wicked eyes working their way around us. And I just stared back at him. The fallen angel of Heaven, who was once God's favourite. The male of music and light.

The morning star.

I was starting to understand how the character of someone was decided by everyone around them, not by who they *wanted* to be. So it was difficult to judge the male before me. Is he evil by who he is, or by how he was treated? Or just because he wanted to be evil. Is it possible that people can make others evil?

Yet without the darkness, we would never truly know the light.

"I know that you think that because I am part human that I am weak. But it does not. It makes us stronger than even *you.*"

"And how did you figure that out?" he sniggered.

But all I could do was smile. "Because our biggest power is holding the pain of so many others without breaking. So do what you will, but you will never break me!"

Silence.

Only the Devil's glaring eyes trying to weigh me down. But they could not. Nothing could.

"Was that you trying to be a badass?"

We all turned.

Overwhelming joy and relief filled me at the sight before us. He was *here.* I wanted to run into his arms and skip our way out of here. But alas, I was not the only prisoner here that needed to be saved.

Kyle was leaning against one of the pillars with his leg crossed over the other. That usual smirk was plastered over his perfect lips. He strolled towards the Devil, each movement overly confident; the body of a lazy panther. He stopped, cocked his head to the side, ran his tongue across his bottom lip, and smirked again.

"Kyle."

He inclined his head. "Lucifer."

"What can we do for you?" The Devil chuckled as he leaned back down into the throne.

"Well," Kyle said. "As you have probably guessed by now, I'm not here because I'm home sick. But I *am* here to bring a certain someone home."

"Is that so."

"Yes."

237

Lucifer scratched his chin and grinned. "And why would I let you do that?"

"Because I have your only weakness," Kyle answered with a vicious voice.

Then he yanked the chain I hadn't realised he was holding forward with a harsh force. God stumbled forward in a heap of shredded robes, blood and sweat. It was surprising how low someone could bring a creature of Heaven down to. She looked up at her son and spat at his feet.

"You will pay for this," she hissed.

His eyes were disturbingly wild. "I already have." And he kicked her forward.

I felt Ari hold me closer to her. To keep me close? Or to reassure herself? I couldn't tell. Maybe it was both.

Lucifer stared down at her, the wild and demented woman before him. Before her lost throne.

Now his throne.

His eyes didn't move, she didn't move; they just sat there, watching each other. Yet even though there were no words spoken, or smiles of encouragement. I think we could all see the bond there, that tether that forever linked them together. And I saw how they could never stop the love they felt for each other because it was a part of them, even down to the way they looked at the world.

The problem wasn't that there wasn't enough love, or enough *fight* for that love. But that they both thought that the love would be the end of the other.

And suddenly, in that moment, I couldn't hate them.

"And what makes you think she is my weakness?" The Devil smirked as he clasped his grey hands together.

"Ok." The blonde male shrugged as he moved towards the scattered woman, pulled her mattered hair back with a rough tug and held a beautifully crafted dagger to her slender neck. The Devil did not so much as flinch. "So you wouldn't mind if I just got rid of her then?"

No one moved. No one dared to. The walls around me hissed and whispered as their ruler sat defiant with her life hanging like a noose around Kyle's neck. Yet her son held no emotion on his face, no lines of guilt or disdain of what he was doing.

They watched each other.

God and the Devil.

They watched each other like how the sun watches the moon. Destined to one day clash together and set the world ablaze.

She could be his kingdom's weight in gold, and he would still pay the price.

And it wasn't until the red liquid that kept us all alive began to stain her skin, stain her once beautiful dress that Lucifer shifted in his chair.

"Think about what you are doing boy!" His grey skin was hard and unchanging as the redness flowed across his once upon a time lover.

"Oh, I have. I have thought about doing this for millions of years. So trust me, I have thought this through." His mother's gurgles filled the decaying room. The look in his eyes, as if his eyes had misted over, and I understood. It was years beyond years of loneliness and hurt mixed together ready to explode. Wanting to explode. He was tired of being alone and being the strong level-headed man everyone wanted to believe he was. And like his siblings, he wanted to break. He wanted to let it all out. To scream and shatter the world. Soon, too soon, I knew it would be his turn to take his vengeance out on everyone who has ever hurt him.

When that time comes, I will pass him his weapons and step back to watch as he brings his chaos and dread. And I will gladly watch as he burned the world to ground. I would help him, aid him. And hopefully when my time comes, he will help me in return.

"How many innocents have fallen beneath your blade, Kyle Hellfire? How many have you watched die?"

I watched as the blonde warrior stood with his weapon at the ready, it piercing his giver of life's neck.

"I may be holding the sword." Kyle's eyes burned as he gripped the weapon to his mother's neck, his hateful stare on her like a vice. "But it was you that brought me here. You cast me out, and it was you that sharpened the blade."

We held our breath.

"I have Lilith!"

Kyle stilled. His face fell, but only enough so that only the people that knew him well would notice the change. The hand that held the knife hovered there against his mother's neck, neither moving away and neither cutting deeper.

"What?" the angel asked, his words a whisper.

Again that cocky, misshapen smirk returned to that grey face.

"She never left." No one had spoken since Kyle had entered the room, but now even the stone stopped to listen. "She has been here all along, waiting for you to return."

I wanted to hold him, the look on his face. It was as if his heart was going to fall through and out of the skies around us.

"Where is she?"

"Let Lola go first, and I will tell you."

He hesitated, but soon obliged. He lifted the stunning knife and let his mother go. She crawled away, clutching at her sliced throat. And instead of coming to us, she climbed the stairs. Not going to her lover, nor her family. But she stood alone. And I realised that all Gods had to. They all had to stand alone, even in the face of death.

"Now." Kyle gripped the dagger harder as he approached the man in the throne. "Where is she?"

No words, not even a crooked smirk, just a wave of a hand. And she appeared.

Among the shadows came a walking pillar of steel and metal hardness. A dark skinned goddess of the darkest nights and the brightest of moons. She had long sculpted legs, as smooth as polished stone. High cheekbones and big full lips, the perfect face to bring a warrior to their knees. Her long black dreads swiped side to side as she strolled into the greyish light around us. They reached her little ankles and hid her well-muscled back; but they didn't hide the fact that she bore no wings. Was she human? Something else? She looked at none of them, not even Kyle as she passed. But she did look to me as she passed by; her eyes were white, no pupils. Nothing. Just an endless white. Time seemed to slow down as she watched me, our eyes meeting. I didn't fear her, but I could sense everyone else did.

Then she turned away.

She climbed the steps to her master's throne and stood beside him, back straight and face proud. She wore a long flowing white robe that matched her pale eyes. It was extraordinary against her mid-night skin. A perfect yin and yang.

"Lilith," the Devil called. "Look who came home to visit."

She looked at her past plaything, grinned to show her even whiter teeth. "Kyle… I've always loved the name Kyle. I've missed saying it out loud." She seemed to roll his name across her tongue.

He couldn't help but stutter. "Thank–thank you. I like yours too." Shocked that the love of his life was right in front of him after so long. It seemed he couldn't come up with anything better to say.

"Idiot," someone muttered from the shadows.

He stepped forward with every kind of weapon I could imagine strapped to every inch of his body. Ready to fight and defend. The joy I felt when I saw Kyle grew by a thousand. And it didn't seem to stop as I let a whimper escape from my lips at the sight of him. He eyes were dark, his glorious wings were out and proud. They held strong against his back, ready for any command. He was wearing the very armour I had envisioned him in for months. That beautifully tinted silver, that darkened metal shone in the window's light. I instantly felt stronger, now braver that he was here.

"Peter," was all I could say.

He did not smile, did not take his eyes away from mine as he approached further into the room. He walked straight up to me, not caring if he knocked anyone out of the way, not caring that the world was hanging around us in tatters. I held my arms out as he swooped me up into his powerful arms and swung me in a huge circle.

"*Lucinda.*" His voice cracked as he repeated my name over and over again. As if he was reciting the sacred words of heaven. "My Lucinda."

He cradled my head as he set me down. No one else would have noticed, but I saw the beginning of tears in his eyes. But I wiped them away before anyone could see.

"You're here, you're really here." I was laughing and crying as I traced his face.

He nodded his head.

"I'm here." He kissed my lips tenderly, savouring the taste of me. "I'm here."

"Oh the irony," Lucifer piped up again. Peter growled as he turned towards his father. He held me to his back, needing the feel of me against him to keep his mind calm. "Now, have you ever heard a more tragic story than not quite doomed love?"

"Let them go!" Peter roared.

"You all keep demanding the same shit too! But what would I get in return?" The Devil held his arms out to us, as if we could magic a present out of thin air.

But the answer we got in return wasn't what any of us were expecting.

"Me…"

Chapter 29

"Beauty will save the world."
– Fyodor Dostoyevsky

Lucinda

"You would give yourself up?" His father didst seem to believe him, and I didn't want to.

"What?" I demanded as I faced him, but he wouldn't look down at me. He just stared up at his father.

The room went into shook. Even that woman Lilith looked unnerved.

"Only if you let everyone go. Lucinda, Lola, Kyle and our sister. Everyone trapped here must be set free. If you do that, I'm all yours."

"No! I won't let you do this!" I looked to his father, to the similar face of the man I loved. *"Please! He is your son!"*

"Maybe in a few years you will learn that power is more important than family," was all the grey faced monster said.

I turned back to Peter. "Please," I wailed. He looked everywhere but at me. "Peter! I'm begging you. Don't do this, we can find another way!"

"This is the only way."

I couldn't bear to look at him any longer. I turned to the Devil.

"Take me instead." I could feel Peter's eyes on me then. "Cut out the star. I give my life instead of Peter's. Take me, not him."

He pulled me back by my arm, betrayal plain on his face. *"What are you doing?!"*

But I said nothing as I looked back to the Devil.

"Deal?"

We all waited for his defining answer.

"I respect you both, believe it or not. But you seem to forget that I am millions of years old," he said. "I am tired. I'm not after all this power for myself, but for my heir. I want to pass onto another world and rest." He stood and clasped his hands behind his back. "I'm sick of playing all these games. I have played *every* game there is. So I respect you want to fight for each other. But it's over. I'm done playing."

"I'm not playing you. I give myself up to you in his place."

His eyes threw accusations and deceit at me.

"Have you forgotten about what he has done? He killed your brother and father. And yet you would still die in his place?"

"I forgive him." I turned to him. He stood there, arms to his side, eyes utterly open to me. No darkness lingered there anymore. "I forgive you. I forgive you for what you did."

"That's it?" Lucifer said.

"No." No, it wasn't. "I can't believe you did that, hurt them, hurt me. And I don't want to imagine what else you have done over the years, before me or after. But we are all sinners here. We have all committed the worst kind of sins that have blackened our hearts. And mine is that I can't hate you for what you have done, for what you are doing now. For saving me and for now trying to leave me." He lifted his hand to mine, and I couldn't stop my own from lacing my fingers through his. "But I will never hate you for it. Even though I should. And that will always be my biggest sin. Loving you when I should hate you."

He pulled me into his arms. And kissed the top of my head.

"Peter, I take your deal," the Devil said quietly, too quietly.

Panic and dread filled me. I tried to push Peter away, push him to fly away and be safe. But he held fast. And it wasn't until the woman Lilith came up behind me that Peter handed me over with a last kiss and a face of apologies.

"No! Stop!" But it was too late. Peter bent before the Devil and did not fight when the guards dressed in black metal pulled his glorious wings back and chained them down. Pain flashed across his face at the awkward position they were bent into. Then they handcuffed his hands behind his back and stripped him of any weapons.

"Peter please! Take it back!"

He said nothing. He only looked at me, and the way he was looking at me.

He knew this would be the last time we would ever see each other…

Everyone roared, everyone tried to run to him. But it was too late. More of the Devil's angels surrounded us. Weapons at the ready and aimed at us all. Jane thrashed in one of the guard's arms as they pinned her down like a wild and crazed animal. Lola tried to run to her children, but an arrow was fired, and with a gurgling scream it pinned her to a pillar. Kyle, with bow and arrow at the ready, aimed it at anyone that came near him. He stood tall. He stood ready to lay his life on the line.

"Brother! Get up! We can fight through this!" He sounded strong. He sounded as if he believed his own words too. But we all knew it was a lie.

I struggled against the women's grip. She was strong, unnaturally strong. She was like a human sized vice around my arms and waist.

And all I could do was scream as the biggest of the guards came up behind the angel holding a long leather whip and a horribly cruel smirk as he first injected him with a silver substance. Then lifted the whip into the air and brought it down with a sound like the clap of thunder.

Yet he did not scream. He did not let out a single sound. He was silent. But he let the pain show on his contorted face. He seemed drunk, dazed from whatever they put into him. But he could still feel all that pain.

"Stop!" I screamed over and over again. But with every strike of that whip, he did not let out a single sound. He just watched me. As if I was the only thing keeping him from breaking. Blood sprayed everywhere around him. His beautiful feathers landed around him like a halo. Then the whip hit his cheek and I snapped. I smashed my head back into Lilith's face, most likely breaking her perfect nose. She flung me forward to cradle her face and I ran towards him. And as the next lashing of the whip came down, I covered him as best as I could. Leaving my own back vulnerable for the slaughter.

"Wait!" Peter screamed while trying to turn to me, trying to shield me once again. But I didn't want him to. I wanted to shield *him* this time.

The first lashing was brutal. It was the kind of pain that was so overwhelming that nothing else had space to cloud my mind. It hit my flesh like the ringing of bells, like the coldness of the ocean in winter. Like the clashing of a thousand swords in mid-war. But I held Peter harder, closer as he let his screams ring through the throne room around us. It was only now, when I was the one being hurt, that he let his screams be heard. The whip came down and down on me like a wave after wave. Over and over again.

Again and again.

Again and again.

Again and again.

Lash after lash.

I could hear in the distance Jane's wailing, that poor broken sound. I didn't even see her come in. But it was Kyle, Kyle's screams that really tore at my heart. He didn't scream for his brother. He cried yes, but he didn't scream. He didn't thrash against the guards. But now he did. For me. He screamed over and over, my name echoing off his tongue like a battle cry of a losing army.

And I let it happen. I screamed and cried as the harsh leather bit my beaten flesh. Because that meant it wasn't touching Peter. It meant he was safe. But then it stopped.

I lifted my sore neck from Peters shoulder, his blood painting my cheek bright red. I looked down at him, at his shocked and pale face.

"*Lucinda…*" He choked on his words and tears fell from his eyes. And I knew that what I had just done. Had hurt him more than any lashing. But I didn't care. If he had to suffer, then I would too.

"That was quite a show," the Devil said while clapping his hands. He lowered from the throne, climbed down from the steps and came to rest before us. "The power of love is truly something else."

He kneeled down and looked us in the eye. He examined his son's beaten flesh, then mine. He scrapped his nail across my raw muscle, drawing out of me a sound that belonged to an animal locked in a cage. He looked at the scraps of flesh now under his nails, no expression of any kind to be seen. He stood up and smirked again.

"Such a shame, and you had such pretty flesh for a human," the Devil snickered.

Peter roared. He roared until his throat sounded raw and burned. Struggling against his chains, he spat blood at his father's feet. But he did nothing. He only waved his hand to one of his lap dogs. And before I could say anything, I was ripped away from Peter. The last thing I saw was the angel look at me one last time before collapsing to the floor in a bloodied heap. His wings covering his split back. I screamed. I screamed until my throat was burning, raw and spitting blood. And I only stopped when something hard and cold hit the top of my head. And I blacked out.

Chapter 30

"I'm caught in between what I wish and what I know."

– Lauv

Lucinda

I think when it comes down to grief, I would prefer the pain over everything else. Why? Because when you lose someone they leave a gap in your life. Pain isn't the worst thing about grief…that hole is. That numb, endless hole. Pain fills it with something. And the worst part of it all is when we don't even have pain to fill it. It's only that sinking, dark gap that will never go away. A reminder for the rest of your life of what you have lost. Pain is the distraction. The nothingness is reality. It is only now that I truly understand it, the pain, the true meaning of lose. Death is not the only form. My loved ones are still alive. For now. But they are still alive. But I have lost them. Lost them all.

I felt the self-hatred and utter self-disgust, like a snake withering through my blood. I wasn't worth the bloodshed that has followed us here, followed me here. I have brought chaos to my family, and all for what? A weapon? A star that now didn't seem like it was worth anything. I couldn't even use it to help anyone. To help myself.

"Astralis…" someone, or something hissed from behind my eyelids.

"Hello?" My lips hadn't moved, but my voice rang out loud and clear. I couldn't see where I was, but it was dark and it was bright. It was cold and it was warm. Everything was in an 'in-between' state.

"You're finally here," it said again. I wasn't afraid of it. Even though I couldn't see it and something in the centre of my stomach told me I didn't want to. I reached out for it. I wanted to touch it. I could feel the loneliness radiate off it.

"Who are you?"

246

It brushed up against my hand and I could feel centuries old scales ripple at my touch.

It seemed to shiver at the slightest of touches. It was defiantly lonely. Even the feeling of flesh on flesh was unfamiliar to it now.

"We have waited a very long time for you Astralis."

"How do you know me?" I pulled my hand away.

"Everyone knows you here. You are a part of every single creature to ever exist." It brushed up against my leg, its scales freezing to the touch. "We have waited for the star to return and save us all. To set us free."

I could feel millions of eyes set themselves upon me.

"Who. Are. You?"

It stopped before me.

"You may call me Serpent."

"Serpent," I repeated, testing it out on my tongue.

"I like it when you say it," it said, voice low. "You don't say it so…Harshly."

"Why are we here? I can't help you."

"And why do you think that? You have all this power at your fingertips. You were born to save us all."

I shook my head. "No Serpent. I cannot help you. I have tried so hard, so very hard to help the people I love. But I have let them all down. I don't want to have to let you down too." I touched my cheek, and tears had fallen from my eyes.

I looked back to it. "I am so broken. Too broken to help anyone."

It took a deep breath before answering. "You see power in everything else but yourself. And for someone like you, that is incredibly dangerous."

It was silent for a few moments.

"We are all broken in our own ways Astralis. Each and every one of us has had our fair share in being broken. But we all eventually overcome it, no matter how long it takes us. We all heal. And most of the time, we don't even realise we have until we look in the mirror, and all the cracks we once saw have glazed over." It slithered closer. "You have loved and lost, shattered and fallen back together. You think that because you have been broken, that you can no longer be strong. But my dear sweet thing." It stroked my face. "By becoming broken, we also become stronger. Stronger than we ever have been before. You are Astralis, Lucinda sky. The human that not only holds a star, but is one. You hold the heart of the Devil's son, you are the daughter of all the past Gods. They

made you, they gave you this power for no one else but yourself."
It let me go. "You are broken, but use that. Let that be a part of your power. Let it drive you so you can save what you have left, who you have left."

"But most of all." It moved away. "Don't allow them to break you any further. Show them, show them the power of which you hold. Show them who you are."

It held its hand out to me, and I reached up. Then I realised I had been kneeling the whole time. I've been kneeling all my life, bowing to whatever the world had seen fit to throw at me.

But now it was my time to stop bowing. I will never bow again. For no man or beast.

And so I gripped its scaly hand, wiped away my tears for the last time.

And arose.

Chapter 31

"And sometimes you held somebody's hand just to prove that you were still alive, that another human being was there to testify that fact."

– 'Rainbow Rowell'

Jane

It was brutal. The blood. The flying pounds of flesh after each whipping.

Is that what I looked like when it had happened to me?

Kyle

When that whip came down upon her smooth back...

I have never wanted to kill anyone so much as I had in that moment. I wanted to kill that guard and make him suffer. I wanted to kill everything in sight.

She was my friend.

And I couldn't stop them from hurting her.

Peter-

I thought about her busted back, how the skin had torn so easily. How I hadn't stopped it. How I couldn't, because if I had tried to, they would have just killed her before us all.

All I have ever wanted to do was hold all the guilt and grief so my family didn't have to. That was how I wanted to repay them for everything they have ever done for me. But I let them down, and now I've let Lucinda down.

And now... now I'm not going to live long enough to say I'm sorry.

Lucinda

My head throbbed. It pulsed uncontrollably through my skull like a ticking-time bomb. But nevertheless, I pushed for my eyes to open. And when I did, I came to find all my beloved faces crowded around me. All but one…

"Peter…" I croaked out of my dry mouth.

No one spoke. They only looked away. I had hoped it was all a horrid dream. But I had to see it to know. And now I know. I sat up, bones cracking as I moved. I looked down at myself. I saw ribbons of clothing that barely covered me now. Blood against the once pure white fabrics.

And all at once the sounds of the whip, the echo of blood landing onto the marble, the screams of my family around me. It all came rushing back, too hard and too fast that I felt nauseous.

Jane held onto me.

"Easy now girl, it's ok. I've bandaged you up. But you need to take it easy."

I sat up all the way. Yet again we were in the cells, but at least I wasn't alone. Kyle sat in the corner, head hanging low. Lola, beaten and pathetic, sat near the door trying to catch some rays of sunshine. Ari, she was by my side holding my bruised hand. Smiling down at me. A memory came back to me. We were children again. I was lying in the middle of the street, knee cut and bleeding into my favourite pair of sparkly trousers. But as we waited for my father to come, she held my hand and wouldn't stop smiling as she comforted me. That smile, so bright and warm. Like my own personal sun to warm my heart whenever I needed it.

I looked back to Jane. "I'm sorry."

From the look in her eyes, she knew what I was apologising for. And I knew that she was sorry too.

"Where is he?" I asked.

But it was Arianne that answered me. "We don't know. No one does. When you both went under, we tried to fight them, but we were outnumbered. They took him. And we were thrown in here."

I sat up all the way, wincing as the pain radiated from my back.

"What will he do to him?"

They all knew what I meant, but this time it was Kyle who answered my question.

"The only thing he can do." We all looked at him. "Peter will never agree to become his heir. He won't be what they want him to be. The monster who brings down the angelic dynasty once and for all. But for Lucinda?" He lifted his head to look at me, using that cold and closed expression to tear me down. "For Lucinda he will do anything. Before we came up here we both knew that Lucifer wouldn't ask him again to be his heir. But for something else. Something worse." His eyes softened ever so slightly, just as he brother's always did whenever they looked at me. "He will ask for his power, his wings. And for you? He will gladly give in to that request."

My heart stopped, then started, then stopped again.

"He can't," I whispered.

Kyle shook his head. "He already has…"

A thought came to me as I looked at Kyle from across the cell. Of how much of an awful person he could be sometimes. But also that he was the one with the biggest heart. The worst kind of people were once the kindest, but then they are ruined. And become what Kyle is now. Bitterly broken.

I felt sick. He couldn't do this. He wouldn't leave me.

But…

If it meant saving my life. Then he would. Even if it cost him his own.

I stood up, crusted blood falling from my ripped back. But I ignored the pain. I didn't want to feel anymore. I thought back to all those months with him, and all those years that I might never get to remember. I thought back to how angry he has made me feel, how furious I was at his choices, how he had decided them without me to protect me. I remembered how he made my blood biol. In the best way and the worst way. I thought back to how he has lied to me, challenged me, challenged my morals and my own choices and beliefs. How every time he touched me…

Right there, I could feel it. A tiny flutter at the very core of my chest. Almost too small to believe that for a second I thought it was just a figment of my insane mind. But it was there, struggling wholeheartedly to beat on for its host. And it has been so long since I have felt it, my heart…

I still had a heart.

He didn't just make me feel safe and beautiful, secure and protected. But he was the man that made me feel everything all at once. And I realised that over the last few months, over the past few years. He saved me. I was empty of everything. I had nothing left inside me. But he brought it all to the surface. Every raw and hideous angry emotion I had for the world, he brought out in a whirlwind. He brought me back to life by showing me it. And in the process, he showed me what it was to love again, what it was to feel something for someone again.

Yet he still thought that after all that, he wasn't good enough for any of it. He thought that the asking price for it all was his life.

There.

There I could feel something.

Anger rumbled through me. Something deep and ancient awoke in the centre of me, and it was flowing through me. Rushing through my limbs, every pore, every cell, every strand of hair was alight with it.

It rushed through me like every piece of energy there was in a storm. As if the sky stored its heart inside my own. I could feel it all.

Everything.

I could feel everything.

I *was* everything.

My ears hummed to its calling. The sunlight warmed my skin even though none of it could reach past these stone walls. I could feel the stone slowly moving, the tiny creatures that lived on our skin breathe. Everything that existed, or ever has, or ever will. I could feel, touch and hear like it was second nature. As if everything was a part of me.

It overwhelmed me.

It all rushed and crushed itself inside my body, my lungs, my heart.

I breathed it all in.

Then let it all go.

Chapter 32

"I know this: you can break before you sleep and start becoming whole again the next morning."

– Juansen Dizon

Lola

Yet again I was dragged before the angel I once loved. Who in some ways I'll always love. He didn't blink, didn't move as I stumbled forward onto the cold marble floor before *my* throne.

I looked up. And he looked back.

"It's over now Lola, you are defeated." He sat up straighter in my chair, and a half-hearted smirk made its way across his face.

I only laughed. "Yet you will never win."

"And what makes you think that?" He chuckled. "Your walls have fallen, so have your armies. Your children that could have saved you are in my cells, soon to die. I have your weapon. You have fallen."

I looked at him. He seemed so happy. So proud.

I remember the first moment I ever looked into those black holes in his beautiful but now greyish face. Something in me broke. Snapped. Fell apart so painfully that I nearly cried out in pain in front of the entire court. And looking back at that moment, I realised that that *something* never fixed itself. As he changed, I changed. As he shattered, I shattered. Like our souls really were the same.

But now…

But now they were so different, twisted into creatures that we could no longer recognise.

We were once each other's salvation.

But now we were each other's demons.

He may have gained the world. But soon he will realise that when he looks around to share in his glory, he will realise he has lost everything else in the process.

253

"Oh Lucifer." He stopped his chuckling. "How thou has fallen," I said in the greatest of pity. He only stared me down, as if I would crush under the weight of his stare.

But it seemed he had forgotten who I was.

I was God.

I can never fall.

He sighed. "I remember when you loved me, loved the way I thought about the world. You wanted the same world as me once. What changed?" he asked, voice strangely gentle.

I didn't answer for a few seconds. I was too scared to speak the truth that I had been hiding for so long.

"In the beginning, you wanted to help me. You wanted to change the world for the better. You wanted to save our two kingdoms. But you lied to me." His face fell. "You didn't want to help me, you didn't want to save the kingdoms. You wanted to rule them, to enslave our people to your bidding. So I had a choice to make."

"Tell me. Tell me why you didn't chose me. I need to hear it." His tone now had a hard edge to it.

I took a deep breath. "My duty is to love my people, my world. Not you."

He turned away.

"What I did with you, what we did, it was wrong." He shook his head roughly. "And I'm sorry, so sorry that I did that to you. But what you wanted, what you were going to do. It wasn't right. What you did to poor Lilith, it was wrong. You have dragged everyone down with you. And you would have done the same to me." Tears fell from my eyes. "But you made me feel alive," I whispered, and his own tears fell from his eyes; but he still wouldn't look at me. "I always wondered what it was like to be human, to feel real emotion. And I will never be able to thank you enough for giving me that wish. But it was wrong of me, wrong to do that to myself, to you. So I chose my duty over my heart because that is who I am. That is who I have always been. That is who I have always *needed* to be."

We were silent.

We were silent as we let the silent tears fall.

We let the tears fall for our hearts, for the young angels whose hearts we broke. For who we are now.

"That's not good enough," he said almost to himself.

"*You were killing me!*" I screamed. "*You were killing me yet you didn't stop, you just didn't care!*"

His eyes snapped to mine.

"I did care!" he hissed. "But you only cared about yourself! You only cared about your precious court and what they thought, never about me. You never stopped to think about how everything you did affected me. So eventually, I stopped doing the same."

"What did you expect? You were wrong and what you believed in was wrong. And in the end, you wouldn't have just broken me but our people too," I said surprisingly gently. I couldn't be harsh. I didn't have it in me anymore.

"And yet," he whispered to himself. "*You* grew to be the one to break *me.*"

I looked at him. And the look I gave him, the way a woman might look at a man; a man she might love, might have the *chance* to love.

It shattered the newly crowned devil completely.

Devils don't possess the ability to hold emotion. They crack under its weight. But as I watched him now, that sparkle in his eyes flashing quicker than any wave under the moon's light. It proved to me that he did hold it. Somewhere deep inside him. He had the gift and burden to feel.

But then it was gone.

As fast as the changing of a second to the next.

"Oh my love," I said. "Don't you know by now? Happiness is the one thing us Gods can never have."

He said nothing as he rose from the throne, climbed down from his pedestal, dropped to his knees before me and held my beaten hands.

"Maybe, but maybe this constant battle between us *is* the happiness we are allowed. And if that is the case, I'll take it. If it means I get to keep a small part of what it is we have. Then I'll take it."

I didn't say anything. And neither did he. We sat holding each other's hands. And it wasn't until his angels came to take me away that he let any part of me go. But that wasn't what surprised me. What surprised me was that when he let me go, for the first time in millions of years, I didn't want him to.

How do you look at the person you love most and accept that it's time to say goodbye?

Chapter 33

"My point is this: the more you have to lose, the braver you are for standing up."
– Craig Silvey, 'Jasper Jones'

He forced himself to let her go, and the clouds began to weep outside the palace walls. And in their naive happiness, they nearly plunged the world into darkness. And so in the midst of their grief, they parted. But it wasn't until the world finally looked back at the devastation it left behind did it realise why it shouldn't have interfered. For now, the world truly knew darkness. The world came to know why the only happiness a God can ever have is to keep on loving her world long after her heart dies. And why the Devil is a monster when they looked his way and a man when they didn't. The God and the Devil fell in love. It was unnatural. Destructive. Chaotic. But in the beginning, when they were still finding each other's heart's, it was beautiful.

Now she protects herself as if she holds the only secret that the world will ever know. And the Devil, he saw something in her he could prune and love until it bloomed for his enjoyment. But instead, he fell in love with her. And in doing so, he wouldn't ever allow himself to pluck her sweet petals. So up until this day, he let her grow, suffer through the seasons and bloom each spring without him.

But that was the way he loved.

And that was the way she lost.

But at the end of the grand scheme of things, love is what truly exists. It is what makes us want to live and what makes us want to die.

Chapter 34

"There is love in holding and there is love in letting go."
– Elizabeth Berg, 'The Year of Pleasures'

Lucifer ordered his minions to hold his son in the lowest cell in the palace. To chain him to the walls, just as his sister once was, to beat him, to poison him with Heavenly fire to sedate him. No one could withstand the burning sensation of the blue flame in their veins. It burned him with each pump of his heart, the poison flowing through his battered body like the dammed River Stix. His cell was littered with his feathers, his blood. But like his brave sister, he never allowed a sound escape his lips when they came to beat him bloody.

He held strong for them.

For Lucinda.

For himself.

Too soon the door opened again. But this time they didn't beat him. In fact, they unchained him and held him up gently so he wouldn't fall to the dirty floor in a heap. They dragged him out, his bare feet kissing the hard floor as they did. He just did not have the energy to fight it anymore. And so he let them drag him up through the mighty staircases and out of the dungeons. They opened a door that, he knew from his distant memory, lead to the open clouds outside his long ago home. He lifted his face to the warm sunlight as the final door burst open. He let it soothe his bruises, his cuts across his bare chest and his ripped up back for as long as he could. Then reality set in when the drums sounded high into the skies.

Hundreds, millions, perhaps billions of angels stood silent as the guards dragged him forward. Then they all moved, parted like the Dead Sea finally choosing to live again, leaving a long walk to where the Devil now stood.

And so on they dragged the fallen angel.

They all stood. Starring as his broken wings left a trail of blood as he passed them. It had been so long since they had seen one of their princes, to see how they had fallen over the centuries, to what they had become now. They remembered how mighty they once were, how beautifully whole they were. Yet now, seeing the mightiest of them all on his knees, bowing to the very thing they all wanted gone.

He was the angel that had nearly cost them their empire. Nearly had cost them their lives, the lives of their children. Still, when as he was pushed down into a heap before Lucifer, they did not cheer. And as yet again he was chained down, along with his wings, they did not roar for his downfall. And as Lucifer ran his speech for what he was about to do to his son. They did not scream for their justice.

But instead they watched the young man. The young angel they remembered as a boy, walking the halls of their temples alone. They saw him when he fell in love, when he fought for it, and when he destroyed for it. They all thought they would finally feel at peace with this act of justice. But if they were telling the truth to themselves, there wouldn't be anything to celebrate when they now just realised: one of their own is about to fall.

Lucinda

I could hear the explosion I could feel it shatter the cell we were trapped in. The dust did not touch me. The vibrations radiated throughout everyone's bodies, just not mine. I was untouched by it all. I didn't look to see if everyone was alright. I just knew that they were. And so I stepped over the rubble, over the dust, and over the past. And followed the light.

Kyle

I watched as the dust cleared. As the ringing in my ears settled. I watched as she walked out untouched, which should have been impossible.

The walls to our cell were no more. They were obliterated in her wake. There was light that grew from her, that *was* her. She didn't see any of us, she didn't hear us as we shouted her name.

So we did not fight as she passed.

Chapter 35

"One must still have chaos in oneself to be able to give birth to a dancing star."

– Friedrich Nietzsche

The world shook, the skies finally marvelled at something other than itself for the first time in centuries. She ran. She caved in every wall she passed, every painting fell from its resting place on the ancient walls. The floors her feet touched shrank back, the darkness that moved within the air around her hissed as her light burned it. With her panicked heart, she finally came to the throne room, yet no one was there. The chair was empty of any soul. She passed it and came to rest finally at the huge crystal window behind it.

Lucinda

I saw him. He was bent at the knee, his beautiful wings chained down and twisted painfully. I pounded at the window, screaming for it to stop. Blood rolled off his lean body and landed on his father's boot. But no one heard me. No one could through this thick crystal glass. My heart was pounding, begging to escape my chest to go to him. Frantically I looked around for a way out, a way out from this maze of white walls and golden horror.

"Lucinda!" I spun round to find Kyle, beads of sweat running down his blush face. He was bracing himself at the throne room door.

"I have to get down there!" My voice was hoarse. He nodded, rushed to me and grabbed my hand.

We both ran.

Twist and turns, doors after doors, then we burst out into the setting sun's light. But I didn't have time to look back at him. I had no time at all. I was completely out of breath. For a moment I thought I wasn't even breathing as I sprinted towards the sea of angels.

Every part of me was numb except for the burning in my lungs and the cold rush in my throat. I didn't look at the angels I pushed out of my way. I could only see him.

Peter.

I pushed my feet forward with everything I was, with everything I *ever* was, with everything I could be. All their faces blurred together, like a tornado blazing through my mind.

I could hear them though. Not the angels, not Kyle screaming for his brother behind me. But everything else. The clouds sang, the shadows of the new night whispered as I passed it. The high-pressured air that I could feel whipping across my face and freezing my cells. I could hear it all. I could feel the setting sun push me on with its last bits of energy to light up the world. The stars, they rang through my mind, through my skin, through it all as my legs burned for me to stop.

I turned to see his face.

Time slowed down, like in the movies when the scene slowed down into slow motion. There he was, his golden brown hair that *still* covered his ears. That nose that was the image of my own. Shock registered within his brown eyes as he saw me.

He hadn't aged a day.

He looked the same as he did the he walked out our door, got in that car. And never came back.

I looked away.

And pushed on with all my might.

I passed him in a blur, but I couldn't breathe. I dropped to my knees gasping for air. I looked up, but I was still too far away to reach him.I screamed for it to stop. For someone to stop it all. But no one did.

Lucifer stood grinning as he stepped back from his empty son that bowed before him. Peter sat kneeling, facing the crowd with his head down. His hands clasped into his lap, his torn wings chained behind him. His chest glistened with sweat and blood. It rose and fell steady and with every beat of the drums.

I looked beyond him to the angel standing behind him.

The world slowed down again. He was holding a sword.

He stepped forward.

And without a single thought.

He raised that mighty weapon.

And brought it down over Peter's head.

"No!"

Everything shone once again. A deepness, a void of light that was quiet and soothing.

It was the throne room. But it was different. More settled, almost peaceful, as if all the power that kept it running died away and just the left the marble structure behind it.

I stepped forward, raising my hand to shield my eyes from the light that was letting me pass. And as I did, I saw a woman kneeling. Her gentle hands clasped before her. Her head lowered and eyes closed. Her pale yet glowing skin covered with shimmering robes, her hair spun into a simple crown upon her head. I stopped before her.

She was kneeling before the throne.

She looked up at me, her eyes burning, raging with something I'd never seen before.

I'd never seen her before in my life, yet the woman kneeling before me…I knew her better than I knew myself.

There was no expression on her face, just that burning nothingness. We existed there for a few seconds, watching each other.

Her eyes mirroring my own.

She had no wings, no divine power radiating from her except for the power that she was born with and not given. She didn't blink once. Just that steady gaze that ripped me apart and spilled the blood from my heart and onto the floor before us.

We were linked. I could feel a pull between us. A chain of private understanding that completed us both.

We've been waiting for each other.

She's been waiting for me to return…

What a sight to behold, a woman kneeling before her throne instead of a man.

I turned away from the kneeling saint to the voice that called out to us.

I was alone.

No more voices.

No more visions.

"Who's there?"

Nothing.

I turned back to the woman. But she was no longer kneeling. I was. She stood before me, and I kneeled before her. Her hands were still clasped before her, as if she was a centuries old sculpture that was crafted from the hands of the finest artist.

No words needed to be spoken because I understood her. I understood myself too.

I knew there was a world outside of this, a world that needed me. I wasn't just a human, or a friend, or a lover. I now knew what my mind was trying to show me, what it has been trying to show me through memories that were mine and some that weren't.

I was every single shred of power that lived within the stars above.

I was power.

I was more than anyone could ever imagine.

I was born of human flesh, but my soul, my heart was crafted from the skin of stars and of planets. The very essence of the dark, black universe that shielded us up together. I was torn away from it as a child. But now I have returned.

I have come for my pound of flesh from the Gods.

She unclasped her hands and held one down to me.

I would no longer kneel.

For stars do not bow…

"Who are you?" she asked. I asked.

I did not answer until I stood before the world, the stars above as my crown, the planets as my body. The universe as my heart and soul.

"I am Astralis Caeli, Princeps Universum, Lucinda Sky." My voice was not my own.

And I have returned home…

Someone unknown

I've heard of the legend. The myth of the human star. How our Lord bargained with the Gods to put their divine power inside the body of a human. But the legend came true when her scream echoed through the world like a battle cry of a war to come.

One moment, there was utter silence as the sword was lifted high.

Then the world exploded.

Her voice rang through us all, her scream shattered our spines like wood. The setting sun became nothing when the boiling light burst from her. It knocked everything down in its wake; it was so fast. So quick. Nothing one moment, then chaos the next.

I was trying to hold my fellow angel down to the cloud with me, my breath being ripped from my chest as the light, hotter than any Heavenly fire I had ever seen, roasted my skin, my wings. My very soul as it blazed from her in a wild frenzy.

I looked up. At the centre of the tower of light that was pulsing across the universe, there she was. Her feet floating, her arms outstretched. Her face looking up to the now darkening sky. The long hair floated around her like her very own halo. Her eyes were wide and pooling the light that was rushing from her in an unending stretch of power that should have never been contained.

Yet there she was.

From all the power I had seen, from the Devil and God; even their own son that was known to be the most powerful angel in all of history. Even more powerful than his own parents.

They were nothing as she let all that power escape her. And for a moment, it seemed to overwhelm her. To seize her. To engulf her.

But then she lowered her head. And faced us all.

Her eyes continued to glow, to brighten the world even more than the sun ever could. We watched her. She watched us.

The light, in a sudden rebound of wind, came rushing back to her. Because it was hers. Not the Devil's, and not God's any more. She *was* the star. Everything the light destroyed in its path came with it. It was swallowed by her power.

And as the Gods up above and the Devils down below watched in awe.

She was reborn again.

Chapter 36

"Is it better for a man to have chosen evil than to have good imposed upon him."
– Anthony Burgess, 'A Clockwork Orange'

She felt every corner of her being in the very second she screamed. She felt every cell, every strand of hair come alive at her heart's command.

She exploded.

She fell apart.

She fell back together again. And when her power spread across the planets and the stars, the dead Gods above her and the darkness beyond that. Her heart screamed alongside her. Her eyes heated with the light from her chest. And she let it all engulf her. She let it warm her, pulse through her, fill her.

She knew it was her star awakening once again. She knew it answered her even though she didn't call for it to listen. It radiated though her body, it burned her and cooled her at the same time.

She lowered her head.

Her once brown eyes were filled with the most terrifying power any creature had ever seen before. She faced the Devil. The Devil who was cowering on the floor, holding on so tightly so he wouldn't fly off from the rushing wind around them. Suddenly, without any warning, lightning struck the temples, the houses, every inch that wasn't taken up with her light. It struck it all down.

Peter, with his beaten body chained down, could only look up in amazement at the woman he loved. The woman who was now surrounded with every inch of the universe.

And he saw it. No one else did. But he noticed every single thing about her. The light that consumed her, framed her as it collected itself to her like a wisp of her very essence. He noticed that the light behind her almost looked like a pair of–

"Peter!" He heard his brother call from somewhere inside the sky of storms and light.

He squinted his eyes. *"Kyle! Where are you?"*

But there was no reply.

Only the screams of all the angels that came to see him fall.

They could feel it all. They could sense their souls begin to break, tiny cracks form between their divine bones.

The Gods above had no power now. She *was* their power. They had given it away to someone, something that could not be controlled.

They have lost their rule.

They had lost.

Lucinda stepped forward, eyes glowing and proud. The storm of her light moved with her. She walked straight past him, glancing quickly over him to ensure he was unharmed. Then carried on towards the Devil.

She stopped before him. Grabbed the front of his cloak and lifted him clean off the ground.

The light swirled around them. She didn't blink as she gripped the front of his cloak and forced him to kneel before her. He's never bowed to anyone. Yet she *made* him. Lucinda pushed him down to the floor, his knees crushing under his heavy weight. His eyes wide, and for the first time in a very long time, he looked scared. He knew he was at her mercy.

The setting sun was nearly engulfed by the edge of the world, the stars up above them started to glow, but tonight, as the light grew taller from the woman standing before them. Not only were they at her mercy, but so was the world. The stars were brighter, as if they were watching their power being realised with complete content.

Lucinda

I felt so *powerful.*

It all rushed through me, cooed at me, filled me. I held the Devil down with one hand. Just one gripping hand. I watched him with eyes glowing while his glowed with horror.

It is all *mine.* All the universe had to offer. *Mine.*

And as she took from the Devil the very thing that he is, she lifted her head upwards to the dark skies.

Eyes burning like a rising phoenix.

For so long now she had worked with the rules, alongside them; she tried to live by them. But how could she now? She had fallen in love with the Devil's son. She had fall for the temptations of power, power that had no shade of evil or good. But power that works both sides of the scale.

But she would defy them all. She will defy whatever the Lords above wanted, what they demanded. She will save the man she loved, she will save herself. She will save them all.

She was no longer a simple human, she was something else…

She was now an unnerving spillage of a paradox. Yet she seemed small and broken, like old piano keys, her heart hidden from the world, yet completely in view. They all knew the human that remained within her. They all smelled the weakness oozing from her…Yet nothing concealed the fear they now felt while cowering before her. Many tragedies conflicted her mind, like many angels and Gods before, but she would be the only one written down in history, the rest to be forgotten. Now as they stood before her, nothing outweighed her power to shake the skies above, or made their hearts warmer than her humanity. And it was her humanity that finally made angels bow before a human. She was now the scale of manic, destruction and compassion that rested equally well upon the world's shoulders that now belonged to her.

The perfect paradox.

And with a whip of light that filled every corner in the universe…

Lucinda Sky and Lucifer Morning Star vanished from view.

And when the light finally recoiled back to their master and everything calmed did the world finally know what it was like to be still.

The angels, their Lord and their heirs turned their heads to where the chaos once was. And all they found was Lucinda. No light. No storm. No glowing shadows that framed her. No glowing hair or eyes.

Just Lucinda.

Her legs began to shake, her body now weak from the power it had to hold. Peter, beaten and broken in every way, was the first to move. His now misshapen wings trailing the mangled cloud behind him as he ran for her. He caught her before she fell to the floor. Concealing her in his arms, gentle as he stroked her tear stained cheeks, he whispered in her ear for her to wake. When she did, everyone hushed back in whispers and cries of terror.

And as they looked upon this new creature that their prince now held, they found something else to be afraid of. This little human that wasn't quite *all* human. But also something else that had shaken them to their core.

They chose her to fear.

His kissed her head, her cheeks, her lips as he whispered against her sore skin to awake. And she did. Her eyes searching for his, and when they found them, those crystal blue eyes that healed her heart, that she fought for with everything that she held within her, she sealed them away into her heart with a bittersweet kiss. Pulling him down to her gently to not hurt him further, she touched her lips to his, sealing the promise that she will fight for him for however long she will be in this world for. And as she did; so did he. He kissed her back with all the strength he had left. Promising to fight for her, to hold her, to love her. To love everything that she was; the ugly, the scared, the beaten. The power that they all knew now lived just underneath her flesh. They both promised to stand by each other.

The son of the Devil.

The daughter of the Gods.

Yet while the two lovers relished in being reunited, they forgot what still sat before them all with its head bowed.

Chapter 37

"But who prays for Satan? Who, in eighteen centuries, has had the common humanity to pray for the sinner that needed it most?"
– 'Mark Twain's Autobiography'

Lucinda

He lifted his head and soft golden curls radiated the centre of the sun. His horns were now coloured like warm, brown-smothered chocolate. His skin was tanned, like sweet caramel, and his wings…They too were gold. When the first God created him, she must have plucked him out of the sun itself. He sat with his head bowed, but when he looked up to us all…I could finally see where Peter had inherited his beautiful eyes from. They struck us all in the centre of our souls. Bright blue eyes that held too much pain…and too much relief…and the first thing they did was look for their lover.

God moved forward. Utter shook rang from her like centuries old bells. Her face more pale than I had ever seen before. Peter helped me stand, but did not let me go. Instead he held my hand, his still shaking from the events that just passed us. We gathered around this stranger, his hands laying in his lap, his eyes raining tears as he looked up at us.

His voice the definition of an angels. "Lola…"

At the sound of her name passing his lips, she fell to her knees before him and cupped his golden face. Both of them crying into each other's hearts.

"Lucifer, I can't believe it." She traced the skin around his eyes, like I did so many times with Peter's. She marvelled at him. And I remembered how long it must have been since she had seen her lover's true face, his true eyes. So long. "Lucifer, oh Lucifer," she whispered over and over again.

"Is this real?" the golden man said as he looked himself over, realising his transformation was real.

He looked back to Lola. "This is real," she said.

He lifted his shaking hand to her face, a smile growing on his own. Yet this time when he smiled, it was beautiful. As if the sun was rising again. No sharp pointed teeth, no darkness that oozed from his whole frame. His eyes, that now shone blue, were a perfect size for his perfect face. Nothing unnatural lived on his body. Except for the heavenly perfection that was now the face of the Devil.

And as the golden horns of the Devil reflected the light of the stars, and after centuries of being apart from the love of his life, he kissed her. He pulled her forward with heart breaking gentleness. She braced herself with both hands against his tanned chest. And kissed him back. Their wings slack as their bodies shivered at the contact. Slowly her arms wound around his neck. Then they worked their way to his horns bracing them with her hands, she lifted herself into his lap. Wanting to get ever closer. And from the way she pulled herself up onto him, it would seem to everyone else around them that she once must have had done it a millions times. I looked away and found Gabriel staring down at them, his purple eyes glowing with something I had never seen before. Something too old and heart tearing to really understand. He must have felt me looking at him. Because he lifted his eyes away from them. Glanced at me once. And walked away. Disappearing within the crowd.

"My Lord." A solider stepped forward. The Gods broke apart. "After many years of war, many of us believe it is your duty to make the Devil stand accountable for his sins now that he is your prisoner."

She said nothing. Lucifer said nothing.

"What do I do?" Lola asked him. Lucifer held her hands within his own, kissed them once. And laid them back down in her lap. But never took his eyes off her.

His answer was honourable.

"I love you." She began to weep. "And I am so sorry for everything that I have done. But know this: know that I love you, but I love you for who you are. For *what* you are. So I will not fight you, I will not run from you anymore. Whatever you have to do, know that I forgive you. As I hope you will forgive me in return."

She nodded her head. "I forgive you my love. I forgive you."

The night was long and so was his trial. Every single angel, fallen angel, dark angel, Demon and saint had their time to speak against him. The courtroom was vast with the amount of souls that filled it. I stood by Peter's side at every turn. Kyle and Jane also. We stood together. And when they passed through the court, they weren't the only ones that stood out from the rest. I did too. All the angels cowered away from us, from me. Peter never let go of my hand once. He held onto my hand like it was the only thing that could save him. As we walked through the seats and were about to sit down, Lola, who was at the head of the entire court, back in a mighty chair that she filled well even though it was not her throne, called out to us.

"I want my children by my side."

We looked at each other. "Yes Lucinda, that includes you too," she said with a hint of soft smile, as much as she could muster.

Without a word to each other, we moved to her side where four marble chairs were ready for each of us. We sat down. Peter on my left, Kyle at my right and Jane at his left.

"Let the trail begin." Gabriel appeared beside Lola's smaller version of her throne. His words silencing the huge room.

He walked into the room. Unchained. Unbound. Everyone holding their breath as his silent footsteps graced the marble floor. His eyes snapped to mine. Full of flickering rage and secrets. A perfect mix of blue, so much like his son's. Entrancing.

Then just as quick he looked away, but I never did. He didn't just live up to all the legends, all the stories. Compared to them, he was immortal…

Lucifer stood in a white booth in the centre on the room. Chained. As he did to his son. His wings were chained down. His now golden wings, chained down. And it was so sad to witness. On each side of the room were thousands of seat filled to the breaking point of men, women, and children.

"First witness to the stand. Lilith, Mother of Demons."

We all turned as she stepped forward from the crowd. Her dark, beautiful legs like steel as she walked before God, bowed and faced the Devil. Her braids hung down her back, her matted robes stark against her smooth skin.

"Lucifer Morningstar. I call upon you to answer to the sins you have committed against me. You have forced me to pleasure you, in evil and in the bedroom."

Kyle reached over and gripped my free hand. We did not look at each other. We just held onto each other's hand.

Lilith continued. "You forced me to take the wings of an innocent angel, to enforce your rule. If I didn't, you said you would kill him. You killed my children. Slaughtered them before me, chained me up so I could not stop it. You have killed two of my husbands, and forced me to hurt the man I loved at the time." Kyle gripped my hand harder. "And while dangling his life before me like a carrot. To do whatever you wanted to ensure you would not end it. How do you plea?" she asked while standing strong.

And without missing a beat, Lucifer answered, "Guilty."

She turned, bowed to God. And sat back down within the crowed.

Gabriel was up next.

He followed the same process as Lilith, bowed to his Lord and turned to his rival.

"Centuries ago you came to us, to me. You gave me a young boy. I treated him as if he was my own. To me, Peter Blackfeather is my son." Gabriel turned to his son and Peter bowed his head in respect. "They are all my children. Kyle, Jane, Peter. They are my children. And over the past centuries, you have hurt me through them. We were once friends. And you have tried to destroy my family in any way you can. How do you plea?"

Again, "Guilty."

Next was Arianne.

Then many from the crowd that wanted to speak of the sins he had committed against them over the centuries arose. Taking their turn for justice.

Then Jane took her chance.

Only this time she did not bow to anyone. She only faced the Devil.

Her back straight, her feet making the only noise we could hear. Her face was a storm that she contained with the will power of only a wisp of air.

"We both know the sins you have committed against me. I won't bother to bore us with the details, and I don't think I should say them out loud with children in the room." She braced her hands on the booth that contained him. "I have suffered greatly at your hands. But here I am, stronger than you, better than you. Yet I will forever be broken because of you. I will forever be condemned to walk these temples as an outcast. A monster, a beast with the scars to prove it."

"I'm sorry," he said, his head bowed.

Tears fell from her eyes.

"Why?" she cried. "Why did you hurt me? I was the daughter of the woman you loved. You helped me after my stripping, you

271

helped me heal. Then you sold me to demons for their entertainment for years. Hadn't I suffered enough by that point?"

He was silent for a few seconds. "There will never be enough time to repent for all the things I have done to you. But I *am* sorry, and I will never be able to explain why I did the things that I did. But I am so proud of you. I have always been proud of you."

"How do you plea?" was all she whispered past her tears.

"Beyond guilty," he said.

Jane said nothing else. She walked back to her seat; wiping her tears away as if they never fell from her eyes. And sat without another word.

Kyle was next.

He squeezed my hand before letting go, rising, refusing to bow to his mother. And then lastly, facing the Devil.

"Lucifer Morningstar. I call upon you to answer to the sins you have committed against me. You have terrorised me and my family for centuries. You slipped a spy into my home, forced her to seduce me, and when she did, you used her life as leverage against me so I would give up Lucinda Sky. And when I refused, you beat the woman I loved before me, chained me down and forced me to watch. After that, you stripped my wings from my back. And harnessed the power of my wings for yourself. You hunted me, so I had to flee to Earth with my siblings and for centuries, I have been on the run. You have kept the woman I love captive. You have hurt her, and in doing so, you have hurt me. How do you plea?"

"Guilty."

Peter lifted my hand and kissed my knuckles. And stood to meet his brother half way. He clasped his shoulder and a silent conversation passed between them. Kyle nodded and sat back down beside me, and this time I reached out to hold his hand.

Peter did not bow to his mother as he took his chance to speak. He faced his father, their faces so alike it almost frightened me, but when I looked at Peter, he calmed me. Reminded me that he was not his father.

"Son," Lucifer greeted his son while looking over his bandaged wings, his battered body.

"Father. I call upon you to answer to the sins you have committed against me." Peter took a deep breath before continuing. "I remember the day you gave me over to the Heaven court. I remember thinking why I wasn't good enough, what I did wrong. I kept looking up at you as we walked towards God's court. And wondering why you wouldn't look back at me. Before you gave me over, we were so close, but now I realise you only showed interest in me because you wanted to use me. But I must thank you for handing me over. Because I found a real father, and I was reunited with my brother and sister. But for centuries after that, you have tormented me, threatened me, and hurt those around me so much that eventually I had to push those remaining away to keep them safe.

"When I finally started to lose my humanity, when I finally started to become cold and exactly what you wanted me to become, I was prosecuted for it across the empire. Both empires. And because of you, when I finally found someone to love, you tried to take her from me, and nearly succeeded. You hurt her, sent people to hurt her, hurt those that *she* loved. All because I refused to be what you are. Father, how do you plea?"

"My son, I am guilty of hurting you. I am guilty of it all. But you will never know how proud I am of how much you tried not to end up like me. But my brave son, no matter what happens to me. There will always be others that will stop at nothing until you become what I have become. You mustn't my son, you must fight everyday with the power you possess, fight them. Even if you like it or not, you have inherited my power. And when I am gone, all my power will go to you. You must learn to control it, and not let it control *you.*"

"*Enough!*" Peter roared, but his father carried on.

"There are forces that are stronger than us all, even stronger than you. And I know you won't believe me, but I have protected you from them all this time. But after this ends, once I am gone, you will need to protect yourself. And I am sorry that I did not protect you better."

He went silent.

Peter said nothing else, and came back to my side.

"Astralis."

"Lucinda," I corrected as I stood. Whoever they were, they did not answer.

I did not bow to God, but I did look up at her as I passed her. I faced the Devil as everyone else did.

"Lucifer Morningstar. I call upon you to answer to the sins you have committed against me." I looked around me, looking at all the faces around me. They all looked back at me, their eyes digging into my own. "There are many things that you have done that have hurt me. You have taken so much from me. You forced your son to kill my family when I was six years old. Not only costing me my father and brother, but my mother too. In her own way, she lost all her senses. Which in many ways made me fend for myself. And lose the rest of my childhood. Then only a few months ago, you killed my mother. Costing me someone else I loved. You forced me to run. To leave behind my newly found family. You made me watch as you killed a young boy in front of me, all because I didn't know how to give you what you wanted. I had to find my mother's decaying body, and watch as her body burned inside my home as it was set on fire. I stood, at six years old, as they lowered my father and brother into the ground. Then just a few weeks ago, I find out that they are still alive.

"I had to become something that terrified me, thrilled me, but changed me for forever more. Because of you, I have to change everything that I believe in. Because of you, I have no idea who I am anymore. To save the people I love, I had to say goodbye to who I am. I had to say goodbye to the human I was and become something that not only scares everyone in this room, but also myself. How do you plea?"

"I am guilty of hurting you. But I am not guilty of what you have become."

"How so?"

"Because you are now what you have always been. You just realised there was more to you than there was before. That power escaped you when it did because it was always there. You called upon it to save the man you loved. And it will escape you again. Many times over. None of us know what you truly are. Not even yourself. My son is believed to be the most powerful being in history. Yet when I saw what you did, I no longer believed that. You have held that in you for centuries. And you will hold it for centuries to come. Blame me for the sin I have committed, but not for the chaos you were born to wield."

"You have no idea what you are talking about."

"Maybe, maybe not. But for all our sakes, I hope you never find out how to use it. I have never prayed before my dear, but I would if you ever did."

The room was filled with anticipation.

"Only for *your* sake, would I pray if I ever did."

I walked away and sat down before the angels. But I did not shrink down in my seat. I kept my back straight. I sat as tall and proud as them all.

"God."

We all went silent, not a breath to be heard. She stared down at him, and he stared back.

"Lucifer, I call upon you–" her words shattered as they left her, "to answer to the sins…you have committed against me," She took a steadying breath before continuing. "Lucifer, my love. You made me fall in love with you, you made me feel emotion and used it to hurt me. You rebelled against me. You hurt my children, you have threatened my kingdom over and over again. You have threatened my reign, killed so many of my people, so many of my angels. Yet–" She took a shaky breath and calmed herself. But even the God of the universe couldn't stop the tears from escaping. "You gave me exactly what I always dreamed of, a day of being normal, human. You gave me everything I could ever want. Everything I ever asked for, you gave it all to me. You made me smile, laugh, cry, hate and love. You broke yourself to give it all to me." She started to cry as she spoke, her words crying with her. "You gave me a beautiful child, who reminds me of all the best parts of us both every single day. But your love corrupted me in the most inhuman, twisted and beautiful way there is. And I thank the first God for it every day." Everyone's eyes were on her, all piercing and brutal. "I love you. But I won't break myself further fighting for someone who isn't worth the fight anymore."

He nodded his head.

"Lola," he said. "My sweet Lola. You forgot to say how much you have given *me.* You have given me so much, you gave me a chance to raise a child. To love, to *live."* He smiled as he said it. "You made me feel like I didn't just have to be the Devil, but for a short while, someone else who could be worth your love. And even though it ended when we thought we would have more time, I am grateful, and I thank the Gods above every day for the time I got with you. And I wouldn't change it for the world. And I would do it all again. I love you. And I hope one day, you find happiness again."

The air in the courtroom seemed to settle, to calm as he finished his speech.

"I plead guilty to all charges, and I accept any punishment that you see fit to give me."

We all looked up to the Lord, awaiting her answer.

"Lucifer Morningstar. For the crimes that you have committed against humanity and the angelic court, I sentence you to the very humanity that you have corrupted."

The court stood up in uproar.

"You will be stripped of your wings, of your title and of any power you have collected or otherwise was born with. And just as before, you will be cast out of Heaven. You will walk among the Earth until judgement day." She stood, her remaining wing shaking as she spoke. "May the Gods above have mercy upon your soul."

They took one last look at each other, and as Lola was about to leave…

Lucifer, the Devil, bowed to his Lord. And without another look to her lover, she turned away and left the courtroom. Gabriel clicked his fingers and the angels of God took the prisoner away. Never to be seen again.

Chapter 38

"I am not much but I'm all I have."

– Philip K. Dick

Lucinda

The temple was silent. The city was silent.

The world was silent.

Many people deal with loss in so many different ways. Some deal with it through expressing anger, harsh words, tears and silence. But tonight, as the moon fell from the sky and as the sun rose to greet us and wash away the sins of last few hours, the world paid its respect to the Devil not with harsh words, or even tears…But through silence.

Weeks passed after the trial. Peter, Jane and Kyle went to help the city after the trial to rebuild. I kissed Peter as he left. He assured me he was fine, and that he was strong enough to go out and help. I wanted to be by myself for a while. I wondered around the temples, going over the past few weeks. The night was coming to an end, the stars were going back to sleep, the moon was climbing down from the sky. I walked across the clouds, their softness comforting me.

"Lucinda."

I walked further and came to the back of God. She was looking out from the edge of the cloud we stood on, her remaining wing low to the floor.

The rays of the newly born sun of today greeted us. I stood next to her, looking out to the vast sky, no longer afraid of its incredible void.

"We never really think about how short our lives are until we lose something we love," she said quietly to me.

"No. No we don't." I reached out and held her hand. "But that's what makes us appreciate it.

She shook her head softly. "I loved him. And now he's gone. Now he's gone."

"That's life. That is how it is." She turned her head to look at me. "Being a God or an angel doesn't stop it. It doesn't change it. Yes it hurts when it all comes crashing down, but before it does, love is the only thing worth fighting for."

"But the pain never goes away…" A single tear fell from her eyes. She wiped it away roughly.

"When it's real, it never does."

We stood quietly for a few seconds, looking out to the peeking sun on the edge of the horizon, and looking over the silent city. I looked back up at her, but she was already looking back out to the horizon. I thought about how old she must be. She looked only a few years older than me, and she was the most beautiful woman I had ever seen. But she's been here for millions of years. Some of the time alone, and the rest at war, losing everything. And I understood her. I understood why she did things she did to us. Why she thought she was protecting us by keeping us apart. She thought she was protecting us from the heartache she knew would come.

"Thank you," I said.

She looked at me confused.

"For what?"

I smiled. "Thank you for protecting me, for protecting us."

She smiled back. "That is all I ever wanted to do. I know now that the way I did it wasn't the right way, but my intention was there."

The sun began to truly rise, its rays chasing the night away. Lola closed her eyes and let it warm her face, a brief but sad smile forming on her plump lips.

"It's hard Astralis. Doing this job, being God. We have all the power in the universe, yet no real power over ourselves. Over our lives." She turned to me, and I turned to her. "The problem wasn't because we didn't have enough love, or enough fight for that love. But that we both thought that the love would be the end of the other. But most of the time, that is the end."

"I knew what I was getting myself into," I said with a voice that was not my own. She was quiet as she listened. "And I knew I would have to give a part of myself to him that I would never get back…a part he needed more than I did. Because I loved him and I wanted to be the one that fixed him." She knew I was talking about Peter because I was sure she could see the gleam in my eyes just like I always did whenever I spoke about him.

"I'm glad he has you."

"Thank you my Lord."

She blinked in surprise, surprise that I addressed her as my Lord. But smiled again nevertheless.

"Lucinda, may I ask you something?"

I nodded and waited.

She almost looked…Weary, unnerved as she spoke.

"What happened to you? That power, where did it come from?"

"What do you mean?"

"When you unleashed yourself upon us, where did that come from?"

I was confused. I thought that was the star protecting me, protecting the ones I loved. I didn't truly understand how I unleashed it. All I could remember was how thrilling it felt, how rushed…How dangerous. But I thought that power came from her, and from the Gods.

"Lola that was the star. That was the star unleashing itself…"

Her eyes seemed to tremble for a moment.

"Lucinda." For the first time since I'd met her, she sounded human. "That wasn't the star."

"What?"

"That wasn't the star. No star can produce that kind of power. No one has ever seen anything like that before. Not even Gabriel. And he has been here since the beginning. A star is one of the most powerful things in the universe, and they cannot do that, not even a—"

She wasn't talking to me anymore. Her eyes trailed down to Earth. Then to the skies above.

"Not even a what?" My voice was barely a whisper.

She looked at me then, her eyes hollow as she watched me. I could see millions of years in her eyes, history as old as time itself. Once, when I was truly human I wouldn't have had the strength to look back, to stand my ground. But now…

Something else stirred inside me now. Something that was a part of me just as much as it was apart. It clawed around me, its light settling down and hiding away until the next time it came out to the world. I could feel it all the time now, as if it sat on my shoulder. We were one. I was *it*. I always have been. I wasn't the only one looking back at the Lord now, and she knew it.

"Say it."

She swallowed before answering.

"…Not even a God can do that."

We stared at each other.

279

Both now wondering what lurked under my flesh. Who I was under this flesh.

I opened my mouth to speak but footsteps sounded from behind us. We turned to see Peter and Kyle approach together, a look of calm restored to their beautiful faces. But as Peter looked to me, smiling, eyes once again bright. It was the most beautiful thing I'd ever seen. His hair shone in the rising sun's light, his eyes like shimmering sapphires, his smile like the sea after a storm. I could see it all so clearly, as if my power was still at my fingertips and not hidden. I could see it all. And as he smiled down at me, I saw where we began and where we ended; deep into the sky and far beyond the stars.

"Lucinda…" he said as if it was all he could say. He reached for my hand, lifted it and kissed it tenderly without looking away from my eyes.

Either Kyle or Lola cleared their throat. We broke away from our gaze.

"Mother," Kyle said. "Would you like to go for a stroll on this fine morning?" He held his arm out for his mother and her face broke into something of pure joy at her son's eagerness to bond. She wasted no time and linked her arm through his. And I saw how much he towered over her, and I saw how she beamed up at him. Together they strolled away, smiles plastered over their Heavenly faces.

Gently and in no rush as the sun started to truly rise for us, Peter pulled me to him by my waist. I closed my eyes and buried my face into his warm, strong chest. He wrapped his slowly healing wings and arms around me, sealing me in everything I would ever need. Him.

He kissed the top of my head. "I have something to tell you," he said against my hair.

"What is it?" I mumbled into his chest. His laugh rumbled through me.

He took a deep breathe. "The court has accepted us back. We can come home."

I froze. My body hiccupped at his words. They could go home, and me…

I would go back. To Earth. Alone. I imagined working back at the pub, without Jane. I imagined going home, walking through the door and not hearing my mum's mumbling through the living room. Or looking over the bar thinking I would see Peter smiling over at me…Yet when I would, no one would be there. Even Kyle,

280

with his foul mood. I imagined going through just one day without his rude comments and sweet looks. What an awful world. What an awful life. A life that was about to be my reality. I turned my face away so he wouldn't see my fallen tears. I pulled away.

"Lucinda?" He tried to get me to look at him. But I couldn't. I couldn't beg him to stay with me. I couldn't be that selfish. He was an angel and I was just…Something else, but I wasn't an angel. He belonged here and I belonged on Earth.

"Lucinda, look at me." He held my arms to him, but still I wouldn't look at him.

"It's ok," I said, voice breaking. "I understand."

"What? Lucinda please just look at me," he said desperately. From the sound of his voice, I looked up at him. His eyes were confused, his perfect eyebrows drawn down.

"I understand. You belong here. And I'm so happy you get to come home. And I wouldn't be that selfish to ask you to stay with me. And I'm so relieved that you are safe, and I would do it all again just to make sure you were safe. Even if it would cost me having you in my life."

I started to walk away. Tears rolling down my cheeks, my hair blew across my face, shielding the wetness of my sadness.

Suddenly, quicker than the breeze around us, he hooked his arm around my middle and lifted me against his front, his chest to my back. I held onto his arms around me, my heart holding on by a thread.

"Lucinda," he said breathlessly into the nap of my neck. "I have waited for *so* long to come home. To see my brother and sister happy again, to see my mother be the mother I have always wanted her to be. To finally see Jane smile like she used to. To see Kyle open up again to the world and let it all in. It's the very thing I have prayed for since I fell. But Lucinda." He kissed the sensitive skin behind my ear. "All of it, everything. It is all *nothing* without you. *Nothing.*"

I held his arm harder. I gripped it like it was my lifeline.

"My love," I said through the tears. "I can't ask that of you–"

"*You don't have to…*" He held me closer. "Because wherever you go, I go. If you became the stars up above, I would burn myself to ashes and carry myself on the wind to get to you. If you fell into the sea, I would dive from the skies to save you. I will follow you *anywhere,* even if you commanded me to stay away. I will always be right around the next corner waiting for you. You *are* my life. They said I could come back, but not without you. Not without you. So they said you can stay with me. But if you decided you didn't, I wouldn't object to that. We can go wherever you want. Together."

I leaned my head back into him, his own resting on my shoulder next to mine.

The whisper was soft, like the inside of a healing heart. "I love you," he whispered.

And there it was.

Those words I heard when I was whisked away into blinding light. Those words I heard in my dreams all those nights I was away from him. Those words that kept me fighting each and every day.

"Turn me around," I whispered.

He did. I faced him. I lifted my fingertips to his gorgeous eyes. His eyes will be the last thing I'll ever remember of this world. I was sure of it.

I traced the skin across his face and wondered how such a cruel world could make such a beautiful man like him. A kind, majestic, thoughtful, powerful man like him.

"I don't know what happens to us when we die. If we become scattered souls or spirits that float around the stars. Or if we become nothing more than ashes and dust. But I know that the last thing that will ever exist of me will be my love for you."

He closed his eyes and smiled, the new sun lighting up his face fully for me to marvel at.

"I love you," I said. I stood up on my tiptoes and took my time before I met my lips to his. I savoured the flavour of them. The feel of them, of the way they moved with mine. Slow and gentle. He held me closer as he kissed me harder. He put the kisses we missed over the past few weeks into this single kiss for me. All the love we weren't able to give each other, into this single kiss, into this single embrace. I wound my arms around his neck, holding him to me, never wanting to let go.

"Sister?"

I froze. I opened my eyes to look up to Peter, but he was grinning down at me, eyes so open and free.

That voice…

It almost sounded like…

No. It couldn't be.

But I turned around anyway, just in case it was true.

And there he stood.

His eyes glowing a melting chocolate brown just as my own did whenever the sun hit them. His golden brown hair that always curled slightly at the top whenever it got too long. I couldn't breathe. There he was. That same goofy smile growing by the second as we watched each other, his lean arms held out to me.

A twelve-year-old cry escaped me as I ran into his arms.

"Michael!"

He laughed as he engulfed me into his strong hold. He smelled the same, he felt the same; the same strong arms that used to hold me up so I could see better; the same smell that always comforted me whenever I was upset. That same smile that never failed to make me smile.

He swung me around.

"I can't believe it. I can't believe it." He put me back down and held me at arm's length to get a good look at me. "You're so grown up."

"I can't believe it either," I said, excitement making my voice squeal.

"I saw what you did, and I'm *so* proud of you. You looked so powerful, so beautiful. I am so proud of the woman that you have become."

I hugged him again. He was real. This was real.

"Where is Dad?" I asked.

"Right here," someone said before Michael could reply. He turned and there my father stood smiling down at his children. The same warm smile I remembered while growing up. The same worn but handsome face that I thought I would never see again.

"My daughter," he said while pulling me into his arms, stroking my hair down my back like he used to.

"I'm sure you have many questions," he said as he leaned his chin on top of my head.

I breathed him in, finally letting my heart remember after all these years.

"Not now," I said. I pulled away and stood back into Peter's arms. He automatically wrapped his arm around my waist, his reassuring heart beating alongside mine. "For now I just want to be with my family."

And there we all stood, our futures unravelling themselves as we watched the new sun wash away the sins of yesterday. I looked around at the people before me. I watched how the sun lit up their faces, how the breeze blew our troubles away. I turned to see Peter not looking at the breathtaking sunrise, but at me. So I didn't look back to the new morning, but I looked back to my new future, my new life. The life I could have with Peter. To the adventure I always wanted. And maybe I would lose my mind through the process, but in the end, that's what makes it an adventure...

Chapter 39

"The world changes too fast. You take your eyes off something that's always been there, and the next minute it's just a memory."
– Michel Faber, 'The Book of Strange New Things'

She stood at the very edge of the cliffs behind her lover's house. The wind was so strong on her face that it froze the pores in her skin. The clouds above were dark and overpowering to others, but they were empowering to her. Storms rumble and will strike the Earth whenever they are disrespected. They cannot be controlled. She thought that about herself that no one could control her thoughts; wouldn't mould her to their ideas of how life should be. The waves below rushed up towards the cliffs, hissing their song for the world as best as it could. She looked out to the ocean, to the world she grew up in. And felt no sadness. She'd chosen her life to this very point. Her heart had chosen who she would love, no matter who he was. And now she would be able to see who else she could be. She would leave the world behind and never again set foot upon its bright green grasses, or swim in its vast oceans, but she would do it for the man she loved. For herself. And for her finally, healing heart. She turned away from the sea, from her old life. And went back to the house instead. She placed the outside walls to her memories for safekeeping. The white paint, the vast woods around them. She stepped through the back door and took her time walking through the hallways, taking it all in. Remembering when she first came her, hoping for something, anything. She remembered seeing Peter standing in the kitchen drinking his feelings away, the kisses that were shared only with the walls, the secret touches as they passed each other from room to room.

She looked upon the hundreds of years of history that hung on its walls. The paintings, the artefacts, the tapestries. All priceless. The mid-day sunlight came through the windows, lighting up the hallways with gold. She remembered the morning she awoke next to Peter in bed, that blissful sleep. The light made the paint come alive, made it breathe with them. The ocean outside the house that morning was dancing with it, living with it.

The sound of shuffling papers brought her back to reality from the study. She followed it in and found Peter collecting the sketches she once put away into his drawers for safekeeping into his rucksack. He'd left the paintings hanging on the wall, bright and beautiful for the world to see.

Yet it wouldn't, because just like her own home they were going to burn it to the ground. Ready to begin a new life.

He looked up and smiled as he saw her.

"Are you sure about this Peter?"

He sighed, came to her and wrapped her up in his arms. She let go of the breath she didn't realise she was holding. And relaxed against him.

"Why wouldn't I be sure?" he asked.

The house was so quiet.

"You're leaving behind so much more than I am. Are you sure you want to leave this house and all your life in it?"

He pulled away and held my face, his hands warming my cheeks.

"It's just a house. These are all just objects. You're what I want. You are all I'll ever need." And with those words he kissed her forehead, then lent his upon hers.

"I've waited so long to have a chance at life with you. I'm ready to see where it leads. Are you?"

She smiled as she looked up into his eyes.

"Yes, yes I am…"

And for the last time, they locked up that beautiful white house and left everything they once were inside of it.

They took one last look and set it ablaze.

Then they turned away together and placing the key into Lucinda's hand, he also placed everything he was or ever could be into them too. He lifted her swiftly into his strong arms. He flexed his glorious wings out to their full length, testing them before they took off. He turned to look at her, eyes dark and the skin around them slightly greyish. Showing only a fraction of the monstrous power that lurked there. But she could only smile.

"Let's go home," she said.

So together they dived from the cliffs. Lucinda held on to him, knowing that if she ever fell, he would surely catch her. And he held her tightly, diving towards the waves below. Then as quick as a warrior's blade, he spread his wings and shot them both into the sky above the Earth. But not before he touched the edge of his wing to the ocean's face, feeling the coolness of it one last time.

He leaned her down, so she could also touch her fingers to the salty waters. Allowing her to bid goodbye.

The Gods up above turned from their centuries old projects and watched as they glided across the blue vastness, and blinked in surprise that something so beautiful had survived the viciousness of the world for this long. Then they secretly hoped that it always would, and turned away once again.

Peter slowly started to lift them away from the sea, holding her closer as they climbed the clouds and blended with the stars.

Then, with a carefree heart, she let the key fall to the ocean miles below them. Watching as it disappeared forever.

She turned away and looked up.

Feeling the power of Peter's wings as if they were her own fly stronger the higher they went. And as they passed the barrier that separated Earth from Heaven, she noticed how her heart was beating as it once did when she was a child. Wholeheartedly.

She blinked.

And they were home.